Outstanding praise for Marilyn Brant's debut,

ACCORDING TO JANE

"Marilyn Brant's debut novel is proof that Jane Austen never goes out of style. This is a warm, witty and charmingly original story of a woman coming of age and finding her own happy ending—with a little help from the ultimate authority, Jane Austen herself."
—Susan Wiggs, *New York Times* bestselling author

"Entertaining, sincere, real . . . well, okay, that the acclaimed author, Jane Austen, speaks across the centuries to beleaguered romantic Ellie Barnett is not quite *real*, but it is fun. An engaging read for all who have been through the long, dark dating wars and still believe there's sunshine, and a Mr. Darcy, at the end of the tunnel."
—Cathy Lamb, author of *Such a Pretty Face*

" 'Where were the true Darcys?' That's the burning question bookish Ellie Barnett has been asking herself since high school when handsome, charismatic Sam Blaine first captured her heart—and then broke it. In this lively, clever novel by Marilyn Brant, Ellie is accompanied along the perilous path of romance by none other than famed novelist and formidable woman Jane Austen, who, for reasons of her own, has taken up residence in Ellie's head. Ms. Brant wittily parallels the two women's difficult journey to the understanding that love has the power to transform even the most selfish of men into a 'true Darcy.' This is a must-read for Austen lovers as well as for all who believe in the possibility of a happily-ever-after ending."
—Holly Chamberlin, author of *The Family Beach House*

Books by Marilyn Brant

According to Jane

Friday Mornings at Nine

Published by Kensington Publishing Corp.

Friday Mornings at Nine

MARILYN BRANT

KENSINGTON BOOKS
www.kensingtonbooks.com

KENSINGTON BOOKS are published by

Kensington Publishing Corp.
119 West 40th Street
New York, NY 10018

All Kensington titles, imprints, and distributed lines are available at special quantity discounts for bulk purchases for sales promotion, premiums, fund-raising, educational, or institutional use.

Special book excerpts or customized printings can also be created to fit specific needs. For details, write or phone the office of the Kensington Special Sales Manager: Kensington Publishing Corp., 119 West 40th Street, New York, NY 10018. Attn. Special Sales Department. Phone: 1-800-221-2647.

ISBN-13: 978-0-7582-3462-9
ISBN-10: 0-7582-3462-7

First Kensington Trade Paperback Printing: October 2010
10 9 8 7 6 5 4 3 2 1

This book Is Dedicated
To Five Extraordinary Women:
Mom and Grandma Lily

&

Wonderful Friends
Sarah Pressly-James, Karen Karris and Joyce Twardock

ACKNOWLEDGMENTS

Like a pair of siblings, when a second book comes along, comparisons to the first are inevitable. Sometimes the new darling is favored and fawned over. Sometimes the firstborn is preferred. Just as some people have a knack for appreciating every child equally while recognizing and valuing their differences, others would just as soon see the whole darn family move to another neighborhood (one, ideally, in a galaxy far, far away). And so it is with fiction.

From the author-mom standpoint, however, it's incredibly exciting to introduce my second novel to the world. And while I may have a bit more experience this time around and know better what to expect before, during and after Release Day, this understanding has only reaffirmed how much it, indeed, takes a village to bring a book from idea to publication.

Friends who specifically helped me with structural plot points or read parts of this manuscript early on were Simone Elkeles, Eliza Evans, Caryn Caldwell and Heather Rebstock—thank you, ladies. Friends who read and critiqued the whole document were Karen Dale Harris, Erica O'Rourke, Sarah PJ and Laura Moore— my appreciation for your time and insights can't be measured. Thanks, too, to Blythe Gifford for her help with 1970s-era song suggestions, and to Lydia Hirt for so patiently explaining the joys of social-networking sites to me. No small task.

As always, my gratitude goes to my friends in my home writing chapter, Chicago-North RWA, as well as to the dedicated staff at The Knight Agency, especially my agent, Nephele Tempest. I had to ask a lot of questions during the past two years, and the incredible team at Kensington was helpful at every stage. Huge thanks to everyone there! An additional note of appreciation to Karen Auerbach and Maureen Cuddy, who both talked me through the brave new world of publicity; Kristine Mills-Noble, who created such gorgeous cover art; Paula Reedy, who made the copyediting process easy and was kind enough to let me correct typos right down to the last minute; and, of course, my wonderful editor, John Scognamiglio.

More than ever, I had a truly kind and encouraging blog community this year—friends who kept me sane in the middle of chaos—and I thank everybody who visited "Brant Flakes," left comments and participated in my contests. (A few extra hugs of gratitude to Erika Danou-Hasan, Josh Bobo, Pamela Cayne and Robin Bielman!) Many thanks as well to friends, librarians, booksellers and readers who sent me enthusiastic e-mails and took time to write such positive reviews of my debut novel. You're priceless.

Finally, to my family—especially my parents, brother, husband and son—thank you for being so consistently supportive that I never, ever have to doubt my footing. It's particularly wonderful to be married to a man so smart and secure that he actually helped me brainstorm plot ideas for a novel that dealt with infidelity—and with such good humor, too! I love spending my life with you, Jeff, and yes: "We may not be perfect, but we're perfect for each other. . . ."

Thanks, everyone.

If certain women walk straight into adultery,
there are many others who cling to numerous hopes,
and commit sin only after wandering
through a maze of sorrows.

—Honoré de Balzac

Where there's marriage without love,
there will be love without marriage.

—Benjamin Franklin

Merely innocent flirtation,
Not quite adultery, but adulteration.

—Lord Byron

✃ 1 ✃

Once Upon a Time . . .

Friday, September 3

They met on Friday mornings at nine because that was the time when Tamara's husband left for his law firm, when Bridget's kids were safely in school and when Jennifer told everybody she had yoga.

Their meeting place of choice was always the Indigo Moon Café, on account of those signature butter-grilled double-chocolate-chip muffins and the mocha lattes.

Really, there was no second choice.

There'd been that one unfortunate February when the Indigo Moon's owners, in an unnecessary display of prosperity and industriousness, remodeled the café's interior (well, in their defense, there *had* been a regrettable plumbing incident the week prior), and the ladies were forced to meet at Bernie's Java Hut on Highway 83 with those dreadful green vinyl seats and weak espressos instead. They tried to forget about that month.

But, on this particularly bright September morning, they sat in a corner booth at their favorite Chicago-area coffeehouse and diner—a familiar trio of married, forty-something, suburban moms in the eyes of the Glendale Grove locals—and settled into the comfort of a well-worn discussion: the demanding nature of their spouses and/or children and the difficulty in keeping their nearest and dearest happy.

Of course, like three very different sisters in an Oxygen Network production of a Grimm's fairy tale, this morphed into an exhibit of markedly divergent mind-sets.

"Oh, please. You know he's an insensitive prick half the time and a workaholic the other half," Tamara ranted openly when asked about what had been going on with her lawyer husband. "He's off on one trip or another, home just long enough to get laid, and then he's flying out somewhere else a week later." She snapped shut the café menu and huffed. "If it weren't for the makeup flowers and the makeup sex, I'd have kicked his ass to the curb years ago."

A blatant lie, incidentally. Tamara—unusually silent yet firm on this point—believed in marriage for life. And, also, she'd exaggerated the amount of makeup sex.

Bridget, keeping her usual disconcerted eye on her audience and feeling stabs of residual Catholic guilt for complaining at all, nevertheless had to get her family grumbles off her chest. "The kids are out of control," she admitted to her friends. "They're just at that *age*. And Graham always leaves it up to me to rein them in. It's exhausting."

The natural abstainer of the group, the quiet chameleon and the one whose knee-jerk response to any question could be described as committedly noncommittal, still contributed to the party line in her own way. "Nothing changes," Jennifer remarked faintly. "Nothing."

Their other-centric behavior at home (even acknowledging that their manner of servitude took different forms) had been an undercurrent in all their lives. It ran below the daily ticker tape of familial activity like an obligatory, perfunctory mechanism. Each had spent years doing little else, and almost as many repressing her resentment.

Of course, the suburban residents nearby would not have guessed this. They didn't know these women, however dissimilar in temperament and appearance, had long ago agreed the world should be wary of pleasers who'd been burnt out by a lifetime of catering to others. But, even had they been privy to the ladies' café conversations (which they most assuredly were *not*), they would've assumed if anyone were to bring up the subject of infidelity it would've been Tamara.

Auburn-haired by nature and toned from countless health club sets of tennis, she'd been described as "brash" and "outspoken" more times in her forty-three years than Hugh Jackman had been declared "handsome" or Daniel Craig "smoldering." Should anyone in their group be accused of saying or doing the most outrageous things, Tamara would be the obvious choice.

But in that, too, curious onlookers would've been more mistaken than not.

Upon the arrival of her tall mocha-hazelnut latte with a double shot of espresso and extra whipped cream, Tamara merely launched into a chat about the start of the school year.

"Benji says he's 'super stoked' about college. The UT campus is 'really sick,' which is apparently a good thing, and the city of Austin is 'un-fracking-believably cool,' so he's happy." She stirred her coffee with a couple of rough, almost angry swirls and took a few sustaining breaths. "He's been there all of two weeks and he's already dropping 'y'all' into his conversation like some fresh-off-the-ranch Texas cowboy. I hate it."

Her friends knew how much she despised her husband's frequent work absences, but now her son was gone as well. Although Tamara didn't say it aloud, she'd never felt more alone. "I miss my baby boy," she murmured.

"Your baby boy is going to be nineteen at the end of the month," Bridget said gently, already three-quarters finished with her skim half-caf vanilla-mocha latte sprinkled with a generous dash of cinnamon. She struggled to show better portion control with her muffin but still nibbled nervously on a corner of it. "It's gotta be hard to let him go, though." *Especially since he's your only child*, Bridget added to herself, but she tactfully avoided saying this aloud.

Bridget had three children versus Jennifer's two and Tamara's one. But, despite her thrill in seeing her youngest off to school full time this year (first grade!), Bridget worried more than any of them that, in the end, Empty Nest Syndrome might hit her hardest.

"Yeah," Tamara said. "His birthday's on September twenty-third. Same as the autumnal equinox. The day my world shifted on its axis and everything became simultaneously aligned and imbalanced, you know?"

Bridget replied, "I know," although she suspected Tamara was being a bit dramatic. But, again, when a woman had just *one* kid she could be inclined toward overfocusing.

Jennifer, as usual, made few comments and none after this exchange. She nodded, however, sipped her small mocha-soy latte made with a squirt of coconut syrup and a hint of nutmeg (a combination from which she never deviated) and regarded the other two with an occasional distracted glance.

She'd been friends with the others for more than four years— ever since her younger daughter and Bridget's oldest were together in summer cheerleading camp and Tamara, who knew Bridget from some community organization or other, helped them secure the park district gym for their practices. Of course, this was followed by infinite library and school district fund-raising events, where they'd been thrown in each other's paths often enough to create a durable bond. Soon the trio had their weekly coffee date in place—an almost unbreakable commitment—which nowadays, because of conflicting schedules, was usually the only time they got together.

Thus, having witnessed it for years, Bridget and Tamara were well acquainted with Jennifer's predisposition toward silence. They understood she wasn't angry with them or even bored. But she'd been slipping into her reflexive introversion more readily than usual over the past three weeks, and Tamara had had quite enough of not getting Jennifer's full attention.

"Something going on with you, Jennifer?" Tamara asked, noting the disturbing strands of gray competing with the streaks of blond in Jennifer's hair. Tamara tagged this stylistic lapse as a form of neglect, feeling justified in her tough-love approach since, clearly, Jennifer's distress had taken a physical turn.

Jennifer shrugged and took another sip of her coffee.

But Tamara persisted. "You're not pregnant, are you?" She realized Jennifer was forty-one and her daughters both teens, but who knew these days? Julia Roberts, Halle Berry, Lisa Marie Presley . . .

they'd popped out their babies at whatever-the-hell age they wanted.

Jennifer's blue-green eyes flew open and Bridget had to cough down half a gulp of vanilla-mocha.

"N-No," Jennifer managed to reply, but even Bridget recognized the trepidation with which their friend answered.

"Have you, uh, gotten any new e-mails?" Bridget asked carefully.

After a long pause during which, in unison, they watched their waitress scurry into the kitchen and out of earshot, Jennifer confessed, "Yes," her tone startling in its quiet intensity.

Tamara raised her coffee mug in a mock toast and beamed. "Whoo-hoo! Here's to your old boyfriend. What's the hottie got to say this time?"

"Shhh," Bridget hissed, scanning the room for listeners.

"What?" Tamara rolled her deep brown eyes. "We're the only ones in this section—nobody'll hear. And, besides, it's not like she's gonna *do* anything with lover-boy David anyway." Tamara turned to Jennifer. "Are you?"

Based on what Tamara knew, Jennifer had only received three e-mails from her college ex, which she always answered dutifully and overpolitely. Never a hint of impropriety. So, Tamara considered Bridget's insistence on discretion rather extreme.

"Um. Probably not." Jennifer twisted the corner of her brown paper napkin and dabbed at a coffee droplet on the table.

Tamara blinked at her. "*Probably* not? Are you fucking kidding me? You're *thinking* of cheating?"

"*Probably* not," Jennifer repeated, a tiny smile of the wry variety rising one millimeter—maybe two—at the edges of her mouth.

Bridget giggled uneasily.

Tamara laughed aloud, unwilling to take Jennifer's claim with any seriousness.

Then the three of them—an unspoken question thickening the air—sat in silence for a full thirty seconds, considering who they'd say "probably not" to . . . if ever propositioned.

David had been the love of Jennifer's life, The One for her, or so she'd been convinced in college. They were of a particular type:

techie geeks who'd found their twin. A type not shared by her poetry-writing, Spanish-language-teaching husband, Michael, a kind man but one who'd never spoken Jennifer's dialect.

Jennifer hadn't told anyone, not even her friends, about the increasingly intimate nature of her e-mail exchanges with David. She'd been careful in her replies, but there were subtleties in his responses—and in her own—others wouldn't pick up on. A suggestiveness hidden in private code. This secrecy made the tension and excitement inside her grow large and potent, like a psychedelic mushroom in a dark closet.

Bridget, meanwhile, had her own secret.

With whole days at her disposal now—the kids in school and Graham at work—she'd transitioned from occasional temping at Smiley Dental to regular part-time hours, which included Tuesdays and Thursdays from ten A.M. to two P.M., when Dr. Luke was in the office.

Bridget *admired* Dr. Luke.

This was what she kept telling herself. Only, sometimes, they shared these glances. Glances that were less about professional admiration, basic courtesy or general respect than about physical appreciation . . . and sensuality . . . and awareness.

For Tamara's part, she'd been highly aware of her sexy, early-thirty-something neighbor guy—five houses down the block, on the left side. She had, on more than one occasion, joked that divorced men were getting younger and cuter all the time but, in truth, she'd also fantasized about this *particular* young and newly available man while getting personal with her BNY-762 Vibrating "Bunny." (Her husband, Jon, was out-of-town *quite* often.)

Twice, maybe three times, though, Neighbor Aaron had sparked her desires even while she was in bed with Jon, a confession she forbade herself to make aloud.

"A quickie affair is a fun fantasy, but it isn't *real,* and none of us would go through with it," Tamara informed them with a certainty that would have been more believable had she not been fidgeting so relentlessly with her stirring stick.

Jennifer, paying full attention to Tamara now, said, "So you have someone in mind then? Someone who tempts you?"

Tamara squinted at her. "All women do. Especially if they've been married for more than a decade. Almost two decades, in my case. But no self-respecting woman acts on it. She'd know better. Husband or lover, it doesn't matter. Men are all the same, especially once they get what they want."

Bridget swallowed, not quite agreeing, but also not quite able to substantiate her disagreement with a logical argument. "Er, yeah. But even if they're *not* all the same, even if they're wonderfully romantic and different from any stereotype, there's that whole 'It's a sin' thing."

Bridget may have been a lapsed Catholic, especially these last few years. And she may have only been going through the motions of attending church sometimes—for the kids, of course—but she still remembered all Ten Commandments with the same devotion she used to recite all ten ingredients in Sister Margaret Marie's Perfect Spaghetti Sauce. Both had been burned into her brain for life during fifth-grade catechism.

Jennifer sighed, her slim shoulders hunched under the onerous burden of indecision. "Yeah. I'm not saying those aren't problems. But what if—" She paused, shrugged, looked away.

"What if what?" Bridget needed to know. Their group had had plenty of deep conversations and, occasionally, some pretty racy ones in their three-and-a-half years of meeting weekly at the Indigo Moon, but none of those discussions had ever taken a turn like this.

"What if it were *more* immoral *not* to test the strength of our marriages?" Jennifer whispered finally. Then, in an unexpected flood of monologue, she added, "We've all talked about our husbands—the struggles we've had, the challenges and, sometimes, the wonderful things, too. We've all had ups and downs. But what if there's a chance we made a wrong choice somewhere? Married the wrong man? Lived the wrong life? What if our *real* task is to make sure we're on the right path? To know, once and for all, without question, that we're where we should be."

Despite eighteen years of marriage, Jennifer hadn't forgotten she'd chosen Michael as her rebound guy after David's desertion. And though she almost never spoke of it, not a week passed that she didn't second-guess her decision . . . that she didn't wonder if, maybe, she should've waited for David just a little bit longer.

Bridget thought of her husband, Graham, and their fifteen years together. The dreams of being a master chef she'd put aside when she got married, the "issues" that had arisen between them since she'd started working more regularly and, if she were being honest, the knotty niggles that had plagued their relationship for several years before that. Her friends didn't know the half of it.

"So, what are you suggesting?" Bridget said. "That for the sake of our marriages we should 'experiment' with other men?" She pushed her thick, dark hair away from her face in a futile attempt to cool herself off.

"I'm not saying anyone *should* do anything," Jennifer murmured. "Experimental or otherwise. Just that maybe we owe it to ourselves, and even to the men in our lives, to know for sure who we want to be with. And why."

"Well, that can only lead to trouble," Tamara said with a distinct snicker.

Not that Tamara considered this a "bad" question, per se. It was one that had floated in and out of her mind a time or twelve since she'd gotten knocked up with Benji at age twenty-four . . . and then gotten married to Jon. Certainly, it would liven up their weekly coffee dates to hear what Jennifer and Bridget learned about themselves as a result of getting friendly with some other guys, but this was one area where she doubted she'd be too opinionated.

People always commented on her candidness and assumed she was fearless, too. But she wasn't some Trampy Cougar Chick, despite her youthful mannerisms and her predilection toward wearing animal-striped stilettos out in public. (Hey, they matched her three favorite skirts perfectly.) She may have had a mountain of bones to pick with her husband but, trapped as she felt by her marriage at times, she took her commitment seriously. And, anyway, she didn't have the guts for adultery.

Still, to be a good sport, Tamara added, "Ah, what the hell? As long as I don't actually have to sleep with the guy, I've got someone in mind I'd like to get to know better. Let's see if Jon can hold his own against a man fifteen years his junior who competes in triathlons *for fun*."

Jennifer raised an eyebrow at this, then turned her gaze on Bridget. "What about you?" Jennifer asked, her voice barely audible above the XM radio station piping in 1970s music overhead. Nothing like the melancholic strains of Firefall for setting a mood.

"You wanna do it, don't you?" Tamara said in a singsongy tone. Adding a saucy expression, she mimed smoking a joint, simultaneously mocking both Bridget's reticence and the standard plea of peer pressure. "C'mon. *Everyone else* is doing it."

Bridget laughed in spite of herself and forced a nod, but she bit her bottom lip to keep from saying the words aloud. The other two understood what she meant because, of course, all three women wanted to allow each other this taboo-laden freedom—just once. But it was embarrassing to admit such a want. The clichéd arm twisting was a requirement in Bridget's case, if only for appearances' sake.

And so it was decided that next Friday, during their morning coffee date, they would share with each other in detail whatever transpired with their extramarital objects of interest over the course of the week. It was promised that such a conversation would be undeniably spellbinding, and all three found themselves most curious (and also rather anxious) to let the spinning of the tales begin.

The ladies may have had differing reasons to contemplate stepping outside their marriages and exploring alternate relationships—reasons both verbalized and deeply closeted. But, as they further discussed the idea in low, charged tones, shivers of realization pranced along the skin of their forearms, giving rise to tiny body hairs and great expectations.

Only one thing proved more startling to them than the revelation that each was at least willing to *consider* having an affair: It was that they thought they knew each other after so many years of chatting and sharing. Understood each other's marriages. Felt they were in tune with themselves, their needs, their desires.

And yet, it turned out, they weren't nearly as in the know as they liked to believe.

It turned out, they weren't even close.

❧ 2 ❧

Bridget

E very woman remembered her firsts:
   Her first kiss.

Her first lover.

Her first blow job gone awry.

Her first crush on a man who turned out to be gay . . . or married . . . or, in Bridget's most unforgettable and inadvertent case, both gay *and* married. And a bad community theater actor to boot.

And, now, a new first: her first time contemplating an affair.

Darn that Jennifer for suggesting such a thing! What had gotten into her friend? The idea was so wrong, so immoral . . . but so horribly compelling. Bridget tried to shove it from her mind, but images of Dr. Luke lingered there, melting over all of her other thoughts like vanilla ice cream on a hot brownie.

She checked her watch (only twenty minutes before she was due at the dental office) and returned to the important task at hand.

"I will choose only whole grains," she instructed herself, eyeing the near-endless rows of packaged bread loaves on the grocery store shelves. "Stone-ground. High fiber."

She inspected a line of breads produced and distributed by the popular Hearth & Harvest Company, all of them boasting the words "New!" "Healthy!" "100% Whole Wheat!" on the wrapping. The blatant enthusiasm and multiple exclamation marks grew more unsettling with each passing minute.

An older woman with blinding white curls and a large daisy print handbag pushed her cart down the aisle with vigor, stopping a few feet away to grab a box of organic honey-wheat pretzel twists. Bridget felt her vibration as she moved. The air currents seemed to dance around the stranger in harmony, like forest animals circling a storybook princess. Could this woman be the Snow White of the Geriatric Set? Bridget couldn't explain it, but she expected magic to occur at any moment.

The lady was at least fifty pounds overweight, but she stood tall, dressed in a classic style with comfortable fabrics and looked supremely confident. Her cart was filled with an array of colorful fruits, vegetables, flowers and gourmet items. Bridget spotted a couple of mangoes, a large bunch of cilantro, fresh asparagus stalks, a bouquet with carnations in three shades of pink and . . . was that a jar of fig jam?

She took a few steps closer and noticed the woman wore a pair of dazzling ruby earrings and, most conspicuous of all, a joyous and welcoming grin.

"Hi, honey," the woman said brightly.

Bridget returned the smile. "Hi. Your flowers—they're lovely."

"Well, you should get yourself some. Plenty of pretty bunches left."

"Oh, I can't. I'm on my way to work. They'd wilt in the car." Plus, flowers were an unnecessary expense, one she never thought to indulge in just for herself. But the vibrant colors of the other woman's bouquet kept drawing her gaze. The carnations seemed so happy, so celebratory. Which might've influenced Bridget a bit more if she'd had something, anything, to celebrate.

The woman nodded as if understanding and pushed her way farther down the aisle.

Bridget turned back to the packaged breads once again, suddenly realizing why the decision of which brand to buy was so difficult: She didn't want any of them.

She wanted something fresh baked. Warm from the oven. Or, at least, not in plastic wrap. She wanted an Italian loaf. Or crusty

French. She wanted to avoid anything presliced. And these wants grew stronger as she watched the lively lady walk away. She wanted to be more like *that* woman. She wanted to have a spring in her step and an irrepressible grin on her face. She wanted to ignore supposedly "healthy" items so full of preservatives they could probably last for a week in her car without a noticeable difference in taste.

Wanting all of these things meant she'd have to come back to the store later to finish her shopping, but she couldn't contain her relief in being able to waltz by those boring old bread loaves.

Before she left the store (only seven minutes until work!), she impulsively grabbed a bouquet of baby roses, their sweet scent filling her with something—hopefulness? eternal spring, even though it was nearly autumn?—and raced to the express checkout lane.

She wanted to clasp the flowers to her chest and drink in the rightness of them, like a cherry slushie on a humid day or a cup of chicken noodle on a snowy night. Sure, they'd been a spontaneous purchase, but sometimes a woman had to honor her impulses. Sometimes she needed to allow herself to step out of her ordinary, uninspiring routines and grab on to something beautiful. Sometimes pleasure, just for its own sake, had to be valued.

She strode into Smiley Dental still clutching her bouquet.

"Hi, Bridget," the first-shift receptionist said. "Glad you're here. I've gotta run."

Bridget nodded. Pamela was nice enough, but she *always* had to run. On Tuesdays, like this one, and Thursdays, too, the office offered early morning hours. So Pamela managed the first shift, then Bridget did her four hours and, finally, Stephie came in until closing.

Pamela pressed the appointment schedule sheet into Bridget's free hand. "Everyone up until here is checked in," she said, pointing toward the middle of the sheet. "Mrs. Roberts called and is going to be about fifteen minutes late. And Ms. Palton is coming in at one-thirty now instead of two o'clock." She grabbed her purse and her sunglasses. "Oh, and Dr. Jim and Amy are working on Mr. Breson in the back. Dr. Luke has little Jake Armarino. And Dr.

Nina is on break, but she'll be back in a half hour. Okay, that's it. Bye." She was out the door before Bridget could answer.

Bridget eyed the two people sitting in the waiting room. Both smiled briefly at her, then returned to their magazines. She glanced at the giant bulletin board on the wall and saw her picture had been added to it. She was really a staff member now! Unable to suppress her grin, she walked behind the desk, deposited her belongings in a drawer—except for the baby roses—and hunted down a sturdy glass to fill with water.

"Hey, pretty flowers," Bridget's favorite hygienist said, rounding the corner, a patient's chart in her hand. "Birthday? Anniversary?"

Her grin broadened. "Nope, neither. I just wanted them." She fiddled with the arrangement a bit more, then took a step back to admire her bouquet.

"That's the best reason, isn't it?" the hygienist said, and Bridget wanted to hug her for reinforcing this burgeoning belief.

Candy (yes, an unfortunate name in her line of employment) was one of the many reasons Bridget loved working there. The young newlywed had a warm, upbeat nature and a delightful sense of humor (she wore a button with a giant smiley face that read: "I'm the only 'Candy' allowed in this office!"), and she was the one who'd enthusiastically recommended Bridget for the receptionist opening based on the handful of times they'd worked together when Bridget was temping over the summer.

Bridget's husband, Graham—bless him—had been right to insist upon her trying out a bunch of positions as a temp first. She soon discovered all day jobs weren't created equal. At Smiley Dental, the other hygienists, the three dentists in the practice and the support staff all proved to be friendly and professional, a far cry from the gossipy snits at the high school central office, the chilly automatons at the corporate library or the collection of backstabbing minions at the real estate company.

And, of course, there was also the added benefit of getting to chat with Dr. Luke—all of the dentists went by their first names— for a little bit every day she was there. She considered it a perk, like the individual flavored cappuccino packets in the staff lounge or the trial-sized cinnamon floss she got to take home.

Ever since Friday, she'd been thinking about him nonstop, but today was the first time she'd been in the office since the infamous affair conversation, the first time she'd have a chance to see him again. She would just be herself, she vowed. Just notice what he said and did. Probably nothing would be too different, even if she kind of wanted it to be.

She finished with the flowers and tidied up the desk area that Pamela had left cluttered with scratch paper and scattered pens. She glanced at the placid face of Mr. Armarino, waiting for his son, and the anxious magazine-flipping of a teenage girl (two cavities, poor kid), who'd gotten out of school early for her appointment with Dr. Jim.

Bridget turned to Candy, who was filing the paperwork of her last patient, and asked her about the morning.

"I've only been here since nine," Candy said with a shrug. Then, lowering her voice so the people in the waiting room couldn't hear, she added, "Long enough to know something's going on with Dr. Nina today. She was a crab when I got in."

Bridget raised her eyebrows. "Really? Thanks for the warning." Of the three dentists, Dr. Nina was the one with the most dramatic swings in temperament. Some days she was on the quiet side, on others she could be livelier. But, in the two weeks Bridget had been on the official staff roster and in the five or six times she'd temped, she'd never seen Dr. Nina in a bite-your-head-off kind of mood, so this news came as a surprise. "Any idea what could be wr—"

"Hello, ladies," the deep voice of Dr. Luke said, interrupting Bridget midsentence and making her forget why she cared about Dr. Nina and her crummy mood anyway. "Where did all these flowers come from?"

"Bridget brought them in," Candy piped up. "Aren't they beautiful?"

He homed in on Bridget's face with the radiant warmth she'd come to associate with him—the unusual combination of exuberance and sensuality, which made her tingle with happiness and nearly brought a blush to her cheeks. "They are very beautiful," he said, every syllable delivered with a bestowal of approval.

And that, just *that*, was enough to make her day.

But he didn't stop there. "We need to get you a prize for being so good, don't we?"

Bridget swallowed. She didn't think a prize was necessary, but she wouldn't turn one down.

"That'd be great!" little Jake Armarino said, and Bridget almost groaned aloud at her mistake. Of course the prize was for the child! Still, she couldn't help but feel a teeny bit disappointed as the cute six-year-old, same age as her son Evan, came into view from behind her favorite dentist to claim his prize.

"Do we have the treasure chest back there, Ms. Bridget?" Dr. Luke asked. "This brave young man deserves a couple of goodies."

"Of course!" she said, overenthusiastically. She pulled out the kiddie box, filled with tooth-shaped erasers, wind-up hopping mouths and "Smiley Kylie" stickers, and held it out for Jake to peruse. "Here you go. Take at least two."

"At least?" the boy asked hopefully. "You mean I can have more?" He stared wide-eyed at Dr. Luke.

Mr. Armarino chuckled as he pulled out his MasterCard to cover the bill for his son's cleaning. Candy grinned, but Dr. Luke laughed deeply, his whole face lit with care and kindness. His age and the air he gave off reminded Bridget of actors George Clooney and Jeffrey Dean Morgan, although, perhaps, Dr. Luke wasn't quite as physically handsome as either. Still, when he sent her one of his lopsided grins, she felt it, like a bolt of warmth to her heart.

He told Jake, "Quick, grab three," and Bridget couldn't help but marvel at the twinkling eyes and affectionate nature of this man . . . and wonder why he wasn't a father. Why he wasn't even married.

What was Dr. Luke's *story*, hmm?

The Armarinos left soon afterward, but the dentist remained, leaning into the reception desk, the very picture of relaxed contentedness—a man comfortable with his masculinity and his easy ability to take up space. He inhaled the scent of the baby roses a few times and made small talk with the nervous teenager, until Candy called the girl back.

Bridget expected Dr. Luke to leave immediately then. Return to whichever room he'd been working in and straighten up, or at least take a quick break in the staff lounge until his ten-thirty appointment arrived.

But he didn't. He stayed with her. She felt an innate thrill at this and, simultaneously, a few prickles of guilt. She probably shouldn't enjoy his company so much, should she?

"You know, my brother's visiting," he said. "He and his wife are in town for the week, seeing Ma, Pops and our sister. And they brought the nephews along this time, so the house is like a live-action video game. Bam! Boom! Bash!" He mimicked kids at war. "Little boys have all this energy."

"I know," Bridget replied. "I have two of them."

"Oh, yeah. They're six and ten, right?"

"Yes." She stared at him in shock. "I'm amazed you remember that." She'd told him about her children only once, and it'd been months ago while she was still a temp. "And I also have a daughter who's twelve."

"Three kids . . . wow. Bet they keep you busy," he said.

"They do," she admitted. "And you?" she asked, already knowing through the office grapevine that he wasn't a father, but hoping he'd reveal other information if they continued along this line of questioning.

"Nope. Maybe someday, though." He locked gazes with her, his brown eyes beaming fondness, though she couldn't tell if it was at her or at the idea of one day being a dad. "Until then, I've got some squirrely nephews who need entertaining, and I'm on Uncle Duty this weekend. They're eight and five. Got any suggestions?"

She did. The Museum of Science and Industry. Lincoln Park Zoo. A Cubs or Sox game. "And there's always Six Flags," she added, "if you have the stomach for it."

"The coasters scare you?" he said with a laugh.

"No. The food does."

He threw his head back and laughed harder, a deep rumbling of sound that she felt down to her unpolished toenails. "Isn't that the truth. Funnel cakes, greasy pizza, elephant ears and the like. It's indigestion inducing. And it's even worse to think about that stuff now. I've been so spoiled lately."

She squinted at him. Spoiled by whom?

He must've read her confusion, because he said, "My Italian mama's been cooking all week and she lets me play wingman. Not just with her homemade pizza with the basil and the fire-grilled porcini mushrooms." He flexed his muscles and mimicked double-handed spatula flipping on a big gas grill. "Ooh, boy. And not only with her top-secret lasagna recipe with the spicy sausage, the sweet red peppers and the Asiago. But also with the cream-filled cannoli and the rum cake and butter cookies. The woman's killin' me."

Bridget had tasted cannoli before, but only the store-bought, ready-made, vanilla-pudding kind. More often than not, they were on the stale-n-soggy side. And once, a few years back, when she and Graham went to a friend's wedding, there were savory cannoli at the reception, which tasted a little odd and were hardly worth the five thousand calories each.

"I've tried a few kinds of cannoli," she said, explaining about the savory ones. "I love the *idea* of a crispy pastry embracing a smooth filling, but that blend of chicken pâté and prosciutto was disturbing when I'd expected something sweet. And the shells never seem to stay hard and fresh for long enough."

He shook his head. "There's no excuse for limp shells. As for the filling, you tasted an unusual variety. There's a style of cannoli that's just like that, and the people who brought them in were probably from Naples or, at least, they favored that style of cooking. But my ma does it the traditional Sicilian way. And hers are sweet. Very sweet. And also very crunchy."

He leaned even closer to her, his torso resting on the desk, the gold cross he wore on a chain around his neck swinging forward slightly. "Imagine—fresh, whole-milk ricotta blended with imported mascarpone, apricot preserves and chopped semisweet chocolate." He gestured a mixing motion, his eyes heavy lidded in apparent pastry-induced rapture. "That's the filling. Not some boring vanilla thing. But it doesn't stop there. For the shells you've got flour, sugar, cinnamon, cocoa powder, sweet Marsala wine and more—kneaded until elastic, rolled over large steel tubes, smothered in canola oil and fried with lethal intent." He smacked his lips. "Pipe the filling into the crisp shells, sprinkle the ends with ground coffee and cocoa, then sift powdered sugar over the whole thing, and *voilà*."

"Oh, my God," she murmured.

"Exactly."

"They sound heavenly." And huge. She tried to ignore all embarrassing thoughts of phallic implications, but she could, nevertheless, picture those large, sweet cannoli in her mind, as if he'd just demonstrated the recipe on her favorite TV cooking show. Dr. Luke was no typical, finicky dentist. Dr. Luke was her pick for the next guest cook on The Foodie Station's *Delectable Dishes, Decadent Desserts* program. And, possibly, a top-ten inclusion in *Chicagoland Cooks!* magazine's "Hot Chefs" issue.

"I'll bring you some tomorrow."

Bridget's elation was as sweet as powdered sugar, and as easily dispelled. "Oh, darn! I don't work tomorrow."

"That's right, that's right. The day after, then," Dr. Luke said. "I'll save one for you and you can try it on Thursday."

Oh, good Lord. That cannoli sounded sinful enough to require a few Hail Marys and all eleven lines of the Act of Contrition. Would he stay to watch her eat one? If so, it'd be just like the famous deli scene in *When Harry Met Sally* . . . only she might find herself reaching an orgasmic high for real.

"Thank you," she murmured, unable to keep from staring at this generous, funny, unexpectedly sensual man.

But, aside from the obvious food fantasies he inspired, something about talking with him always made her feel *buoyant*. Well, when she wasn't feeling guilty. He made her feel as though she was on the right path somehow. Observing the way he'd conducted himself throughout their few exchanges had convinced her the feelings he aroused weren't evidence of some silly crush she'd quickly get over. That her interest in him wasn't a mere physical thing. He might be fifty and the tiniest bit stout, but it was his boyishness and enthusiasm that turned her on. A person could try to ignore attraction, but it wasn't like you could totally get rid of it, could you?

No. And there was a special quality about *this* man. The way he had more pull on her now than ever. He seemed to epitomize the direction she was heading in her life and her understanding of it, whereas Graham—not that there was anything *wrong* with him (she *loved* her husband, of course!)—was very much where she'd been. Things were different now between them, and Graham was a living remnant of her younger, less mature manner of walking in the world.

Dr. Luke leaned a couple of inches closer still, as near as he could be to her without actually making contact. "Do you wanna hear about the rum cake?" he asked, which to Bridget seemed as much a line of seduction as saying, "Do you wanna talk about lacy undergarments and, perhaps, a few kinky sexual positions?"

She bit her lip and began to nod, just as the office door swung open and a very tense-looking Dr. Nina strode through. The dentist clenched her bony jaw with a rigidity strongly discouraged by the American Dental Association, slammed the heavy oak door behind her and marched toward the desk, her wiry arms pumping at her sides.

Bridget and Dr. Luke pulled apart as if they'd just been caught kissing in a coat closet and were about to be scolded by Bridget's old catechism teacher, Sister Catherine Anne. No one ever dared to cross the fiery nun.

"Hey there, Nina. How are you doing on this fine afternoon?" Dr. Luke asked with his usual amiability, although Bridget couldn't help but detect something forced in his tone.

Dr. Nina narrowed her eyes at him in response, then glanced between him and Bridget in an assessing way that left no doubt they were being judged—and not pleasantly. She said, "I'm not in the mood for any crap. From anyone."

Dr. Luke's eyes widened. Bridget blinked at the woman. So much for the "friendly, professional office staff" she'd thought she'd found.

Dr. Nina dropped some new business cards on the desk and stalked off in the direction of the staff lounge.

Dr. Luke lifted one of the cards, read it and winced. "Ah." He flipped it around so Bridget could see. "She did away with the hyphenated last name," he explained. "She was Nina Brockman-Lewis. Now there's no more Lewis."

"Does that mean there's also no more husband?" Bridget asked in a low voice.

"I think that may be an excellent deduction." Dr. Luke lowered his voice to match hers. "There've been problems at home for a while." He tilted his head toward the back hallway. "I'm gonna go check on her." But before he turned to leave, he looked directly into her eyes, the kind of warm, affectionate gaze that liquefied her insides to a Ghirardelli hot-fudge-sauce consistency. The kind of glance that had kept her awake past midnight more than once in a futile attempt to interpret it. The kind of knowing glimpse into her soul that would be impossible to explain to her friends without cheapening the interaction.

It was a sensation that lingered long after he'd left, but once he'd physically walked away, Bridget busied herself with filing paperwork and fielding phone calls. A few new patients came in. A couple of others left. Over the next hour there were a handful of chaotic moments punctuated by stretches of pure, blissful silence.

Around one P.M., though, Candy all but sprinted into the area behind Bridget's desk, rummaged through a drawer and snatched her purse. "I'm having my lunch break *out* today," she said, rolling her eyes in the direction of the hallway. "Too much drama back there."

"Why? What's going on now?"

Candy, sotto voce, said, "Dr. Nina's spouting off some, um, colorful phrases between patients. I just overheard her talking to Dr. Luke about her soon-to-be ex and his PR assistant. She referred to the woman as 'That Little Blond Whore with the Britney Spears Wardrobe Who's Somehow Fucking My Impotent Husband' so . . ." Candy wrinkled her nose and frowned.

Bridget grimaced. "Did Dr. Luke have any luck calming her down?"

Candy shook her head. "Dr. Luke's a good guy, but he's not a miracle worker. Or a shrink. Dr. Nina needs at least one of each."

Bridget smiled and seized the opportunity to ask more personal questions about her favorite dentist. "When he rushed back to talk to Dr. Nina earlier, he seemed really sympathetic," she said. "I thought it was maybe because he'd gone through a divorce or something, too. Any idea?"

"I don't know much. He never talks about it, but I did hear he'd been engaged once. Something happened, though, and they called it off." The hygienist shrugged. "I know he's had other long-term relationships since, but he's never been married." She took a couple of steps toward the door and shot Bridget a semiwicked grin. "He might be more expressive than most guys, but he *is* straight. *And* single," she mouthed. "Maybe he and Dr. Nina will . . . um—" She made a suggestive hand motion, then flashed another grin. "Might cheer her up."

Bridget forced a laugh but felt vaguely nauseated by the idea. *Her* Dr. Luke with the cool, too skinny and now rather irate Dr. Nina? No.

Not that Dr. Luke didn't deserve to find love. But if Bridget couldn't have him, shouldn't he at least be involved with a joyful woman who didn't look like she desperately needed to eat more than a ninety-calorie oat-n-nut bar and a cup of raspberry yogurt for lunch?

Bridget thought so.

Unfortunately, these impulses made her feel uncomfortably callous. Based on what little information she'd gathered, it seemed Dr. Nina was the injured party in her decomposing marriage.

But what if Dr. Nina's husband had had a *good* reason to cheat? Bridget hadn't ever seen this rude and enraged side of the female dentist before, so maybe the woman just put on a well-behaved show in public. What if she was a raving witch at home who'd scared her husband into submission and *that* was why he'd strayed?

Might that be an excuse or was that still wrong? Still a sin? And was it immoral to even ask these questions?

When Bridget's shift ended, she made a quick trip to the lounge to put away some coffee mugs, passing Dr. Luke, who'd just finished with his latest appointment.

"Quick. C'mere." He motioned her to enter the room as he

waved goodbye to the elderly gentleman. After doing a cursory hall check, he unzipped his blue Smiley Dental shoulder bag and retrieved a thick white box about the size of one of Graham's carpentry manuals. "Don't tell Candy," he warned as he opened it.

Bridget gaped at the contents. Every inch was packed with brightly colored, individually wrapped pieces of saltwater taffy. "She'll wring your neck if she walks by."

He winked. "I know, but they're worth it. Soft. Tangy. Packed with flavor. My brother's from Atlantic City and they make it fresh there. He always brings me a box when he visits." He glanced again at the open door and lightly tapped her arm with his fingers. She felt his brief touch like the tantalizing buzz of a smoothie blender, vibrating against her skin. "Hurry," he added. "Grab a handful for the road. Don't let anybody see you."

She plucked five pieces to take along. "Thanks."

"Welcome." He smiled conspiratorially. "Have a great afternoon and, uh, Bridget?"

"Yes?"

"Watch your fillings."

She laughed. "See you Thursday, Dr. Luke."

His behavior was perfectly innocent, just another example of his generous nature, but she couldn't help but feel as though his words and deeds that day were all part of an unintentional kind of foreplay uniquely tailored to her. And she couldn't stop her heart from becoming floaty and light from just their little bit of contact.

She glided out of the office, purposely leaving her pretty baby roses on the desk—a gift to joy, life, beauty and also, perhaps, as a reminder of her to Dr. Luke. Then she sped back to the grocery store. When she recalled the high that had washed over her as Dr. Luke described his mom's cannoli, it made her second food-shopping excursion of the day feel like a wholly different task from her first one.

She all but skipped down the aisles in search of interesting meal options. How about a circular loaf of sweet Hawaiian bread, imported orange marmalade, sliced Muenster cheese and a rainbow of organic fruits for breakfast the next day?

Yes.

And for dinner that night, why not buy a bottle of white wine and some sparkling pear cider for the kids and get the fixings for Vietnamese spring rolls (with fresh mint and hoisin-chili dipping sauce!) as a healthy appetizer? Add a side of roasted red pepper hummus and a bag of sea-salt-sprinkled baked pita wedges? And finish it off with a main course of pecan-encrusted tilapia, steamed broccoli florets with slivered almonds as the evening's vegetable and a luscious dessert of tart lemon sorbet?

Sure!

Minute after minute ticked by on her Timex, and she knew she had to get home to unload her groceries, do the dishes and toss a batch of laundry into the washer before the kids got back from school at three-thirty. But Bridget couldn't tear herself away from the delightful abundance of cans, boxes and sealed plastic bags. She gave in to her desire to linger. She reexperienced the jubilation of shopping as if she were an alien visiting the planet, her cart rolling in front of her and her former self a shadow tiptoeing behind.

So what if her purchases made her gain a few more pounds? She was healthy. She exercised (a little). She wasn't an unhappy Twiggy type. She could learn to love her hips, which, thanks to three pregnancies and her more recent perimenopausal changes, were several inches wider than they'd been a dozen years ago.

She walked by a table of bruschetta samples and snagged one. The texture of sun-dried tomato bits and fresh mozzarella chunks on a crunchy cracker. The scent of basil. The flavor burst of really good olive oil. Mmm. A tangible reminiscence of her long-held daydream of going to culinary school and making such delicacies . . . at least before she was reminded of practical considerations.

Nevertheless, she could bring little elements of the foodie life into her regular one. She could! The table could be set beautifully, pleasurably, artistically. No fast-food junk. Meals could be a feast for the eyes and the senses, as well as for the taste buds. The kids—and Graham, too—should expand their dietary horizons. They should eat something besides mac-n-cheese or burgers and fries or frozen pizza, for goodness' sake. They should be willing to take a chance on a new dish and put their litany of food aversions aside for a night—if not for themselves, then for *her*.

Infused with desire for a blissful dining experience, she strolled up and down all seventeen aisles one last time, feeling ever more like the fun, white-haired woman she'd met that morning. And just like that woman, Bridget picked up a carnation bouquet to bring home—red-tipped yellow ones—and placed it in her cart as her final item, economy be damned. Because life was worth celebrating, "just because," right?

Home, however, wasn't nearly as receptive to the beauty of flowers as the dental office had been.

"Mom, I need to go to the library," her daughter said, dropping her social studies textbook onto the kitchen counter and crushing the petals of two carnations unlucky enough to be in the vicinity.

"Cassandra!" Bridget reached for the bouquet, still wrapped in floral plastic and tied up with rubber bands. "Please watch what you're doing."

Bridget had gotten back just as the school bus puttered into their subdivision—too late to start either the dishes or the laundry—but she'd been desperately trying to get all of the groceries put away before the kids stampeded into the house.

She glanced at the bruised yellow petals and sighed. Perhaps she should've put the flowers in a vase before refrigerating the bean sprouts and the shrimp for the spring rolls, huh?

"Can we go *now?*" Cassandra asked, tapping the toe of one dingy sneaker against the wooden baseboards.

"No, your brother has a soccer game at four-thirty," she told her.

"Today?" This came from Keaton. A child unable to remember which day of the week it was let alone when he had his sporting events. Sporting events he, incidentally, had insisted upon signing up for this fall. "But I told Josh I could play football with him outside."

"Well, untell him," Bridget shot back, "because we have to leave in half an hour. And where's Ev—"

"But, *Mom!* I need to go to the library to*day*," Cassandra whined, now openly kicking the bottom of the counter. "I have a *project*"—kick—"that's *due*"—kick, kick—"on *Friday*."

"Go take those shoes off, Cassandra. Right now." Bridget snipped the wrapping off the bouquet, trimmed the stems and plunked the carnations into a vase. She flicked on the faucet and filled it with water.

Kick. Kick. Infuriated grimace. Kick. "You're *not* listening, Mom! I need—"

"No, *you're* not listening. Go take off those shoes this instant. And stop. Making. Demands. We'll discuss this in a moment." She turned toward Keaton, who'd grabbed her cell phone and was angrily punching in his friend's phone number, his rigid fifth-grade back to her. "Where's Evan?" she asked him.

Keaton tossed a look over his shoulder, made a How-Am-I-Supposed-To-Know? face and shrugged. "Hey, Josh," her elder son said into the phone. "My mom's *making me* go to soccer now, so I can't play with you today. . . ."

Bridget gritted her teeth. "Evan?" she called out. "Evan, are you in your room?"

No answer.

She focused on her daughter, who'd pitched one of her grimy shoes down half a flight of steps. "Evan got off the bus with you, right?"

Cassandra rolled her eyes. "Y-*es*."

"Then where is he?"

Her daughter huffed and crossed her arms. "In the backyard," she said, as though this should have been obvious.

Bridget struggled to keep a hold of her tempter. "Thank you, Cassandra." She took a full breath. Then another one. "I'll drive you to the library with plenty of time to get your project done before Friday, but we have too much going on tonight, so it'll have to be tomorrow after your catechism class, understand?"

"Whatever," Cassandra muttered. "I'm gonna go read."

"Fine. But you'll be coming with us when we leave."

Her daughter groaned. "Do I have to—?"

"Yes," she said, and then went in search of her youngest child.

Cassandra's grudgingly released information was accurate, however. Bridget discovered her six-year-old son sitting outside on the back patio steps, picking at rogue blades of grass that pushed through the cracks in the concrete.

"Hi, Mommy," Evan said.

She sat next to him. "Hi, honey. Everything okay?"

"Yep. It was just a long day."

"I know the feeling," she murmured. She loved her children with her heart, her soul, her life—even when they were being annoying. But many times she feared this wasn't enough to protect them.

"I kinda felt like throwing up after lunch."

She instinctively pressed the back of her hand to his forehead. No fever. "Does your stomach hurt? Are you sick?"

He shook his dark head.

She thought back to what she'd made him for lunch. A peanut butter and grape jelly sandwich, which he loved. Applesauce. Fruit snacks. Milk. All fine choices normally. "Did you eat something you didn't like?"

He shook his head again. "It's a lot of hours to be there, Mommy." He pressed his soft lips together. "And some people can't be nice for that long."

She reached for his hand and held it. "I'm sorry to hear that, sweetheart." She sighed quietly. Oh, her baby. Out in this big, mean, often confusing world. If only people could just be *happy*. Find the things they were passionate about. Seek joy. How much more pleasant it would be. For everyone. She tried to think of something comforting to say to her son. Some way to help him navigate the rough terrain of first-grade society.

Before she could come up with anything remotely profound, Evan said, "I'm kinda hungry now, though. Can I have a snack?"

"Of course." Still holding his little fingers, she led him into the house, fixed him and his siblings plates of crackers and cheese, got everyone dressed appropriately for the soccer game and made it to the field with two whole minutes to spare. Some days, hitting these marks—transitioning from one activity to the next—felt like a little miracle.

By the time they got back to the house, it was late, Graham had just gotten home from a day at the construction site (a new addition to the town hall), the kids claimed they were starving and the dinner—her gourmet feast of Vietnamese spring rolls, broccoli florets and pecan-encrusted tilapia—had yet to be prepared. She tried to rally the enthusiasm to make it.

"I bought some tasty things at the store this afternoon," she called to her husband cheerfully. He'd squeezed her shoulder when she and the kids walked in the door, but then he'd moved past her, down the hall, to flip on the TV in the family room. ESPN.

"That's great, hon," he called back. "Pull it out. Put it on the table. Let's eat!"

"Well, um, I still have to cook it." And she had no idea how long to expect the tilapia to take. She had a recipe card somewhere but hadn't preheated the oven, prepared the pecan topping, or even washed the dishes so she'd have the pan she needed. Plus, she had to roll the spring rolls. Mix the dipping sauce. Steam the broccoli.

"Microwave it," Graham said, not understanding. He turned up the volume on the TV to drown out the sound of the kids jockeying for a position in front of the screen. "Shouldn't take more than ten or fifteen minutes, right?"

She bit her lip and dug out the recipe card. Total prep plus cooking time was listed as forty-five minutes for the tilapia. "Well . . . I can try." Maybe if she pan-fried it instead? She tried to engage him in a little more conversation by mentioning Keaton's impressive goal attempt during his game.

"Super," Graham said. "Hey, just let us know when you want us to show up for dinner. I'm gonna catch a few minutes of this Bears recap." She could almost hear him tuning her out.

She released a long breath, sank to the floor tiles near the refrigerator, rested her back against a cabinet and stared up at her carnations, still sitting in the vase on the counter in an attempt to brighten up the kitchen.

A study in futility.

She sighed and tried to fight a shakiness that'd started in her bone marrow and was working its way out to her skin. She wanted to reach for a calming handful of M&M's but was too far away from her chocolate drawer. She settled for the last piece of saltwater taffy she had left in her pocket.

How had her life become this? Graham focused only on his construction or installation jobs and his world outside the house. Although he was never cruel to her, he seemed to barely notice her inside theirs. The kids had school and extracurriculars that snatched their attention. Her function in all of their eyes was that of a dutiful wife and mother who'd unquestioningly get them what they needed. So, really, as long as she hit *her* marks, it didn't matter what she did or what kind of changes she tried to make to their routine. The family either didn't want such changes or she didn't have the necessary time to do them justice.

She immediately flashed forward in her mind—not to her fantasy projection of the five of them sitting around a beautifully set table, talking about their days and dipping expertly prepared spring rolls into hoisin-chili sauce with peanut sprinkles—but to the likely reality of such an evening: Cassandra pouting (because that was what pubescent girls did), Keaton declaring that she should *know* by now how much he hated shrimp, Evan quietly picking out every last bean sprout and Graham benignly oblivious to everything but the football scores on TV and in the *Chicago Tribune*'s sports section. They'd each find something wrong with the hummus, too, she realized, and the broccoli, and the tilapia.

With a wave of despair forceful enough to bring on cramps, she pushed herself to standing and yanked open the freezer. Maybe Jennifer wasn't so off base with her questions. Maybe what'd been right for Bridget fifteen years ago wasn't right now. Maybe, rather than feeling guilty about her enjoyment when she was with Dr. Luke, getting to know why she was so happy in his company and so frustrated at home would shed light on her situation. That, in this context, maybe it wasn't such a sin to explore a relationship outside the family after all. No matter what her favorite priest, Father Patrick, would have said on the subject.

She pulled out a couple of large frozen pizzas, checked the cooking time and blinked back a tear. Why keep fighting it?

"Okay, everyone," she called out. "Dinner'll be ready in exactly twelve minutes."

❧ 3 ❧

Tamara

"I wouldn't call a scallion an *undignified* plant," Tamara told her aunt on the phone that afternoon, unable to camouflage a smirk at this latest conversational thread. "Spiny or wild, perhaps, but hardly indecorous." Tamara held her ultrasleek cell phone in one hand and her new Weed Extractor in the other, rooting out unwelcome thistles in her vegetable garden while talking with her favorite relative. Aunt Eliza, a thousand miles away in the rolling Vermont countryside, was employing her time in a similar manner.

"They're coarse. Uncouth," her aunt insisted, no doubt riffling through her extensive mental Rolodex of good Scrabble words to pound home her meaning. "Why on earth did I bother planting them? I much preferred the refined cherry tomato. The sleek bell pepper. The well-mannered pumpkin."

Tamara laughed. "Pumpkins are *not* well mannered. They're viney, they twist and they take up way too much space. They're the most badly behaved plant of them all. Plus, they have the nerve to be *orange.*"

Her aunt giggled on the line. Yes, giggled like a girl—even at the age of eighty-one. The woman was beautiful, wonderful, hilarious . . . and a serious nut job. But, in spite of her persistent prejudice against the scallion and its horticultural cousins (the onion, the leek and the chive), Aunt Eliza hadn't inherited the critical gene that her baby sister, Tamara's mom, had in such abundance. Which was why Tamara called her aunt every other day and her mother only once a week, at most.

"Perhaps I should plant more broccoli next year," Aunt Eliza said. "It's so good for me, though, which isn't in its favor. I can't stand having yet another Good For Me thing on my to-do list."

"Oh, you're so spry, Auntie, you don't need to eat more broccoli." She fought with an especially prickly thistle and won. "Ah! Got that sucker. How's your weeding going?"

"Eh, I'm getting there. I love my Speedy Weedy. I have to finish this up soon, though. Got a date tonight." There was another giggle on the line. "Don't you breathe a word to your mother."

Tamara stopped digging and sat on the parched grass. "What? Of course I won't tell Mom, but who's the lucky guy? Is he tall? Dark? Unbelievably hot?"

"His name's Al. He's a younger man. Seventy-four. I tell you, it's like cradle robbing."

"Oh, seven years is noth—"

"And he's got a New York Giants bumper sticker on his Lexus," her aunt added.

"Well, in that case, maybe you should reconsider," she said with a laugh. Aunt Eliza's late husband had been a staunch Green Bay Packers fan, which had been a point of contention between them for all forty-seven years of their otherwise idyllic marriage. Not because her aunt had anything against football—quite the contrary—but because she only cheered for the Patriots.

"Maybe I'll give him one date. See if he redeems himself," Aunt Eliza mused. "If this Giants thing is just a passing fancy, he might get lucky."

"Auntie," she said, "behave yourself." She laid her head down on the grass, kicked off her gardening Crocs and grinned up at the cloud-streaked sky. "And be careful. Don't do anything I wouldn't do, okay?"

"Ha. Not a chance. You think I'd follow a dictate like that, Tammy-girl? You talk a good game, but I'm a well-seasoned woman. I wanna get my kicks while I'm still kickin'. And, anyway, Al and I are road-tripping to Boston to see *La Bohème*. Not a lot of laughs in that one, so I may have to find something interesting to keep my attention. At least until intermission when I can get myself a dirty martini."

"Wait—does that mean you two are staying overnight? Um, together?"

Her aunt snorted at this. Yes, snorted. She must really like the guy. Aunt Eliza was very loyal to the people and organizations she liked. And very generous, too. Her being a liberal and having lots of money helped, of course.

Tamara knew there was no reining in her aunt once she'd set her stubborn mind on something. "Go for it, Foxy Loxy, but don't—" She was interrupted by that distinctive low beeping, indicating she had another call. She checked her phone. "I'm sorry, Auntie, I've got to get this. It's Jon."

"No problem, honey. I'll call you tomorrow . . . if Al and I don't skip the opera tonight and get hitched." And with a final giggle, she hung up.

Tamara smiled, took a sizeable breath in preparation, then clicked to Jon's call. "Hi," she said. "How are things going in Portland?"

"Fine," he replied, his tone brusque. "Where *are* you?"

"Where *am* I?" she mimicked. "I'm at home."

He huffed as if he didn't believe her.

She could hear through the line the bustle surrounding him in the Oregon courthouse. Jon wasn't traveling to prosecute a case of his own but, instead, to support a fellow lawyer from the firm who was on trial himself. Not a good situation, which probably explained his less-than-merry mood. Although, let's face it, when had Jon been in a *jovial* mood in the past five years? In the past ten?

She tried to project a cheerfulness she didn't feel in hopes he would lighten up. That worked sometimes. "Are you still flying back on Monday?"

"Yes."

There was a pause and she could hear some guy coming up to Jon and asking him a question, which he answered in a surprisingly friendly tone, employing polysyllabic responses and everything. It'd been ages since she'd heard him speak like this. She'd kind of forgotten he could sound that way.

Now someone else joined the conversation, and the three men were chitchatting and laughing, the other two apparently oblivious to the fact that Jon had her on indefinite hold. She could've sworn one guy slapped Jon on the back and said, "Way to go, man," like they were in a bar and he'd just scored a date with the busty cocktail waitress. Well, golly gee. Hand those boys a beer bottle, shine a camera on 'em and they'd be a fucking Bud Lite commercial.

She exhaled hard and shook her head. So, what was the deal? What'd she done to piss him off this time? And why wouldn't he talk to her—his wife—in the friendly manner he used to talk to a couple of strangers?

As tempted as she was to just hang up, she couldn't stop listening to her husband's conversation. It mesmerized her:

Guy 1: You really calmed Garrett down, man. I've never seen that dude look so nervous.

Guy 2: Yeah. He was shakin'. But you set a good example for him of patience and humility, especially right before he faced the bench.

(Jon? Patient? Humble? Yeah, right.)

Guy 2: And your consideration of the judge, too, when he passed us in the hall—

(Jon? Considerate? Like hell.)

Guy 1: It was just awesome, man. His attorney totally loved you. Don't know what Garrett would've done . . .

This snippet of dialogue alone was amazing. Like being in high school and eavesdropping on a description of some cute boy in town, thinking you might really like this warm, kind, enlightened guy being discussed by a couple of adults, but then suddenly realizing the boy in question was that teen psychopath down the street who chewed wads of tobacco behind his parents' shed, ogled twelve-year-old girls on the school bus and, for entertainment, set fire to his kid brother's pet gerbil.

Lucky her to be the only one around privy to her husband's split personality—complete with full access to his jagged and spiteful side. His West Coast pals didn't know what they were missing.

After nearly five minutes of male bonding, the other men left and Jon addressed her again. "Look, Tamara." His voice resumed the degree of coolness it'd had before. "I need you to check a file for me. Since, as you *say*, you're finally at home."

"Where the hell else would I be?" she shot back. His implication that she was lying to him and really painting the town at two in the afternoon was so freakin' irritating. But even worse was the way he treated her, like she was some pesky personal secretary he had to tolerate until the next company downsizing. Sometimes she still couldn't believe she'd abandoned a promising marketing career and left her master's degree unused for this life of servitude.

Then again, Benji had been worth it . . . though now he was gone, too.

Jon sighed, acting as if she'd been the one insulting *him*. "Listen, I tried our home line four times and you weren't there. You're always running around somewhere—shopping or coffee or manicures. Is it too much to expect for you to spend a little time in the house?"

She tossed her weed-removal tool to the ground and marched toward the front door. "Patience" and "humility," her ass! Where the hell was his "consideration" now?

"Jon," she spit out, "you may want to think *outside* the fucking box. I've been at home. But *out* in the yard. I was working on the goddamned garden, and destroying my manicure fingernail by fingernail. However, since you asked me so very *nicely*, I'll go inside now. And help you. Okay?"

You self-centered kumquat.

She could hear the clipped vowels of her own speech still hanging in the air, blanketed by the angry sheen of sarcasm. She almost didn't recognize herself. Not only didn't she feel like the same woman who'd been sprawling on the grass, giggling with her goofy aunt just a few minutes before, she didn't sound like that woman either.

"You can stop with the expletives now," he ground out.

"Only if you stop with your shitty insinuations."

"Fine," Jon said, forcing civility. "Just go into my office and double-check something for me—*please*. It's on my desk in the blue folder on the right-hand side. Look on top of the *Attorneys in America* text. Do you see it?"

Tamara stomped through the door and up the stairs to his office, where she scanned the top of his desk and, yes, spotted the blue folder. "I got it. Now what?"

"Open it and tell me if, in the left pocket, you can find a certificate of deposit for Mid-Atlantic Bank dated around March first of last year."

She riffled through the papers, half expecting to find something incriminating, until she came upon the CD. It, however, looked totally normal. "Okay, I have that."

He breathed a relieved-sounding sigh. "Good. Just tell me who, besides me, signed it."

She read the bank manager's name on the certificate.

"Good," he said again. Then, "Uh, hang on a minute." And suddenly he was back to yakking with somebody else who'd walked by. A woman this time—whoo-hoo. And, again, out popped that über-amiable vocal tone he'd used before.

Tamara squeezed her eyes shut. This was so typical of him—spewing his crappy attitude all over her while faking a Mr. Nice Guy front to the rest of the world. He had such a volatile personality. Calm one minute, argumentative the next. How many times had he done something like this to her? How many of her days did he routinely ruin with his unpredictably foul moods? At least one per week? Maybe two? Regardless, he'd already reached his quota, and she wouldn't let him wreck another one.

She let out a breath she hadn't realized she'd been holding, opened her eyes and glanced out the window in time to see a figure down the street. A tall, muscular figure. One who was working out in his front yard with his light gray T-shirt so drenched in sweat it was sticking to his very buff torso.

Aaron.

Her neighbor worked from home. Must be break time. She admired his cut physique from afar as she waited for her husband to finally finish up his conversation, the view helping her to resent Jon's terseness toward her a little less. As Jon blathered on to this new acquaintance, she tried to push the idea of Aaron's lean, well-defined body from her mind. But it was so easy to imagine him stripping off that damp T-shirt, then peeling off those formfitting blue jeans and—

"Thank you, Tamara. That was all I needed," Jon said coolly, the woman gone and his voice Exhibit A in a case on Dispassionate Interest and Impersonal Contact.

"Um, you're welcome," she murmured, waiting for him to say something else. Apologize for his snappish behavior, perhaps. Ask her about her day. Tell her, like a normal husband would, that he missed her (despite all evidence to the contrary) and was looking forward to seeing her soon. He usually came up with some excuse for his offensive conduct or made an attempt, however paltry, at smoothing things over. It was a pattern she'd grown accustomed to over the years.

But, this time, Jon did none of these. "Enjoy the rest of the week," he said stiffly. "I'll see you on Monday."

And he waited until, at last, she said, "Bye," and hung up on him.

She shook her head, clapped her cell phone shut and resisted the urge to slam it on Jon's desk. Fine. Screw him. She left the phone on his freakin' blue folder. She'd go back outside, she'd work in her garden and she'd be damned if she'd take any more calls from him or from anyone.

She strode out of the room, paused at the top of the stairs and bowed her head. Turning on her toes in a half pirouette—the one thing she remembered from her six years of ballet—she returned to her husband's office and grabbed the phone. No, she had no intention of speaking with Jon anymore, at least not for a couple of days, but there was someone else whose voice she wanted to hear.

She punched in the Austin phone number and waited for her son's answering machine to pick up. "Hi, y'all. This is Ben. Sorry I missed ya. I'm probably at the library studying right now—" This was followed by a few loud guffaws from his roommate. "But if you leave me a message, I'll call you back soon. Thanks for calling, and hook 'em, Horns!"

Despite a pang of loneliness so strong it nearly made her double over, she couldn't help but be flooded with warmth at his message.

Her Benji (so he'd abbreviated himself and was "Ben" now?) was growing into a man. With a voice so deep, so adult. But best of all, he sounded so very happy with his independence. He was free from all parental constraints. The world was a playground of possibilities. And he knew it.

She clicked off without leaving a message. She didn't want to embarrass him with an unnecessary call from Mom when he came home from whatever he was really doing that night (one thing she knew for sure, it wasn't studying at the library). He'd gotten into the habit of calling her on Sundays and, a few times in the past few weeks, when she'd gotten really lucky, he was inspired—or bored—and called her on a random weeknight. She lived for all of those calls.

Meandering outside again, she picked up her Weed Extractor and began a full-fledged attack on those malicious thistles.

"Listen up, you prickly bastards, I'm gonna get you. Don't think you can hide from me, scratch me or infiltrate something I love and not feel the wrathful blade of my sword," she informed the thorny weeds in her lowest and most vengeful tone. She brandished her tool, pointed a chipped index fingernail at the nearest thistle and added a threatening, "Prepare for battle."

Just as she lunged toward the first villainous clump of barbed leaves, she heard a masculine chuckle behind her and a voice rich and resonant saying, *"En garde."*

She swung around. Oooh. Young Neighbor Guy. Still in that sweaty T-shirt, too. "Uh, hi, Aaron."

"Tamara," he said with an amused nod. "I'm afraid I'm interrupting your . . . your, um . . ." He motioned toward the garden.

"Crusade against the Evil Thistle Empire," she finished for him. She grinned and forced herself to project the kind of cool confidence a "woman of her type" (a circular description Jon once used to categorize her) was supposed to project.

"Exactly. It sounded like you were gonna kick their spiny little asses," he said, wiping a few drops of perspiration from his brow. She was about to lob back some flippant reply when his amused expression morphed into a compassionate one. "Frustrating day?"

Before she could verbalize it, her body was saturated with a combination of emotions befitting a woman on a Big Day in her life, not a random Wednesday. A day, perhaps, of either her marriage or her divorce—but not a simple day of weeding. She knew she shouldn't feel so *affected* by his concern. And, yet, she was quivering just beneath the surface, and she could honestly say:

Hell, yes, she was frustrated.

She missed her son.

And her husband was such a callous, insensitive jerk sometimes. Why couldn't *he* have been the one to ask her about her day instead of this (very) cute but uninvolved neighbor?

She tried to sweep away every thought but the one of her own image—the veneer she'd polished until she all but sparkled with self-assurance. "Yep," she answered with practiced carelessness. "Broke a nail fighting these suckers. They're gonna pay."

He shrugged and laughed briefly with her, but his empathetic look still lingered, and she hated that he didn't completely buy her charade.

"Well, I saw you out here and had a favor to ask." He paused as if waiting for permission.

"Of course," she prompted, her imagination running like a cheetah through the possibilities. Did he want to borrow a cup of sugar? Was he hoping she'd collect his mail while he was out of town on some romantic cruise? Was he in desperate need of a tennis partner for a game tomorrow? Hey, she'd play a set or two with him. She flipped her hair off her shoulders and tried to keep from further imagining what *that* would be like. Both of them very hot, very sweaty and—

"I wondered if you might have a handheld trimmer I could use, just for the afternoon. I was about to charge mine, but I'd foolishly left it on the basement floor where my ravenous dog found it and chewed through the power cord."

She laughed, surprised. "Really? Sure. Ours may need to be charged, too, but it might still have ten or fifteen minutes of juice left in it." She studied him, all long-limbed and relaxed. Except for his neck where she could see the tendons tensing. She rethought her reaction. "I—I don't mean to make light of what happened, though. Is your dog okay?"

He broke into a full grin. "Thankfully, yes. The cord was un-plugged. But Sharky's a feisty one. I've come to expect these little disasters."

"You named your dog Sharky?"

"Yep. He's a two-year-old German shepherd I got from Pet Rescue a month ago. Still not quite polite enough to meet the neighbors. We're going to obedience classes," he explained ruefully. "But that devil dog is all mouth. His goal in life is to chew on everything, dig up my backyard and make a nuisance of himself. He's got the energy and the manners of a hyperactive teenager." Aaron's affection for the pooch radiated off him. "Don't know what I'm going to do with him."

"He probably just needs to get laid," she muttered.

"Pardon?" he said, his deep blue eyes blinking at her, the amused expression returning full force.

"Nothing. Sorry." She flushed and race-walked toward the garage so she could grab the trimmer. She needed to make sure her own mouth didn't get her in trouble here. It wouldn't have been the first time, but for some reason she didn't want to come across to *this* man as "flamboyant and frivolous" (yes, another of Jon's flattering descriptive phrases for her). She considered trying to say something serious, but she couldn't think of anything that didn't sound insipid.

She snatched the device off the dusty metal shelf and swiveled around to walk back to him, but he was only two steps behind her. "Oh, okay," she said, almost breathlessly. He was standing so close! "H-Here you go." She placed it carefully in his hands.

"Thanks, Tamara."

Ahh, she loved the way he said her name.

"I'll bring it back tomorrow."

"No rush." She sent him a casual nod. "Keep it as long as you like, Aaron. I've got my work cut out for me here. I'm not doing any detail stuff until I can see my cherry tomatoes in clear rows and be assured they won't be overrun by the Bristly Bad Boys."

He nodded and strolled back toward the garden with her. "I think your cherry tomatoes look great," he said, appraising them. He raised a single eyebrow in her direction before reaching toward one very ripe, very red Sweet Chelsea on a branch near them. "May I?"

God, he was so polite. "Be my guest."

He plucked it, rubbed it against his jeans and held it up for her to see before popping it into his mouth and chewing. "Mmm, good." His lips were so . . . so . . . indescribably intriguing.

Huh.

"So, they're to your satisfaction then?" She feigned a mild interest in his reply and barely glanced at him. Inside her chest, though, her little heart picked up the pace.

He stopped in place and waited until she met his gaze. "I wouldn't worry about perfect rows when you've got a product that tastes this good." Then he broke eye contact with her and scanned the yard. "Why aren't the guys helping you out here? Work? School?"

She explained Jon was on yet another business trip and Benji was officially away at the University of Texas.

He whistled, low and smooth. Lordy, the man was Sexiness personified.

"Big step, starting college. Kind of a big deal for both of you, huh?"

Staggered again by the suddenness of her shifting moods, she drew a shuddering breath at this and tried to brush off the pummeling of emotions that raced like the Running of the Bulls through her system. She strained to smile but couldn't speak.

"Really," he said, tilting his head and edging closer to her. "How are you doing?"

Now, what could she say to this? That she was a fucking mess? No one wanted to hear crap like that. All anybody ever really wanted from her was an "I'm fine" or a "Doing great" or, at most, an "It's been a long day."

But for some reason, as she looked deep into his serious eyes, she found herself unable to maintain her well-honed masquerade, not in the face of all this concern. "Truthfully? N-Not well."

He nodded. "Yeah, I sort of figured that. It's gotta be hard."

She swallowed. "It is."

They walked in silence for a few minutes, making a paisley pattern on the grass with their meandering footsteps.

Aaron rubbed the ridge of his jaw. "I was the youngest kid in a family with three older sisters," he told her, his voice soothing and slow. "When I left, it was tough on my mom. She loves my sisters like crazy and they still get together all the time, just the girls, but it was real difficult for her losing me. Not only because I was the last one to leave home, but because I was her *son*." He met her gaze again and held it for a long moment.

She finally had to look away. She spotted her weed remover a few feet to her left. Snatched it up from the grass. Fiddled uselessly with it.

"My mom and I communicate really well," Aaron continued, "but not in the same chatty way she talks with my sisters. Our conversations are less verbal. It's more about just hanging out together." He sighed and stopped walking. "So, my being gone created a different kind of absence for her, know what I mean?"

Tamara's breathing grew more labored. *Dammit.* "Unfortunately, yeah."

She studied the features of this increasingly alluring but, in essence, unfamiliar man. Tall, lean, strong—yes. But there was something more about him. She was overcome by his intuitive ability to express what she'd been trying to understand about herself and her relationship with Benji but, for some reason, hadn't quite been able to pinpoint. Sure, Aaron was more articulate and in touch with emotions than most men—a characteristic she attributed to his profession as an online men's health magazine writer. Or was it editor? Some literary thing, anyway . . . but still.

She felt her throat tightening and a tempest brewing within her. If one of them didn't change the subject fast, she knew a crying jag would hit. One uncontrollable and torrential enough to rival a tropical rainstorm.

But, despite her efforts to hide her rising emotion, Aaron persisted in noticing it. Noticing *her*. He didn't let her construct her usual facade. He stood next to her as a couple of fugitive tears leaked from her eyes and dropped onto the dry grass.

"I don't know if any of what I said helps." He waited until she wiped her cheeks with the back of her hand and stopped sniffling. "But it's easy to see what a great kid Benji is, even from the few times I've talked with him. You must miss having him at home."

And gently, very gently, he reached out his hand and touched her forearm. Just a couple of fingertips, but they burned his kind words into her skin and warmed her.

"Thanks for understanding," she murmured as he pulled away and took a few steps toward the curb.

"Hey, it's okay. Hang in there, you hear? I'll see you soon." He raised his palm in a quick wave and added, "Thanks, again, for letting me borrow this." He motioned to the trimmer.

"You're welcome." She swiped at her eyes and smiled a little. "Just bribe Sharky with a nice leather loafer or something—I'd suggest some tasty Armani—so he stays away from cords."

He chuckled. "I will."

And as Aaron strode back toward his house, she stared after him. No longer thinking about his sweaty shirt or even his cut physique. Her only prevailing thought, which spooled like a never-ending mental loop through her addled brain, was, *What could've induced any woman to divorce* him?

He was, in Tamara's not-so-humble opinion, a man without fault.

❧ 4 ❧

Jennifer

Thursday, September 9

"The dish towel caught on fire," Jennifer's husband, Michael, informed her as he dropped the singed green terrycloth into the sink and turned on the faucet.

She watched steam rise from the stainless-steel basin and counted the seconds until the fire alarm would likely go off. Five, four, three, two—

The blaring noise assaulted her ears. Jennifer eyed the alarm. Couldn't be too much power left in that battery after all the use it'd been getting lately. Good thing daylight savings time was coming to an end soon. She needed an excuse to make Michael change the 9-volt.

The latest problem, of course, was the toaster oven; the dish towel was merely an innocent bystander. Something invariably went wrong daily between 6:10 A.M., when Michael stepped out of his hot shower, and 7:20 A.M., when he grabbed his briefcase filled with student quizzes, his *¿Habla Español?* teacher's guide and the keys to his Toyota before heading off to work.

How did she know this? Well, because yesterday's problem had been the hair dryer.

And the day before it had been the rechargeable shaver.

And one memorable morning last week it'd been the microwavable omelet maker.

She and Michael had had a month of appliance malfunctions with which to mark the deterioration of morning conversation from "Hi, honey, how'd you sleep?" to "Quick, grab the fire extinguisher!"

If she didn't know better, she'd think Michael was set on destroying the house one electrical device at a time, simply to get out of asking her how she was doing, what she was thinking or why she was spending so many hours glued to her computer screen.

Thus far, his strategy had proven effective.

"I'll turn off the alarm," she said.

"Great, thanks," Michael called to her as she opened up a kitchen window, then fanned the smoke alarm with last month's issue of *At Home with Bits-n-Bytes* magazine until it stopped its high-pitched alert. "I can buy some new dish towels this weekend," he added.

"Don't worry about it," she said evenly. Michael was not exactly Mr. Bed, Bath & Beyond. He'd be more likely to get distracted at the strip mall, wind up at a Starbucks and write an "Elegy to the Earth" on one of their paper napkins about how "the scorched jade of the cloth was like seared bamboo shoots; foliage burnt by human avarice and neglect. . . ."

Which was precisely why *she* handled all the practical matters in their household.

The girls came trudging down the stairs. Shelby, "almost thirteen," as she liked to say, sniffing and wrinkling her freckled nose as she walked. "What's burning now?"

"Nothing, sweetheart," Michael told her reassuringly. "The edge of the towel just got caught in the toaster oven. But, hey, I made you girls some cinnamon toast. Want a slice?"

"We're *women*, Dad," Veronica, Resident Freshman, said with a tone that would have been ironic had she not sounded so pleased with herself.

Michael, having been admonished by his nearly fifteen-year-old daughter to refer to her as a "lady" or a "woman" and not a "girl" (ever since the advent of her period some three years ago), had been more successful than not in "avoiding the perpetuation of sexist stereotypes within their home." However, sometimes

Jennifer just wished he would go a little alpha male on her. Be a fix-it man for a change.

"Sorry, sorry, *ladies*," he said with a good-natured laugh. He picked up a plate stacked with cinnamon toast and offered it to their children.

Shelby gamely took one and put hers on a small plate. "Thanks, Dad." She sat down at the table and nibbled on the corners.

Veronica took one, too, kissed her father on the forehead and ate her slice over the sink, bits of sugar and cinnamon clinging to her lip gloss and reminding Jennifer of a little girl with fairy-princess makeup.

"Want some?" Michael asked Jennifer, his voice hopeful.

She nodded and took a piece, even though she wasn't hungry. Even though, after eighteen years of marriage, he should know how rarely she ate breakfast. But Michael so wanted to please "his girls," and she didn't want to disappoint him.

"Well, I've gotta go." He squeezed Veronica, pecked the top of Shelby's head, kissed Jennifer on the cheek and grabbed his briefcase and a slice of toast for the road. "Hope you *women* have a great day."

"Bye, Dad!" the girls called out in chorus.

"See you tonight, Michael," Jennifer said a few beats later.

And though he'd already reached the door, he peered back over his shoulder at the three of them and grinned. "Love you all."

"Love you, too," cried the girls.

Jennifer didn't answer. *What about ME do you love?* Always, she wondered this.

She sighed as she heard him start his car and pull out of the driveway. She understood instinctively what he loved about their daughters, but he'd never answered the question sufficiently enough for *her*. When she worked up the nerve to ask, he'd always mumble something about how "he sensed her quiet cleverness" or how "she navigated their family waters with astute tranquility." But, aside from a nod at her intellect and her ability to remain calm in a crisis, these weren't concrete qualities—qualities that by themselves would or should inspire "love."

Rather, his words had the ring of a line from one of his poems.

Embellished and a touch contrived. Though, to be fair, Michael proved himself to be a good husband, a good father, a good *man*. Only problem was, he dwelled in a wholly different universe from hers (and not just in his bizarre preference for Macs over PCs). He always had. But, then, that was what she'd been looking for when she got married.

Jennifer checked the digital clock above the stove. "School bus," she announced, glad their district was small enough that both her daughters could still leave at the same time on the same bus. That the junior high and the high school were right next to each other. It made Veronica's transition to the "big building" a bit easier this year.

Veronica, who seemed to be filling out a little more every day (or maybe her shirt and her jeans were just tighter?), was busy downing a tall glass of milk to accompany her second piece of toast. She rolled her hazel eyes and sniggered. "*Seriously*, Mom, we can tell time." Self-possessed and just a tad condescending, she directed a mocking grin at her sister. "Bet I can beat'cha out there."

Shelby, with the poise of a duchess and the long-suffering sigh of a younger sibling, glanced at Jennifer and smirked. "You know she only says that, Mom, because she thinks if we race I won't notice she's wearing my leather sandals." She pointed a triumphant index finger at Veronica, who'd hidden her feet behind the kitchen counter. "Ha. Caught you!"

Veronica giggled. "You said I could wear them if I let you wear my black tee. Remember?"

"Oh, yeah."

"Yeah. How quickly we forget." Veronica brushed some crumbs into the sink. "So . . . race ya anyway?"

Shelby feigned a pensive look, then shoved her chair back, jumped to her feet with a squeal and pushed past her older sister to the door. They somehow snatched their backpacks and their hoodies and were on the porch with a shout of "Bye, Mom" in stereo before Jennifer could even make it to the window to watch them.

Snorting with laughter, her daughters sprinted toward their bus stop. A few leafy trees blocked her view, so she couldn't tell who'd won the race. Didn't matter, though. The girls—nay, the *women*—loved each other. And she adored this about them.

Jennifer paused and listened to the inebriating silence within the house, punctuated only by the hypnotic ticking of the grandfather clock in the foyer and the clackity-click of the lilac branches tapping a coded message against the family room window.

She released a long, slow breath. Alone at last.

She ambled down the hall to her PC and, finally, *finally*, was able to flip it on for the day.

Beep.

The whirl of her computer coming to life made her feel like a gambling addict facing a favorite casino machine. Who knew what she'd find in her Inbox today? A single message? A strike out? Or a lucky streak of three in a row? She wouldn't know until she typed in her password and checked her Yahoo! account.

Nine messages.

One for a Viagra-like product. Two for cheap Rolex replicas. A few for oil-change offers and restaurant coupons . . . Oooh, 20 percent off her total bill at the Happy Szechwan. And one—just one—from David.

She clicked on that first.

He wrote:

Damn. We have a morning meeting scheduled with the IT squad. Might run late. Can we IM at 10:14 instead?

She suppressed a smile and found herself scrolling to the bottom of the page, trying to keep from reading their correspondence in reverse. She wanted to review her e-mail history with David from the beginning, which had become an odd preoccupation for her, like a new OCD acquired and made instantaneously habitual.

His first message had been sent on August 13.

Subject: CPU Reunion!

Jenn—it's been a while. Bet you didn't expect to get a message from me, huh? Got your e-mail address from the alumni office, along with all 26 members of the CPU Club during our four years in college. You remember

Mitch, right? He and I are planning a reunion for the weekend of November 13 and wanted to let everyone know. More details to follow, but I hope you can come.

David Saxon
CPU Club President

Like she wouldn't remember who he was or that he'd been their president. And, of course, there was the matter of their club's name, which university administrators always assumed meant "Central Processing Unit"—the brains of the computer or, in this case, the campus.

Anyone who knew *David,* however, knew it wouldn't mean something that obvious. With David, hidden messages were expected. And if they weren't mathematical in origin, they were sexual.

She'd worked up the nerve to respond three days later:

Hi, David,
It WAS a surprise to get your e-mail. A reunion sounds fun. I'll tentatively put the date on my calendar. Are spouses and children invited, or is it a party just for club members?
Jenn

And, yes, she signed "Jenn" not "Jennifer" because with him—and *only* with him—she used that nickname. It always made her feel like a different person. "Jenn" was the focused, sharply observant, almost confident college girl—quietly energized by possibilities. "Jennifer" was the mousy, retiring, vaguely bored married woman she'd morphed into—silently dissatisfied by routine.

Within forty-eight hours, David had shot a reply back:

I heard you were married. Any kids? I've been with Marcia (an old friend of my sister's, maybe you remember her?) for 11 years now, married for 9. Our boys are 2 and 6.

As for the party, it was supposed to be alumni only—members from years 1–4. But I'll check with Mitch and see if he's interested in changing that.

Of course he had to mention his sister. Ugh. So, Sandra had finally matched him up with Little Miss Betty Crocker after all. Well, good for them. Jennifer hoped he still liked pecan pie. She wasn't convinced Marcia could cook anything else.

She tried to wait it out, but she didn't hear back from him about Mitch's opinion. Since David had asked her specific questions, she finally gave in and returned his message a week later, her fingers skimming across the keyboard like a child pretending to play a baby grand. Only, Jennifer hit every intended key:

Michael and I met not long after graduation. (A bit of a dig since David had left her just BEFORE graduation.) *His parents are great people, and mine just adore him.* (Another dig, but David deserved it. Her parents hadn't approved of David AT ALL.) *We got married after 8 months and have been together for 18 years.* (Double his marital length, so ha! Take that.) *We have two daughters, one almost 15 and the other who'll turn 13 this winter.*

About the reunion—a small gathering is fine. No need to change plans. I just wasn't sure what to expect. Did you have a time in mind? (She wrote this even though it was ridiculous. This was DAVID—of course he had a time in mind. Most likely, a very specific one.)

Four interminable days went by before his response came:

Yes. I'd planned on Saturday night. Drinks at 5:07, followed by a few games of Monkey Pong. Dinner to start at 7:02 sharp. What do you think?

She shook her head. Why, why, why did this guy still get to her? How, how, how did he know exactly what to say?

Her: *Sounds like old times.*

Then the messages followed each other in a flurry of text and type—each posted within twelve hours or less of the last.

Him: *Where do you live now?*

Her: *Glendale Grove. A northwest Chicago suburb. You?*

Him: *Just outside of Springfield.*

Interesting and odd. Because while Springfield was Illinois's capital city and it had its share of data-related jobs, it wasn't exactly the Technological Hotbed of the Western World. She hadn't pictured him working for some small tech company. She'd imagined him in Northern California all these years. On business trips to Germany, Singapore, Japan. Or living in Champaign-Urbana at the very least. After all, U of I was based there and that had been their rival computer school, with more grads placed at Microsoft than any other university in the country. Even more than C-IL-U, their college. And that was saying something.

Her: *You're not in Silicon Valley?*

Him: *Nope. Look, no one signed up for the location committee, wanna volunteer? I could use a few suggestions. Maybe we could IM for a couple of minutes next week? Just about possible spots for the reunion. I'd appreciate your input.*

Oh, God. That was almost like talking live for them. More than 60 percent of their college "conversations" had been through on-line messaging, back even before AOL (when they used Quantum Link) and long before the rest of the nongeek world joined in the fun.

Her: *Sure. Next Thursday would work. I'll be at home all morning.*

Him: *Thanks. We can chat then. Say around 9:49?*

Her: *Ha. Okay.*

Because, of course, thirteen had been their lucky number. Naturally, he would have e-mailed her first on the thirteenth of last month, planned the party for the thirteenth of another month, chosen every single digit or clock time he could possibly manipulate to be a multiple of thirteen (507, 702, 949 . . .). Something no one but the two of them would have known or understood.

But she'd known: It was David's apology.

And she'd understood: It was his way of making sure she knew he remembered what they'd shared.

And now this new message on the day he was supposed to IM. So he had an info tech meeting this morning? Shocker. She'd be here at 10:14 A.M., but she just didn't want to make everything so easy for him. He'd always reeled her in with such little effort. She typed: *Make it 10:27.*

She rolled her eyes. Yeah, she was really playing hard to get. She hit SEND anyway.

And sure enough, precisely at 10:27 A.M. Central Standard Time, while she was halfheartedly working on one of her commissioned Web designs, her computer alerted her to his incoming instant message.

David: *Hi, Jenn.*

Her pulse sped up. She put her fingers to the keyboard and tried unsuccessfully to keep them steady.

Jenn: *Hey, there. How are you?*

David: *X-ellent. You?*

God, he still typed that word the same way he did at age twenty-two.

Jenn: *Great, thanks.*

Except for the night sweats she got at half past ten this morning and the fact that her fingers were trembling so badly she could barely hit the keys. Yep, she was great.

David: *Been nice being back in touch with you after all these years. Brought back a lot of memories.*

He'd hit return after this, but she could see the little message at the bottom of the text box telling her he was typing another line.

David: *So, is your husband home right now? Or your kids?*

Jenn: *No. Shelby and Veronica are at school—seventh grade and freshman year. And Michael's at work. He teaches high school Spanish to juniors and seniors.*

She'd expected a reaction, and she got one—quick.

David: *Spanish? No shit?! Did he manage to teach you any of it?*

She picked at the cuticle on her thumb for a second before typing back.

Jenn: *Un poco. A phrase here and there. Not much.*

David: *Wow. But still . . .*

And she could almost see him standing next to her, grinning. The freckles dotting his nose. The wire-rimmed glasses reflecting her adoring gaze back at her.

David: *We barely made it through Spanish 204, remember? F*king foreign language requirement.*

Jenn: *True. But we DID pass.*

She couldn't type any more than that, though, because to comment further would lead only to bringing up additional memories.

Like the night they'd crammed for the Spanish 204 final. The drinking and computer gaming before they studied. The making love after.

David: *We did.*

And although he agreed, he was also noticeably silent on any follow-up reminiscences.

Jenn: *What's Marcia been doing these days? Still baking?*

Okay, she couldn't resist a little dig here.

David: *Funny you'd remember that . . . yeah. She works part time at a restaurant. One my sister owns.*

Jenn: *Really?*

Of course she did. Those two were inseparable.

David: *Yep. She and Sandra are still best friends. Which, actually, surprises no one. Half the time I think Marcia married me just so she and Sandra could officially be sisters. Ha!*

His laugh, even in electronic form, came across as forced. Especially with his follow-up line.

David: *Sometimes they're a more compatible couple than Marcia and I are. LOL.*

Hard to tell, but wasn't there a tinge of bitterness in his response? To her it seemed so.

Jenn: *Oh.*

David: *Anyway, she's . . . content with life.*

And then there was a pause in their IM'ing, long enough to let his meaning sink in, as Jennifer was sure he knew it would.

This was pure David Saxon, Cipher Man. Purposely butchering Karl Marx, David always used to say, "Contentment is the opiate of the masses." During college, he'd complained about his sister's "pesky friend Marcia" to Jennifer. "You'll never believe what a dope she is!" he'd exclaimed, in full irritation mode one day. "I was talking to her about Marx, and she said, 'Richard Marx? Like the singer?' I could've strangled her."

But, instead, he'd married her.

Jenn: *I see.*

She was determined not to get drawn into some marital weirdness and discord although, clearly, David was not content with his wife's contentedness.

She typed a new line to change the subject.

Jenn: *How about your boys? What're they like?*

David: *Ah, John's in first grade. He's into dinosaurs and a wide variety of reptiles. Paul is our two-year-old and he's pretty much all about trucks these days.*

She laughed aloud before responding, tracking his latest clue.

Jenn: *What? Not a guitar between them? (*grin*)*

David: *Now, now. I chose John's name, okay. But Paul was Marcia's idea.*

Jenn: *Oh, sure. And you did nothing to persuade her? Why don't I believe that . . . ? Does she realize you'll expect a George and a Ringo, too?*

David: *Nah. There won't be any more kids. Plus, believe it or not, she's not a Beatles fan.*

She rolled her eyes before firing back a reply.

Jenn: *She's gotta like Wings. Everybody liked them.*

She hit return and began to type a new line. She got as far as *Or what about John Len*—before her message was interrupted by his.

David: *Nope. Not "Silly Love Songs." Not Lennon's solo stuff. She called "Imagine" BORING once.*

Jennifer didn't know what to say to this. How about: *That's what you get for leaving me after nearly three years together, running away from our future plans and marrying a little twit five years younger than you.* Tempting as it would be to fling this back at him, she refrained.

David: *Anyway, I've gotta get back to work. I wanted to run some places on campus by you, but I've got a better idea now.*

She waited as he typed a new line, literally holding her breath and wondering what his "better idea" would be.

David: *Mitch e-mailed me a list of possible bars, restaurants, dining halls and stuff. But it's been a while since I visited C-IL-U. Have you been there recently?*

Jenn: *No.*

David: *Maybe we could check it out together. It's been so long, I'm not sure what'd be good anymore. Plus, it'd be nice to catch up in person before the reunion, maybe even take a trip to Russia.*

Translation from David-Code: Visit *their* restaurant. The Winter Palace. The one that served the best Chicken Kiev west of St. Petersburg.

Oh, God. Go back to campus? With HIM?

Jenn: *Is it still there?*

David: *I think so. I HOPE so. I know it's a lot of time to be gone in one day, but if you're able to, I'd really appreciate your help. Your husband wouldn't mind, would he? You hanging out with an old friend for a few hours?*

Michael wouldn't be aware of the degree of danger—that was what she *thought*. But that wasn't what she *typed*.

Jenn: *No. Would Marcia?*

David: *Nah.*

The reply came back perhaps too quickly, and she was confused by the turn their messaging had taken. It was followed by a line far more confounding, however.

David: *It's just an innocent get-together to scout locations. And we could meet somewhere we both know well. At the front doors of the library, maybe. How far of a drive is it for you? 2 hours?*

Jenn: *A little less. You?*

David: *About 3. But it'd be interesting to see some of those campus hot spots again.*

With her?

Jenn: *Well, yes . . .*

He didn't wait for her to construct an excuse.

David: *What are your Fridays like?*

Jenn: *Not good. I have yoga.*

David: *Yoga? WTF?!*

Even in text form, he couldn't disguise his shock. In his defense, she'd been pretty anti-floor-exercise in college. Unless he counted the number of times they'd had sex on his sleeping bag in his parents' basement.

Jenn: *It's for health reasons.*

She didn't bother explaining she'd had to do *something* to counterbalance her techie side. She lived so much of her life in her head. And, besides, her doctor had ordered her to do it to "manage her anxiety," which she always tried to keep hidden. But her blood pressure told the truth, so she'd had no choice but to sign up for classes.

Jenn: *I've been going every Friday morning for the past couple of years. It's a nonnegotiable part of my routine.*

This, of course, wasn't strictly true. She met her friends an hour before yoga was set to begin. She actually left the Indigo Moon Café in time to make it to the gym only about once every third week. But her ex-boyfriend didn't need to know this, particularly since her husband didn't.

David: *Well, you always were flexible.*

She swallowed and tried to push away the memories that pummeled her at these words, not to mention his insinuations. She didn't answer.

David: *So, okay—not Fridays. How about a Thursday then? Not next week. I've got a presentation scheduled, but maybe the next one?*

Jenn: *Bluetooth?*

She was, of course, aware that even though he wasn't living in California he was still working full time in the high-tech computer world. But she could only guess at what, specifically, he was doing.

David: *You bet'cha.*

She could almost hear his pride.

David: *I'm with Syn-Sig Tech. We specialize in GPS receivers, but I'm also working on a project with our Swedish branch on internal notebook cards. You'd love this stuff, Jenn. You're still in the field, aren't you?*

Oh, how best to answer him? Much as she would've loved to embellish, she opted for honesty.

Jenn: *Yes, but I'm just designing basic Web pages at home. Mostly for local businesses.*

She didn't add that these easy jobs had allowed her the autonomy to be a stay-at-home mom, which had been a priority for her, particularly when the girls were little. Or that they needed her income to supplement Michael's teaching salary. She especially didn't mention how much she'd dreamed of being truly innovative in the field or how, maybe, she might have lived up to her programming potential if she and David had stayed together.

David: *I'll bet you do great work. E-mail me a few links to your projects. I'd like to see them.*

Jenn: *Sure. Thanks.*

Like hell she would.

David: *And, if you help me out with the reunion, maybe I'll bring you a USB dongle as a gift. Ours are ice-cream-cone shaped, and they come in special neon colors. . . .*

Like condoms. *Sure, David. Talk dirty to me.* He had a way of making even talk of flash drives sound filthy. She squeezed her eyes shut and typed:

Jenn: *That won't be necessary.*

Then she pulled her fingers away from the keyboard.

David: *C'mon, it'll be fun. Would two weeks from now work for you? Thursday the 23rd?*

She knew she had nothing special on her calendar for that day. But should she drive all the way back to C-IL-U? To *their* college? Just to see David again? She needed to buy time before answering.

Jenn: *I'll have to get back to you. Let me check our family calendar and verify a few appointments. I'll e-mail you next week.*

David: *Thanks. And, Jenn?*

Jenn: *Yeah?*

David: *I've missed talking to you.*

Jenn: *Same here.*

She clicked off their connection and took several of those deep-cleansing yoga breaths, which supposedly removed toxins and prevented hyperventilation. But would it release all her pent-up feelings about David Saxon from her body?

Not likely.

As much as she didn't want to have to confess what'd been going on to Bridget and Tamara, she needed to. She had to talk to somebody about this. Thank God tomorrow was Friday.

She wasn't sweating quite so profusely anymore, but her skin was clammy and her hands still shook. It was a strange sensation, right down to her fingertips—like clipped wings regenerating but still not long enough or strong enough for flight. And, wow, was the process ever painful.

David's leaving had swept the wind from beneath her in college. She'd felt so unbelievably deflated, all the progress she'd made toward confidence and self-assurance having blown away in his absence. Being no longer sure of her footing on the ground, she was unable to lift off and fly after graduation. Not like she'd hoped.

Michael was David's opposite and, perhaps, too far a swing in the pendulum of relationships. She'd desperately wanted someone who didn't remind her of David *at all*, and Michael fit that bill like no other:

He was flowery in his speech and mannerisms, whereas David was direct to the point of bluntness.

Poetic-linguistic whereas David was mathematical-logical.

Sappily romantic vs. sexual, bordering on kinky.

Technicolor vs. black and white.

Openly loving vs. secretive, skeptical and shielded.

Michael was so much *easier* to love than most men, and he clearly cared about her, too. So, Jennifer didn't know why she was still drawn to a challenging man she hadn't seen or even spoken to over a phone line in eighteen years.

No. That was a lie. She knew exactly why.

She had loved David *first*. He'd flipped on her switch and never turned it off. On a certain level, she was as binary in her thinking as the processing chips inside her HP tower—a characteristic that David fully understood in a way her husband didn't and couldn't.

And she wouldn't be the least bit surprised if David, intentionally or not, used this knowledge against her. He was capable of a great many trespasses.

David, unlike Michael, didn't exaggerate, didn't embroider. Not ever. David had once called her a "talented mute who could type fast," and he meant this literally. Yet, she could believe his declaration, even though it bordered on unkind. A part of her almost reveled in the sting of it, craved the tangibility of the insult.

She Googled her alma mater's home page. So many acronyms. C-IL-U (the school—Central Illinois University). TJH (the dorm—Thomas Jefferson Hall). CPU (the club—Carnal Pundits Unlimited).

Seeing snapshots of the places she'd loved in this isolated, two-dimensional forum was painful, too. A part of her still existed in that world. If she squinted, she could almost see her body walking around in the pictures. In many of them, holding hands with

David. But *that* Jenn had been neglected . . . betrayed not just by an old lover, but by herself.

Realizations like these kept her up at night. They lived in memory's infamy and tended to pop into her consciousness at the oddest possible moments. While paying bills. Or driving to yoga. Or cleaning up Michael's latest morning disaster. Of course, IM'ing with David again had made it worse. They'd been so right for each other. But *still* he'd walked away. Lame excuses and all.

She'd cry about it if she could, but she'd shed her tears decades ago. So, instead, she just listened to the crickets inside her computer tower with their twitters and beeps. She could've sworn they were chirping an old song she'd heard again at the café not long ago. Carole King. "It's Too Late."

Was it? And for which relationship?

❧ 5 ❧

The Trio

The café was hopping at nine A.M., but the ladies, sequestered at their favorite corner table, were oblivious to the concerns of their fellow Indigo Moon patrons.

Not only were none of them late on this sunny and rather temperate morning, all of them were at least ten minutes early. (Even Bridget, who tended to cut things close.)

Each woman had found the week an exercise in fluctuating emotions, discovering the dividing line between titillating and terrifying to be precariously narrow. All had an incident to share—and advice to seek—but each worried about how her friends would perceive her.

Tamara spoke up before the other two. "Okay. We've gotta talk."

Jennifer gave an owlish blink, cleared her throat and said, "I know."

Bridget bobbed her head. Catching Tamara's eye and twisting her lips upward on one side, she added, "I think we could use some brain wave energy first."

Their waitress brought them a tray of their usual mocha lattes—crafted to individual specifications—and a platter of grilled double-chocolate-chip muffins. Bridget, in desperate need of comfort food, did not concern herself with calorie counting or portion control on this day, nor did Jennifer claim lack of appetite.

As David Gates and the rest of Bread crooned "Make It with You" on seventies XM radio, the women (immersing themselves in carbs of both the aural and oral variety) devoured the muffins with a voraciousness fitting a pack of *Survivor* contestants at their final, prevote buffet.

"That helped," Tamara commented. "But I had a . . . weird day yesterday." She squinted at Jennifer and Bridget, remembering Aaron's return of the trimmer to her house, his visit to her kitchen and the peculiar conversation that followed. How much should she tell her friends?

"Oh, God! Me too!" exclaimed Bridget, brushing crumbs from her lips and chin. Muffins or no muffins, she'd eaten one of Dr. Luke's heavenly cannoli at the dental office yesterday afternoon and remained incapable of getting that taste out of her mouth.

"Me three," murmured Jennifer, thinking, of course, about her IM session with David the morning before. Then louder, "Really weird."

"What happened with you?" Tamara asked Jennifer, figuring if she quizzed the others first she'd get a clue as to how much to reveal.

"David instant messaged me," Jennifer told them. "He wants us to meet. In two weeks." She gulped two long, consecutive swallows of her latte. "Should I do it?"

Bridget crumpled her napkin, trapping a few errant chocolaty morsels. "What did he say? What led up to this?"

Jennifer explained about scouting on campus for a party location and tried to put into words the pull of a man who wooed her with multiples of thirteen and talk of Bluetooth devices. Her friends were understandably perplexed.

Tamara frowned. "When he left you, at the end of college, did he explain why he was breaking things off? Talk with you about it personally?"

Jennifer shook her head. "But he faxed me a note a week later."

Bridget pivoted toward Tamara for confirmation. "Did she just say he *faxed* her?"

"She did," Tamara said. Then, to Jennifer, "What did this post-breakup fax say?"

At this point, Jennifer had to career a little bit away from the truth. As always, there was what David *said,* and there was what David *meant.* Outsiders could never decode his words correctly.

"He explained that he needed space to make a few decisions. That he didn't want to lead me on if he couldn't follow through. He apologized for not being strong enough to tell me this in person, but he hoped I'd forgive him someday. That it was all for the best."

"Did you believe him?" Bridget asked her.

"No. N-Not entirely."

"Then why do you think he *really* did it?" Tamara said.

"I think his sister got into his head." Jennifer took a deep breath and downed the rest of her latte. "I think that bitch had an ulterior motive."

Bridget blinked. Unlike Tamara, Jennifer only swore on rare occasions and usually under her breath. Plus, these curses were directed inward. Jennifer didn't make a habit of name-calling so, to Bridget's mind, David's sister must've been one serious Medusa.

Tamara's eyes widened as she heard this, too. Her gaze and Bridget's locked across the table before Tamara, not about to let social niceties prevent her from getting the dirt on the ex-boyfriend, turned her attention fully on Jennifer. "Huh. Wanna elaborate?"

Jennifer inhaled deeply and cleared her throat, unaccustomed to delivering long speeches or sharing such personal stories, but she was willing to make a partial exception this time. "Sandra is five years younger than her brother and me. David and Sandra's parents didn't have the best marriage. Not so much shouting and overt aggravation"—*unlike her own family,* Jennifer thought—"as it was a continual freeze out." She shivered remembering the war being waged in front of her eyes during her few visits to their house. The battleground of raised eyebrows, clenched jaws, deadly silence during mealtimes. Or worse, the forced joviality. "They had a really stiff, undemonstrative family life and, as the only kids in the house, David and his sister formed a special bond. Almost like a sibling pact, actually. It was an unspoken decision to ignore their parents' coldness."

"So, the two of them are pretty close," Bridget said.

Jennifer nodded. "Well, Sandra came up for Little Brothers and Sisters weekend one time, after David and I had been together for about eight months, but before I'd met his parents. Even though I was really nice to her and showed her around the dorm and made her s'mores, she moped around the whole time and kept looking at me like I was the devil incarnate. David tried to tell me that she was just overwhelmed, a small-town girl on the big college campus. But I'd overheard her telling him that he seemed like 'a different David' when I was around."

"She was threatened by you," Tamara inserted. "And she thought you were going to come between her and her only family ally."

"That's really sad," Bridget said.

"Oh, yeah. I pitied her at first, too. Then summer vacation came and David invited me home with him for the weekend." Jennifer shuddered at the memory. "We were between our sophomore and junior years in college then. Sandra had just finished her freshman year of high school. In her words, since David got to have 'a friend' stay overnight, she should be able to have one, too. Her parents agreed, and Sandra's 'friend' was a flirty little airhead named Marcia. A teen as different from Sandra's brooding, manipulative behavior as humanly possible. Maybe because Sandra wished she could be as easygoing and bubbly as her friend, or maybe just because Sandra could control her so well, she had a soft spot in her frozen heart for Marcia."

"And David was attracted to her?" Tamara asked.

"Not at all." Jennifer paused. "Well, not at first. At first he thought she was a dork. Marcia had no academic talents. She was very much a C student, which David—being brilliant—looked down upon. But she was lighthearted, made Sandra less grim to be around and even I thought she was kind of fun. David told me how much he appreciated seeing his sister happy, so he continued to encourage their friendship."

Bridget leaned forward. "But?"

"But Sandra was just setting up her master plan. She wanted David and Marcia in her life, and she wanted me out of it. So she convinced Marcia that David had a secret crush on her but couldn't

act on it because of me. And anytime David was home from college, Sandra would parade Marcia around in front of him. We both
thought it was funny and juvenile at first, but as the girls got
older—high school sophomores, then juniors—it started getting
more serious.

"The last time I was there, it was spring break of our senior year
in college. Not even two months before he broke things off with
me. Marcia was seventeen by then, tall and pretty. She'd had a few
short-term relationships that I think Sandra managed to talk her
out of, and she still held a torch for David. Sandra knew David and
I had been making future plans. We weren't ready to get married
yet, but we were talking about getting jobs in the same area,
putting a deposit down on an apartment, moving in together. But
Sandra just wouldn't let up on the Marcia thing, and David had
stopped complaining about how irritating it was that Marcia had
this crush on him and was always baking pies and things with Sandra at their house. He said it was like having 'another little sister,'
and I, convinced he and I had a life together, tried to ignore the
way his sister kept working to exclude me.

"We'd just come from two days at my parents' place, where
we'd had an argument because he felt my parents, especially my
dad, didn't like him. Dad kept grilling him on his career plans and
asking if he'd consider grad school, etc., etc." Jennifer didn't explain to her friends that this was her father's modus operandi, however. That his interrogation style of conversation and overbearing
presence had been a painful constant in her life. Nor did she add
that David's slides into pompousness and his tendency toward
game-playing were transparent to her, often funny, and seemed,
by contrast to her father's interpersonal conduct, a minute behav-
ioral infraction. That David's manners were in many ways a reprieve from what she'd grown accustomed to. "So by the time we
got to David's house, he was already defensive and nothing I said
was the right thing.

"Sandra made sure we had almost no time alone to work things
out. She'd whisper stuff to him and to her friend when I was just
out of earshot, and she made sure that every night I stayed over,
she and Marcia had a sleepover, too. The last straw was her en-

couraging Marcia to model the latest Victoria's Secret sleepwear they'd picked up on their most recent shopping trip that week. It was a sheer ivory teddy, which left little to the imagination. I walked out of the room, but David stayed and watched, saying to me later, 'Aw, c'mon. It was hilarious.' The next day I told him to drive me back to my parents. He did and, on the road, he told me he was just humoring the girls but was sorry I'd felt uncomfortable . . . and blah, blah, blah. We sort of patched things up and, once we were back at school, everything seemed normal—"

"Until he suddenly left you," Tamara said.

"Right."

"Jennifer, didn't David go to graduation? Did you really just not see him again anywhere for those last couple of weeks?" Bridget asked.

"No, he managed to avoid me very well. The only exams he had left were in classes we didn't have together. He was living off campus with a few buddies that semester, and whenever I called there, I got their answering machine. When I stopped by, no one opened the door. I know he completed his class work and all the requirements for graduation, but he skipped the ceremony altogether. He disappeared from my life as if he'd never been there." Saying it aloud, remembering it, reliving it, brought the rush of pain back into her body as if those eighteen years hadn't buffered her from it at all.

"That sounds just horrible," Bridget said, her voice so sympathetic Jennifer had to resist the embarrassing impulse to cry in public. "It does seem like his sister had something to do with your breakup."

Jennifer sucked in some more air and forced her emotions back under wraps. "I'm not doubting it. The question isn't whether or not David was manipulated. The question is how much—or how little—he regretted his choice. I'm inclined to believe it wasn't enough."

"Well," Tamara said reasonably, "any college guy who could be so easily manipulated by a couple of high-school girls isn't worth much in my book. But maybe there's some important tidbit of information you're missing. If you meet him at your old college campus in two weeks, you can find out for sure."

And this promise of certainty took hold in Jennifer's brain, tempting her to tinker with it like a stray bit of code, unfinished and seductive to her puzzler's mind. "That's true. . . ."

After extracting a promise from Jennifer to let them know what happened next, Tamara then turned to Bridget, who was worrying her lip, her pale forehead deeply creased. Tamara knew she could gently suggest a few good creams to moisturize away those wrinkles, but if her friend kept grimacing that way, nothing would prove effective. "You said you'd had a weird day, too. What happened?"

Bridget tried to suppress the smile that always seemed to rise to her lips whenever she thought of Dr. Luke. "You know that dentist from my office? The one I talk about?"

Her friends nodded.

"Well, he brought me a cannoli dessert yesterday. One he and his mother made. And I know I can't describe it well enough to do it justice, but it had this amazingly rich cream filling with slivered bits of chocolate and a hint of Marsala. And he'd kept the shell separate so it would stay crispy. But at the office he piped in the filling right in front of me and *insisted* I try it right away. He watched me eat the whole thing! It was unbelievable, but the weird part was afterward. We had this . . . moment. This really long moment when we just looked at each other. It wasn't exactly flirting. It was more like recognizing some quality in each other." She glanced at the other two women, trying to gauge their reaction.

Jennifer bobbed her head slowly in a show of quiet understanding.

Tamara squinted at her. "Let me get this straight. The guy you're so hot for is that chubby old dentist? And he—like what? Lives with his mother?"

Bridget felt heat rush to her cheeks. "He's not old! He's, maybe, five or six years older than we are. And so what if he's got a little paunch? Other than that, he's in pretty good shape. Just not a beanpole. He's one of those stockier guys, which I happen to like." She rolled her eyes at Tamara. "And he doesn't *live* with his mother. They just cook together sometimes. Jeez."

"I can see how you'd like him," Jennifer offered, her voice soft but kind. "I usually go to Dr. Jim for cleanings, but Dr. Luke has a warmth about him, and he seems to love to cook, just like you do."

"Thank you," Bridget said, feeling a little better and more than a little grateful to Jennifer for this comment. But still. If Tamara was going to be so judgmental, she wasn't going to bother trying to explain her feelings anymore.

"Hey, it's okay with me," Tamara said, grinning. "Whatever turns you on."

Bridget realized Tamara was being her normal, in-your-face self, but knowing this didn't stop her from resenting it. She and Tamara had had their differences in the past, but she had never been so irritated by Tamara's insensitivity before. She'd been trying to be open. Get a handle on her emotions and experience. Ask for advice from two women she thought she trusted.

But Tamara's response made her want to fire back a nasty retort. Only, she couldn't think of one fast enough. At least not one that wasn't blatantly rude. So she settled for narrowing her eyes a fraction and pausing while she tried to regain her composure. Then she added, being careful to stamp the sarcasm out of her voice, "What happened with you and the younger man?"

Tamara looked at her dark-haired friend, instantly regretting her flippancy. She knew she'd been behaving less than charitably toward Bridget, and she had no excuse besides panic. She could feel her anxiety rising higher with each ticking second that they continued to sit there discussing this topic. She'd been fighting to retain some small measure of self-control and had to resort to her "tough girl" demeanor to do it.

She feigned a shrug. "Not much, I guess. I mean, he was out working in his front yard again, looking cute in his little running shorts." She forced a laugh. "He'd borrowed my grass trimmer on Wednesday and brought it back yesterday."

"You said you'd had a 'weird' day," Bridget persisted, not about to let her off the hook that easily.

Tamara acknowledged this and tried to sort out the "weird" part of the scene in her mind before openly expressing it to her friends. In a twenty-second flashback, she ignored the inquiring stares of the other two, took several sips of her coffee and reviewed her mental tape:

Aaron, showing up at her house yesterday, had been dressed in a faded red T-shirt with black running shorts, which revealed his tanned and muscular legs. He stood in her doorway, holding the trimmer out to her like a harvest offering.

"Morning, Tamara. Just wanted to drop this off," he said, a smile on his face and in his voice. "Thanks."

She managed some trite reply but, mostly, just stared at him. She hadn't been expecting company. Hadn't showered. Was dressed in her rattiest cutoff jeans and an old lilac-colored sweat-shirt. And she'd turned on the stove to make tea, so when she heard the doorbell ring, she didn't think it was for anything more important than one of the UPS deliveries Jon was always getting.

She took the trimmer and forbade herself to smooth her hair and give away her insecurities over her appearance. "You sure you don't want to keep this? Come back tomorrow and do my lawn, too?" (Yes, she'd said *my* lawn, not *our* lawn. Huh. Cutting Jon out of the picture already, eh?)

He laughed. "Not a chance, neighbor. Your Thistle Empire is part of your domain."

She said, "Fine, fine. Be that way." Then the kettle whistle blew, a noise startling enough that Aaron spun around looking for its origin. "That's just my tea," she explained.

"Oh, I'll let you go then." He took a step back.

But she read a look in his eyes, a flash of disappointment cloud-ing the light blue irises, so she impulsively said, "Want to have a cup with me?" The tooting got ever louder, making it impossible to ignore, adding a sense of pressure.

He entered her house. "Sure. Anything to make that scary sound stop. I thought we were being bombed."

She motioned for him to join her in the kitchen as he kicked off his dusty Reeboks. She raced toward the stove. Within seconds he was right behind her. What an unsettling habit, that stealthiness of his. She could feel his breath just two feet behind her as he laughed and said, "Tweety Bird. How cute."

He'd been pointing to her designer kettle. "Cute" was a new and refreshing descriptor for it. Jon had always called it "infantile."

She murmured, "Thanks," then asked, "Do you like Jasmine Blossom?"

"No idea. Never heard of it, but I'm sure it'll be great."

She tended to chatter when she got nervous, so she prattled on about how it was a traditional Chinese tea that dated back to the Song dynasty of the ninth century. "It's mild and lightly floral. I'm usually more of a coffee drinker, but I've always appreciated this one."

"Wow. History, botany and high tea all in one. Think you're pretty smart, don't 'cha?" And he laughed. Was it *at* her or *with* her? Either way, she didn't know how to defend herself against his mockery. It was mild and good-natured, though, unlike Jon's abrasive snark, and she hadn't had an interaction like this with a male—bantering but not confrontational—for so long. She felt lost, vulnerable in her too-comfy clothes, unprotected against his judgments. But his eyes kept smiling at her, and so, she fought for balance. Tried to think up an appropriately scathing reply. He surprised her, though, by adding, "Well, I guess you *are* pretty clever," a concession her own husband had never willingly made.

It rendered her speechless.

Aaron glanced around the kitchen, seemingly oblivious to her faltering. "Do you want me to grab spoons, napkins, creamers or something?"

"Umm, no," she managed. "I've got it."

"Seriously, I have three older sisters, remember? I won't faint if you ask me to pull the half-and-half out of the fridge."

She couldn't take much more of this. She either had to lasso her fear of speaking her mind in front of him or kick Aaron out of her house. She had a big personality and she *refused* to be intimidated by some guy she could've babysat for as a teen. Now was the time to draw her weapons. "Why are you being so nice to me? Do I seem that pathetic to you? That in need of self-esteem bolstering?"

He squinted at her. "What?"

She couldn't allow herself to back down an inch. She had to

come on strong, forceful, opinionated. Take control of the conversation and shape it to her own specifications. She had to rip into him. Project confidence even if she were nowhere near to feeling it. "Oh, I'm onto you," she claimed. *A lie. A total lie.* She had no freakin' idea what was running through the man's mind. "I know all this flattery and helpfulness comes with ulterior motives. You don't just want tea, do you? You want cookies, too."

He laughed again, as if finally getting the joke. "Oh, you just *think* you know my Machiavellian plan. Not likely, neighbor."

Her breath caught in her esophagus for a split second, but she pushed it out, laughed lightly and pulled two Tweety Bird mugs (they matched her kettle) from the cabinet. She poured. "Milk? Cream? Sugar?"

"None of the above."

She raised an eyebrow at him. "Grapes? Pistachios? Snickerdoodles?"

"Snickerdoodles." He grinned at her.

"Okay." She broke the seal on the package she kept stashed in the pantry and reached into the bag. She plopped a couple of cookies on a plate, wishing she could have baked homemade ones like Bridget. "You can have more if you want."

Aaron took his plate and teacup and sat down at the table. "Why are you being so nice to me? Do I seem that pathetic to *you?*" he mimicked.

She shook her head and, again, forced herself to laugh. But she made the mistake of catching his eye, and he leveled a very steady gaze across the kitchen at her. Was he challenging her? Was this flirtation? What kind of game, exactly, was she playing with him?

As if in answer to this question, he intensified his stare—a bright blue-eyed burning—and, for a moment, it was as if they'd physically touched. As if her well-crafted veneer had been stripped away and he could see the girl underneath. Whatever the game, she was going to lose against him, and that knowledge scared the shit out of her.

After that, he'd gulped most of his tea and chomped down one of the cookies before she'd even made it to the table. The conversation that followed was jerky, awkward and brief. He grabbed his second cookie for the road, thanked her for the snack and said he needed to finally get in his run ("an easy 10K") before his conference call with an advertiser that afternoon.

"See you around," he said, shooting her a guarded glance over his shoulder on his way out.

"Yeah," she whispered.

She'd mocked Bridget's "moment" with the flabby dentist, but only because she couldn't believe the terror she'd felt in having experienced a similar instance with Aaron. She did everything in her power to push those unsettling emotions away.

But Bridget and Jennifer were still waiting for her reply. And Bridget asked again, her tone slightly irritated, "What weird thing happened?" And Jennifer kept staring at her, her blue-green eyes round and luminous.

"Sorry," Tamara murmured. "All that happened was that he rang the bell, I opened the door, he handed me the trimmer, thanked me for its use and ran away. Literally ran. He does a minimum of five miles per day. What was weird was that this was all he said. That our conversation was so short," she lied.

"Oh," Bridget said, sounding disappointed.

Tamara shrugged and turned her attention to the task of people-watching in the café. She couldn't eat more than half of her muffin and felt physically ill over lying to her friends. Sure, she'd omitted information here or there in the past, and certainly she'd exaggerated a time or two, but she hadn't actively misled them before or told full-scale falsehoods. At least never about something so important.

She inclined her head toward a young couple sitting down four tables away. "Look at those two. College kids." She rolled her eyes dramatically and threw in a smirk for good measure. "He's staring at her like he wants to undress her right there in front of the donut counter. Should I yell, 'Get a room'?"

"No!" her friends exclaimed in unison. And, with that, Tamara successfully redirected the spotlight and remained free to keep her disconcerting interaction with Aaron to herself.

Jennifer didn't say anything, but she'd noticed the way Tamara kept twitching and stabbing her grilled muffin with a fork. She'd seen Tamara do the same thing after Benji got his UT acceptance letter and, also, one time when Tamara had confided in them that Jon threatened to put their house on the market and move them all to Atlanta to take a job with another law firm if Tamara didn't agree to let him increase his work travel.

So, no matter what Tamara *said,* Jennifer had reason to believe there were issues she'd left unspoken.

Bridget, on the other hand, was happy not only to let the subject drop but to ignore Tamara altogether for a while. As they parted company an hour later, Bridget vowed to be more guarded the next time she met her friends for coffee. Her "moment" with Dr. Luke meant something to her, and she wasn't willing to be criticized by Tamara again—whether her behavior was a result of meanness or merely thoughtlessness.

Her tall, slim friend didn't know what it was like to censor herself the way Bridget did. Tamara always got to play the Outspoken card, which was fine and good for *her,* but Bridget was determined to get to the bottom of her own problems and concerns. And while she'd hoped for her friends' support in doing so, she didn't require it.

Bridget, Jennifer and Tamara left the Indigo Moon Café with affected smiles and professed delight in their next coffee date, just seven days away. They openly lamented their inability to see one another sooner than that, or even talk for long on the phone, due to their "crazy schedules." It was their usual parting ritual—a well-worn script that they'd clung to out of habit. And it had once been completely true, at least when they'd first created and reserved these Friday mornings at nine for each other.

All three of them, however, grimaced, frowned or scowled respectively when they were in their cars and safely out of view of the others.

As they each drove away, all three reflected on the obligation of telling the truth in intimate friendships. Was it really such a necessity? Or, beyond a set point of general veracity, was there such a thing as too much information?

❧ 6 ❧

Jennifer

Sunday, September 12

The first text message came in the middle of their family drive to the mall to get new sneakers.

As Jennifer flipped idly through some paperwork Veronica wanted her to sign, Michael navigated the Camry through the leisurely Sunday traffic and chatted to the girls in the backseat about music. Her husband, with clear intent to torture their daughters, kept commenting on the lyrical relevance of every song that played on the radio. The girls would retaliate by laughing and, in some way or other, insinuate that their dad was a very old man. This was a long-standing game.

"Do young suburbanites use phrases like 'my crib in the hood' when discussing their four-bedroom homes in their gated communities?" Michael inquired, his tone thoroughly mocking.

Shelby sniggered. "*Daaad!* It's rap. They're supposed to use street language."

Michael turned up the volume a notch and listened to the next verse. "Now, see, that phrase is unclear. Was he saying 'pimping' or 'primping' right there?"

Veronica groaned. "Mom, tell him he's being obtuse!" She'd been enjoying the use of that word and employed it whenever possible. "That line makes perfect sense to anyone not born in the Pleistocene era." She sighed loudly. "It's 'pimping,' okay? Gawd."

"You sure?" Michael smirked and began bobbing his head like an unlikely hip-hop artist. In wild distortion of the lyrics, he rapped, "I'm *primpin'* in my car, yo. Gotta get my hair done. All this wind 'n' rain, yo, is messin' wid my fun." He paused and pumped his open palm forward a couple of times. "Yo, yo. Yo!"

The girls dissolved into giggles in the backseat, and even Jennifer couldn't keep from laughing.

"You're such a geek, Dad," Veronica said affectionately. "I'm *soooo* glad you don't teach at my school."

"Oh, c'mon, I'm cool. Right, Shelby? You'd want me to teach in your school, wouldn't you?"

"*Daaad.*" Shelby shook her head and rolled her eyes simultaneously, as if one form of negation were insufficient.

He winked at Jennifer and reached with his right hand to squeeze her left. She squeezed back. "What you women need is to hear some *good* music. A little Joan Baez. A little Santana. They've got songs in real English and, if you're determined to listen to stuff you don't understand, they've got a bunch of Spanish tunes, too." He began riffling through the CDs in the nook underneath the car radio. "Let's see what we've got here."

"Mom!" Veronica cried. "Make him stop before he puts Billy Joel on again."

"I like Billy Joel," Jennifer said, because she did but, also, because she wanted to make Michael laugh.

"Finally. An ally," he said, still searching for a decent CD.

"Besides," Jennifer continued, "we'll be at the mall in a few minutes." She pointed to the sheets Veronica had given her. Permission slips, it seemed, to be part of some Homecoming Dance committee. "So, this is a release to let you get out of study hall every Monday and Wednesday for the next four weeks, and this other one is to agree to let you stay after school for two extra hours every Tuesday night?"

"Yeah. Only until the dance, though," her fourteen-going-on-forty-year-old daughter said, not giving away any more information than that. "October fifteenth."

"Why the sudden interest?" Jennifer asked her. "Didn't you al-

ways say how much you hate planning things like this before?"
She swiveled in her seat to glance back at the girls.

Veronica shrugged. "But I'm in high school now. I just wanna
try it this year. Get involved, you know?"

Shelby had her lips pinched together as if holding back a tide of
commentary.

Michael, settling for the Eagles and their *The Very Best Of* collection, said, "Aren't you the little joiner. Trying to get in good with
the popular crowd?" This was more to hassle her than because he
meant it. Unlike Jennifer in junior high and high school, Veronica
had always been blessed to be pretty and part of the popular
crowd. As far as Jennifer knew, there hadn't been any recent
change of status, although her eldest had been getting mouthier
lately. And more secretive. Dressing in a range of clothing that
could best be described as "formfitting." Even moving a bit differently, a bit aggressively, if Jennifer thought about it. Was her
daughter getting to be *too* popular?

"So, are Ashley, Joy and Heather going to be doing it, too?" Jennifer asked. "Because, if so, maybe we can carpool with their parents to pick all of you up."

There was an unnaturally long silence. "Umm," Veronica said.
"Heather was, uh . . . thinking about it."

"Oh, c'mon!" Shelby burst out. "Tell them already." She poked
her big sister and cackled. "Her friends all think it's lame, but Tim
Taylor is on the committee, so she wants to be on it, too."

Veronica shoved her. "Shut up, Shel!"

"Who's Tim Taylor?" Michael asked.

"Just a guy in my grade." Veronica fidgeted with her fingernails
and shot evil glares at her sister.

"A guy who *likes* her. A guy who wants to go out with her. Not
just on a date. He wants to be with her forever and ever."

"Shel. Shut. Up."

But Shelby did not shut up. "He's neighbors with my friend
Krissie and rides her bus. And he keeps Veronica's school picture
from last year in his wallet. And he talks to his best friend the *whole*
way to school about how beautiful Veronica is and how much he
loves her and—"

Veronica slugged her sister.

"Ow!" Shelby bellowed.

"Ladies, stop that," Michael commanded. Then, after a beat, "You gave this guy your school picture?"

"Arrrrghhh!" Veronica screeched. "Just gimme a break, okay? Is it a crime to wanna try something different? It's just a stupid committee."

"It's not a crime, and you can absolutely try it, sweetheart," Michael said, his voice soothing. "Has, er, Tim asked you out? To this dance or something?"

Their daughter forced the air out of her lungs like she was under doctor's orders and, eventually, mumbled, "Maybe. Yeah, kinda."

Michael grinned and winked again at Jennifer. "Maybe, yeah, kinda, eh? Well, he's a guy with good taste." Then, to Jennifer, "What do you think, honey? It seems our daughter has her first real date coming up."

Jennifer sat paralyzed in the passenger's seat, her heart pounding, her fingers gripping the permission slips with both hands. "It seems so," she managed to say.

She stole a peripheral glance over her shoulder at her two girls: Shelby, a look of pride gracing her face, probably thrilled she'd succeeded in outing her sister, but Jennifer wasn't certain. And, Veronica, wearing an expression Jennifer recognized all too clearly—caginess coupled with a simmering excitement. It was exactly what she'd felt when David asked her out for the first time. For *her* first date.

"So, you'll sign the forms?" Veronica asked, trying desperately to appear nonchalant and not remotely capable of pulling it off.

Jennifer nodded, unwilling to grill her daughter yet on her relationship with this Tim guy or launch into the list of necessary cautions for dating teens but, oh, she had many questions and even more warnings. She couldn't believe how Not Ready she was for this stage of parenthood. She forced herself to release her death grip on the permission slips and reach into the glove compartment for a pen.

The opening strains of "Hotel California" began to play and, for a moment, all four of them paused and listened to the haunting guitar solo that stirred her soul and inspired a sense of wanderlust. As the other instruments joined in, she took a deep breath. She could do this. She could put the past behind her so she'd be able to deal effectively with the present. She clicked the pen and glanced out the window. They were less than a mile from the mall.

Her cell phone beeped, making her jump. "Oh," she said, laughing uneasily. The girls and even Michael rolled their eyes and shot her amused looks.

"Someone's texting you on a Sunday?" her husband asked, grinning. "Don't they know this is a day of rest and mindless consumerism?"

She smiled faintly. "Guess not." She flicked open her phone and pressed her lips together like Shelby had done earlier, an attempt to keep herself from gasping.

David.

His text message read: *Zup? Abt 9-23, r u in? TML8r n LMK.* (Translation: What's up? About September 23rd, are you in? Text me later and let me know.)

"Anything important?" Michael asked.

"No." She snapped the phone shut. "Just some computer stuff. I'll take care of it when we get home."

"Okay," he said, and she knew he assumed she meant one of her Web design clients. She also knew how easy it was to mislead him.

When they'd pulled into the mall parking lot and finally hunted down a space, Michael and the girls jumped out immediately. Shelby, who was cold and regretted wearing only a T-shirt, wanted to extract her old unfashionable Windbreaker from the trunk, where it was buried under a picnic blanket and a few boxes. With everyone else out of the car and momentarily busy, Jennifer grabbed the opportunity to reply to David's message.

She texted back: *CU on 9-23. TTY 2moro.* (See you on September 23rd. Talk to you tomorrow.)

Then she changed the setting on her phone to vibrate.

When the girls were in bed that night, she and Michael sat on the downstairs sofa with a couple mugs of decaf, reviewing their commitments for the upcoming week.

"We've got a staff meeting on Tuesday afternoon," Michael said, "but I should still be able to swing by the school to pick up Veronica. She'll be done by five?"

Jennifer nodded. "That's what the form said." She warmed her hands on her mug. "About this Homecoming Dance and this guy—"

"Tim Taylor," Michael supplied with a smirk.

"Yes. Tim Taylor. Isn't she too young for something like this?"

"A dance? Nah. It's cute. It's romantic. All of my students have crushes and go to overblown events like this. It's natural at that age. They 'date' for two weeks and break up. And considering how well-adjusted Veronica is socially, I'm surprised there haven't been more boys asking her out. Though, I guess, they're doing that group-date thing for longer now."

Jennifer remembered the many times she'd taken Veronica and her *Twilight*-loving friends to the movies or the mall only to have them meet up with a group of guys while they were there. They'd all go out for pizza or ice cream afterward, and it was dating of a sort, but it seemed far less worrisome than this one-on-one, formal dance situation. The kinds of things this Tim Taylor guy was saying to his buddy, well, it came across as so . . . possessive.

"Aren't you concerned she'll get too serious too fast?" she asked Michael. "This kid seems *really* into her. All this talk on the bus to his friend. I don't know. I don't want her to end up with some stalker guy."

He laughed. "I see high school boys every day, honey. And, yes, they're sex-crazed and insecure, but very few cross the line into stalkerdom." He shot her one of his typical amused glances. "You're really funny about this. You know what it's like to be a teen. One minute you're 'in love' with someone, the next you have no idea what you ever saw in them. I know you dated other people before me—"

"Not in high school, Michael."

He shrugged. "So, okay, you were shy in high school. And I was awkward. Sometimes I'm still awkward around someone I'm trying to impress." He shot her a sheepish look, blinked a couple times, then glanced away. "But even in college we were still trying to feel our way with the whole dating game. And we weren't all that serious about the people we had relationships with back then, even when we were nineteen or twenty."

Speak for yourself, she thought, but she only cleared her throat.

"And it's not like either of us ended up getting engaged to anybody or anything," he added. "Though I think you were a little more into that computer geek guy than I was into my college girlfriends." He gulped the first half of his coffee. "What was his name again?"

"Who?" she whispered. Then, "David?"

"Yeah. David. I know he was your first real boyfriend and everything, but even you didn't get all hung up on him forever after it ended. A few weeks, a month, sure, but you got over it. And you two dated for a lot longer than Veronica will probably be with this guy." He took another slurp of his drink. "I'm not worried."

Jennifer wished she could be so unaffected. Then again, this was yet another example of how Michael didn't understand her. Yet another projection about her thoughts and emotions based on *his* thoughts and *his* emotions. So, fine. Michael may not have been hung up on any old girlfriends for longer than a week, but Veronica, if she were anything like her mother, could get hung up on a guy for two decades. And these were the kinds of things that Michael would never comprehend. Would never see.

But, of course, it wasn't as though she could ever explain it to him. She took one sip of her now-tepid coffee and dropped the subject. What was the point?

As a silent reminder of her alternate reality, her phone pulsed in her right back pocket. She'd slipped it into her jeans and could feel it quivering between the denim folds. It'd been vibrating for the past hour, but she hadn't wanted to steal away to check the message.

She knew it was from David. He'd already sent her two other texts after she'd replied to his first, the intimacy of his tone escalating exponentially, even in electronic form. And she, of course, had responded in private to both of those messages, too.

She feigned a yawn. "Well . . . good night," she told Michael, kissing him lightly on the forehead. "You coming up?"

"In a little bit. I'm going to finish my coffee, maybe grade quizzes for a half hour down here."

"Okay. Don't stay up too late."

He laughed, kind of. It was more like a snickery exhale and accompanied by a gaze she couldn't readily identify. "Yeah, you either."

She smiled carefully at him. "I'm going to bed right now."

"What? No final e-mail check for the night?"

She shook her head.

He looked at her as though he wanted to believe her but didn't. He'd been doing that more often lately, and she wasn't sure what accounted for it. What signals he was receiving. "Well, okay, then. Sweet dreams," he said.

"You, too."

She dumped out her remaining coffee, meandered upstairs and then changed into her nightgown. Finally, when she couldn't stand the suspense an instant longer, she locked herself in the master bathroom and flipped open her phone.

Cant W8 2 CU. Keep tkg abt it. R U?

Was she thinking about seeing David again? Oh, God, when had she ever stopped? Did lonely, geeky girls ever get over missing the hero who'd ridden into their lives and changed it forever? Who'd rescued them . . . and then run away?

Hell, no.

She typed: *U know the answer. G-nite.*

7

Bridget

"A month?" Bridget exclaimed when Candy told her the news that morning. "Dr. Nina's going to be gone that long?" She glanced around the dental office. Though the waiting area bustled with patients, she all but hugged herself. Wow, would this place ever be peaceful without The Crab Lady snapping at everyone.

"She needs time to get her head together," the hygienist explained. "At least that's what she told Dr. Jim on the phone. And I wish her well but, boy, I'm not gonna miss the drama of last week. I don't think I've ever seen anyone that pissed off. I thought for sure she'd crack Mrs. Kinney's crown the way she kept jabbing her Remington Scaler at it. And poor Mr. Ashburg. She practically attacked him with a foot and a half of dental floss."

Bridget remembered. There'd been a stream of traumatized patients at the gagging end of Dr. Nina's magnified mouth mirror last week, and you didn't want to be anywhere near her number 14 metal probe. "Did you ever meet her husband? Has he come in before?" she asked.

Candy nodded. "A couple of times. Seemed like a nice enough guy, but you never really know about people."

"True," Bridget murmured.

Dr. Luke rounded the corner, his eyes crinkling at the corners when he spotted Bridget. "Hey, ladies. Who's up next?"

"Mr. Ingersole at ten-fifteen," Candy said.

Dr. Luke shook his head. "We're racing today, aren't we?"

Being one dentist short, it was going to be a busy week—heck, a busy *month*—for all of them but, still, Bridget preferred an absent Dr. Nina to a verbally abusive one. She pulled a sealed Tupperware container out of a plastic bag. "I know you won't have any long breaks, but I brought something for you guys to try whenever you have a free moment." She peeled the lid off the still-warm container. "It's chestnut ravioli." She glanced at their faces and both her friend and her favorite dentist looked bewildered and more than a little reticent. Her heart dropped to her knees. She'd worked for hours on this recipe. "I know it sounds like an . . . an odd dish, but I saw it in an Italian cookbook ages ago and always wanted to try it. It—It's okay if you don't like it or you think it'll be—"

Dr. Luke clasped his hands together like a priest, reminding Bridget that she wasn't the only Catholic in the office. "Bless you, Bridget," he said, sounding very much like the monsignor at her mom's old church. "You have no idea how much brighter you just made my day, do you?"

"Um," she said, lost in the kindness of his deep brown eyes.

"I've never heard of chestnut ravioli," Candy murmured, "but you're putting my boring old ham-n-cheese sandwich to shame. I can't wait to try it at lunch."

"The hell with waiting for lunch," Dr. Luke said, rummaging through one of the drawers for a box of toothpicks. He slid one out of the box and speared a plump ravioli with it.

Bridget watched him as he popped the whole thing into his mouth. She caught every one of his facial expressions as he savored and analyzed the taste—surprise, puzzlement, delight. She remained glued to his reaction as the flavor sensation washed over him and held her breath until he groaned.

"What is *in* this?" he whispered, eyeing the rest of the ravioli in the container. "The filling—it's smooth, rich, earthy and spiced." He locked gazes with her. "And I wasn't expecting the sweetness. It tastes like autumn."

She grinned at him. "It's supposed to."

He grinned back and thrust the box of toothpicks at Candy. "Try one."

As Candy taste-tested the "tender pasta pillows," as Dr. Luke called them, he forced Bridget to detail every single succulent ingredient in the recipe and the exact amounts she used, from the chestnut puree to the amaretto liqueur to the hint of grated chocolate. She wasn't left wondering if her efforts had been appreciated. Dr. Luke took *notes* on what she said. He listened to her. And when he bit into his second and then his third ravioli, he gazed at her with heavy-lidded, bedroom eyes.

No one would ever believe her if she said it, but their exchange was almost better than making love. Oh, God. She wanted her life to feel like this moment. The intoxicating sensuality overwhelmed her. She craved this kind of intimacy and appreciation . . . and she couldn't stop the powerful tsunami of gratitude, leveled at Dr. Luke, for giving her both.

"I can't tell you how glad I am that you both like it," she murmured, feeling her face flush as Candy, too, expressed her raptures over the pasta. For a few seconds, she'd forgotten Candy was even there.

Of course, much as she enjoyed her friendship with the good-natured hygienist, Bridget hadn't completely deluded herself. She knew very well that it was *his* praise, *his* pleasure she sought. She couldn't have been more invested in Dr. Luke's good opinion if they'd been in bed together or, possibly, if he'd been on the Culinary Institute of America's board of admissions.

Her CIA man was smarter than a secret agent, though, at least when it came to flambé techniques. Faster than anyone with a spatula and grill scraper. Able to roll pastry dough singlehandedly—

"Uh, Bridget?" Dr. Luke said, waving his palm in front of her. She blinked. "Yeah?"

"Thank you. I'm in your debt." His eyes twinkled as he licked, then smacked his lips. "I'll be thinking of a way to repay you. I promise." And with a final wink, he swiveled back toward the exam rooms and told Candy to bring Mr. Ingersole to number three whenever she was done "savoring Bridget's magnificent indulgence." Bridget's four-hour shift had never flown by so fast.

At home, she sat at the kitchen table and sifted through the three-hundred-plus cards in her recipe box. She flipped through her fourteen favorite cookbooks. She paged through the "Coordinated Culinary Feasts" she'd marked with Post-it Notes in her back issues of *Midwest Cooking* magazine. The possibilities were endless!

She considered what to make for Thursday: the rice-and-meat-stuffed grape leaves or the vegetarian penne in vodka sauce? Oooh, or maybe lamb stew—everyone always loved that. But what would Dr. Luke love? Of course there was the potent allure of spice. A biryani curry, perhaps? Or chili-chicken and bell-pepper fajitas?

The front door flew open, and Keaton flew through it.

"Hey, Mom," he called. She could hear him panting at the foot of the stairs, so he'd obviously raced home. He stampeded up to her. "Can I play at Josh's? He's got this new game for his Xbox 360 and I—"

"May I," she corrected automatically. "And what about your homework?"

"I just got a math worksheet and one chapter to read for stupid English—"

"Keaton," she said in warning.

"It's *nothing*, Mom. I'll be done with both in twenty minutes. A half hour tops. And I'll do them tonight, I promise."

"Lots of promises today," she murmured.

He stood behind her, still panting, and peered at the shrimp jambalaya recipe card she was holding. "Aw, gross. You're not making that for *us*, are you?"

"No," she said regretfully, "I'm not."

"Oh, okay." He studied her profile for a second—she could see him peripherally as he scanned her, making judgments. Then, to her surprise, he said, "Sorry. You know I hate shrimp."

"Yes, Keaton. I know. You've made that perfectly clear since preschool."

"Yeah, I know you know. But sometimes you want us to 'be adventurous eaters' anyway and try stuff we hate." He wrinkled his nose and shrugged. "I'm *never* gonna like shrimp."

"Never say never. People's tastes can change. Even yours." She half smiled at him, but he only sighed and bounced from one foot to the other, clearly having had enough Mom 'n' Son Chat Time for one day. Who were those idiots who always prattled on about "quality family time" and such? They must not have had kids so anxious to be away from them that their offspring actually kept jogging in place so as to be better able to zip away once permission to leave was granted.

What Keaton had asked to do wasn't something bad, it just happened to squeeze at her heart and bring to light the parental-child divide. It painfully underscored yet again how little she was needed anymore beyond the mandatory household chores. Mindless and impersonal duties, which, in performing them, made her time at home feel more like *work* than her time at the dental office. There, at least, she was seen as a person. Spoken *to* not *at*. Appreciated for her efforts.

The front door banged twice in quick succession. Cassandra. Evan. Her daughter bounded up the stairs issuing demands in the form of questions with every step. "Can I take the phone into my room? I need to call Emily to talk about our science project, okay? And can I just grab a granola bar for a snack? I wanna eat it while I talk to her. And I won't get any crumbs on the carpet, all right?"

"May I," Bridget corrected faintly as her daughter, a whirlwind of need, riffled through the pantry for her snack, snatched the phone and bolted toward her room.

Keaton, still bouncing nervously behind her, gave another impatient sigh.

"Fine. Go," she told him. "But be back by five-thirty. And I want you to get your homework done immediately after dinner."

He was out the door before she could finish the sentence, not even a hasty "thanks" thrown over his shoulder at her as he passed his kid brother on the staircase.

Evan heaved himself up the flight of stairs liked he'd just run the Chicago Marathon. He glanced at her and waved wearily. "I'm gonna take a nap," he informed her, dropping his backpack in a heap at the foot of the kitchen table before trudging off toward his bedroom. She heard the door click behind him and the distant sound of giggling coming from Cassandra's room farther down the hall.

She grimaced to no one but herself, then chose a simple chicken, rice and sautéed-veggie casserole to make for dinner that night (very *safe*), laying aside the more "adventurous" recipe cards for later.

As she reluctantly hid her stack of fun in a cabinet and gnawed on pretzel sticks to stave off her irritation, she couldn't avoid a realization that'd been dogging her for the past several weeks: She looked forward to going to work on Tuesdays and Thursdays. But, more than that, she looked forward to it like most people looked forward to their weekends off. How sad and scary was that? And what did it say about her and the state of her life?

When Graham got home, she tried to draw him into a discussion. "How was your day? Anything new happen?"

He shrugged and pecked her with a top-of-the-head kiss. "Nah. Repaired some windows down at the bank on Main. Got a contract for a job at the professional building on State and Kennedy for next week. 'Bout it." He sniffed. "Smells good in here. When's dinner?"

She stifled a sigh and glanced at her watch. "Fifteen minutes, maybe twenty."

He grinned. "Good. I got time to check the score on the—"

"Graham. Wait. Please. Can we just talk for a few minutes?"

"Why?" He stopped and squinted at her. "Something wrong? Kids doin' okay?"

"Oh, no, nothing's wrong. Cassandra's talking to half the school on the phone, Keaton's playing with Josh outside and Evan's in his room, still napping, I think. I just thought that, maybe, with them occupied, we could have a real chat before dinner. Just the two of us."

He stared longingly down the hall in the direction of the bedroom TV for a split second before plunking himself on the edge of a chair. Bridget felt a rush of guilt for keeping him in the living room, apparently against his will, but the sports scores wouldn't be going anywhere and in just a few moments their window to talk privately would be gone.

"You good?" he asked. "You worked today, right?"

"Yes," she said enthusiastically, and she told him about Dr. Nina taking a month-long leave of absence. Then she segued into how she'd made chestnut ravioli for her coworkers and that they'd loved it. But somewhere in the middle of her description of the dental staff's reaction to the pasta, she caught him gazing down the hall again, and his inattention made her feel silly. She didn't know how to engage him in conversation anymore. It was like she was wandering around in their marriage alone and had lost her sense of direction. "Um," she began, floundering, "what games are on tonight? The Bears?"

Graham laughed lightly. At her. "No, hon. Today's *Tuesday*. They played last night. I just wanna take a look at what's been happening in the college leagues and get a recap of the NFL games I missed over the weekend. No big deal." He batted the subject away with a sweep of his palm. "I know you're not into it."

She swallowed. No, she wasn't—as he put it—*into it*, but she had tried to watch football games here and there *for him*. Not that he would ever think to talk with her about it. He had decided she wasn't a football fan in their first two months of dating, and his opinion never wavered in the years since.

Bridget stood up. It was useless to keep him prisoner here. "Well, I'm going to check on dinner then. Why don't you go watch your sports show? I—I'll call you when it's ready." She forced a smile.

He sprung up and beamed a joyous smile at her. "Great! Thanks." And before she could blink, he was down the hall.

Two days later, Bridget was reminded of her love for her work environment yet again as she caught herself all but bubbling over with excitement at the prospect of going to the office. It was crazy. She was like one of her kids on the morning of a big school field trip. Every time.

She dressed for work carefully, knowing she'd be looked at. Knowing she'd be the object of some admiration once they tried her latest creation. She'd found the perfect recipe, and the joy of getting to share it was almost too thrilling to handle. Despite the juggling act that was her home life, she'd managed to shop for and assemble all the necessary ingredients and then carve out the hour it took to make it from scratch. She slipped on her cooking apron and giggled like a schoolgirl.

Imperial Roman Risotto!

It was beyond beautiful. Way past eye-catching. More than flavorful. A far cry from even delicious. It surpassed all of these to produce a total taste sensation.

She cooked the short-grained round rice briefly in olive oil, so as to coat it with fat. She added white wine. Waited as it absorbed, then evaporated over the medium flame. Next came the hot stock, dribbled in, plus diced pats of cold butter and sprinkles of finely grated Parmesan cheese. Then the garlic, the mushrooms, the herbs, until it was blissfully al dente. She had to time it perfectly; she hadn't a minute to spare. When finished, the risotto must be eaten at once or it threatened dryness. She wasn't about to take chances like that.

She spooned the risotto into a lovely blue and white china bowl, covered it carefully, whipped off her apron and grabbed her car keys along with a bag with plastic cups and forks for immediate tasting. Then, with a gleefulness she couldn't contain, she drove to work.

Smiley Dental had the relaxed atmosphere of a diner after closing. A couple of patients were in the back, and Candy was with one of them. Pamela, as usual, was about to bolt, but smelled the aroma coming from the bowl and paused.

"What is that?" she asked. "Your lunch?"

"Risotto." Bridget set the china bowl on the front desk and removed the foil. "Wanna try?"

"Hell, yeah. I heard about the ravioli I missed."

She handed Pamela the bag of plasticware, and the other receptionist dug out a fork and scooped a generous portion of the still-hot dish into a cup. She blew on her first forkful and lifted it to her mouth. Then tasted. Pamela's timing couldn't have been better. Just as she was saying, "Girl, this is fabulous," Dr. Luke rounded the corner.

"What has our brilliant Bridget made for us today?" he asked, eyeing the bowl with a curiosity bordering on lustfulness.

Bridget told him.

"Is there some for me?" he asked, looking worried that there may not be any left soon. Pamela was on her second cupful already.

"Of course," she said, handing him the appropriate plastic utensils and offering him a serving.

He, too, tried it. He, too, raved. And he, too, had seconds when he finished his first cup.

Pamela snatched up her belongings and added one final scoop of risotto to her cup before heading toward the door. "I hate to go. Thanks, Bridget. That was amazing." And for the first time since Bridget had known her, Pamela paused to really look her in the eye. To let Bridget see how much she meant those words.

"You're welcome," Bridget replied, encouraged she wasn't crazy to have this secret dream of a culinary life. Other people—people out in the real world, people who weren't even her friends—loved her cooking! But it was more than that. She knew she'd been going beyond sharpening her skills with a few tricky recipes. As she crafted each new recipe, she'd been honing a whole new personality.

Dr. Luke cleared his throat. "You've kept me from wanting to eat my lunch twice this week," he told her, feigning sternness. "And the thing is, Bridget, those were *good* lunches. But your dishes were just better." He stared at her with those huge brown eyes for a long minute, and she rejoiced in having taken extra time with her hair and makeup this morning. Sighed in relief at having worn the forest green shirt that always made her feel kind of pretty, not like her usual dowdy-mom self.

She smiled at him. "I'm glad you enjoyed them. It was nothing."

"No, actually, it was something." He fiddled with the plastic fork, bending one of the tines until it snapped off. "Look, I thought of you when I was at home yesterday. You seemed to like the cannoli and—"

"I loved the cannoli," she said aloud, interrupting, but all the while her brain shouted silently, *He thought of me when he was at home?!*

He grinned. "Good. And you made that incredible chestnut

ravioli on Tuesday. And now—risotto." He paused to swallow or catch his breath, Bridget wasn't sure which. "It's pretty clear you're an Italian food lover. So, I've got a restaurant for you, and I'd really like it if you'd let me treat you to lunch sometime soon so, you know, I can thank you for helping to make this tough time in the office a little easier."

He didn't give her a chance to answer before starting to flip through the calendar next to the reception desk. "Oh. This might work. You know the office is going to be closed on Thursday, October fourteenth. Hygienists have a conference. I know it's not for a few weeks yet but, if you haven't already made plans for that day, maybe I could take you out then?"

"I—um—" *A lunch date with Dr. Luke?*

"Do you need to check your calendar?" he asked, taking a step closer to her so their sleeves almost touched. "Or . . . ask your husband?" She couldn't describe the expression on his face. It was hopeful and fearful and some other emotion she'd need more time to figure out. As for herself, she felt those same mixed emotions and more.

But he was waiting for her. Looking at her. Listening to *her*. And, God, how she appreciated that. So she shook her head. "I don't have any plans." She paused and met his gaze. "An Italian lunch sounds really fun."

❧ 8 ❧

Tamara

It was just shy of ten A.M. when Tamara, glancing through the big glass windows of The Rake & the Hoe, spotted Bridget walking toward the dentist's office across the street, kitty-corner and to the left.

The lively lady co-owner of Glendale Grove's lawn and garden shop, who'd been telling Tamara about their latest deals on bug spray and cedar wood chips, paused midsentence to ask her husband a question about cherry saplings. Even though Tamara knew Bridget couldn't see her, she took the opportunity to slide into the shadows of the hose and sprinkler aisle and watch as her friend, carrying a large bowl in her hands, wrestled with the front door of Smiley Dental.

A staff birthday, maybe? Bridget wore an attractive dark green blouse and an irrepressible grin. Why did she look so happy? So put together? Was she bringing chicken soup to someone with a cold . . . or something else to that dentist friend of hers? Tamara didn't know why that unsettled her so much.

She backed farther into the aisle and grabbed an extra watering can. Then, in other regions of the store, she collected a new pair of gardening gloves, a bundle of brown bags for cut grass and, because the blades of her old rose clippers were getting dull, another pair of those, too.

She thanked the owners and drove home with her purchases in the passenger's seat. As she passed by Aaron's house, she spied him in his yard, hunched over a stack of chopped wood in front of his garage. He looked up and waved. She was too close to ignore him, and she'd been staring too intently at him to simply wave back and drive away, so she inhaled deeply and slowed down. As he sauntered over to her, she stopped the car completely, pasted a smile on her face and lowered the window.

"Hey," he said.

"Hey," she said back. It'd been a week since she'd seen him. A week since their little tea party in her kitchen. Why couldn't she get over feeling so awkward around him? "I'm going to be doing some yard work today, too. Nice morning for it." An inane comment by any measure of intelligence, but at least she was taking command of the conversation and not just stupidly staring at him.

"It is. And it's an excellent break from typing, too. Been up since five-thirty working on the new issue." He paused and glanced over his shoulder at the woodpile. "Lived here a year and a half. I plan to actually use my fireplace this winter," he chuckled, more to himself, she thought, than to her.

"Are those vegetables I see over there?" She pointed at a small garden patch on the side of the house.

"Yep. Gonna be doing some serious broccoli harvesting soon." He met her gaze and grinned. "I dare you to top that, even with your hundreds of juicy cherry tomatoes."

She laughed, remembering when he plucked that tomato off one of her plants and, also, thinking of her Aunt Eliza and her reviled broccoli crop. "You dare me, huh? Well, I'll see your broccoli, and I'll raise you two bell peppers, a head of lettuce and an eggplant."

He blinked at her. "You grow eggplant? Show-off. Fine. Bring it on. We'll have to compare produce sometime. I know I've got a blue-ribbon bunch of superior cruciferous goodness here."

She loved it when he pulled out the multisyllabic words. "Ha. I'll take that as a challenge. And those flowers over there . . ." She waved her hand at the meager growth of goldenrods in his front yard. "Are they award winning, too?"

"Hey, just because I don't do roses like *some* people—"

She found herself giggling. "Fine. You admit you're not skilled enough for roses, but c'mon. No lively snapdragons? No delicate violets? Not even a handful of impetuous poppies?"

"Neighbor, you're pushin' it. I am *very* skilled." He ducked his head to hide—unsuccessfully—a smirk. "I just grow dignified, manly plants."

"Whatever you say, but I still think I've got you beat."

"Oh, we'll see about that." He met her eye this time. Then, when she sensed she'd stayed long enough and had nodded good-bye at him, he winked, turned his back on her and headed again toward the stack of wood logs littering his driveway.

She drove the short distance home, her hands trembling faintly as she steered. This was ridiculous. He was just a *guy*. And he probably used that playful manner when he talked with everyone. She gripped the wheel tighter until she could no longer see the shaking. But she still felt it. Deep inside her fingers. Hidden by a camouflage of skin and jewelry.

She frittered away the next several hours with mindless tasks like vacuuming, dishes and dusting (Jon would be home that night and he hated "untidiness"), but she was unable to concentrate on much beyond that. Jon's flight was due to touch down at O'Hare around five, but he was often late and had a habit of just taking a taxi back to the house. So, it would probably be hours before she spoke with another human being in person, and there was an undeniable pang of loneliness at the thought that her only remaining conversation of the day would be with her husband.

She didn't want to bother Aaron, even if he worked from home and had flexible hours, but she couldn't help but think about him when she picked a pail full of veggies from her garden. It would be funny if she dropped some off for him, right? An extension of that light mockery they always had between them.

So, she spent half an hour trying to choose a pair of jeans and a long-sleeved tee that said "casual and clean," even while aiming for "cute and clever." Then, just before four, she clipped three of her most perfect white roses, locked the door but left the garage door open and headed to Aaron's, a plastic bag of vegetables in one hand, her house keys and the flowers in the other.

When she got to Aaron's front step, she noticed the main door was open and the screen allowed her an easy view into his house. She could see him, well, part of him, sitting in a chair one room over, his back to her. She wasn't sure what he was doing, but his sturdy shoulders appeared stiff and his level of concentration so intense that he didn't hear the scuff of her shoes on his welcome mat.

She observed him for a moment, holding her breath, wondering how a woman who'd fallen out of love with him would perceive him. Would the shoulders Tamara considered broad and strong be seen by his ex-wife as rigid, tense and unyielding? Would the verbal repartee Tamara attributed to him as evidence of witty banter be viewed by his ex as examples of argumentativeness and hair-splitting? Would a rose by any other name . . . ?

"Hey," he said, spotting her and waving her inside. "You're back. You can come in, you know."

"Thanks." She opened the screen door and stepped in. "You seemed involved in something. I didn't want to interrupt."

He shook his head. "Just editing. The next issue goes out on Monday, so I've got the weekend to finish up."

"The next issue of—your magazine?"

"My company's magazine," he corrected. "I'm one of the co-founders. We send e-mail issues out to over one hundred twenty thousand subscribers, twice a month." He pointed to his laptop, which, now that she was in the house, she could see resting on the table in front of him. He quoted from the site: "'*The Enlightened Man* is for today's Renaissance Warrior. It's the only e-zine for men that specifically addresses health and fitness matters alongside in-depth features on relationships, clothing, entertainment, cars and culture. We cover everything that a Man of the Millennium needs to know.'" He paused to nod at her. "Sounds good, doesn't it?"

"A top-notch publication," Tamara agreed. "Almost makes me wish I were a Man of the Millennium myself, just so I had an excuse to read the articles."

He snickered. "Sure you do." He logged off his computer.

"Well, maybe if your husband is very good, Santa will get him a year's subscription."

"I doubt that'll happen." She kicked off her shoes, seeing as his sneakers were there, too, and crossed the light beige carpet with her vegetable and floral offering. Just as she was about to make some flippant remark about how her bell peppers were undoubtedly greener than his broccoli crowns, he made a comment that halted her midstep.

"Why's that? Because your husband hasn't been very good or because Santa already has a different gift in mind?"

"Um—" She tried to laugh it off, but he was waiting for her reply. What did a woman with a marriage like hers say to a question like this? The approved answer would be the latter, with some well-rehearsed sexual allusion tossed onto the flame of innuendo for good measure. The truth would be the former, but one didn't make such an admission aloud. Especially not to mere acquaintances. And especially, *especially* not to other men.

She cleared her throat. "Jon doesn't have much time to read," she said, marveling at her ability to lie so smoothly and, indeed, so often over the course of just one week. What would she claim next? That she was a tennis champ who could rival Venus and Serena at Wimbledon?

"Oh," he said, shrugging. "Too bad."

"Yeah." She spotted a snapshot taped to the shelf above the computer. Aaron with an elderly man who looked to be his dad, an elderly woman most likely his mom and another female—a sister, maybe? She pointed to the photo. "Your family?"

"Two out of the three. My parents are in the middle. The woman on the right is my ex-wife. Isabelle."

"Oh." She studied the younger woman in the snapshot more closely. Long light brown hair, pretty grayish eyes, delicate bone structure. Features so petite they made Tamara feel like a Midwestern version of Xena, Warrior Princess. "You must still have a really good relationship with her to keep her picture up."

He laughed, a sound that came so swift and strong it surprised her. "Not at *all*." He laughed again until tears gathered at the corners of his eyes. "But it's a real nice photo of the four of us, isn't it?"

She nodded.

"Exactly. I keep it up to remind me that appearances can be deceiving." And with that, he pushed himself to standing and took the plastic bag from her fingers. "What have you got in here, neighbor?"

Her head still reeling from his admission, Tamara mumbled something about how her roses could outdo his goldenrods any ole time, and her vegetables were *waaaay* better than his vegetables.

He raised one disbelieving eyebrow. "Are not."

"Are, too. And," she added, "where the hell is this famous broccoli of yours, anyway?"

He inclined his head in the direction of the kitchen. "Got a fresh bunch on the table."

"Well?"

He plopped her bag full of peppers, cherry tomatoes, lettuce and eggplant on his oak table. "Feast your eyes, neighbor." Centertable and ready to eat, the broccoli glistened with a just-washed sheen. It was cut in easy to grab florets, and Aaron pulled a small bowl of ranch dip out of the refrigerator. "Try one."

So she dabbed a small floret in the dip and took a bite. Smooth stalk. Crisp but baby tender. Flavorful and fresh. "Not bad."

He rolled his eyes. "It's excellent. Say it."

"Not till I try it steamed."

"What?" He laughed. "You're a hard woman to please." He moved to place her roses in a thin, clear vase he'd filled with water, then reached for the steamer pot on the stove.

"Aaron! You don't really have to do that. I was just hassling you."

He raised his eyebrows at her. "Oh, I know. But you threw down the gauntlet, and I'm gonna win this round."

As he steamed a couple of stalks, she glanced outside and saw Sharky chasing after a rabbit in the yard. Then, when the rabbit bolted under the fence, Sharky jumped up and down as if pleading for the bunny to come back. Barking, "Don't leave! We're not done playing yet."

Aaron caught her watching and said, "He's an extrovert. What can I say?"

"Are you going to bring him inside?"

"In a little bit. He's been cooped up a lot today. Besides, he's not real polite about waiting for attention when he wants it. He'll snatch your keys or something until you play with him."

She smiled. "Better to ask forgiveness than to ask permission, though, right?"

"So they say."

And Tamara really didn't know how or why what happened next happened. It probably wasn't anything noteworthy in anyone else's book, but to her their conversation fell into a rare easiness, one almost mystical in origin, at least compared to what she'd grown used to.

As he inspected her garden's produce, their chatting took a personal turn. They talked about their favorite relatives. He mentioned his crazy Grandpa R. J., the one who always took him fishing—a couple dozen times at least—but they only caught fish twice. She told him about her Aunt Eliza. He laughed when she explained her aunt's gardening antics, Al the "younger" man and her latest road trip . . . this time to a Patriots game.

He insisted on chopping up her vegetables to accompany his broccoli, both raw and steamed (turned out, she preferred the latter), so they could have a taste test. And, eventually, after they'd tried some of everything, he broke out a bag of molasses cookies and let Sharky back inside. A canine whose love of bacon treats, she soon learned, eclipsed even his love of jumping on people.

"Your dog's hilarious," she said, watching Sharky attack one of Aaron's running sneakers with the exuberance of youth and the teeth of a baby wolf.

"Yeah, he's funny. My very own teenager. But, he's also kind—energetic, but in a good-intentioned way. And loyal." He exhaled long and hard. "Never lived with anyone like that. Not as an adult."

She shot a look at him, not knowing whether she should ask directly or wait for him to explain, but then she thought, How freakin' ridiculous. Since when was *she* afraid to ask a man a question? "So, things with . . . um, Isabelle, they ended badly?"

He didn't hem, haw or remotely hesitate. "Things with Isabelle ended like the Agony of Defeat, Tamara. Like the most disastrous skiing wipeout imaginable."

Oh, she wanted to know more. To probe for details and explanations. To have her theory confirmed that Isabelle played the role of *bad* spouse and Aaron the *good* one. Because—c'mon—only a female villain would've given him up. "She was disloyal to you, right? She let you down?"

He glanced sharply out the kitchen window, suddenly fascinated with a squirrel or something in the yard. "We let each other down," he said finally. Then he looked her in the eye. "In a bad marriage, it's never just one partner's fault, you know?"

She shrugged. "I suppose not." Though she didn't quite believe that. Then, to break eye contact with him, she glanced at her watch. Seven P.M. *Shit.* Where did the time go? Jon might actually be home by now. "Oh, God, it's getting late, Aaron. I didn't realize . . . I should head home."

"Okay." He pointed to the veggies and cookies on the table. "Wanna take some with you?"

She shook her head. "No, but it was delicious. Well, I mean—" She feigned a shrug of indifference. "The broccoli was just *okay*, but my vegetables were outstanding." She stood up.

He stood up next to her and gave her the elbow. "Shut up, neighbor, or I won't invite you back for the zucchini harvest."

She grinned at him, even as her hyperawareness of his body's proximity to hers intensified. He was so close, and he'd *touched* her. Not that this meant anything, but it created in her a strange kind of *zing* she hadn't felt in years. Decades, perhaps. "You were gonna invite me back? Gonna make me zucchini bread or something?"

"Not if you keep being so mouthy." He called Sharky to come say goodbye.

"Thanks for talking," she told him, completely serious for a second. Completely meaning it.

"Welcome. It was a nice break for me, too." His Adam's apple jumped as he nodded at her, and then the man and his dog watched her as she walked away—she'd glanced back to check—Sharky wagging his stubby tail, Aaron just standing there, a half smile on his handsome face.

She shivered as she strode back toward her house. There was a chill in the evening air that hadn't been there during the afternoon. Though maybe her emotions contributed to that. She felt a range of them, managing to be both excited and at peace simultaneously. Maybe because being with Aaron at his house had been that way: interesting and engaging without being overstimulating, but equally quiet and calm without that pervasive sense of loneliness she'd grown so accustomed to in her own home. She could relax in his company in a way she hadn't been able to do with anyone, not even her best friends, for a long time.

That sense of peacefulness was shattered the moment she spotted the closed garage door. Oh, damn. Jon had beaten her back. She sped up, unlocked the front door and there he stood, in full reprimand pose at the top of the staircase, glaring down at her.

"It's after seven," he spit out. "Where the hell have you been?"

"Just down the street—" She pointed her thumb behind her as if to say "right there" without giving away specifics.

"Didn't you remember when I'd be back? I've been wondering for an hour when you'd show up, Tamara."

"Well, now that burning question has been answered, hasn't it?" She slammed the door shut, her temper rising, a predictable thing these days. It twisted and snapped like firewood into shards of well-practiced irritation. "You're gone for *days* at a time, but what? You expect me to wait by the door for your return like some little nursemaid whose only purpose in life is to attend to your fucking needs?"

"No. But the garage door was wide open—like you were just out for a few minutes. You didn't have your cell with you. I couldn't reach you. I didn't know if you wanted me to makeshift a dinner or if you were out picking something up. Your car was still here, though, so, unless someone else drove you somewhere, I didn't think you'd gone far."

"So, that's the real reason you're so pissed off? It's about *dinner?* Because you didn't know if you'd be required to make yourself a sandwich or heat up a can of soup?" Of course, he was upset because of *that*, not because he was worried about her.

He shook his head. "Look, I'm tired of always arguing with you. It just would've been courteous to let me know where you were. A note or something."

She kicked off her shoes. "You know nothing about courtesy, Jon."

He laughed. A nasty, sarcastic sound. "Well, you're so damned angry and aggressive, I'm not sure you'd be one to recognize it."

She stared at him. "Me?"

"Yes, *you*. You don't want to have a meaningful discussion with me about anything. All you want is to incite a new argument. Even when you're clearly in the wrong."

What she *wanted* was to yell at him, to react in some way, but her interest in engaging him for one more measly second of debate suddenly abated. A bad habit she'd grown weary of keeping. Instead, she studied him. His fair skin, black eyes, dark hair still thick even as he approached fifty. That crease between his brows where he collected his frustration. The hint of stubble on his tensed jaw.

How could he know so little about her? How could he, after nearly two decades of marriage, not realize how much she craved a true conversational connection with him? It wasn't that she didn't want it. No. It was that she'd given up—years ago—the hope of ever getting it.

She shrugged and said, "Think whatever you want. You're going to anyway."

He regarded her with an expression she'd most closely describe as contempt before shrugging and turning away. "Oh," he said, making it clear he wouldn't waste unnecessary words on her. "Your cell kept ringing. I finally checked the number. Wasn't one I recognized. Vermont area code, but not your aunt's number."

"Thanks for telling me." She waited until he'd disappeared into the black hole of the hallway, more than fine with the prospect of him not returning for a few hours. She saw the light in his office switch on. The door closing behind him.

She spotted the day's mail. Jon had brought it in but left it in a heap in the middle of the living room coffee table, of course, so *she* would have to deal with it. She sifted through the stack as she listened to her cell phone messages. The caller had tried three times but only left one message. It was the voice of an older man unknown to her, at least not at first.

"I'm calling for Tamara," the man said. "I was hoping to catch you in person, but I didn't have luck in reaching you directly. My apologies for telling you this via message. I'm Al Jeffries, a good friend of your Aunt Eliza. I'm sorry to say, your aunt has been rushed to the St. Augustine's Medical Center in Montpelier. She had a stroke and is in critical condition. I just—"

Tamara dropped the gas bill and the drugstore circular back onto the coffee table and struggled to listen to the rest of Al's message. Pretty much all she could grasp after that was that the man would keep her posted and, if she had any questions, she could feel free to give him a call.

She immediately hit Callback.

"Hello, Al? It's Tamara. I'm so sorry I missed your call," she said when he answered his phone, but that was all she could manage before the tears overcame her. Not soft, gentle droplets. These were sobs. Sobs loud enough to drag Jon out of his office to peek at her. To actually walk down the hall to see what the big problem was.

"Tamara, dear. I'm glad you reached me," the older gentleman told her.

She sniffled. "Is she okay? Or at least kind of stable now?"

There was a telling silence. "No." He cleared his throat. "No, we lost her a half hour ago. But there wasn't a thing either you or I could've done to stop it. She slipped into a coma right after the stroke, and the medics weren't able to revive her. Even had you known, there wouldn't have been anything you could've said or done—here or there—to turn back the clock." He gulped some air. "She was a stubborn one, that aunt of yours. Always said when she was ready to go, no one would stop her. . . ."

Tamara could hear the affection mingling with sadness in his voice, both so powerful she could feel them through the line. "I can't believe it, Al," she whispered, and, for a few moments, that was all she could say. The immensity of the loss engulfed her. Then, "I wasn't—I wasn't ready for her to go."

"Me, either."

After that, they just stayed on the line for a while, saying nothing, really. Clinging to their phone connection as if it were their last link to Eliza herself.

Before Tamara hung up, she told Al she'd fly out to Vermont right away to handle the funeral arrangements. He said he'd be more than willing to help. Then he added, "I'm sorry we're meeting for the first time under these circumstances, my dear, but I'm glad we'll have a chance to get acquainted finally. Your aunt loved you immeasurably. Her phone conversations with you brightened her days. Some people—" His voice broke as he said this. "Some people only remember their elderly family members when they die. You were there for her in life."

When she clicked off, Jon was standing behind her, not even pretending not to have overheard. "Sorry to hear the news," he said, his voice gruff but, for once, devoid of his usual tone of accusation. "I know how much you loved her."

"Thanks," she whispered. She gazed at him and, for a brief, rare moment, she felt a glimmer of the closeness they'd once shared. But the moment passed, so she ambled to the bedroom to begin packing. Alone. Jon had commitments, of course, but was it too much to offer to help? To even give her a consolation hug? Apparently so.

After booking an online flight out east, she e-mailed Jennifer, whom she knew would be checking messages. *No Indigo Moon for me tomorrow,* she typed, explaining quickly about her aunt's death and the funeral. *Please pass along the news to Bridget for me. Have fun, though, and I'll see you both soon.*

But she didn't know if she would. For the first time in three and a half years she was relieved to have a good excuse not to go out for Friday coffee. Appreciative of the upcoming days away, regardless of the reason. Grieving yet somehow grateful.

❧ 9 ❧

Bridget & Jennifer

Friday, September 17

Jennifer arrived three minutes early and slipped through the front doors of the Indigo Moon Café, not surprised to be the first one there. She'd received Tamara's message, of course, and would relay the news to Bridget upon her arrival, but she more than suspected her dark-haired friend would be late. Which suited Jennifer just fine this morning.

She'd come prepared for calm—and quick—pleasantry, and she'd dressed accordingly. She'd fixed in her mind a set departure time, and the greater the number of minutes that passed before she had to enact her charade of normalcy in front of Bridget, the less time she'd have to spend onstage overall.

She unbuttoned her light, beige overcoat, designed for both appropriate warmth (the fall mornings could be chilly) and anonymity. The latter she accomplished by eschewing all marks of distinction, such as colorful silk scarves or identifying broaches. There would be no golden oak leaves or bright red apples pinned to one of Jennifer's coat collars, thank you.

Of course, David would laugh at her if she wore anything with an apple—decorative or not. "Turned into a Mac person now, have you? Christ, what's the world coming to?" So, the fewer items she wore worthy of comment, the less she'd be forced to reveal.

Jennifer let the hostess lead her to the usual corner table. She made herself as comfortable as possible on the squishy vinyl, picking at her short fingernails with the edge of the laminated menu and contemplating prospective opening lines for when she and David met next week. *It's been a long time.* Or, *Hey, nice to see you. You haven't changed a bit.* Or, *Before you take even one step closer, tell me why you left me.* Well, maybe not that last one.

At precisely 9:09, Bridget burst through the front doors, spotted her and made a beeline for their table.

"Sorry I'm late," she panted, removing a maroon Windbreaker with a faded red, white and blue "Obama Mama" button on it and tossing the jacket on the seat beside her. The thin jersey Bridget wore beneath was an eye-popping swirl of teal and lavender, the visual equivalent of smelling salts on Jennifer's psyche.

"That's okay," Jennifer murmured as she tried to blink away the color cacophony. Didn't work.

"The kids were driving me insane this morning. 'Where'd you put my granola bar?' and 'Are my new jeans washed yet?' and 'Can I go over to Leo's or Kara's or somebody's house after school?'" Bridget mimicked, plopping herself onto the vinyl cushion next to Jennifer. "Evan almost didn't make it to the bus because the two older ones kept—" She stopped midsentence and glanced around, the dark hair swinging behind her like a superhero's cape. "Hey, where's Tamara? Is she running late, too?"

Jennifer told her about the funeral.

"Oh, that's just awful!" Bridget exclaimed. She covered her mouth with her palm and glanced down, but she didn't know if she did it quickly enough to mask her relief. It wasn't that she wanted Tamara's aunt to die—no! It was just that she'd kind of needed a break from Tamara. Jennifer, while quiet and often so hard to read, was at least an easier companion.

After the two women had discussed with sufficient solemnity the sadness of their friend's loss, they took concurrent deep breaths and ventured down a less grim path of conversational exchange. The result—the morning's relative cold snap—coincided with the arrival of their waitress, her pen poised for order-taking.

Bridget had been being careful again about her calories. She'd made an effort to "dress for success" more often these days (she could hear her mother pithily quoting those words to her some twenty years ago), and she'd noticed her wardrobe choices expanded exponentially when she was down eight or ten pounds. So, she waved off the tempting muffin options and focused on her skim-vanilla latte, which she intended to redress with dashes of cinnamon and lace with sprinkles of cocoa powder.

"And for you, a small mocha-soy latte made with a squirt of coconut syrup and a hint of nutmeg, right?" the waitress asked Jennifer.

If pressed, Jennifer would've said it was the air of smug triumph in the waitress's voice that pushed her to finally choose a different beverage option, but that wouldn't have been the whole truth. In just six days she would see David again. The unnatural jitteriness caused by anticipating this disquieting event made her certain she must forgo all forms of caffeine—coffee and otherwise, today and all week—and opt instead for a soothing decaf chai.

Bridget looked stunned by her choice, the waitress duly chastised for presumption, but Jennifer would have shouted to the world at large, "Don't be so sure you know me!" had she believed more than a tiny handful of individuals would've cared.

Bridget continued to stare ominously at her for several seconds after the waitress disappeared. "So, um, what's been going on in your life? Any . . . news?"

Having no interest whatsoever in self-disclosure, Jennifer began to mumble something about getting a few new Web design clients in the past week, but Bridget interrupted her. "No, I meant from David." She paused, tearing a series of millimeter-sized rips in the side of a Splenda packet. "What are you, um, hoping will happen with him? What do you want by seeing him again?"

Jennifer squeezed her eyes shut until she could see the David of her youth in her mental viewfinder. He wouldn't look like that guy anymore, she reminded herself, but it had never been his physicality that had drawn her in anyway. It was that essence of him. It was that quality of a potent understanding between them. A connection.

She opened her eyes and glanced at her friend, fighting to rein in the truth but finding herself being candid anyway. "I'm hop-

ing—I think—that in seeing him again I'll know more. I'm counting on . . . a feeling, I guess. Of rightness or wrongness. And I—I
don't usually rely on feelings, but in his case . . ." The sheer honesty of her own statement was enough to glue Jennifer to the vinyl
and paralyze her tongue, but Bridget didn't look nearly as surprised by her disclosure as she had by her order of a new beverage.

"I rely on feelings a lot," Bridget said with ease. "I don't think
there's anything wrong with making decisions based on logic, but
sometimes it's just better to give yourself over to intuition. Know
what I mean?"

Jennifer did *not* know, but she nodded anyway.

Bridget continued. "I can feel in my bones that I made the best
choice for me way back when in marrying Graham, but things between us are different now. I wonder whether the people we are
today would've chosen to be together if we'd met this year instead
of all those years ago. And, how bad is it, really, to want to sort of
step back from a relationship that isn't working so I can be a part of
one that might?"

Jennifer nodded again. She could discern the importance of
Bridget's struggle. Indeed, in many ways, she shared it. For herself
she wanted closure. To know her rebound guy was the right guy
after all. Or, at least, that the original guy *wasn't* the right guy, and
she'd made the correct decision in moving on (or trying to) all
those years ago. However, this notion of being able to "feel in her
bones" that one choice had been the best—at *any* time—was beyond her grasp.

Bridget, meanwhile, marveled at her understanding of Jennifer's problem, though mere issues of certainty weren't at the
forefront of her mind. Her battles differed in that, despite the
shakiness of her faith, she still believed she had God as her judge,
not only herself. It was the intrinsic rightness or wrongness—of
the *act*, not just the feeling—that concerned her. The sin or the
not-sin. Dr. Luke was Catholic, too. If the situation didn't involve
him directly, she'd have asked him his opinion. Was infatuation
just one of God's tests or a sign of something else? Was marriage,
after a decade or more, something that must simply be *endured* for
most couples? Or, was it part of God's divine plan that she must

fully become the woman she longed to be no matter *what* the consequence?

Somehow Bridget didn't think her childhood priest, Father Patrick, for all his gentle kindness, would sanction the latter.

Jennifer mumbled some platitude about how she was sure "Graham would meet her halfway," and asked if she had "talked to him at all about her feelings."

Bridget's cynicism shield rose. She knew when she was being fed a pat response. Jennifer may have been momentarily open with her, but Bridget was aware of her friend pulling back again.

So, she murmured that, yeah, her husband was a good guy and, perhaps, she could try to work up the courage to discuss this with him, carefully. They both laughed lightly at that and returned to superficial chitchat: a pregnant PTO friend, gossip about a school-board member who was leaving, whether Kip and Leah Wiener would host their annual Halloweiner Party at their McMansion next month and, if so, how they could get out of going. The usual.

All the while, Bridget couldn't help but think of what a kind but closeted soul Jennifer was. So reserved. So different from Tamara. It was funny, the closest Bridget ever came to Tamara's abrasive manner was with Jennifer. She always wanted to shake her up. Get some emotion flowing in her. It almost didn't matter if it was positive or negative. Bridget just wanted the other woman to feel *something*.

Of course, she might get a reaction if she told Jennifer about Dr. Luke and her upcoming lunch date with him. She waffled on it. What if Jennifer judged her as harshly as Tamara did? What if Dr. Luke cancelled out? Then it would look like she'd made up the invitation.

Before she could talk herself into sharing, Jennifer announced, "I'm going to have to leave for yoga in ten minutes." She pointed toward her light gray sweatshirt with the petite pink Downward Dog pose encircled inside the Glendale Grove Yoga logo on her left shoulder. Only then did Bridget notice the black yoga pants she also wore and the easy-to-slip-off white sneakers.

"Oh, no problem," Bridget said, hurrying to finish her latte but wondering why someone who was already so quiet, so calm and frequently so expressionless had to go anywhere to "get centered."

As they paid the bill and collected their few belongings, Jennifer brought up Tamara again. "It must be so sad for her. She was really close to her aunt." Bridget acknowledged this, but didn't say anything when Jennifer added, "I'm sure she wishes she were here having coffee with us instead. I wonder what she's doing right now."

Tamara, however, one thousand miles away in a tiny northeastern section of Vermont, was not wishing she were drinking coffee, wondering whether her friends were talking about her or remotely curious about what they (or her husband, for that matter) were doing in her absence. She was standing next to the man who'd loved her dearest relative and choosing a coffin.

"I don't know which one to get," she whispered to Al, unable to see the models at all clearly because of the watery blurriness in her eyes.

As she reached out to touch the ivory fabric lining the inside of the mahogany one, she felt Al's hand cover hers and squeeze.

"This one looks fine," he whispered back. "Your aunt would've said, 'Life's too short for such unpleasantness, especially when the results are irrelevant.'"

Tamara nodded. "That sounds like her. She would've been right. As usual."

And when they buried her aunt in that very coffin on Sunday afternoon, Tamara fought—and lost—against a torrent of silent, angry tears. How could Aunt Eliza leave her? Who would give her the levity in her day, the strength to face the frequent annoyances, the unconditional love she knew she could count on, if only from one source?

Tamara's mother had driven up from Massachusetts for the funeral, arriving only a few hours before the service. She stood—not beside her daughter, of course, but across the grave from Tamara—head bowed, staring coldly and with dry, resigned eyes at the mahogany box as it was lowered into the ground.

Tamara's mom and Aunt Eliza . . . sisters . . . had never been close, which Tamara had always thought was a shame. Now she realized it was far more than that. It was a loose end that could never be tied. A lingering dance of unrest that would never cease its motion.

Tamara felt her anger abate as she tossed her obligatory handful of moist New England earth onto the shiny coffin.

Goodbye, Auntie. I'll miss you. I'll always love you. I'll do at least one truly wild thing every season in your honor. One joyful, crazy, risky, loving thing. I promise. . . .

As she stepped back, she knew one truth was truer than ever: that, while she'd deeply miss her aunt, she didn't have so much as one tiny regret about their relationship. Tamara glanced at her mother again, knowing this feeling was not universally shared. Tamara's loss wracked her body with aches, but the pain was pure. It was a single, powerful strand, but it was untainted by missed opportunities, closed hearts or any hint of relief.

She also knew, more than the legacy of financial riches Aunt Eliza had willed to her, that the knowledge of life's fleeting nature was her most precious inheritance. The bestowal of wisdom. The parade of happy memories. The joy of real conversation. Gifts her aunt had given her freely and, now that Tamara knew of their power, she'd no longer be able to ignore them again.

❧ 10 ❧

Jennifer

Thursday, September 23

The MapQuest directions informed Jennifer that it would take precisely ninety-two minutes to reach the C-IL-U campus from Glendale Grove—her first time returning since graduation. The MapQuest directions did not take into account, however, her shaking hands, her three dire rest stops or her bizarrely inconsistent driving speed, which had her racing sixteen miles per hour above the speed limit, then crawling at thirteen miles per hour below it, depending on the nature of her thoughts.

She'd tried to block out those thoughts—first with talk radio and then with music. She'd switched from the talk station to the music after ten minutes because they were discussing some sports thing that bored her so much she'd tuned it out and begun daydreaming about David.

Unfortunately, after a trifecta of brokenheartedness on the easy-listening station (Jackson Browne's "Love Needs a Heart" followed by David Soul's "Don't Give Up On Us" and, finally, to round out the maudlin set, the Carpenters' "Hurting Each Other"), she figured her own reflections couldn't be as damaging as what she was hearing. She snapped off the radio completely and drove in silence for most of the way there.

Five minutes from campus, however, she felt as though she'd been abducted by youthful aliens in a time travel assault, then forced into captivity in their parallel universe. There were places that looked familiar, only they weren't. There were groupings of people she had once been a part of, only they now had a wholly different membership.

That corner grocery store on the way out of town—Kirby's— was still standing, but its colors had all changed. The distinctive green door was now beige. And who knew what the shopping was like there these days? Used to be they'd had the cheapest peanut butter and generic bags of chocolate chips on campus for when she and David were in the mood for a late night dessert pizza. They'd get all the other ingredients there, too: the mix-n-bake pizza dough for the crust, the bananas, the occasional bag of mini marshmallows.

The video rental place that had once been right across the street from Kirby's now had a "Verizon" placard where the neon "Hot Video" sign used to be. That was where she'd first gotten a copy of *The Abyss*, which almost made her breath stop watching it. And David, perv that he was, always rented *A Clockwork Orange* just to torment her.

She slowed as she approached the campus proper. She spotted two sets of couples. One pair loitered in silence by the Fine Arts building. One pair held hands on the walkway toward the Catacombs, the student union.

There was a clique of girls clumped together who—Jennifer's heart clenched—looked barely older than Veronica and her friends. Oh, God. Her little girl would be huddled in a group like this and giggling over similar nonsense in just a few years. She felt a sudden and very deep pang of empathy for Tamara, who'd been experiencing this teen-to-adult transition with Benji.

She saw a dozen different girls of all variations, including one twenty-something with glasses, dressed in a premeditatedly sloppy way, surrounded by a small cluster of boys. The girl was cute-ish but far from a beauty queen type. However, she had a presence Jennifer could detect from half a block away. She stood with such a confident posture that the unified gaze of all four guys was fixed on her.

Jennifer suspected from the number of students roaming the

sidewalk that a class session had just ended and that this girl was in one of the heavily male-dominated courses. Nothing caught a geek boy's eye faster than a woman who could hold her own in a ten to one male-to-female ratio class like quantum physics, actuary science or computer programming.

And something else Jennifer noticed—or, rather, *felt*, which was always a surprising sensation: The air outside her car practically hummed with the breath of possibility. All these kids—the princesses, the jocks, the computer geeks—were on the verge of a great unknown. They were *alive* in a way she was not.

She rolled down the window to inhale the aching scent of Uncertainty mated to Excitement—the act flooding her lungs with both oxygen and the intoxication of youth. It'd been so long since she'd felt the latter, she scarcely recognized herself. Like a former version—Jennifer 2.0 BETA—even though she'd been upgraded to the well-tested but safe and uninspired Jennifer 5.0.

Just to be sure there was no match between her emotional rush and her appearance, she flipped down the driver's side visor and stared at her reflection in the mirror. Nope. She was no longer twenty-two. No longer single. No longer free to consider the world a 3GB hard drive full of possibilities. And yet—

"Watch it, lady!" a college boy on a skateboard shouted, his expression pissed off, his accompanying hand gesture decidedly rude as he skimmed through the crosswalk she'd been obliviously driving into. Hmm. She glanced to her right, only now noticing the stop sign.

She waited until he and a handful of other kids passed by, forcing herself to concentrate on this last leg of what had become an eighteen-year journey. It wasn't just driving to a library in another town and finding a parking spot. It was returning to David and the life of possibility they'd left behind.

Like a programmer doing a code check of a new design before going live, Jennifer did a full analysis of all her parts before stepping out of the safety of the car. Head. Body. Style. The CSS of her physical and emotional state. What was consistent?

In her expert opinion as a designer, there were too many emotions competing for precedence within her, crashing discordantly, like when there were too many fonts on a Web page. Only one, maybe two, should be dominant. Choosing the style of type to be used for the header, subheader, small text was always a critical design task. Selecting a lead emotion should, likewise, be expected. No more of this mishmash of feelings. Was Anxiety her primary emotional font or merely the subheader? Where did Curiosity, Excitement and Relief fit on the page of this strange, long-awaited day?

Finally, she ought to get some answers. Perhaps that was her key to these odd sentiments and internal signals. She felt that peculiar vibration deep in her gut, like the sensation she had right before launching a new site. She may have designed it and have had a strong sense of what the final outcome would be, but she never knew *exactly* what it would look like until she viewed it live for the first time.

Jennifer jumped out of her car, feigning an air of spontaneity. She skittered along the small path to Hooke Library, wondering if she blended well enough with the coeds on the walkway, or if they were as acutely aware of her inability to fit in as she was.

Stepping at a brisk pace up to the front doors, she scanned as surreptitiously as possible for someone as equally anachronistic with the current time and place. After studying a score or more faces—and David's not among them—she began to feel a whole new sensation. One that was a mighty leap up from mere anxiety.

But she fought her worry. She'd give him five minutes, maybe ten. She glanced at her watch. Well, okay, maybe fifteen. She'd driven the whole way here, after all. But she somehow had to find a place to stand where she could be at once watchful and inconspicuous. Visible to David, if he should materialize, but neither overly eager nor unduly apprehensive in the eyes of the library staff (she was trying hard not to look as though she were casing the place for a break-in), the students walking by or David himself when—or, heaven help her, *if*—he spotted her. Somehow she had to control the first impression he might have of her in nearly two decades, provided, of course, that she could project all of these semicontradictory qualities at once.

She shuffled to the side of the outdoor entranceway, repositioning herself with her back to the bricks and her body poised to pay riveted attention to a steel pole with flyers taped to it.

She skimmed over the offerings for what felt like an hour, though only a few minutes in reality: a punk band playing the next night at the student union. A request for a second-semester roommate. A pet iguana for sale.

Out of the edge of her vision, she spotted a figure moving inside the library, on the other side of the panes of the nearest window. A hovering, distinct figure. One that craned between shadow and light to watch her.

David.

She couldn't see the significant details of him—the color of his clothing, the expression on his face—but she could feel his intensity piercing her. She posed for it, for him. Reaching out to smooth down the edge of a flyer for a university trip ("Spend Christmas in Cozumel!"), she snuck a glance at her watch and considered making her impatience visible.

After another two minutes of feigning fascination with calculus tutors and auditions for *Man of La Mancha*, and still not having him appear, she deliberately checked the time on her watch. He was a full twelve minutes late. Ah, now she understood. Thirteen.

Fine. He was up to his old games, but she didn't have to put up with it. Thirteen minutes was one minute longer than she was prepared to wait out his game. She took a few steps out of his viewing range and, with the acuity of her peripheral vision, noticed the instant the dark figure swished past the window to his next hiding place. Still observing. She pretended not to notice.

Thirteen minutes past the hour. Time to call his bluff.

She checked her watch conspicuously one last time, tapped the face of it and strode with forced purpose back toward her car. She'd barely cleared the library's walkway when her cell phone beeped. A text message from David. Shocker.

It read: *Look behd U.*

She sighed and turned slowly around, cell phone in hand. Sure enough, he was leaning up against the pole with the flyers as if he'd been the one waiting for her all along. She paused before beginning her approach, suspecting this was what he'd wanted from the start. Her walking toward him. Him manipulating the game.

She didn't say his name when she reached him, just raised one silent eyebrow and waited for the forthcoming explanation.

"Hi, Jenn," he murmured. "I was running late. Had trouble finding parking," he lied, pointing vaguely toward Lot C. "How're you doing?"

She raised the other eyebrow and shook her head. "How long, David?"

He blinked. Shifted positions. Then grinned at her. "C'mon. You already know. A good eight inches at least." His grin broadened, obviously enjoying the opportunity to twist her words.

But David was in for a surprise if he thought she'd react like the easily deceived college girl he'd left behind. The one who always refrained from asking him direct questions. "How long were you waiting in the library and watching me from the window?" she said evenly.

His expression registered astonishment. *Good.* He inhaled. "I—um—" And then the smug, overconfident look reclaimed his face. "I couldn't find a space in Lot E, so I—"

She swiveled on her heel and headed again toward her car. Screw him.

"A half hour, Jenn."

She stopped. Waited.

"Forty minutes, maybe. I didn't want to take the chance that I'd miss you, okay?"

She pivoted back and could see the truth of it floating across his eyes, knew the tone in his voice—on the "okay?"—when he'd stopped struggling to be the cool Dungeon Master in this real-life game of D&D.

"Don't lie to me again, David."

He nodded but didn't reply, and she didn't push him any further. This was the first opportunity she'd had to look at him— *really* look—and the compare and contrast, past to present, was unmistakable. When he was in the library, she'd sensed the aura of him, which had remained unchanged. The specifics were, of course, a different story.

She laid the image of her twenty-year-old mental snapshot side by side with the reality of the forty-something man standing before her. Receding but still dark brown hair. Slightly paler, more washed-out complexion. Marginally puffier in the face, especially around the eyes. Body still slim but not that sinewy lean of her memory. Clothes far more stylish than the threadbare jeans paired with "The Who" T-shirts of their college years. The squinty lines at the corners of his brown eyes were deeper, too, than they had been, but the purpose behind them was the same. David was studying her, taking an inventory of his own.

"You look . . . good," he mumbled.

"Thanks. You, too." Undoubtedly, they were both far more adept at being insincere these days.

As if by extreme force of will, he pushed away from the pole to join her. He motioned for them to walk toward the center of campus and fell into step alongside of her.

A new class session must have been just about to begin because students were being siphoned off the paths and into the various buildings like dwindling streams of liquid. They were abandoning her.

David laughed suddenly, an almost violent release. "I hadn't expected it to be this awkward, you know? After all the times we'd talked online and texted each other. The in-person thing, it's, well—"

"Weird?" she supplied.

"Very. Though I imagined us doing this—more than once. More than a hundred times, really."

"A hundred raised to the power of thirteen," she murmured, remembering this was something he used to say. Something he'd said the first time he told her how much he loved her.

"Yeah."

He didn't add anything further, and they kept walking.

Finally, she halted. "Do you have any specific spots in mind that you want to check out?"

He nodded and dug into his pocket, retrieving a creased piece of paper. He unfolded it and rattled off a list of locations painfully familiar to her. Each would seem innocuous enough to a casual observer but, in her case, every one of those places came complete with an accompanying photo scrapbook tinged with a sound track only the two of them would recognize.

"How about we start at the Weaver Center?" he suggested.

The Weaver Center. Home of the campus's best strawberry milkshakes. Comfy, ratty chairs great for all-night study sessions. That spring dance they went to where the DJ kept playing Supertramp because he thought it was funny.

"Sure," she said, trying to look expressionless. Indifferent.

"It'll hold a lot of people," he told her. "Not that we'll need room for more than twenty."

She glanced at him sharply.

"Mitch heard back from a few people already who can't make it," he explained. "Other commitments and stuff."

"So, you and Mitch split up the club members? You each contacted half?"

"Something like that. Well, actually, I delegated a bit."

He looked away, busying himself with putting away the list, but she knew for certain, right then, that this was entirely a setup. That the reunion was David's idea, but he'd roped Mitch into helping. That she was probably the only club member David had contacted personally. And that this idea of being on the "location committee" with him was just a ploy, but she couldn't figure out what had set him in motion.

"Why? Why after all this time did you want to see me again?" she asked, feeling oddly bold for someone who'd almost never challenged him when they were together.

He started walking again and, for a moment, she thought he'd try to ignore her. But then he said, "For the same reason you agreed to meet me." He quickened his pace. "Unfinished business."

She considered this. "But what made you think it was unfinished for *me?* Before we started e-mailing? And you said in one of those early messages that you'd heard I got married. From *whom?* I didn't keep in touch with anyone from college that you'd have known, David."

He batted away those questions with an annoyed gesture and a grimace. "I did a little research."

They were right in front of the Weaver Center entrance, but she pulled him back from the door. "Wait. You cyber-stalked me?"

"I people-searched you, I didn't stalk."

"But you looked me up? Found photos of me? Already knew where I was living?" How creepy. And, yet, how strangely gratifying that he'd been that interested.

"Oh, c'mon. It was nothing. Some pictures of you at a kids' cheerleading camp fund-raiser. Fall PTA minutes. Web credits for your design business. You're not fucking invisible, Jenn." And from the fierce look he gave her, she knew she wasn't. At least not to him. "So don't bullshit me. It's not like you've never done it. I know how sneaky and subversive you can be. Playing at innocence while gathering up data to use against someone later. Stripping away a person's defenses in your mind and digging at their insecurities while acting all mousy and serene."

He glared, deep and feral, and it was a spike to the heart, this knowledge he possessed of her. She'd let so few people into her inner circle, but he'd been one of them. Once. Unfortunately, much of what he'd learned about her still remained true today. Still true because it'd always been true . . . and because she'd let him see her real self. Big mistake.

"Look me in the eye, Jenn, and tell me you never Googled my name."

She closed her eyes and bowed her head.

"You want me to play fair?" he spat out. "You have to play fair back. You want me to be honest? You have to be honest, too."

She took a deep breath and returned his glare. "Fine. A few times but, last I checked, there were ninety-six living David Saxons in the United States. A handful in Illinois alone. And, besides, I thought you'd have moved out of state a decade or more ago."

"How many David Saxons were in my age bracket?"

"Twelve that I could identify," she shot back.

"How many with the middle initial O?" David's middle name was Oliver.

"At least six, but there were a bunch that weren't listed."

"Don't tell me you didn't look at the ones in Illinois and wonder if one of them was mine. That you didn't do a reverse phone number search or check out the aerial view of a few of the addresses. That you didn't see my parents' names recorded in the 'relatives' section by one or two of the listings. Or Marcia's."

"I didn't see Marcia's name anywhere. Anytime. Ever." That was true. But, in many ways, David was right. She certainly qualified as compulsive enough to hunt down the details of his life, and she *had* made a start on it. So, the greater truth was that she was curious to a point but then simply scared. She'd suspected a connection between him and Marcia, yes, but she hadn't wanted to look long or deep enough to have it verified.

"Then you weren't looking too hard, were you?" He studied her, the intelligence in his eyes undeniable, and the amused delight in the wry twist to his lips unmistakable. He *saw* her.

She had been trying to work up the courage to ask about those last weeks of their senior year, to corner him and ask why he'd left, but he was the king of conversational pacing. He had turned her momentary imbalance to his advantage.

He broke their eye lock and pushed open the door to the Weaver Center. If Jennifer had wondered where they packed the students on the C-IL-U campus, she had to look no farther. The interior was swarming. Even busier than when they were students. Some kids were there for meals (the building housed the main cafeteria), some for small group seminars, some for tutoring and many simply to hang out in the lounges and study in those comfy, ratty chairs.

Jennifer and David wandered the long corridors of the rec center for a few minutes, peeking into the rooms set aside for the larger lectures or student gatherings.

"You could host a wedding reception in this one," David said, pointing through the open door to a "lounge" that could easily seat two hundred.

"If we're going to have less than twenty people, maybe we should look for something more, um—"

"Intimate," David finished for her.

"Well, yeah. The Center is just too big." And they hadn't even bothered to trek through the lower level where the dances and performances were held. They already knew those wouldn't provide any kind of cozy, chat-with-old-buddies atmosphere.

"I think we should give TJH a chance," he said. "I don't know if they still have those party rooms on level three, but they'd be about perfect for what we're looking for."

TJH, or Thomas Jefferson Hall, was the upperclassmen dorm. The dorm she and David had lived in, just one floor apart, during their junior year. Every hallway housed a memory. Every study room a recollection of their relationship. Jennifer wasn't sure she could handle being in there again. Of course, anything was better than the Vat Building, which David also had on his list.

"Okay, let's go there," she said, resigning herself to the lesser of two evils.

But unexpected news befell them before they ever got out of the Weaver Center.

They passed by a campus information booth, manned (womanned?) by a perky blond thing, a student guide whom David, apparently, couldn't resist questioning. "Hi, there," he said. "Perhaps you can help us."

"Sure!" Perky Girl said with an unnatural level of enthusiasm. Jennifer tried not to scowl at her.

"We were interested in renting out one of the party rooms in TJH. Who on campus should we speak to? The dean? The dorm director?"

The girl regarded them blankly. "Um, party rooms?"

"Right. On the third floor. You know, those large rooms where people gather?"

Jennifer could hear the polite condescension in his voice, something a typical eavesdropper might miss. He looked so pleasant, but the glint in his eye, the measured enunciation and the marginally terse tone gave away his impatience and irritation. Good to see that one of his core traits had remained unchanged through the years. And that, no matter how nubile the woman, David still didn't suffer fools cheerfully.

Though there were exceptions. He'd married Marcia after all.

"My friend lives in Thomas Jefferson Hall," the girl said, squinting at them. "They have a few kinda small lounges up there for residents, but I've never seen big party rooms. I mean, some guys live on level three and they, you know, have *parties*"—she blushed prettily—"but not, like, *officially*."

"They must've converted the space to dorm rooms," Jennifer said, the tension in her chest loosening at this news. Now they wouldn't have to go there.

David nodded, bit his lip, turned back to Perky Girl and slowed his speech even further. "Is there *anywhere* on campus that might have rooms alumni can rent out?"

Perky Girl batted her eyes as she stared, unfocused, into the distance. Thinking, presumably. "Um, maybe somewhere in the Vat? I think they have, like, places just for responsible adults and stuff."

"Responsible and practical adults," David murmured in an aside to Jennifer. "Dependable, sensible, respectable adults."

"Acceptable, presentable adults. A vegetable," she murmured back with a grin, parroting a mixed-up version of the famous Supertramp lyrics from verses they'd once had memorized. Words they'd danced to in that very building.

Perky Girl looked confused. "A vegetable? You mean, like, you wanna bring food in there?"

"Not necessarily," David said with feigned sweetness. "We just want a room where we can joyfully and happily be intellectual, logical, clinical and cynical, uh, *adults*."

"That would be a magical miracle," Jennifer contributed in her most serious voice.

David snickered.

Perky Girl no longer looked so perky. "You'll have to ask the dean," she said with a sniff. "I totally don't know."

"Thanks, anyway," David said, pushing Jennifer away from the booth before they both started laughing.

"That was mean of us," Jennifer said once they were outside, even though she couldn't stop giggling. "Funny, but unkind."

"She was a dope," David said with a dismissive shrug. "But I think we may have to go over to the Vat and see what's available in person."

Jennifer sucked in some air. She knew she couldn't express to

David how very much she didn't want to go back there. Not with him. Not with anyone, really. The words she wanted to say got stuck in her throat, however, and all she could do was nod mutely. A gesture that he, of course, took to mean acquiescence.

"It'll be kind of strange to walk around in there after all these years, don't you think?" he asked.

Strange didn't begin to cover it. Again, she sort of nodded at him.

"God, the hours we spent in that lab . . ."

No kidding. The Vat Building housed the university's main computer lab. She, David and their friends had treated it like their true campus home. If the rooms in TJH presented painful flash-backs, every nook and cranny in the Vat caused the equivalent agony of a two-hour-long torture film.

Nevertheless, to the Vat they went.

Bizarre how someplace could be altered—room elements switched around, new equipment incorporated, even additions put on the building—and, yet, two decades later, still look and feel exactly the same.

The room that was the hardest for her to walk into was the Techie Lounge. It had the ancient familiarity of her childhood bedroom, and despite its emptiness, or maybe because of it, she felt teleported through time when she crossed the threshold. There were new vending machines, of course (though they still were stocked with Coke, Snickers bars and bags of Doritos), a few pieces of different furniture (old and moldy, but not as old or as moldy as the ones that'd been there when she and David were students), a marginally less horrible valance above the window over-looking the quad (but still *very* ugly).

Even David paused, speechless, by her side. They gaped in stunned silence at the room—one that was "just right" for their gathering, whereas the Weaver Center had been too big and Thomas Jefferson Hall too small.

She was thinking about this for several seconds before she became aware of David's breathing. It had turned hard and labored, his eyes becoming glassy to the point of wateriness.

What the hell? Was he having a heart/asthma/panic attack? She stared at him in alarm. "David? Are you all right?"

He shook his head.

She grabbed his wrist and felt for his pulse. It raced beneath her fingertips, but he just stood there, immobile. "David?" she said again. "Talk to me. Tell me what you're feeling." She fumbled for her cell phone. "You need to sit down. I—I can call for an ambulance or at least get a doctor out h—"

He turned to face her, twisting his wrist out of her grasp and, instead, taking her hand. Gently. "What I'm feeling," he said, still panting more than breathing, "is regret. That I'm sorry, Jenn. So sorry I left our life together. So sorry I left . . . you."

Jennifer, held fast by both his grip on her hand and by the circle of magnetism he always seemed to create around himself, gazed at him. She realized with shock that the water in his brown eyes stemmed from tears, not pain. Well, at least not physical pain.

"It was a long time ago," she whispered, again wanting to ask him for the details of his departure but unable to voice her question for fear of setting off in him some kind of relapse.

"Doesn't seem so long."

"No," she said. "Not in this room. But it was."

He pulled back then, released her hand, looked away. She heard him mumble something that sounded like "Maybe. Maybe not." She wasn't sure, though, since he'd walked away from her and toward the window. He seemed strangely fine again.

With an abrupt motion, he snatched at the dangling cord and pulled, opening the blinds until they smacked the underside of that ugly valance. "Let's get some light in here, huh? Take a look around."

She figured they had already had plenty of time to look around, but since color had begun seeping back into his lips and cheeks, she humored him. Still, she couldn't help but say, "Are you sure you don't want to check out any of the other rooms? They built that new wing in the back—"

"Nope. This is the spot. Everyone in the club knew it well." He met her gaze directly. "Dreams were formed and abandoned here.

People met each other, then moved away. And isn't that what re-unions are all about? Returning to an influential place and facing those dreams, and those people, again? Seeing if the present real-ity in any way mirrors the hopes of the past?"

How poetic, she wanted to say, feeling the anger bubbling in-side her at his words. How easy to speak of abandoned dreams like they were a figurative concept. And blithely pulling out the phrase "hopes of the past," as if he were giving some valedictory speech meant to be inspirational and not merely trying to excuse his own lousy behavior.

Instead, she glanced at her watch. "I have to go soon."

His eyes widened. "Really? But it's nearly lunchtime. I was hoping we could grab a bite at the Winter Palace."

She pressed her lips together. "I don't think—"

"Just wait." He moved toward her, shooting her one of his Gimme-A-Chance-And-I'll-Charm-You looks. Funny. He could still pull that off. "Let's see if we can secure a reservation on this room, and then we'll talk about lunch, okay?"

She shrugged. He'd have to drag her in there, North America's Best Chicken Kiev or not. As for the Vat, maybe they'd get lucky and be told by the university administration that the chosen loca-tion was unavailable. Then they'd have to hold their CPU reunion in the psychology building or something. Somewhere she could feel numb and indifferent.

But it turned out to be no problem for two alumni to rent out the Techie Lounge for a night—given a couple of months' ad-vanced notice, given the purpose was for a former campus club's reunion and given their readily available $150 deposit check writ-ten out and handed over to the C-IL-U treasurer.

The Winter Palace was, to Jennifer's relief, not so easy a place to secure a reservation, however. Not for lunch. Not for anything. The building was gone.

"Aw, crap," David said, staring at the empty lot just off campus where "their" Russian restaurant had been. "They tore it down." He craned his neck to scan up and down the block. "Maybe they just moved to a new location."

But when they asked a college boy on a bike, and then an elderly lady with a dog and, finally, some businessman in a dark blue suit if any of them knew what had happened to it, they all said, "No."

A store owner in the mini strip mall next door explained the rest. "Tore the place down, 'bout three years ago now. Owners moved to Florida."

As the man answered a few more of David's questions, Jennifer's cell phone rang. She backed away several feet, recognized the number and answered. "Hi, Michael. What's going on?"

Her husband could not, thankfully, see her grimace or spot the tremors in her hands, but David missed nothing—not even while finishing up his conversation with the store owner. Jennifer could feel his eyes on her—watching, waiting, analyzing.

Michael, who sometimes called on his lunch break, babbled on about the school's standardized testing, some student-adviser meeting he had that afternoon, the grading he needed to finish up that night. She mostly murmured, "Oh, okay," to anything he said, including his suggestion that he could pick up a pizza on the way home if she and the girls wouldn't mind eating an hour later.

She sighed. What did it matter?

Michael wasn't a bad man, despite his cluelessness, nor was David purely evil, despite how he'd hurt her once. Being sandwiched between them—Michael jabbering in her ear and David scowling in her line of vision—she couldn't help but wonder how she was to have been attracted to (and to have, at one time, attracted) these two very different men. These two sides of her. Did either of them really know her? She doubted it, but perhaps that was her fault. Perhaps she had never been fully honest with either of them about herself. Perhaps she had projected just enough of what they had wanted to see and hear that each man assumed she was who they had wanted her to be.

When Michael finally rang off, she snapped the phone shut, only to have to deal with David, who had finished his conversation with the store owner and moved to within a foot and a half of her, the intensity of his gaze always startling at so close a distance.

"He doesn't know you're here, does he?" he asked her point-blank, his tone a mix of accusation and curiosity.

She shook her head, surprised by his surprise. "But," she fired back, recognizing the probable source of his insecurity and consequent attack, "I'll bet Marcia doesn't know *you're* here either."

He didn't immediately answer, but she saw she'd struck at the truth. "In the ways of sneakiness we always were well matched," she whispered, a torrent of memories accompanying her words. She and David, lying convincingly to the resident assistants about their whereabouts in the dorm during a series of unnecessary fire alarms. Blatantly cheating on their end of the year Spanish project. Stealing a couple of programming tests off the professor's computer—not that they'd needed help with the class. Just to do it. Stuff she probably wouldn't have even thought of doing had she not been following David's lead. But, nevertheless, she had pulled off those pranks without a hitch, which said something about her, didn't it?

David had enough sense not to challenge her or question her meaning. "The Winter Palace is gone," he said instead. "But that doesn't mean we can't grab a quick lunch somewhere else. You up for burgers or something?"

"Thanks, David, but no." She glanced pointedly at her watch. "I'd like not to have to rush home. If I leave now, I'll get there about fifteen minutes ahead of the girls."

He nodded, but she knew David never gave in easily. She could almost see the board game behind his eyes, the strategy in his moves, as he said, "See you on November thirteenth, then? It'll be here before we know it."

"True." She broke away from his magnetic circle and took a few independent steps in the direction of her car. He motioned to follow her, but she waved him off. "Until November."

And even though he got in the last word—"We'll be in touch, Jenn," he called after her—she felt relief bordering on euphoria that she was the one who got to leave *him* behind this time.

❧ 11 ❧

The Trio, Reconfigured

Late September through early October

For the three consecutive weeks that followed, the Glendale Grove trio did their best impression of Shell Game Friendship.

Tamara would run into Bridget and both would quickly scoot away. Jennifer would slide into the middle of the other two but, after a momentary pause, would soon be elsewhere herself. There was a great shuffling of insincere greetings and relieved departures, their biggest problems remaining hidden beneath an impenetrable bowl—like a tightly cupped palm over their hearts—with no one admitting to what lurked, alone and hard, underneath the smooth veneer.

The day after Jennifer's face-to-face encounter with David, she left a message on Bridget's home voice mail (when she was certain the other woman would be showering), pleading illness and her inability to make it to the Indigo Moon that morning. In truth, she needed time to herself, time to think, the lack of which had caused a particularly painful malady that Jennifer reasoned could surely fall under the subheader of Sickness.

Thus, considering Technology Avoidance to be her Rx for the day, Jennifer did not respond to Bridget's phone call of concern, Tamara's e-mail asking how "the event" at the university went or even David's follow-up text message saying: *Thx 4 the visit*. Really, they all just needed to give her a damn break.

In light of Jennifer's absence, Bridget considered cancelling out on the Friday coffee date herself. But she knew it would be a cowardly reaction, and she'd been practicing boldness in cooking (amazing what curry could do!) and wanted to extend the experience to life.

However, the visit itself proved dissatisfying to both women, though Glendale Grove onlookers would have noticed nothing amiss, except the notable lack of one regular member of the threesome. Not so unusual considering their several years of get-togethers. Even inevitable, one might say. But the morning's omission really threw the remaining two off course.

Bridget's resolve of boldness was doused by Tamara's strained demeanor. For once, the latter was cagey and nearly introspective. She answered Bridget's inquiries about her aunt's funeral with measured civility and only one brief instance of moist emotion, but she divulged little else of a personal nature.

Bridget, having already learned her lesson about sharing her fears with Tamara, wouldn't give away anything either. She merely deflected Tamara's halfhearted questions back to their speculative discussion on Jennifer and how the meeting with her ex-boyfriend the day before might have gone.

With focused effort and forced graciousness, the pair managed to stay at the Indigo Moon all by themselves for one hour and seventeen minutes. Not that either was counting.

Tamara, acutely aware of the slipper of mistrust that had wedged itself in the door between her and Bridget, could not, nevertheless, work up the energy to yank it loose, let alone remove it altogether. She had too much on her mind anyway to be playing junior high clique games. She didn't blame Jennifer for canceling out, and she couldn't bring herself to feel hurt by their friend's avoidance.

Bridget, by contrast, had always felt instinctively more comfortable when Jennifer was present at their morning meetings, and so found herself startled by the suspicion that a rift may have begun long before—not just with Tamara, but with Jennifer, too. She'd noticed a drifting between them that had been present back in the summer and, possibly, even in the spring, but she'd tried to shut it out and think only of the three-plus years of good discussions and warmth. But the clues were in the little things. The increasingly longer conversational silences. The unanswered phone calls. The lack of *realness* when the problems turned deep and dark, despite the many hours the women had spent together in the past.

Perhaps, Bridget thought, Jennifer had been easier to be around simply because she'd hidden herself so successfully. And perhaps Bridget had been fooled over the years into believing they'd had a genuine intimacy when it may have merely been careful self-protection on Jennifer's part, drenched in a sheen of polite attentiveness. It hurt her to think so, but she couldn't rule it out.

So, when the next two Fridays brought with them a natural reprieve from the stresses of their coffee gatherings (parent/teacher conferences one week and the four-day, wraparound Columbus Day weekend the next), none of the three women experienced any emotion akin to disappointment.

Of course, while all of the ladies may have had a much needed break from each other, they were hardly immune to the troubles at home. In fact, their required and concentrated attention in *that* quarter only intensified those problems.

Jennifer, for instance, was getting the sense that too much time scrutinizing the behavior of her elder daughter would lead to little good for either of them. And parent/teacher conferences, never one of her favorite events under the best of circumstances, proved to be a gateway to a series of uncomfortable yet unavoidable discussions.

She'd been pretending to listen with rapt attention to Veronica's U.S. history teacher, Mr. Ryerson, a wiry, genteel man who had the gaze of an impassioned hawk. Having survived all of Shelby's conferences relatively unscathed ("Your daughter is a bright student but quiet in class discussions . . ."), Jennifer had not expected to encounter any difficulties with the reports of her more talkative daughter. But Mr. Ryerson had no less than six pages of notes on Veronica.

"She doesn't have trouble with the class work," he told her, "when she pays attention to it. But I've noticed a steady drop in her concentration over the course of the first quarter."

Jennifer fidgeted with her watchband. "Uh-huh." Veronica was a teenager—what'd he expect? She'd gotten a B for the grading period. It wasn't like she was failing.

As if guessing her silent argumentativeness, Mr. Ryerson continued, "I realize high school history is about the last thing a typical fourteen- or fifteen-year-old would be interested in, but I suspect Veronica's lack of attention has far more to do with a triangular drama that's playing out in the classroom than with any real resistance to the Boston Tea Party."

"A triangular drama?" she said, finally making eye contact with the man.

"Yes." The teacher sifted through a few pages of notes. "Not to name names, but your daughter seems to be . . . socially involved with two of the boys in the class."

"Two of them? I only knew about Tim Taylor."

He nodded. "Tim is one of the boys. He sat to Veronica's right for most of the quarter until I had to move their seats a few weeks ago. They'd taken constant texting to new levels."

Jennifer squinted at him. "But the school has a policy about cell phone use. They're only allowed between classes or after school."

Mr. Ryerson gave her a significant look. "Exactly."

"Oh," Jennifer said. "So, I take it you took their cell phones away for the class period and then . . . ?"

"And then they borrowed phones from friends. After I discovered that ploy, they resorted to old-fashioned note passing. But as distracting as this behavior was, most of the teachers in the building are fairly lenient about cell phone infractions and the like. So many kids text each other in secret, we would have class sizes of ten if we sent everyone who'd abused the policy once or twice to the office. No, it wasn't until another boy—Erick—started getting involved that the situation worsened."

Jennifer murmured his name. "She's never mentioned an Erick."

"Erick sat directly behind Veronica until I moved his seat, too.

He's a new student this year, a sophomore, actually, and very charismatic. He and your daughter have really, uh, hit it off."

"They're flirting?"

The teacher laughed. "Teen *flirting* in public is generally a non-verbal thing. Lots of looks and smiles, the occasional rude gesture. Sometimes, when the kids are popular and confident, it morphs into giggling, chatty conversation and suggestive language. It does not routinely include inappropriate touching or grappling, or it crosses the line from flirting into wrestling."

Jennifer gulped. Tim and now this Erick guy have been *grappling* with Veronica? "They're touching her?"

He shook his head. "Most of the time, she's the one touching them. Even with their seats in opposite corners of the room from hers, she'll often make a point to pass by one of their desks when she gets up. The class tends to find it all very funny, so even when I don't see it happening, their laughter gives her away."

Jennifer felt a spasm of embarrassment as she thought of her extroverted, popular daughter. Was this really how Veronica acted in class? "I'm so sorry she's been this disruptive, Mr. Ryerson, but why is this the first time I'm hearing about this problem? I would've liked to stop it immediately."

"It's progressively worsened," he said. "Initially, I'll admit, I didn't think the kids' behavior was anything out of the ordinary, but since the Homecoming committee's activities have accelerated in the past two weeks, so have their in-class antics. I had a discussion with the three of them after class on Tuesday, and all of the kids promised to tone it way down. The boys made an effort on Wednesday and Thursday—Tim, in particular, was quite subdued—but Veronica kept at it, primarily by sneaking up behind Erick and running her hands down his chest . . . and a little lower."

"Oh, crap," she whispered, not quite under her breath.

Mr. Ryerson smiled kindly, though his gaze pierced right through her skull. "You're going to need to talk with your daughter. I spoke with the principal this morning, and Veronica's on probation in my class. She'll be suspended for two days and moved out of my room within one week if that behavior continues."

* * *

At Glendale Grove Elementary, Bridget was hearing equally disturbing news from Evan's first-grade teacher, Miss Welsh.

"I'm glad you were able to come in today," Miss Welsh said, gently but not at all like her usual, bubbly, third-year-teacher self. "I've kept the next conference slot open, so we'd have a little extra time. Mrs. Molinelli, the school social worker, is going to stop by in a few minutes."

The social worker? "Why?" Bridget asked in alarm. She kept Evan clean and well fed. She made sure he got enough sleep and wasn't late to school. She never forgot to pack his lunch, his mid-morning snack or his gym shoes. She wasn't a negligent mom, was she?

"You know, I'm still pretty new to the school district," the teacher said. "So there's a lot about the kids' emotional development that I'm still learning. But I've been noticing how Evan's been really withdrawn lately and, when I question him about it, he gets irritated. There *does* seem to be something bothering him, though, yet he always denies there's a problem. Have you noticed him acting differently at home or showing signs like these?"

Well, of course Bridget noticed *that!* But she had three children. Each of them had their own personality. And Evan had always—*always*—been her supersensitive one. She tried to explain this to Miss Welsh.

The teacher nodded. "I can see that about him. He's very attuned to the needs and hurts of the other kids. But—" She paused at the knock on the classroom door and the subsequent appearance of the social worker.

"Hello, ladies. I'm Mrs. Molinelli," she said with a smile at Bridget. "Thanks for letting me join you."

"Hi," Bridget murmured, the worry in her gut expanding.

Mrs. Molinelli jumped right in. "I've observed Miss Welsh's class several times," she explained. "And we're both concerned about Evan's behavior this year. Back in the spring, I'd spoken to him and his classmates when I observed the kindergartens, and there was no sign of the frustration we're noticing in him this year. Are there any . . . situations at home that might be upsetting him? Any kind of family issues that could be affecting his routine?"

Bridget began to shake her head but then stopped. "I started working again in the summer," she admitted. "Just part time, though, and it's only during the hours the kids are in school, so I'm still always home when they get back. You think that could be it?"

Mrs. Molinelli scribbled something in a spiral notebook. "It's possible, but there are a lot of possibilities." She scribbled some more. "Has he mentioned being disturbed by anything in particular lately? A classmate? A sibling? Did you have a pet or family member pass away in recent months or experience any kind of marital discord that might cause him trauma?"

Bridget blinked at the woman. She knew the school had to ask questions like these. That they were bound by law to report any potential abuse or to follow up in situations where a child might be in physical or emotional danger. But for all of Evan's sensitiveness, Bridget couldn't believe there was something going on behind her back at home that would affect him so profoundly. And, sure, she'd had some marital concerns lately, but Evan couldn't have picked up on *that*, could he?

"No." But then she remembered that day in the backyard when he said his stomach hurt, and she told the two women about that. And about him mentioning some kids being mean. "He didn't mention any names, though. And he's really tired by the time he gets home, so maybe it's just the longer day."

Miss Welsh agreed to an extent. "The transition from half-day kindergarten to full-day first grade is a challenge for many of the children. But school's been in session for almost six weeks now. Most everyone else who had difficulty with the extra hours seemed to adjust several weeks ago. But it's possible that's the problem. He may just be more sensitive to change than most."

Bridget's heart tightly embraced that theory.

"We are, however, noticing Evan going further and further into his shell," Mrs. Molinelli said, flipping to an earlier page in her spiral. "The behavior we're seeing in him—his hesitation in playing with other children at recess, his inhibition in the classroom, his unwillingness to be engaged by either adults or other kids and his quick temper when forced to interact—all of these are especially unusual given the report from his kindergarten teacher that he was 'a kind, bighearted boy who loves to laugh and play with blocks and other building material with his classmates.'" She looked up from her notes. "We'd like you to talk with him. Keep an eye on him at home. Perhaps he's not getting enough sleep, or he's being bullied by a sibling or someone on the bus. He *has* been really tired lately, so maybe whatever the problem is has been keeping him awake at night and the fear of the conflict is giving him stomachaches."

Bridget took in all the information and readily agreed to do whatever she could to help—talk with Evan, her other children, her husband. She zombied her way through Keaton's conference (thank goodness she'd had Cassandra's the night before) and rushed to her car, calling Graham on his cell phone while still in the school's parking lot.

"Okay, okay, Bridget. Calm down. We'll figure out what's going on with Evan," her husband said, sighing. "You get too emotional. He's just a growing boy. Moody like the other two. It'll sort itself out, so just relax, would'ya?"

Relaxing wasn't in the cards for Bridget. Easy for Graham to tell her to calm down! A problem like that didn't just "sort itself out"—a parent had to help. She fumbled in her purse for a licorice twist and a pack of gum. Then she chomped agitatedly until she thought she could drive safely. It took ten minutes, one Cherry Twizzler and two pieces of Trident Cool Mint before that happened.

Tamara, meanwhile, was nowhere near any of the Glendale Grove schools. In an odd (for her) tea choice, she was working her way through a rather large pot of Berryblossom White and losing herself to the sentimentality of *not* getting to go to parent/teacher conferences this year.

For the first time since Benji had been five, she was home on this day with not a single teacher expecting her. A whole day with no one to tell her what a smart, amiable, creative son she had. And it just sucked.

She'd heard some nonsense once about women who cried when menopause hit and they stopped getting their periods. Sobbed like infants, for chrissake, right in the middle of the Tampax aisle. Even now she rolled her eyes thinking about it. She planned to drink a pitcher or two of raspberry-lemon-drop martinis when *that* blessed day occurred.

But nobody had told her to prepare for *this* day. Nobody had ever said, "You're gonna be a wreck while every other mother in town is listening to some fifth-grade dragon lady criticizing their child's spelling or a leather-skinned industrial arts teacher praising their kid's birdhouse. Make yourself some soothing tea, buy yourself a box of tissues and don't talk to anyone. It'll be embarrassing."

And, of course, Jon was away again. Indianapolis this time. Not that he'd be nearly as affected by missing out on conferences as she was. He'd barely made it to one in four when Benji was a kid, and he hadn't gone to a single one when their son was in high school.

She blew her nose and poured another cup of tea, envying Jon the distraction of his job. Perhaps the time had come for her to really consider getting out there again. She had an MBA after all. She was marketable. Mostly. Not that she'd used any of her business skills in years—at least not to further her own career—but they were still there. Just waiting until she was ready to pull out her portfolio and unleash them. With the economy the way it was, a lot of people who'd been out of the workforce for a while were going back if they could get a position somewhere. She'd be proud to be one of them.

She pulled out a sheet of lined paper and began listing anything that could legitimately fit on her résumé:

* BS degree in marketing from University of Illinois–Urbana-Champaign, 3.86 GPA.
* MBA from Northwestern University, 3.73 GPA.
* Three-month summer marketing internship at Lewis, Darvis & Webstock in Chicago.
* Two years experience in the marketing-promotion department at Tower Graphics, Evanston (part time, while in grad school).

* Nineteen years of working a room for her husband at incredibly boring law firm cocktail parties and supporting his career.
* Excellent PTA negotiating skills as evidenced by a new playground, a revamped hot lunch program and the best Teacher Appreciation Brunch in a decade (when Benji was nine).
* Top-notch Boy Scouts fund-raiser—sold LOTS of popcorn tins and holiday wreaths (when Benji was twelve).
* Can type . . . pretty fast.
* Has no problem—morally or physiologically—with two-martini lunches.
* Likes dress clothes.

Okay, well, maybe she'd have to reword everything after her time at Tower Graphics, but at least this was a start.

What other skills did she have?

She could coordinate outfits pretty well, grow vegetables and a handful of robust flowers, use Microsoft Word and Excel, e-mail attachments, fax documents, collate, copy, talk on the phone—

The knock on the door startled her. She hadn't been making any noise and there were no house lights on (well, it was ten-thirty in the morning). Maybe, if she sat really still, whoever was there would leave.

Or not.

Three more knocks followed, louder this time, followed by a ring of the doorbell.

With a sigh, she forced herself out of the kitchen and to the door, where she spotted Aaron through the side window.

Oh, boy.

"Hey," she said, swinging the door open and noticing the brown bag he had clasped to his chest. "What'cha got in there?"

"Just some my-produce-is-better-than-yours proof." He grinned. "The bag's kinda heavy. Can I set it down for you somewhere?"

She squinted at him. It didn't look *that* heavy, but she said, "Sure, thanks. There's an open spot on the kitchen counter." And she stepped back so he could come in.

Once he'd set down the bag, he opened it, rummaged through half of it and pulled out his first offering.

"Just take a look at this." He held up a perfect, soccer-ball-sized pumpkin. "Happy October, neighbor."

"Wow," she said, genuinely impressed. "Suitable for painting, carving or reenacting *The Legend of Sleepy Hollow*."

"Damn right." He sifted through the bag some more, this time unearthing two smallish cantaloupes. "What d'ya say to this?"

"Braggart." But then she thought about what she was seeing. "Those *grow* in the Midwest?"

He looked triumphant. "Yep. I've got five more of 'em in my kitchen. They're small, but pretty tasty, if you let them ripen." His hand dipped into the bag yet again.

"Lettuce?" she guessed, staring at his latest retrieval.

"Cabbage," he corrected, setting it down on her counter before pulling out two beautiful zucchinis, several bunches of broccoli, a smattering of Roma tomatoes and a small spray of wildflowers, which he handed right to her. "I lied. I do have poppies and a few wood violets. No buttercups, though. But I keep them hidden in the backyard. It was an experiment. I used one of those floral seed packets from the grocery store," he explained. "Didn't turn out too badly, though."

She stared at him.

"You're not allergic or anything, are you?"

She shook her head, swallowed and then instinctively brought the bouquet to her face. She inhaled. It was odorless, but still—she nearly hugged the blossoms. It'd been so long since anyone had brought her flowers. Even for an occasion as innocuous as this one. "Thanks, Aaron," she murmured.

He grinned, crossed his arms and struck a confident pose. "Well, there you go, Ms. Smarty Pants. How're you gonna beat that?"

"Well, I don't know yet, Mr. Green Giant, but I *will*." She wrinkled her nose at him, then turned to fill a tall glass with water for the wildflowers. "A marginally impressive little show you just put on."

"*Marginally impressive?*" he cried with mock indignation. "That was a slam dunk, and you know it."

She relented and laughed, which was not how the game was played, of course. If she were totally *en pointe*, she would have teased him for far longer. Made him work for any hint of defeat and her ultimate admission. Been nonchalant. Feigned obvious boredom. Dragged out the charade so it'd be more fun for him. But she couldn't hack the simplest of tasks that day. Not even elementary level flirting. "You caught me at an off hour," she confessed. "I'm truly at a loss for words."

He took a step back, dropped the alpha male pose and raised a dark blond eyebrow. "Everything okay?"

Her gaze shot to the piece of paper/pseudo résumé on the other end of the counter. "More or less."

His gaze followed hers, squinting to read her heavily slanted scribbles. "Job search?"

"Maybe." She snatched up the sheet before he could get to the embarrassing stuff farther down the page. "So, working at home. Pros? Cons?"

His expression turned thoughtful. "Kinda depends. On you. On your relationship." He exhaled for somewhat longer than she thought necessary before continuing. "Not to be sexist about it, but some of the disagreements Isabelle and I had over it might not affect you because you're a woman and Jon is already accustomed to your being at home during the day. For men, it has its challenges, though more guys are doing it now, so it isn't seen as quite so strange. Still, I worked for a company for a couple of years before I launched the magazine. Isabelle had a hard time adjusting to my suddenly being home when she wasn't. She resented having to be the one to go out on cold mornings, start the car, deal with the commute, put up with the social dynamics of the people at her law firm and—"

"Jesus, she was a lawyer?"

"Yep. Was and still is." He rolled his eyes and couldn't hide a painful grimace.

They shared a moment of mutual, though nonverbal, commiseration. It was hard being a lawyer's spouse. At least with certain lawyers. Draining to always have to put on a show for the other people in the firm, who—let's face it—often looked down on a stay-at-home mom as being a dependent slacker. She had spent her entire marriage struggling to prove to most of Jon's colleagues that she wasn't "a brainless housewife" (one of Jon's partner's favorite terms), and even then they would usually dismiss her as soon as someone more interesting showed up.

Heaven only knew how many little digs guys like that would have given Aaron at those tedious cocktail parties. How, in major ways and minute ones, they would have shown how little they respected someone who wasn't wearing a tailored suit and clocking billable hours at a "real" office somewhere, no matter how successful he was at home.

"For you, it might be win-win. Though it's still a *career*," he said cryptically. "There can be other issues you won't be immune to."

"Like?"

"Like knowing when your workday is really over. It's tempting to check your e-mail 'just one more time' or fix 'one last document' or make 'only one super-quick phone call.' And, before you know it, it's eleven o'clock and you haven't had a conversation with your spouse about anything other than the mundane operations of the house."

"I can see how that could happen," she said.

"Also, there are other people who don't understand how much you actually do need to work. They don't realize you have to call clients or freelancers during regular business hours. That you might be less rigid as far as timing, but not all the people you work with have the same flexibility."

She agreed. And, though she didn't tell Aaron this, she'd heard Jon make such assumptions about his few nontraveling, corporate-lawyer buddies who worked from home as consultants. Jon still considered this to be a cushy job for "old" men. Something done for fun in between golf games.

"Pros, though, are many," Aaron said. "You do set your own hours. You base your work on what's most significant to you. You can more easily screen out phone or e-mail distractions—or at least postpone them to more convenient times. You can work on your garden for an hour before lunch and mull over project ideas or take your dog for a walk when he needs to run around. If you need to schedule a root canal in the middle of the week, you don't have any hoops to jump as far as taking time off or filling out paperwork.

But, unless you work for an established company, you also don't get any built-in health or dental insurance, paid vacation time or other special perks. I'm sure you know that."

She bobbed her head. She loved the way he logically ran through the details and was willing to explore all the options with her, but he didn't do it condescendingly. He accepted without question her intelligence as being sound, and he treated her immediately as an equal. The law spouted off about equal opportunities and mandatory women's rights and blah, blah, blah, but that didn't mean this was her day-to-day experience. Not by a long shot.

"There are financial issues to remember, also. Start-up costs and such that you'll want to explore with your husband, because they can be seriously high at first."

She'd run into Aaron the week before and, when she told him about her aunt's death, he expressed his condolences and asked her about the funeral services. She told him about Al and about her few days in Vermont. She did not, however, tell him about Aunt Eliza's will, and the inheritance bequeathed to her. As the details had yet to be divulged to the other recipients, Tamara hadn't mentioned the sum to anyone. Jon hadn't asked, but even *he* didn't know the full projected amount once estate taxes and other fees had been deducted. Tamara, however, knew her start-up costs wouldn't be an issue, even if Jon didn't agree to spend a cent.

"The deal is," Aaron said, "if you can learn to maintain some kind of balance that works for you, working at home is a beautiful thing. The flexibility, the control, the environment, the opportunity to mesh your real life with your work life and tailor your unique skills to a career you largely create . . . it's phenomenal. For me, it helps me stay passionate about what I do. Since I'm accountable for everything, if I'm finding I hate some aspect of my job, I can't blame that dissatisfaction on the boss in the other office. I have to work to either creatively fix the problem or to eliminate it."

"How long did it take you to achieve a balance like that?"

He paused, his gray blue eyes scanning the ceiling unseeingly as he considered. "A little over three years." He shrugged. "Most of my marriage."

"Ah," she said.

After Aaron left, she read through her résumé, such that it was, again. She wasn't without skills, no matter how little experience she'd had in the corporate world. But much of what Aaron said appealed to her, especially since she could fashion numerous aspects of a new career to the abilities she did possess, slowly building up her experience and, eventually, taking on work opportunities she might not be privy to now. She'd always wanted to be a marketing consultant. To help small businesses look their best. To get their products recognized and purchased by the right buyers.

But money couldn't buy everything. Not skill proficiency. Not client respect. Not marital support. She wouldn't deny that money was extremely helpful . . . simply not an all-inclusive solution.

She continued to ponder this during the remainder of the day. Quite honestly, the allure of having an identity beyond her role as wife and mother was as strong as the opportunity to, at last, flex her career muscles. Jon would be home that night and maybe, just maybe, he would prove both supportive and insightful. It was not a matter of intelligence with him. He would *understand* the issues in an instant. It was merely a matter of inclination.

And, indeed, it turned out that Jon *did* surprise her, though not at all in the manner she'd expected.

"Got any plans for next weekend?" he asked all of four minutes after he'd burst through the front door. His face was unusually flushed, an expression more smile than smirk gracing his lips.

"For Columbus Day?" She thought about it, coming to the almost immediate conclusion that, no, she hadn't put anything pressing on the calendar. She told Jon this.

"Good," he replied. "How about we go visit our son in Austin?"

And in that instant, all thoughts and feelings of new careers and marital frustrations fled. She actually rushed into Jon's arms, squeezing him, unable to keep the tears from flowing down her face and splashing onto the shoulder of his white dress shirt.

"Oh, Jon. Thank you."

To her surprise, he squeezed her back just as tightly. And when she looked into his eyes, they were damp, too.

ᔐ 12 ᔐ

Tamara

Tamara and Jon flew out of O'Hare Airport the following Saturday, just before noon, while Bridget and Jennifer dealt with their families—and their respective problems—at their individual homes.

Tamara was relieved to go to Texas for several reasons. First and foremost, she'd get to see Benji again. But, also, she hated to be alone in their house without him. Her friends might complain about the noise and general chaos of life with their crew of little ones and teens underfoot, but the other ladies didn't know what the alternative was like.

"Want a glass of wine?" Jon asked her moments after takeoff. She'd noticed he'd been trying harder lately to be solicitous. To anticipate her needs a little more. To be kinder. At least since Aunt Eliza's death.

"Sure. White," she said. "Thanks."

He ordered for them both, wines and luncheon sandwiches, and then got comfortable in his leather seat with his *Chicago Tribune*. They were flying business class—free because of all of his frequent-flier miles—and it occurred to her they could do this anytime. They were limited not by expense or even by distance, but by whether their son would welcome the intrusion.

Not that their visit was in any way unexpected. They'd cleared it with Benji before purchasing tickets. It was just that she couldn't shake the feeling they were somehow disrupting his life.

"What do you think of this Lance kid?" she asked Jon, after the flight attendant had poured their drinks and moved halfway down the aisle. "You've talked to him more than I have."

Her husband glanced up from the Real Estate section. "The roommate?" He shrugged. "He's okay. Kind of squirrely, but I've seen worse. At least he's from a bigger city in Georgia or South Carolina or somewhere like that, so he's not too much of a hick." He shrugged again. "Still Southern, though."

Jon wasn't fond of Southerners. Or most Northerners, for that matter. She noticed he immediately returned to reading his paper.

"I meant more in terms of him being a friend to Benji. Do you think they're a good match? Neither of them knew anybody before starting at UT. Do you think they're becoming real friends or just hanging out together so much because they don't have anyone else?" Both boys were drawn to UT because of its stellar engineering program, but maybe that was all they had in common.

Jon sighed and folded his paper shut. "We'll see what it's like this weekend, but I don't know if I'd expect any long-lasting friendship. They've got the facade of youth right now, but it won't last. Especially this early in Benji's college experience. Everyone he gets to know this year is in the same place. It's like the army."

"What? No, it's not." She shot him an annoyed look and gulped half of her wine. "They're choosing their own classes, learning to manage their time, differentiating themselves as much as possible from—"

"College is a leveler, Tamara," he said, with more than a hint of irritation. "They may all be from different backgrounds coming into it, but when they get there they're struggling with the same mean calculus prof, the hard-to-understand career counselor, the hot new girls on the floor above them, the cramped dorm rooms. They're bonded—both by being young and by being new to the big campus. And, for a while, that bond masks a person's deeper, truer qualities. It all changes once they've chosen their majors.

And it changes even more once they start their careers. Their real priorities emerge and, a couple of years after graduation, they're not in touch at all anymore."

She remembered that this had been Jon's experience exactly. That his two best friends from his undergraduate years stopped calling not long after she and Jon got married. That Jon always acted as if this were irrelevant, but how could it not hurt? How could he not care?

Jon unfolded his paper again. "We've just got to hope Benji doesn't do something stupid and end up committing to some girl before he knows who he is and what he wants out of life."

The undercurrent of criticism and regret was unmistakable. She and Jon hadn't met as college freshmen, true, but they did as Northwestern grad students. He could have easily been talking about them and how—as a law school hotshot—he'd curtailed his career options and done "something stupid" by tying himself to a business student with few connections, limited cultural experience and a high student loan balance.

"I'm sure Benji won't be *stupid*," she murmured, snatching the in-flight magazine from the seat pocket and pretending to read an article entitled "North America's Top 10 Horticultural Marvels" until Jon returned to his newspaper. She didn't ask any further questions.

As it turned out, roommate Lance was absent upon their arrival to Benji's dorm.

"Hey, Mom and Dad," their lanky and still boyishly good-looking son said, side-hugging them in the lobby. His straight light brown hair flopped into his eyes and he brushed it away in a move reminiscent of the goofy little kid he'd once been.

Tamara's heart overflowed with a month-and-a-half's pent-up adoration. She didn't know how to turn it off. Like too much water in a bathtub, anything Benji said or did only added to the increasing level of feeling, until her love for him displaced every other possible emotion and sploshed and spilled everywhere.

"Don't cry, Mom," Benji whispered, glancing furtively around the packed lobby, and she saw Jon's jaw tighten. Neither liked teary displays.

She swiped at her eyes and turned to face the wall, not wanting to embarrass her son further or incur the wrath of her husband. "Sorry, Benji."

"S'okay," her son said, moving quickly away from her. She pressed her lips together to try to rein in the hurt. But her boy was back a couple of seconds later. "Here," he said, prodding her arm gently with a small box. "I was just looking for the tissues. They keep 'em at the front desk." Then he hugged her again.

She grabbed one, dabbed her eyes with it and pocketed two more. She had no doubt she'd need them.

Meanwhile, Jon asserted himself into the middle of the lobby and said loudly, "Good to see you, *Ben*," overemphasizing, Tamara thought, the shortened version of their son's name. "Want to show us around campus?"

"Yeah. That'd be cool," her kind, thoughtful, amazing son replied. "Let me just grab my keys and stuff."

So, they trailed after him to his room. The place looked studiously clean, and Tamara surmised the guys had spent a whole half hour at least sprucing it up.

They'd met Lance and his dad in August when all the students were moving in. The roommate and his father seemed like a friendly pair, but they'd all been preoccupied with the unpacking and the transition, so they'd just shaken hands, chitchatted superficially for twenty minutes and then parted, mostly in relief. Tamara had spoken to Lance on the phone all of twice since then and wondered what he'd been up to in the intervening weeks.

"So, uh, where's Lance?" she asked, hoping the answer wasn't "scoring drugs in Zilker Park" or "out getting his gun license."

"Crashin' with this ho' he picked up at a party last night," Benji replied evenly.

She stared at him. Jon's eyes widened, too.

Her son glanced seriously between her and his father several times before breaking into a grin. "Totally kidding, you guys. Lighten up!" His smiled broadened. The same sweet grin he'd had as her darling ten-year-old. "Lance is a hard worker. He got a job at one of the stores in SoCo, the South Congress district," he explained. "Lots of coffee shops and some kinda wild stores, but it's a pretty safe area. He's working until six, which is what he usually does on Saturdays, and he's a good guy, okay?"

Tamara could see he was being utterly sincere, and she relaxed enough to smile back. "Okay. Well, maybe he can join us for dinner or something tonight. We could take you both out to a restaurant you like, a late movie even. And if you want to stay—" She'd been about to suggest that Benji could have a couple nights of luxury at their four-star hotel, but the expression on his face stopped her.

"Oh, um, no. Not for Lance. But thanks. He's already got plans for tonight. Tickets to a concert downtown." He chuckled at some private memory. "This is a wicked cool music town. There are some really hot acts that come here, and we saw these local guys at the Austin City Limits Music Festival two weekends ago that are performing by the riverfront tonight. So, Lance'll be at that."

Tamara swallowed, suddenly understanding. "And you had a ticket, too," she guessed. "You cancelled out because of us, right?"

"Hey, it's no biggie," Benji said, suddenly interested in the contents of his upper-left desk drawer. "Someone else'll be able to use it. I get to go to stuff like that all the time, but I don't get to see you two very often." He exhaled fast and beamed another of his trademark grins at them.

He meant it, Tamara realized. He really did. But she hated to make him sacrifice a single thing on her behalf, not when it was within her power to prevent it.

"When are your friends leaving tonight?" she asked.

He scrunched his eyebrows together. "Oh, I dunno. Seven, maybe? But—"

"We can have you back by then, right, Jon?" She shot a Say Yes look at her husband and nodded for emphasis.

"Sure," Jon said. Then, to Benji, "You've still got your ticket?"

"Yeah, but it's really no big thing." Benji shrugged, but the want and the hope in his eyes gave him away.

Tamara felt the tears begin to prickle again and dampen her lashes as she realized there'd be no late-night chats tonight, like they'd had sometimes when he'd been in high school. No midnight movie or room-service breakfast with him at their hotel. At least not this time.

"It *is*, though," she told him, forcing her brightest smile at her bighearted and unbelievably loving son. "We don't want you to miss anything good."

She knew her smart, beautiful boy wasn't doing stupid things, and he wasn't making shallow friendships. He was *thriving* away from home, and she needed to facilitate that. Honor it.

They let him walk them around *his* campus, show off the sites. Several times he waved a greeting to some girl or group of guys. They took him to dinner at a burger joint he'd heard raves about and listened with rapt interest to his tales of Professor-this or TA-that. Those four and a half hours flew by too quickly.

"Hey, see ya both tomorrow," he said, as they dropped him back off at his dorm. "I've gotta get a little studying done somewhere in there, but we can do whatever you want for most of the day, okay?"

They agreed, watched him disappear into the building and then sat in their rental car in silence.

"You want to just go to the hotel now?" Jon asked her. "Or would you like to have a cup of coffee somewhere?"

"Whatever you'd prefer," she whispered, because, really, it didn't matter to her. Without Benji along, all options were equally uninspiring.

Jon chose a Starbucks a mile from their hotel. He went up to the counter to order and she was in charge of selecting the seats. She collapsed into a chair by a window table and studied the passing traffic.

It'd been a day of primarily good things—no drama or big arguments with Jon, quality time with Benji—so, really, she'd had the opportunity to spend a Saturday in the most enjoyable manner possible, and there was still Sunday to look forward to. Maybe shopping in the open-air Arboretum mall or a scenic visit to Lady Bird Lake? The nature of the activity was unimportant—she'd be with her son. But with Jon, tiny dissatisfactions niggled at her and she tried to pinpoint why.

One thing was their hotel room, which they'd checked into before going to Benji's dorm. How it had these overly fluffy, rose-colored pillows on the bed. Tasteful but easily discernable heart patterns everywhere—painted in the abstract wall pictures, carved in the ceiling's crown molding, embedded in the hand soap. The subtle implication that there would be romance in the room that night.

But there wouldn't be.

Her physical relationship with Jon had deteriorated to almost zero. They had sex less than once a month, and only when he initiated, and she wasn't getting those let's-get-it-on vibes that night. Most of the time, she wasn't convinced even *he* wanted to do it, just that it would have been increasingly more difficult to get in the mood if they waited too long. She suspected they both kind of forced themselves into it and that he, like she, had someone else he fantasized about. Maybe all couples went on automatic pilot after a decade or more of marriage. Maybe every spouse had daydreams about the hot neighbor down the street at some time or other. Stuff like that just happened.

But here, at the Starbucks, Jon deposited a couple of nice lattes and a bag of almond biscotti on their table. He seemed in as much of a reflective mood as she was as he blew on his coffee and stared at the flickering lights.

"Our son seems happy," she said, going for an easy opener.

He nodded. "It's good to see."

"Yeah." She didn't have an appetite for biscotti, but she played with one anyway just so she had something to do with her fingers.

Jon, too, seemed to need something to fidget with. He pulled out his BlackBerry, scanned it for messages and then just kind of squinted at it.

She hadn't checked her cell phone for most of the day and wondered if Al had left her a message. The two of them had both been trying to keep the other out of the pit of depression and, strangely, her elderly aunt's boyfriend was the one person she never had to pretend to be cheery around. She was so grateful to him for having loved Aunt Eliza. So grateful he understood her loss.

"It's been a stressful fall," Jon said suddenly. "Ben leaving home. Your aunt passing away. Our . . . frustrations with each other." He met her eye and, in that quiet glance, she saw the soul of the man she'd once admired. The man with whom she'd married and had a child.

"It *has* been hard," she admitted. "We—we aren't always on the same page, are we?"

He shook his head. "Hard to know what makes a friendship last. What makes a couple grow together. Or apart." He drank a little of his coffee, but then set it down. Pushed it away. "Sometimes I'm not sure, Tamara, if I'm really the man you wanted. Or thought you'd gotten." He let out a long breath. "I'm not sure if *you* know, either."

She studied him as he said those words. He wasn't being sarcastic, caustic, acerbic, nor did he pair any of his usual criticisms with his typically exasperated-with-her facial expressions. He just stated—simply, plainly—that he was a man confused. That her signals regarding her love for him were unclear.

"But you *are* sure?" she asked him. "About me? You believe there's hope for us to be happy?"

He gave her one of his almost smiles. A resigned, nearly tender look. "I've always wanted to think so," he said.

A moment later, they left their unfinished coffees, and he took her hand, took her to their hotel and made love to her for the first time in weeks. Made it feel like the first time in years. The softness, longing and familiarity could be felt viscerally, entwined with decades of kinesthetic memory. For a soundless instant, a mere heartbeat in time, every part of her remembered *knowing* this man.

It wasn't until their early-Monday flight home that she realized Jon's answer to her questions had been inconclusive. He hadn't said an unequivocal "Yes." He'd said it'd been what he'd "wanted to think." And those were *quite* different responses.

Some of the glow from their weekend of connectedness dimmed for her, and she was left with a small but piercing ember of anxiety burning uncomfortably within her abdomen. Too tiny to mention to him for fear of being seen as petty and, yet, intense enough to be impossible for her to ignore. She wondered, did Jon feel anything like this? Or, if he did, would he dare to utter it aloud?

ᓆ 13 ᓆ

Bridget

Thursday, October 14

B ridget felt like a chubby Mata Hari, and not a very sexy one at
that. She parked her silver Honda Pilot in the otherwise empty
Smiley Dental lot at ten A.M. precisely (for once, she wasn't even
one second late!), the start of her regular shift. But she wasn't
working today. She was meeting Dr. Luke for a chat and, whenever they got to their mysterious location, a private lunch.

What she knew about their "date" could be listed in three short
sentences:

Place: somewhere Italian.

Dress: business casual.

Emotion: anxious to the point of nausea (but also kind of excited).

Well, that was *her* emotion. She had no idea what *he* was feeling.
Especially given that he wasn't here yet.

She did a quick check in her visor mirror for fallen eyelashes,
smudged lipstick or anything else that smacked of disarray. She'd
never been good at sneaking around, even if there wasn't any real
reason for subterfuge. But it was just a luncheon, right? No need to
be so nervous.

As she flipped the visor back up again, she spotted Dr. Luke's
black car turning into the lot. He pulled up beside her, rolled down
his window and said, "Hey, great day we've got. Poor hygienists,
having to be stuck indoors all day at their conference."

She smiled at him. Definitely enthusiastic. He looked . . . kind
of excited, too, but maybe he just liked weather that was mostly
sunny and sixty-two degrees. "Yes," she said agreeably.

He glanced around the lot. They'd agreed to meet here just like
it was a normal work day, and she had assumed she would follow
him in her own car to wherever they were headed. But Dr. Luke
must have had a different idea because a sudden look of concern
crossed his face.

"You know, I don't think there's a town ordinance or anything
for parking here when the business is closed, but just in case—"
He pointed to a space across the street from them, near Franklin's
Diner. "Why don't you leave your car there and jump in with me.
No reason for us both to drive."

He stated this as if it were a perfectly logical suggestion, but she
sensed something else. Was he a little bit anxious, too? Was he
worried someone might recognize her car in the empty dental lot
and ask her later why she'd left it there?

But Bridget wasn't Tamara. She couldn't bring herself to ask
pointed questions like that. What if she made him feel uncomfortable or something? So, she said, "Sure," and moved her car.

But when she slipped into his sedan—a Volvo? she thought that
was what the symbol on the steering wheel meant—her awkwardness started to get the better of her. The last time she had been
alone in a car with a man (who wasn't her husband, a male family
member or a hired taxi driver) was years ago. Zach-somebody,
whom she'd met when she was still single, at the wedding of a college friend. Zach drove a dark blue Corvette, and all she could
really remember about him was how he was so much more interested in showing off his prized car than in getting to know her.

"Everything okay?"

"Huh?" she said, staring at the warm, kind man driving the
Volvo. A man who, again, was not her husband. "Oh, yeah. Everything's great, Dr. Luke."

He grinned and focused on the road. "Just Luke. Please. At
least while we're out of the office."

She bobbed her head jerkily, and for a few moments she observed him. His nice gray dress slacks. His maroon pullover. He

looked like he'd just stepped out of men's Suburban Casual clothing catalogue.

But then Dr. Luke—or just Luke now—broke the ice by telling her a funny story about his kid brother. The one with the nephews who had been visiting. "Matthew's a great dad," he said, after explaining about some camping outing, complete with toads in their tent and a coyote scare. "But he was a handful as a child. My mom was happily naming her brood after the saints and was prepared to devote her mothering to seven or eight of us. She stopped after three because of Matthew."

Bridget laughed. He'd already told her about his older sister, Teresa, who lived in Philadelphia with her family, but the Matthew stories were fun, and Luke clearly adored his nephews. So, despite her normal lack of courage, she had to ask, "Did you ever want to do that, um, Luke? Get married and have kids?"

An odd expression crossed his face, at least she thought so. He kept his eyes fixed on the road, so she couldn't be sure. After a few lengthy seconds, he said, "A long time ago. I was going to do it once, but the bride, she . . . she had a troubling habit."

She blurted, "Really? Smoking? Drugs?"

"Nope." His smile was tight and unreadable. She didn't think he was going to say any more, and that was fine with her. She was curious, sure, but she didn't want to pry. Finally, though, he added, "Getting sick. Terminally, the last time."

She caught her breath. "Oh, I'm so—I'm so sorry."

He shrugged it off.

Oh, God. Why did she have to ask him that? It just went to show that she should never be curious. She should never ask inappropriate things that weren't any of her business or she would be punished somehow. She should never be alone in a car with a man like—

"She got sick for the first time about a month after we got engaged," he explained. "Her kidneys were failing, and she needed a transplant. Her sister turned out to be a match and immediately insisted on donating. Close family, you know? Good people . . ." His voice trailed off.

Bridget didn't know what to say. She tried to project sympathetic understanding at him. Oh, poor Dr. Luke.

"If that had been all, it might've still worked. Turned out, the doctors missed a little tumor in their diagnosis. Ovarian. The *silent* cancer," he said, his voice a touch sharper than she had ever remembered hearing it. "The kidney failure had masked some of the disease symptoms, and it had already metastasized to several lymph nodes by the time they found it. She was twenty-seven then. She died four months later."

The same age Bridget had been when she and Graham had gotten married. She tried not to personalize it too much or to keep focusing on the tragedy of it, or she knew she'd lose it. But the anguish in Luke's expression was hard to ignore. Seeing him so vulnerable and recognizing the depth of his loss brought her tears too close to the surface. She tried to blink them away. Tried to speak without her voice trembling in empathy.

"I—I can't imagine how horrible that must've been. What"— she took a deep breath—"what was her name?"

He mimicked a cheerier smile and, for a few moments, fingered the gold cross he wore. Then he tucked it back inside his shirt and laughed—a sound closely approximating his real one. "It was Hope, actually. Her sister Bethany and I made some terrible puns about that on the day of the funeral. Privately, of course, but we couldn't stop ourselves. 'We'd lost Hope.' Morbid stuff like that. We'd been living with the fear of that day for so long by then, it helped to have someone else to cope with. To share the pain in a way we knew Hope would've found kind of funny if she hadn't, you know, been dead."

They drove in silence for a several minutes. Bridget, having lost the battle with her tears, turned to face the window so she could furtively swipe away the droplets with the back of her wrist.

"No more sad stuff today, okay?" Luke said as he took one of the downtown Chicago exits off the expressway. "Don't you want to hear about the restaurant we're going to?"

"Of course," she said, injecting jollity into her voice. "What's it called?"

"Ah, that's one of the many beautiful things about it. It's Buona

Cucina Italia, near the Italian Village." His tongue lingered over the name and Bridget shivered at the sensuality of it. "Opened up about a year ago and, oh, my . . ." He turned to look into her still slightly watery eyes. "They do things with freshly grated Parmesan that should be illegal."

She laughed with as much relief as delight. He was putting her at ease. On purpose. In spite of his own grief, he was so caring and thoughtful that he was concerned about *her*. What a fantastic person! She really and truly *liked* him. And who wouldn't? He was such a wonderful man. It was hard to believe God—or even Graham—would be so coldhearted as to disapprove of her friendship with The Good Dentist. Which was all this was. They were *friends*. And having friends, she reminded herself (and God), wasn't a sin.

Traffic had been light, so, even after driving into the city and finding a parking space, they still had plenty of time to window shop for a half hour and then settle in for a leisurely lunch before Bridget would need to be back. A few hours, actually.

Her companion didn't seem to notice the return of her anxiety upon being seated at their little table. Bridget appreciated the niceness of the place, but it felt kind of, well, intimate to her. She soaked up the atmosphere as Luke got settled in—the golden lighting, the colorful wall tapestries, the smallish rooms that collectively made up the restaurant . . . each one capable of holding a cozy grouping of perhaps seven or eight couples.

One other couple was midway through their meal on the other side of their room, but Bridget knew there were many other couples scattered in similarly snug rooms nearby. Keyword: couples. None of the diners seemed to·be families or a group of sisters or any other configuration. Buona Cucina Italia was a place for lovers.

Their server brought out menus and recited a list of specials that sounded like the featured recipes in one of her favorite issues of *The Gastronomical Gourmet*. She bit her lip and scanned for something that looked to be in a reasonable price range. (He'd insisted several times that he'd be treating her, and she didn't want to take advantage.) But each entrée was so beautifully described, she lost herself in the lustfulness of reading them.

Zuppa di Orzo e Fagioli—a hearty soup with dried borlotti beans, pearl barley and handfuls of succulent vegetables.

Tonno con Capperi e Cipolle—braised tuna with capers, onions and dry white wine and served on a bed of fettuccine.

Calamari Imbottiti alla Griglia—grilled squid stuffed with bread crumbs, ham, raisins and garlic.

"Oh, my God," Bridget murmured after reading these.

"Ooh, what'd you see?" Dr. Luke asked. "Get to the Sicilian frittata yet?"

"What?" She flipped through the menu until she came to it. "*Frittata di Verdura e Formaggio*," she read aloud, swallowing a few times at the description of the Sicilian dish made up of wild greens baked into a crispy, cheesy frittata. "This is unreal." She scanned more of the menu in amazement. "Listen to this one." She pointed to the explanation of the *Ravioli all'Uova con Tartufi*. "Giant egg ravioli with truffles. And ricotta. And, oh, the Parmigiano-Reggiano cheese!"

"We're ordering that one for sure," Luke said. "And you've gotta read this one. Perfect for us Catholics during Lent or just any ole time. *Pesce al Forno con Pinoli e Uva Passa*. Roasted sea bass with rosemary, pine nuts and raisins."

She gasped. "Good Lord."

"It's pure food porn, this menu," he said with a wink.

Bridget felt herself blush. Naturally, she was familiar with the expression, but hearing those words coming from his lips made a few impure thoughts bubble to the surface of her mind. She banished them, of course (a woman shouldn't think of a *friend* that way!), but she couldn't as easily dismiss the comparisons that were arising between Her Friend Luke and Her Husband Graham.

Like the fact that Graham never got excited about a dish written in a foreign language. When they were first dating, and during their early years of marriage, he was a little more exploratory. At least he'd *tried* a few unusual cuisines. These days, though, he would just wrinkle his nose at the weird pronunciation and ask her why the restaurant couldn't just have "your basic hamburger, for chrissake." She'd actually stopped trying to get him to go anywhere that didn't serve buffalo wings or slabs of pizza because, really, it was no use.

But Luke. Wow. He wasn't putting on some show for her just to be nice. He loved this stuff, too. He was as zealously focused on those dishes as she was. And she couldn't help but wonder—fleetingly—what it would be like if she were with someone every day who shared her similar passion for specialty foods.

They went back and forth, with ever-rising ardency, for several minutes. The *Insalata di Gamberi alla Sarda*. No, wait. Look at the *Lasagne di Magro*. Ohhh, or what about the *Bruschetta di Pomodori?*

After their waiter had returned twice, Luke finally took the reins and just ordered for them. He chose the bruschetta appetizer and, also, a platter of stuffed portobello mushroom caps. He also ordered the truffle ravioli, a meaty polenta casserole *(Polenta Pasticciata con Ragù di Carne)*, crisp salads with Kalamata olives and a raspberry vinaigrette dressing and two glasses of the Tuscan red wine. "It's the house favorite," he explained. "And no matter what you do, save room for dessert."

She laughed. "You must be insane," she said when their server brought a tray filled with just the appetizers and proceeded to load their table with the beautifully arranged platters. "There's no way we'll be able to eat these, our entrées and dessert, too."

He leaned across the table until he was only about five inches away. "Trust me. We will find a way."

She blinked, sent him a quick smile and glanced at a couple striding past their table. The man, dressed in a business suit, was oblivious to them, but the woman stared at Luke strangely and shot a scowl at Bridget that bordered on hostile. Luke noticed none of this. Instead, he engaged her in a conversation about salad dressings for twenty minutes and, slowly, she began to relax.

When the main courses arrived, Bridget studied her half-eaten salad. Delicious, but she was already getting full, and Luke was in the process of divvying up the polenta and the ravioli. He touched the back of her hand with his forefinger to get her attention, then offered a plateful to her. Her senses were momentarily overwhelmed by both the physical contact and by the gorgeous food display. "Take a bite," he urged. "Tell me what you think."

She began with a forkful of the polenta casserole, and Luke did the same. Both of them sampling it at the very same time. The flavors swirled around in her mouth, teasing her with their subtleties. The spices in the meat. The richness of the sauce. The multiple cheeses. She gave an involuntary groan and reached for her wine. It was the perfect accompaniment.

"I hope you know you're ruining Franklin's Diner for me," she said. "I'll never be able to order their Wednesday Night Italian Special again."

He laughed, looking pleased with her reaction. "I've had the Chicken Vesuvio at Franklin's. It's not bad, but it sure as hell isn't up to Buona Cucina standards."

She remembered seeing the Buona Cucina version of Chicken Vesuvio on the menu when they arrived. It was a Chicago specialty, so she wasn't surprised they had it. Having now tasted first-hand the unique combination of sides and sensational spices used in the Buona Cucina dishes, she could only imagine the way this restaurant would upgrade the Chicken Vesuvio to a gourmet level.

She fell into the reverie that sometimes happened when she envisioned a beautiful entrée, and she started detailing her thoughts to Luke. "I can almost taste the chicken, see it practically falling off the bone, the skin delectably crisp. The potato wedges are sautéed in extra-virgin olive oil, dotted with garlic and oregano, and white wine is added for a burst of flavor. A handful of green peas are tossed in at the end, accenting the otherwise earthy colors on the platter." She broke out of her trance. "Right?"

He was staring at her, his mouth partway open, his warm brown eyes luminous. "That's exactly right, Bridget. What else do you see?"

She shrugged but, with his encouragement, she soon found herself in another daze of food creation, telling him how she'd like to experiment with the polenta recipe—adding a dash of basil and several tablespoons of dried porcini mushrooms. "And wouldn't it be interesting if we used veal instead of beef?"

They were working their way through the ravioli now, but he nodded at her in a way that made her certain she had his full attention. "I hadn't thought it possible to improve upon these dishes, but my Italian mama would be giving you a standing ovation." He exhaled and beamed a look at her that was two parts admiration, one part hunger. "I'll bet your husband feels he's the luckiest man in the world to come home every night to your culinary creativity."

The comment skewered Bridget's heart like a shish kebab. Thankfully, she had her mouth full of a perfectly al dente wedge of ravioli, so she wasn't required to answer right away.

And she needed the time.

The thing was, whether it was intentional or not, Luke had taken a sideswipe at her marriage. She knew she couldn't be so disloyal to Graham that she would be able to laugh aloud at Luke's suggestion, but she, likewise, couldn't bring herself to lie either and claim her husband was remotely appreciative of her cooking skills.

So she chewed slowly, smiled, then deflected the comment with a remark about how difficult it was to get kids to eat anything "adventurous." But, thinking of Evan's stomach upsets as well as Graham's lack of interest in her "exotic meals," she couldn't help but frown. This was something Luke apparently picked up on, although he attributed her discomfort to only one source: Evan.

"Hey, how's your little boy doing? Any improvement with things at school?"

"No, it's not good. He's a very sensitive kid. We're trying to do what the teachers suggested—make sure he gets enough sleep, eats healthy meals, talks out his problems instead of internalizing his frustrations. Stuff like that. But I'm not sure how much it's helping."

She'd told Luke and Candy about her conference a few days after it'd happened, and both had been very sympathetic. Yet another contrast between the dentist and her husband, she couldn't help but reflect, and with a touch of bitterness.

Luke was solicitous of her opinion and tried to suggest possible reasons for Evan's behavior change ("Could it be a bully in his classroom? A food allergy?"), while Graham dismissed most of her concerns outright with lines like: "It's just a phase" or "Probably growing pains." His idea of *handling* Evan's problem was to pat their young son on the head, tell him to "be truthful" and to "make sure to poop" when he needed to and "not hold it in." Very helpful.

She didn't mention any of that to Luke, although she admitted to having gotten another phone call from teacher Miss Welsh, and she explained that Evan's siblings were going out of their way to, as Cassandra put it, "cheer up their depressed brother."

"It's sweet, the effort Cassandra and Keaton have gone to," she told him. "It's nice seeing them do something besides trying to torment their little brother."

But she didn't add that the recent sibling kindness had had an unexpected effect: She was a touch . . . jealous. There. She admitted it, at least in the privacy of her mind. Her older children couldn't make Evan's stomachaches go away, but they'd managed to make him laugh, which made her feel both powerless and a bit of a parental failure. She couldn't even do the simplest things to help her baby boy. In fact, the only place she felt remotely successful these days was at Smiley Dental.

On that subject, though, it was almost as if she'd had too much success. "I wish you'd consider going to full time at the office," Luke said. "Jim and I have been talking about adding more receptionist hours. Something you might be interested in?"

She'd heard rumors from Candy about this but hadn't wanted to be presumptuous. "I don't know," she blurted. "I'm still adjusting to working part time."

"Well, think about," Luke said. "Keep it in the back of your creative mind. We could use more Bridget hours."

She smiled. Oh, yes, she'd consider it.

They'd talked so long and eaten so leisurely that, when the time finally came for dessert, Bridget found she could be cajoled into splitting a treat with Luke. "Seriously. Two bites, though. That's all I've got room for," she told him.

"You say that now, but wait until you taste their *Bellissimo Tiramisù.*"

Bridget didn't need to shift her imagination into overdrive on that one. Even at average Italian restaurants, there wasn't much that could ruin the combination of ladyfingers soaked in espresso and rum and then layered with sweetened mascarpone cheese. She made some mention of the weight she'd gain from this luncheon, but he cut her off.

"No. A woman like you, with a healthy appetite and a good attitude toward delicious food, is a rarity. People—mostly women—they get all caught up in calories and nonsense. What's a few extra pounds? If you usually eat reasonable portions of well-made food and enjoy the dining experience, you're treating your body and your spirit far better than those myopic folks who stuff a meal—healthy or not—into their mouths without tasting it. Who deprive their bodies of something delicious and nourishing just because of some strange power play. That's not good. And it's not attractive," he said, implying with a tilt of his brow that she *was*, as long as she didn't dare turn down dessert.

Quite honestly, she wouldn't have dreamed of doing so.

When it came, along with the two spoons Luke requested, he raised his wineglass and motioned for her to do the same. "A toast to world peace. May everyone dine as richly someday, and may they realize the sweetness of fine food is more powerful than the bitterness of human discord."

They clinked glasses and drained the remainder of their red wine. As she was licking her lips, her empty glass still in her right hand, her spoon in her left—poised for digging into the tiramisù—her male *friend* winked at her. "You'd better do justice to your half," he mock-threatened.

Giddy with the joy of the day and, perhaps, a little high on the rich scent of mascarpone, she threw her head back and laughed. And right at that moment, her laugh still floating in the air above their table, that couple from before—the one with the scowling lady—walked by again. They were headed in the other direction but, on this pass through, the woman didn't just scowl. She stopped.

"Luke?" the forty-something woman said, her greenish eyes narrowing, her vocal tone chillier than a pint of Häagen-Dazs.

He saw her this time around. His only response to the woman—who'd handed a big box of leftovers to the guy next to her and had crossed her sticklike arms in front of her flat chest—was an expression of surprise and an exclamation. "Hey, Nancy. How're you doing?" Luke raised his hand in greeting to the man in the business suit, who seemed preoccupied with figuring out a way to escape the restaurant.

Nancy's male companion flashed a return wave at them, jauntily held up the Styrofoam box and then announced he needed to get the car from the parking garage.

After he'd scurried away, Bridget returned her gaze to the woman whose eyes were, if possible, even narrower than they'd been. There was something oddly familiar about her, but Bridget couldn't place her. She didn't think she'd ever seen this Nancy person before, but she couldn't shake the fact that she felt she should know her.

"A long way from Glendale Grove just for lunch, eh?" Nancy said, directing her frigid remarks at Luke but eyeing Bridget's hands as she spoke.

Bridget set down her empty wineglass and tried to inconspicuously lay the spoon on the white tablecloth, but it hit the dessert plate and clattered. Despite the noise, the woman kept focusing on Bridget's fingers. What was up with that?

Luke said, "Yes, but Bridget and I needed to make a trek here. Bridget, this is Nancy. She's Dr. Nina's sister. Nancy, this is Bridget, one of our fabulous receptionists at Smiley Dental." He grinned. "Plus, she's an amazing cook in her own right. No one makes a chestnut ravioli like Br—"

The woman shifted away from Luke and stuck her bony hand in the vicinity of Bridget's face. "I'm Dr. Nancy Brockman-Bertelstein," she said, her words clipped and cold with a dash of smug. Bridget shook her icy hand. "I don't believe we've met at the office, but I've seen your picture on the staff board, and my sister has told me about you."

Bridget blinked at her. "Oh?"

"Oh, yes. Nina and I are very close. We talk a lot." Nancy gazed at her coolly enough to convince Bridget the commentary hadn't been favorable.

Bridget wondered, was she the problem or was it Dr. Luke? Had he taken out other staff members for lunch before? Did

Nancy and Nina think he was, like, some kind of serial Italian food seducer? But, of course, she didn't say any of this.

"So, you must know I'm part time, then," Bridget mumbled. "And kind of new."

"And married," Nancy said, her gaze returning to Bridget's fingers. Oh, her wedding band. That was what she'd been staring at.

"Yes," Bridget said. "I am." She forced a grin at the witch. "Are you a dentist, also?"

"A surgical gastroenterologist."

"Ah." No wonder she was so skinny. She probably dissected all her food before eating it.

Nancy bestowed upon them a pinched smile, which, to Bridget, looked more like a grimace. "Well, nice to meet you. Enjoy your—" She waved her palm at the sweet confection in the middle of their table as if it were a platter of live roaches. "Your dessert." And with a parting glare in Dr. Luke's direction, she floated away.

The encounter was almost enough to ruin Bridget's appetite for the tiramisù, and that was saying something.

"Well, she's, um, interesting," Bridget ventured. "I didn't know Dr. Nina had a sister. Do you know her well?"

Luke shook his head. "Not really. She pops into the office every once in a while. But she lives in Chicago, and I think she doesn't much care for the untamed suburbia of Glendale Grove." He laughed, forced a few spoonfuls of tiramisù on her (so spectacular!) and essentially played off the incident as if it were nothing.

But, try as Bridget might, she couldn't shrug it off as easily. Not even after they'd left Buona Cucina Italia behind and Dr. Luke—he was definitely *Dr.* Luke again—had returned her to her vehicle and she'd thanked him profusely for the lovely lunch.

At heart, she may still have been a naive Catholic girl, but she knew being spotted by someone like Dr. Nina's sister could present complications in her . . . her *friendship* with Dr. Luke. Innocent though it was. She knew the Who of the problem (Nancy!) and she suspected the Why (the woman despised her—what had Dr. Nina said?), she just wasn't sure about the How, the Where or the When. But she figured she'd better be prepared for anything.

❧ 14 ❧

The Trio

They wandered into the Indigo Moon Café at varying times: Jennifer first, who privately clocked their arrivals and worked to slow her breathing—part of her never-ending quest to incorporate yoga techniques into everyday life.

She was followed by Tamara (two minutes later), whose mood had taken an optimistic turn on account of both seeing her son the prior weekend and actually having good sex with her husband—even if it had just been that once.

And, finally, Bridget raced in (five minutes after that), and she, too, found herself almost content, but not because of her family and certainly not because of her luncheon with Dr. Luke but, rather, because each member of their threesome seemed, oddly, okay.

Well, "okay" was the wrong word. It was more like "familiar." Too often lately she hadn't recognized her friends. They'd been distant, withholding. And so had she. But she didn't sense the same degree of tension on the faces of the other two women that morning, so it felt like a return to old times. At least initially.

"It's been a while since we've all been together," Bridget said cheerily. "The fall's been sort of stressful, so it's . . . nice to be back again. How are you both doing?"

Jennifer inhaled, nodded, exhaled. "Good."

"Much better," Tamara said, reacting immediately to Bridget's words. They were a reiteration of Jon's comments about the difficulty of the past couple of months and, also, they offered a ready excuse for her less-than-charitable behavior toward her friends during much of that time. She wasn't going to pass up an opportunity to take it. "We went to see Benji over Columbus Day."

Her friends exclaimed at this news with predictable enthusiasm and pressed her for details on the visit. For a few joyous minutes, Tamara reveled in playing the part of the proud mother again, as opposed to the depressed, pathetic and abandoned one.

She echoed Bridget's sentiment of it having been a tough start to the autumn and she said, by way of subtle apology, "This past weekend was the first time I felt like myself since Aunt Eliza died. Or, really, since Benji left for Austin."

Bridget smiled at Tamara, fully and genuinely, compassion flooding her rounded body, and her lingering apprehension slipping away. Like a UFO chaser, she *wanted* to believe. And, like a (kind of) good Catholic, she also *wanted* to forgive.

Tiny prickles of hesitation poked at that desire, of course, much like tiny freckles dotted the creamy skin on her nose. But just as she often tried to mask the freckles with a pat of powder, she likewise covered her niggles of disbelief with a cool film of determination and the protective coating of forced faith. She fervently avoided questioning Tamara's sincerity in their friendship because she so actively wanted to avoid questioning her own.

Soon it was Bridget's turn in the spotlight, however. Tamara, being unusually solicitous, asked about her family and inquired— almost gently—about her "work relationships."

"Oh, the office was closed yesterday," Bridget said by way of breezy evasion. "But things are going fine." She reasoned it would take too long to explain about the restaurant visit with Dr. Luke and, anyway, it was just a fun lunch with a *friend*. There was nothing to report, right?

Instead, she launched into an explanation of what'd been going on with Evan. "I'm worried about him," she confessed, because it was a safe admission. "I think the extra sleep is helping, though. I just wish he weren't so sensitive to everything. That he was more of a Just Do It kind of kid and didn't think so much."

Jennifer, who'd often been accused as a child of being overly sensitive (her parents' favorite method of dismissing her fears, in fact, until she'd learned to conceal her anxieties) and too much of a thinker in just about everyone's opinion, nodded. She found this conversational turn very interesting indeed, but largely because of Bridget's curious omission. Glendale Grove might be near Chicago, an anonymity-allowing metropolis, but at its essence, the suburb remained very much a small town. Bridget, sweet though she was, ought to have the sense to know she wasn't invisible in it.

Jennifer repressed a grin as Bridget prattled on about the foods her son didn't like to eat anymore and how he wasn't himself in class. Jennifer had been at Franklin's Diner the day before, picking up carryout for their dinner, and she had seen a very smiley, not-remotely-worried-looking Bridget slipping out of Dr. Luke's car and into her own. But, hey, if Bridget didn't want to kiss and tell about her adventure with the dentist (what did they do?), Jennifer sure wasn't going to make her. They would have to drug Jennifer with a truth serum before they would be able to pry any real feelings out of her about her meeting with David.

Not that Tamara didn't try.

"So, we never really got the details on the whole campus visit thing," Tamara said eventually, getting comfortable on the vinyl cushion and taking a long swig of her latte. "Did seeing him again put things into perspective for you or did it just make you wanna jump his bones?"

"I did *not* jump his bones—" she began, but Tamara cut her off.

"Not what I asked," Tamara said mischievously. "Did you *want* to?" Tamara had been pretty much fixated on the idea of bone-jumping lately, a problem that intensified for her whenever she saw Aaron working out in his yard, which had been the case the previous afternoon. Even reasonably good sex with her husband didn't completely obliterate her desire to see their handsome neighbor with far fewer clothes on, and she had this recurring fantasy involving him wearing his tool belt and a pair of handcuffs. . . .

"No," Jennifer said, taking care not to speak too quickly. It wasn't a lie. She may have found David attractive, even after all of these years, but she was still furious with him. And she couldn't sleep with anybody who made her so angry.

"Well, what'd you two do down there? What'd you talk about? Spill." Tamara had a persistent streak.

Jennifer halfheartedly obliged, giving a cool rundown of the places she and David visited and their ultimate decision to hold the reunion at the Vat Building. Jennifer knew the other two wouldn't understand its significance, and she wasn't about to enlighten them. "We really only talked about the locations," she said, which was a sweeping falsehood, even by her standards of restraint. And there was no way in hell she was going to reveal the heightened degree of confidence sharing, the intimate questions asked and the frequently inappropriate commentary of their IM'ing sessions and phone calls since that day. Not a chance.

"Was it painful to be with him again?" Bridget asked, her voice tender, her soft hand squeezing Jennifer's forearm. "Did he show any signs of regret at the way he'd ended your relationship?"

Jennifer bit the inside of her cheek. How much could she admit to before she'd find herself in danger? At what point would the level of disclosure be too high for her personal sense of self-protection?

"It was awkward," she confessed, figuring she had to tell her friends *something*, "but I didn't ask him for any reasons or explanations."

Tamara huffed at her. "You had him right there and you didn't ask? Jeez, Jennifer. *Talk*, would ya?" She massaged her forehead with both palms. "So, okay, maybe you weren't feeling a huge connection with him, but did seeing him at least answer your question of wanting to test your marriage? Do you feel you made the right choice in moving on or are you still questioning that?"

To Jennifer, this inquiry showed that Tamara knew her Not At All. When wasn't she questioning? With more ineptitude and appliance malfunctions at home à la Michael, and more impropriety and suggestiveness (to the point of near phone sex and sexting) with David, how could she decide anything?

She feigned a light shrug. "Maybe I'll know more after the reunion." Then, taking a page from Bridget's book, Jennifer finally succeeded in shifting the conversational focus onto her family. "But I do know it's tough being the mom of a teen. Veronica has been pushing a lot of buttons lately." She told them about what'd been happening in Mr. Ryerson's U.S. history class. About the two boys. About the Homecoming Dance, which would be held that very night.

"Veronica's been doing all that?" Bridget said, her tone one of surprise. But Jennifer suspected this was more out of politeness than any real shock. Bridget had a spirited daughter of her own and had grown up with a couple of sisters. Bridget knew what girls were like.

"Oh, yes. She's been behaving much better in class these past two weeks because we told her if Mr. Ryerson kicked her out, we'd forbid her from attending tonight's dance. But she isn't making life easy at home, and we just found out Tuesday that she's not going to it with Tim anymore, the guy she'd liked so much she just had to join the Homecoming committee. No. Now she's crazy about this new guy Erick." Jennifer shook her head. "I guess he's meeting her there. I think that way they figured they could avoid having to deal with Michael, me and our questions."

In a stroke of hypocrisy so profound she'd stunned herself, Jennifer had actually had a conversation with her daughter last weekend about "figuring out who she really liked" and "needing to be honest" with both boys. And while Jennifer did not openly tell her friends this, both Bridget and Tamara were indeed thinking some variation of the phrase "Like mother, like daughter." Tamara's was a somewhat harsher and more judgmental version than Bridget's, however.

For all of her renewed spirits after having seen her beloved son again, Tamara's restlessness kept rising up within her and taking the form of silent jabs. She wanted to scold Jennifer on the freakin' ridiculousness of not asking a guy she hadn't seen in *eighteen years* why he'd bolted. C'mon already. Grow some bloody guts.

And then there was Bridget, who kept absentmindedly fondling the salt shaker at their table like it might change shape with just a little nurturing. Argh! Tamara was *this close* to blurting out a crude comment about giving it a hand job but, instead, she gulped her coffee, pasted a smile on her face and tried to behave.

Until fucking Fleetwood Mac came on.

"I hate this song." She groaned. Loudly. "Turn. It. Off," she commanded the Bose speaker levitating in the upper-left corner of the café's ceiling and piping out its endless excrement of seventies music. Goddamn XM radio.

Not surprisingly, the song—"Dreams"—kept playing.

"What's wrong with it?" Bridget asked, recognizing that, while it'd been overplayed to death and that Stevie Nicks woman looked like a druggie flower child in platform boots who'd been locked in the attic (kind of the way those crazy ladies in Gothic novels always were, and *they* always wore a lot of lace, too), there were far more annoying singers from that era. Like the Captain & Tennille. Or Debby Boone. Ugh. She'd take "Dreams" over "Muskrat Love" or "You Light Up My Life" any day.

"I have never been able to figure out what these lyrics mean," Tamara ranted. "Not even after listening to this nonsensical song five million times." She set down her coffee and squeezed her fists as if choking a couple of invisible offenders. "The only thing I'm sure of is that Stevie must've been having some pretty strong hallucinations when she was writing it. Listen."

The second verse started and Tamara stabbed the air with a venomous index finger, shooting death wishes at the ceiling speaker. "Hear that? Here she goes again seeing 'crystal visions.' She *says* she keeps those visions to herself, but she doesn't." Tamara crossed her arms and struck a pose of pure irritation. "Her voice is scratchy. She has a serious enunciation problem. The words that aren't slurred are depressing as hell. It's a sucky song, and it should've been banned from all airplay thirty years ago."

Jennifer shot her an impish grin. "Any further commentary?"

"No," Tamara said. "The prosecution rests its case."

Bridget bit her lip but didn't suggest that, perhaps, Tamara had been too long in the company of her quick-tempered and often irritable lawyer husband. She set down the salt shaker she'd been toying with and was about to reach for the pepper when, in a most unusual display of contentiousness on Jennifer's part, their quiet friend stated, "It's one of my favorite songs from that decade, Tamara. What part of it, exactly, don't you understand?"

Tamara blinked at her, then laughed. "I don't understand *any* of it. Seriously. Start anywhere."

And, to Bridget and Tamara's astonishment, she did.

"I think it's about resignation," Jennifer began. "A woman is being told by the guy she loves that he wants his freedom. She senses his attitude toward her and their relationship—like other men she'd dated before him—is more indifferent than it should've been. That he feels he can get another woman whenever he wants one. But, in her opinion, he's not thinking about the reality, not anticipating the loneliness he'll feel in quiet moments later, if he allows himself to feel deeply. She's been through this before and she knows. But it's no use trying to convince him now. He's set on leaving, so she's resigned to the fact that she understands the situation better than he does. She sees with crystal clarity what he's giving up, but she lets him go and lets go of the dream of their future together, knowing that one day he'll recognize his mistake. But, of course, it'll be too late then to recover their relationship."

Bridget thought Jennifer was, perhaps, putting herself a bit too much into the lyrics.

Tamara, convinced she'd inadvertently found herself stuck in the middle of one of those horrible literary discussions where earnest young poets or songwriters tried to ascribe meaning to the works of their famous and often dead predecessors, said, "Gah!" and rolled her eyes at Jennifer. "What? Did you and Stevie get together for happy hour one night and lament your lost loves?"

Jennifer, drained from so much speaking, clenched her jaw. "You're not required to believe me, but you *did* ask."

Tamara held up her hands. "Yeah, yeah, I asked. It just seems way heavy handed in some spots. The whole crashing of symbols with the thunder and raining part. And going all Edgar Allan Poe with that madness-inducing heartbeat. The rest is just incomprehensible to me." She shrugged. "How d'you crack the lyrics anyway?"

Jennifer gave a small smile. "I Googled them."

"Figures." Tamara played with her stirring stick and stared into space. She hadn't thought to Google anything. Not even Aaron. She might just have to do that.

Jennifer didn't mention that she'd also read about the song on Wikipedia. That singer Stevie Nicks wrote it in ten minutes during a time in the band's history when she and guitarist Lindsey Buckingham were breaking up after eight years together. Vocalist and keyboard player Christine McVie was separating from her husband, bass player John McVie, and the band's drummer, Mick Fleetwood, was getting a divorce. Clearly, this was a group of people who knew something about deteriorating relationships.

But it did no good to try to explain this to friends who didn't want to listen. Tamara was showing no interest in hearing any more about the music, and Bridget, while feigning attentiveness, pretty evidently had her mind elsewhere, too. Jennifer was just about to excuse herself for yoga—which she *should* go to, even though she really didn't want to—when a force she was incapable of circumventing burst into the Indigo Moon and rushed their table.

"Oh! I spotted you three from the window and *had* to say hi," Leah Wiener said, with more energy and exuberance than should be allowed in a woman pushing retirement age. "I *just* sent out the invites last night." Her eyes crinkled everywhere as she beamed enthusiastically at them. "You know it's that time of year again. Kip and I hope you and the hubbies can all come to the party." She whipped out her BlackBerry, punched something into it and announced, "Saturday the thirtieth. From nine in the evening until the Witching Hour. Mark your calendars! We'll mingle and catch up for a bit and then, at midnight, we'll have some tasty pumpkin cake and do a beheading, okay?"

Bridget sucked in some air and kind of nodded.

Jennifer blanched.

"Sounds . . . un-missable," Tamara said for all of them. "As always."

"Yeah," Bridget echoed faintly.

"Great," Leah enthused. "Then I'll put down six yeses. No need to RSVP again. Just show up with your darling hubsters at nine o'clock sharp." She whirled around and took a flurry of steps toward the door. Halted. Shot a look at them over her shoulder.

"And, oh, it's a fairy-tale theme. Don't forget to wear costumes!" She cackled gleefully and waved goodbye.

"Oh, my God," Tamara muttered when Leah was out of view. "I'm so sorry. I couldn't think of a single excuse with her standing right there."

"Don't feel bad," Bridget said. "I couldn't either."

Leah and Kip Wiener were the town's most avid Halloween aficionados, as well as bigwigs on the public library's board of trustees. They knew *everyone* in at least three counties, put up more house lights in the month of October than some entire neighborhoods at Christmas and had roped Bridget, Jennifer and Tamara into years of library fund-raisers. Their annual adults-only "Hallowiener Party"—a "reward" for their scores of fund-raising volunteers— had become a Glendale Grove tradition and one that inspired weeks of post-event gossip. Although it puzzled Bridget exceedingly how a woman as sweet and grandmothery as Leah could host such horrifically gory gatherings.

Last year, Leah, Kip and a few of their friends performed a midnight reenactment of the movie *Saw*, followed by "refreshments" of bloodred fruit punch and ax-shaped sugar cookies decorated with real razor blades. She couldn't imagine what this year's party would have in store.

"She isn't someone you can say no to," Jennifer commented, thankful that Michael had experienced being cornered by Leah or Kip more than once in the past and wouldn't hold her assumed acceptance of the invitation against her.

Bridget and Tamara nodded and, if in nothing else, the three women were united in their dread of this particular event. The last of Jennifer's motivation to attend yoga fled, despite how much she could have used help with her breathing. She drained the final drops of her beverage and grimaced at her friends, thankful in a small way not to have to discuss relationships—broken or otherwise—for the remainder of their morning together. "Guess we'd better coordinate our costumes, huh?" she murmured.

Tamara flagged down their waitress. "We're gonna need more coffee," she informed the young woman.

"And more muffins," Bridget added.

❧ 15 ❧

Bridget & Friends

Thursday, October 21 & Friday, October 22

Bridget, who'd foolishly dismissed Dr. Luke's idea of her son having a food allergy because Evan wasn't the kind of kid who'd had a reaction to any food in his life, now studied the contents of her refrigerator, hunting for glutens—hidden or obvious.

A wheat allergy, Evan's pediatrician had suggested, when she pulled him out of school early and took him in to be examined this afternoon. And possibly rice, barley and other grains. "Test Evan for a reaction to glutens first," Dr. Statenbach suggested when her son's blood work showed signs of anemia. "It's possible it's an intolerance or a mild allergy. Or, it's possible it's celiac disease."

The word "disease" didn't sit well in Bridget's gut. It created an intense and immediate pang of terror, actually. But, in the brochure the nurse had so helpfully handed to Bridget on the way out of the doctor's office, the various symptoms of celiac disease *did* seem to mirror those she'd been noticing in her son. Symptoms that had finally gotten her to call for a doctor's appointment. The list included: abdominal cramping, bloating, irritability, decreased appetite, various bowel ailments, vomiting, anemia, fatigue and even depression. Now that she thought about it, Evan hadn't gained any weight in a few months. Odd for a growing six-year-old boy. She should've guessed something medical was wrong sooner.

She sighed and snatched a gluten-loaded loaf of Hearth & Harvest from the middle shelf. For eight weeks, there would be no wheat, farina, durum, matzo, semolina, rye, barley, spelt, udon noodles or modified food starch for her son. She didn't think she'd have to worry about rooting out couscous or bulgur—both were off limits, too, but neither item was on Evan's dietary radar. Breakfast cereals were another matter, though. So were biscuits and pastas. Coming up with meals for Evan without these would be a culinary challenge she wasn't sure even she was prepared to handle.

Cassandra's dark head appeared over the top of the fridge door. "Hey, Mom. Can you take Emily and I to the mall tonight? Her mom said it's okay with her."

Bridget stood up and stared blankly at her daughter.

"Mom. I *said* can you—"

"It's 'Emily and me,'" Bridget replied. "And, no, I cannot."

Cassandra huffed and crossed her wiry arms in front of her still-flat chest, dramatic as always. "Why? Can you give me one good reason why we can't *ever* do what *I* want to do?"

Bridget didn't know what came over her, she just knew she was sick of having to explain herself to everyone. Almost without thinking, she shut the fridge door and lobbed the loaf of bread at her surprised daughter, who caught it with an expression of shock.

"Nice catch, kiddo."

"Uh, Mom. Why'd you—"

"Find the 'Ingredients' section of the label," Bridget commanded.

Her daughter tentatively twisted the package in her hands, scanning for the list. "Yeah, okay. So what?"

Bridget strode briskly over to the pantry and swiped a soup can from the middle shelf, but she didn't hand it to her daughter yet. "Now, read it. See if you can find any of these words on the bread's plastic wrapper." She pointed to the kitchen counter where the celiac disease brochure lay open and the gluten dangers highlighted.

Cassandra studied the paper and then, the bread loaf. "Oh, yeah. There's like three of them on here."

Bridget grinned at her eldest child. "Thanks. Put it on the counter and check this one, too." She tossed her the soup. Cassandra caught it, a hint of pride registering on her face this time, and, predictably, she found glutens.

"But why are we doing this?"

Bridget and Evan had returned from the doctor's office just fifteen minutes before her other two children had gotten off the bus, and Bridget hadn't had a chance to explain the situation to her daughter. Keaton was outside playing some version of football with his buddy Josh, and Evan was napping after his stressful afternoon at the doctor's office. Bridget decided to level with Cassandra. "Because these are all foods Evan can't eat for a while. And maybe never again."

Her daughter's eyes widened. "Whoa. That sucks!"

"It does," she agreed. "Why don't you grab a black marker and put a note or something on everything Evan should avoid, okay?"

Cassandra no longer seemed so preoccupied with the mall. Thank God for small blessings. "Okay. What should I write?"

Bridget leaned over and kissed her daughter's forehead. "I'll let you decide that. Just nothing that'll make your brother feel bad if he sees it."

Cassandra bit her lip, a behavior she seemed to have inherited from her mother, Bridget realized ruefully. "Thanks, Mom."

"For what? You're helping *me*."

"For trusting me," her nearly teenage daughter said. "For knowing I could do it myself."

And in that instant, Bridget realized that was the truth. She kept forgetting how Cassandra was growing up. How her little girl was more than capable of helping. Soon she wouldn't need Bridget at all. Time . . . it just went by too fast, didn't it?

"Sorry to have been so distracted lately," she told her daughter. "It's been, well, an adjustment going back to work, and these past several weeks with Evan being sick a lot have been pretty hard, too."

Bridget thought of Dr. Luke and the couple of times she'd seen him since their lunch date. He'd been just that little bit warmer, just that dash more conspiratorial, at the dental office. Not enough to ring any bells of impropriety, but enough so Candy could pick up on it and make a joke or two. Just this morning, Candy had said that Dr. Luke considered Bridget "his most favorite person" in the building on account of their "shared gourmet sensibilities." Dr. Nina, on the other hand, had returned this week from her month-long sabbatical and didn't seem to care about Bridget at all or, indeed, notice much of anything. She'd been acting withdrawn and, in Bridget's opinion, thankfully inattentive.

Of course, next week was a new week. Who knew what lay ahead?

Cassandra, busy deciphering the ingredients on a box of Hamburger Helper, didn't immediately reply to Bridget's meager apology. After another few minutes, however, her daughter commented, "You like working there, though. A lot. Don't you?"

"Yes, absolutely." Bridget raised herself on tiptoe so she could better search through one of the higher kitchen cabinets. "I like the people at the dental office—" Well, most of them, she added to herself. "And the work environment is very pleasant. I think people should try to find jobs where their skills are appreciated and where they feel comfortable."

Bridget enjoyed a few moments of basking in the pride of her parenting and getting to speak in the blissfully nonconfrontational manner of a woman to a young friend, as opposed to a harried mom to a quarrelsome daughter.

Then, in a burst of insightfulness not entirely foreign to prepubescent girls (but always disconcerting when it happened), Cassandra glanced up from her box and said, "Yeah. I can tell. You look different on the days you go to work. Like Emily does when we're in math with Adam—her crush. So"—she speared Bridget with a laser look—"is there someone at the dentist's office that you think is cute?"

The following morning, Tamara winced when Jennifer told her the news: Bridget's youngest son was still sick with stomach ailments and the doctor said he might have, as Bridget described it, "a condition." She'd called Jennifer last night and told her she wouldn't be meeting them for coffee. She wanted to keep Evan home from school until Monday "to watch him and to try out some new meal ideas." She sounded very shaken.

"I always hated those days," Tamara said, unable to keep the note of wistfulness from her voice alongside the orchestration of sympathy. "Not only did it throw off the whole week's schedule, but you couldn't help but be constantly anxious."

Jennifer nodded. "It's really hard when they're sick." She thought about Bridget's son Evan and knew how fretful his mother was about "his possible disease." She knew Bridget had been up with him for multiple nights in the past few weeks, not knowing if his stomach pains were due to the flu, to food poisoning or, since he was a worrier like Bridget, to a tendency for a stomach ulcer. Or something worse. Jennifer could understand why Bridget would be very concerned, even if celiac disease was a more manageable issue than many other potential disorders.

Jennifer and Tamara each sent Evan good-health wishes in silence and, then, due to their mutual fidgetiness and proximity to a number of Glendale Grove gossips (the Indigo Moon Café was unusually crowded that morning), they decided to grab coffee to go and walk off some of their residual nervous energy.

Tamara zipped up her brown leather jacket and turned to Jennifer, who blew on her latte but was otherwise silent for their first several yards. "So, c'mon, what's the story with you? You seemed to have a lot on your mind when I called. What's been happening?"

Jennifer understood, logically, why one-on-one discussions resulted in greater disclosure on her part, despite her resistance to them. There was neither the danger nor the protection that came from getting lost in the crowd (something that happened even with a trio, since she could easily sit back and let the other two interact). Tamara had called her a few days ago to check up on her and find out how the Homecoming Dance went but, with the other family members at home, she'd been cryptic on the phone and, besides, she hadn't yet processed everything well enough to discuss it. No such excuses anymore.

"It was kind of a disaster," she admitted.

Tamara's eyes widened. "Did Veronica have a terrible time? Did the first guy she was supposed to go with cause a huge scene at the dance? Or did the second guy try to maul her or something?"

Jennifer, well accustomed to Tamara's dramatic side, didn't physically roll her eyes, but she thought about it. "No, none of the above. At least, not that I know about." She paused on the sidewalk and took a cautious sip of coffee. "Michael and I had a big fight about it. I really didn't like the way he handled the night."

"Like a yelling and screaming kind of fight? Throwing vases and stuff?"

This time Jennifer did, actually, roll her eyes. She snickered, too. "In all the years you've known me, when have I ever yelled at anyone or thrown anything? And you know Michael, too. Does he come across as a screamer to you?"

Tamara smirked and waggled her eyebrows. "You tell me, honey."

Jennifer laughed. "No. And he's not that kind of screamer either." She drank more coffee. "We have quiet fights. Battles of will. But this laissez-faire way he has of parenting is really starting to bug me."

Tamara shrugged. "That's pretty common among guys, though. Not all of them, maybe, but Jon was really hands-off with Benji in most areas. He always left the details to me. And he's not nearly as laid-back a person as Michael is."

"True, but it's the *reasons* he's giving for being hands-off that are annoying me. Because he's a high-school teacher. Because he sees teens all the time. Because he knows himself and, thus, projects that knowledge onto Veronica and this situation. What he's missing is that she's *my* daughter. That if she's even kind of like me, it doesn't matter what *other* teens would do. It's what *she* would do." Exhausted from this rant, she paused again for more coffee.

Tamara paused, too. "What does Michael say when you tell him that?"

"He fucking laughs it off."

Her friend laughed aloud. "Sorry. You just sounded so much like me for a second there."

Jennifer grimaced and they resumed walking. "Michael said that Veronica's extroversion makes her act differently than I would have in a similar situation. That she needs to control her behavior in class, of course, and that he'll talk to her social studies teacher and the principal, if it ever comes to that, and work with them on any problem. As if I didn't handle things well enough during the conference, but his buddy-buddy high-school teacher self would just smooth everything over perfectly."

Jennifer squeezed her fists. "Michael says I have to trust Veronica's judgment, of which, I must say, she hasn't shown much since this school year started. And, even though I said I was only going to go to the dance for twenty minutes to take a quick look at this new boy, this *older* boy, Erick, and that a lot of parents peek in on the kids without being obvious—he refused to let me go. He insisted on dropping off Veronica and picking her up himself. He told me not to *interfere* so much. That I'd be doing damage to her. That she wouldn't trust us if she felt checked-up on. Then he went into the kitchen and somehow managed to break the opening lever on the dishwasher, so we need to get *that* fixed now."

"Sounds frustrating," Tamara said, her mind drifting momentarily to Aaron and that tool-belt-wearing, handyman fantasy she had involving him. She pulled herself back to reality.

"Yes, but I'm not wrong, am I? You're an extrovert. Just because someone is talkative, it doesn't mean they're wise."

Tamara stopped and stared at her. "Nice."

Jennifer sighed. "Oh, c'mon. You know what I *mean*. I'm just saying emotional maturity isn't tied to verbal openness. Just because Veronica's more popular and chatty than I ever was, it doesn't mean she's capable of making better decisions. She's just more apt to talk about them. And not, incidentally, with *us*."

Tamara grinned. "Her best friends have probably gotten an earful, though."

Jennifer nodded.

"No," Tamara said. "I don't think you're wrong. You and Michael just see Veronica's behavior differently. Maybe you're both projecting your personalities on her, and she's actually someone else entirely. Someone neither of you can fully recognize." As Jennifer considered this, Tamara—wanting to take advantage of her friend's unusual loquaciousness—couldn't help but bring up another point of some personal concern. After her friend had had another minute or two to reflect on the topic of her daughter, Tamara initiated a related discussion—that of their husbands.

"You know how you asked us last month about whether we felt *sure* in our choice of husband," Tamara said, "and that maybe we needed to test out our marriage to know?"

"Yeah?"

"What was your day with your ex really like? I know you said the reunion would help you clarify. That you'd probably know more after that. But you can't tell me you spent all that time touring your old college campus with David and still have no impulses one way or another. No sense of intuition about which man you feel more connected with."

Jennifer sighed. What *was* it with her friends and their bizarrely innate sense of *knowing*, which they were always pushing on her? "Look, Tamara, I'm really not sure how to explain it. . . ."

"Try."

She inhaled deeply. "Okay, but you'll think it's weird, because it's not as easy as an either-or situation, much as I'd like it to be. David and Michael exist in different planes. Sort of like their space-time continuums are completely separate from each other." She glanced at Tamara, who, indeed, did appear to find her explanation an odd one. She pressed on anyway. "The world I inhabit with Michael disappears when I'm with David, or even IM'ing with him. Meeting Michael, after David and I broke up, was like journeying to another dimension. Same planet, but a million minute differences."

"Huh." Tamara finished her coffee and tossed the paper cup into a nearby trash bin. "But if it's the same planet, as you say, then when and where does the transition actually happen? For instance, what about when you're completely alone?"

"You mean, which dimension do I live in then?"

"Yes. Is the journey really *out there*, between Michael and David? Or is it within you?"

A tiny voice in Jennifer's head was the first to answer. A voice she, for once, didn't quash. "It's been so long since I was really alone, I don't remember." She paused. "And as long as I keep the two men apart, I can't know for sure. I—I'm pretty sure I'm not ready to know, though. Not yet."

"Fair enough," Tamara said. "Maybe that'll change after the reunion."

"Maybe." Of course there was a rather large piece of the puzzle Jennifer omitted. A couple of pieces, if she were to be completely honest.

One was that she hadn't even told Michael about the reunion weekend yet. She'd kept her calendar open, sure, but she hadn't committed to the event in the eyes of the family for fear she'd unwittingly give herself away. That everyone else in the world had this instinctive sixth sense that her DNA didn't possess. That if she mentioned David's name out in the open at home, her husband and daughters would somehow deduce there was something going on.

Then again, Michael was so busy destroying the house, appliance by appliance, maybe he wouldn't notice. And maybe he wouldn't understand the specifics of the text messages David had sent her—if he were to see them, and she was careful he wouldn't. That was the other unspoken piece. She kept her cell phone with her at all times, except when she was showering or sleeping. (And then she had it turned off and hidden in a zipped compartment of her purse.) But somehow she suspected Michael's liberal-artsy, poetic side would *intuit* the meaning behind David's carefully crafted messages, which had, in typical David form, begun nearly innocuously before mutating to an entity just shy of cybersex.

At first, it was about the reunion directly:

Got all RSVPs. 10 for sure. 6 maybes. Thx 4 being in the 1st group! (And ten to sixteen people made quite an intimate group for a reunion, really.)

Then it turned cutesy:

U gotta check out this YouTube vid. Monkey Pong Live! Will e-mail link. (A reference to the computer game their friend Mitch had programmed, which had been a perennial favorite of the club members. Only the video link David sent wasn't of the real Monkey Pong, but of two real monkeys that were filmed kissing with very raunchy captions below the video.)

Then it became a series of texts—once he'd engaged her in conversation, had gotten her into a habit of answering his messages right away and knew which times of day she could respond quickly:

Look at this ad. (With a link to an online lingerie store featuring mannequins dressed in underwear, wrestling in Girls Gone Wild style.)

To: *What kind RU wearing?* (She didn't answer that one. And she immediately deleted it.)

But it was followed the next day by:

Just heard Meat Loaf. (Which she answered cautiously with, *I always liked him.*)

Then it morphed into:

I know. Rembr. that rainy Sunday? (Which, of course, she remembered. Late August of their junior year. Just back to school after the endless summer break. A room to themselves. Listening to "You Took the Words Right Out of My Mouth (Hot Summer Night)" and "Paradise by the Dashboard Light" from the classic *Bat Out of Hell* album. And touching each other. So, she typed, *Yeah.*)

He wrote:

I rembr. yr #26 shirt. (Which was really *his* #26 shirt.)

And then in separate texts that he didn't wait for her to reply to:

I locked the door.

U took off my fave blues. (His favorite pair of Levi's jeans.)

My hands, yr legs . . .

Got rid of yr B & P. (He made quick work of undressing her, yes. Her bra and panties didn't stand a chance.)

Like an ice-cream cone. (She blushed at that memory. He liked . . . going down on her. But, at this, she typed, *Stop it.*)

He defended his texts with:

Just a memory. Nothin wrong w. that.

Only there was. She wasn't so self-delusional that she could miss what David implied with every keystroke or how Michael would react to his wife taking part in a cybersex reenactment with her old boyfriend.

She was not telling Tamara about any of this.

Through some deft manipulation on Jennifer's part, and some very general whining about the cluelessness of husbands, the subject eventually twisted and turned to Tamara and Jon.

"We get used to different things—whether we like them or are irritated by them," Tamara said. "Jon and I have essentially had a convenient marriage for a couple of decades now." A reference to her shotgun, city hall wedding because she was pregnant with Benji. "He's good at some things, but I'll never like his temper or his snarkiness. Those qualities are a pain but, after a while, enough time goes by and it's hard to imagine being with anyone else and getting used to a whole new set of bad habits. So, none of Jon's carrying on really bothers me anymore."

Jennifer raised one stealthy brow. "Really?"

"Well, yeah. I mean, it's not ideal. It's not the fairy tale. But what relationship is? What *long-term* relationship?"

"But relationships aren't general, Tamara. They're specific. Very specific to the two people involved."

Tamara shrugged. "I made a choice. I think once people make that choice, the specifics don't really matter."

Jennifer actually laughed at this. "And, yet, that's not exactly what you said when we talked about Jon's plan to move to Atlanta that one time. I remember you telling us that he'd already taken away your choice of life mate, and that you weren't going to let him take away your home, too."

Tamara tried to bat away Jennifer's doubts. "Look. I guess 'it doesn't bother me' is the wrong way to put it. But what can be done about it?"

Jennifer blinked and tilted her head annoyingly.

"I do *not* still harbor resentment over the forced marriage," Tamara insisted.

"*Forced* marriage, is it now? Interesting choice of words."

"Oh, Freudian slip. So what?"

Jennifer shrugged. "You tell me. If you don't know your feelings—" *Or acknowledge them when you do,* Jennifer added to herself, not that she was an expert at that skill personally. "How could I possibly guess them?"

Tamara fought the rise in her level of defensiveness, which created an internal churning and unease that pissed the hell out of her. "I'm the last person anyone ever accuses of hiding my feelings," she said. "I'm not the least bit reserved. I'm not remotely withholding."

Jennifer squinted at her in disbelief. "You *seem* so open, that's true, but I'm always surprised by how little you actually reveal."

"Well, I have to have some secrets, don't I?" Tamara blurted, and then stopped in the middle of the cracked pavement. As she puzzled through understanding her own admission, she couldn't help but recognize the parallel between what Jon had said to her in Austin and other times before, which she tended to dismiss because he could be such an A-hole, and what Jennifer had just said, which, while irritating, wasn't nearly as challenging to her self-esteem. It was, however, virtually the same message: If she didn't know what she wanted and didn't express it when she did, how could anyone else know?

"And just what kind of secrets do you have?" Jennifer asked, a small smile playing at the corners of her small mouth.

Tamara thought of the fantasies she'd been having lately. All of them featuring Aaron. But *everyone* had fantasies, and what she felt about him she knew wasn't *love*. It was . . . weird, yes. And strangely powerful. But, even in her most serious moments of staring head-on at her attraction to him, she doubted it was more than an odd case of very exclusive and directed lust. Which had her identifying too readily with Samantha on old episodes of *Sex and the City* and taking altogether too much interest in the courtship and consequent marriage of Demi and Ashton. And it certainly had her convinced that the libido of a strong, forty-something woman could rival that of any hot younger man. But, still, those were all just mental games. None of it was real.

She *knew* real.

"The only thing I know," Tamara said, sidestepping her friend's question, "is that you can't change a man. No matter what you might think before marriage."

Jennifer halted. "No. No you can't," she agreed. "But you can change yourself."

Something inside Tamara blossomed at those words. They rang

so true for her and filled her with such a sense of relief. So obvious and, yet, so right. Even *knowing* Jon wouldn't change didn't keep her from *hoping* he might. She could finally see that clearly. Could finally let go of that girlish myth she'd clung to for all these years. Like chopping off a superfluous part of her—like the silly ponytail she wore in her youth—and tossing it out the window. It was that deft a cut.

Perhaps she hadn't been fair to Jon. Perhaps she ought to give marriage to the *real* man a try, and not secretly pine for the idyllic shadow of him she'd created. And, above all, perhaps she needed to express to him what she wanted in their relationship. It may yet be possible to achieve it.

They had zigzagged several blocks, wound around in circles, but were now back on the same street as the Indigo Moon. She felt drained, but it was an exhaustion ribboned with exhilaration. And it came with golden threads of gratitude.

"Good point, Jennifer," she said. "Very good point."

The other woman smiled at her and downed the last of her latte.

"You want another one of those?" Tamara asked, pointing to the empty cup. " 'Cuz I could go for a second one."

"Sure." They were a few yards from the entrance, and Jennifer reached into her purse to pull out her wallet.

"Oh, you know what?" Tamara said. "This one's on me. And I'm grabbing us a couple of scones to go, too."

"Thanks," Jennifer said. "But I'll only eat it if it's shaped like a guillotine and has a real blade at one end."

Tamara laughed. "Eight more days, and your wish just might be granted."

❧ 16 ❧

The Hallowiener Party

Owing to the impending event the following evening, the trio elected not to get together on Friday the 29th. A conservation of energy would surely be required to make it through the Hallowiener Party and, quite possibly, an emergency coffee meeting might be necessary early the next week as well. All three women doubted they'd be able to postpone discussing the festivities until the following Friday.

However, amid a flurry of phone calls and costume coordination (none of the women wanted to choose the same fairy-tale outfits to wear), it was promised they would keep an eye out for each other while at the party and, if Kip or Leah Wiener threatened to make them or their husbands take part in any beheading performance, they would have each other's backs. And necks.

Bridget, who felt a natural affinity for anybody who brought food to loved ones in wicker ware, dressed as Little Red Riding Hood. She was rather pleased with her hooded red cape, and she'd filled her woven basket with home-baked cookies and a few other low-fat, heart-healthy goodies in the event that the treats provided by the hosts proved too scary or inedible.

She and her husband, Graham, the Woodsman, were later than many of the partygoers. But, surprisingly, they were the first of the three couples to arrive at the Wiener house, where plenty of costumed wolves were in attendance, including Kip's brother, the town's chief of police.

"Be careful where you swing that ax, Woodsman," Wolf Wiener said, crossing his arms by the front entrance before breaking into a grin.

The men shook hands.

"Nice to see ya again, Chief." Graham and his crew had installed eighteen new windows at the police station over the summer. Bridget was glad there were always guys he knew invited to this event, so, in that way, he could enjoy a little male camaraderie as they experienced the spectacle of the night. "Did Kip make you the bouncer again?" Graham said with a chuckle.

The other man laughed, his fake wolverine teeth bright white in the glow of the sparkling house lights. "You know it. Reckon you two are over twenty-one, though. They got some wild brew inside."

"Any beer?"

"Yep," the Wolf/Chief Wiener said. "There's a keg next to the food table. Go grab yourselves a couple glasses. And, uh, don't be too shocked by the color."

"Red again?" Graham asked, with a hint of apprehension.

"Nope. You'll see."

Bridget pulled out two specialty jams from her basket, one with a black bow, the other with an orange one. "I brought strawberry and peach preserves for Leah and Kip," she said. "Is there a good spot to put gifts?"

The Wolf/Chief nodded. "Leah's adding the finishing touches on her Spider Sandwiches." He pointed in the general direction of the kitchen. "She'd love for you to pop in and say hi."

They thanked him and wandered inside.

Jennifer and Michael arrived shortly thereafter with an autumn bouquet for the Wieners. Jennifer's two daughters had been employed in the task of babysitting Bridget's three children, and Jennifer had taken a few extra minutes at the house to ensure that Veronica and Shelby understood the detailed instructions her friend left on which snacks Evan could have versus those for Cassandra and Keaton.

Dressed as Goldilocks and the (one) Bear, Jennifer and Michael approached the Wolf/Chief with some caution.

"Welcome, friends!" Kip's brother's voice boomed into the twilight.

Jennifer smiled wanly and Michael shook his hand.

"You're gonna be here through the show, right?" Wolf Wiener said.

They nodded, but Jennifer thought, *Not if we can escape sooner.* And Michael couldn't muster the enthusiasm for a verbal reply.

"Great." The police chief waved them into the house and told them to help themselves to some refreshments.

Unlike Bridget's husband, Graham, Michael did not find anything about the annual Halloweiner Party diverting—not the bizarreness or even the beer. Despite his overall outgoingness, he unequivocally hated coming to this party, but he knew, for his wife's sake and, really, for his own, he had to attend. Jennifer understood this as well. It was a See and Be Seen event in their community, and their absence would have been noticed.

Didn't mean they had to like it, though, which partly—though not entirely—explained their somber moods upon entering the house.

Tamara and Jon were the last of the trio to arrive, toting a bottle of Chardonnay for the hosts.

Of the three husbands, Tamara's spouse was the one with the greatest appreciation for the peculiar goings-on, largely due to the fact that anyone who had the fortitude to withstand the dust-dry conversation of a law-firm cocktail party could easily maintain his stamina amid the Pied Piper of Hamelin, the Frog Prince, the Ugly Duckling and all of the Bremen Town Musicians.

The Wolf/Chief extended his hand and his welcome to them as well, and they—dressed as Rapunzel and the Prince—entered the large house, set aglow by windowsill jack-o'-lanterns flickering squiggles of light into the darkness.

The first thing Tamara noticed when she set foot in the dimly lit foyer was the armored knight statue acting as sentinel. She stopped in front of it and grinned. She remembered the life-sized toy from the last three years. "Hello, again, Knight."

"Behold, visitor!" rumbled the Knight's artificial voice. "Are you a princess, an enchantress or a wench?"

"A wench," Jon answered for her, tugging on the sleeve of her peasant blouse. "C'mon. I saw Mayor West's Mercedes out front." Jon, who considered the event a three-hour networking opportunity and a chance to drum up business for the firm (his ability in collecting new clients always impressed his fellow partners), did not want to waste time talking to inanimate objects when the mayor was available. Even if the town's highest official bore a striking resemblance that night to Rumpelstiltskin.

Tamara sighed and followed Jon through a sea of women in party gowns, made up to look like good or evil queens, an overly abundant number of men dressed as princes or kings (everybody wanted to rule the world) and at least five of the Seven Dwarfs.

They got as far as the refreshments table, where Tamara spotted Bridget inspecting the spread of goodies and Bridget's husband chatting with another guy (Sinbad the Sailor?) a few feet away. "You go look for the mayor," she told Jon. "I'm gonna have one of, um . . . those things before I mingle." She pointed at a random food item—no idea what it was—and winked at Bridget.

"Yeah, okay," Jon mumbled, and he was gone.

Bridget took a step closer to Tamara as soon as he'd cleared the room. "Don't know if I'd risk it," she whispered.

"Risk what?"

"The, uh, Jack and the Bean-Dip." Bridget tapped her finger near the folded orange index card labeled with the name of the dish.

Tamara studied the lumpy brown glob in the bowl surrounded by green-tinged wafer crackers and laughed. "It does look . . . questionable," she whispered back. "Anything here you'd recommend?"

"Well, the Princess's Pea Soup isn't . . . *bad*, and the Golden Goose Deviled Eggs are kind of, um, interesting."

Tamara winced.

"Graham seems to like the Three Bloody Pigs in a Blanket," Bridget suggested, motioning for her to take a look at the ketchup-covered, biscuit-wrapped wienies.

This time Tamara shuddered.

Bridget reached into her basket and surreptitiously withdrew a large oatmeal-raisin cookie. She hid it in a "Halloween Is Spooky!" napkin and handed it to her friend. "Here. Eat this."

"Oh, thank God," Tamara said, taking a bite just as Jennifer wandered into the room, an odd expression on her face. Tamara lifted her free hand in greeting and took another bite of Bridget's treat. Damn, that girl could bake.

Just then, a guy wearing a large gold crown, a small pair of beige-colored briefs and *nothing else* pranced through the room, waving to everybody. Tamara almost dropped her cookie. "What the hell was that?" she said, probably too loudly, but who cared? It was a party, for chrissake. Guests were supposed to be loud, right?

"The Emperor," Jennifer said, rounding the food table and coming to stand next to them. "Dressed in his New Clothes."

Bridget handed her a cookie, too, which she took gratefully but didn't eat.

"Are you feeling okay?" Bridget asked her.

Jennifer shook her head. She'd gotten a barrage of text messages from David that week and even more of them during the day. She had set her cell phone to vibrate and would have turned it off altogether, but what if one of the kids called?

"I'm a little frustrated," she said, squeezing the hem of the stark white apron that covered her blue and white gingham skirt. "I told Michael I'd bring him a drink, but I really just want to get away from all the noise and interruptions and . . . everything." Not that she could. She glanced around the party room they were in—one of probably fifteen areas in and around the Wiener house that was packed with people—and realized this was not nearly quiet enough. Her cell phone vibrated again. Damn.

She pulled it out of her skirt pocket and pressed a button to check the message:

Once upon a time there was a v. curious grl who went deep in2 the forest.
She sighed.

"Is it the kids?" Bridget asked, her voice worried.

"No." Jennifer seriously regretted ever having told David about this party and about her dressing up as Goldilocks. She was about to put the phone back into her pocket when a new text appeared: *She was v., v. hungry and not real law abiding.*

She shot a look at her friends, who were regarding her with concern. "I need to turn off this phone," she told them. "Right now. Bridget, could you call the kids and tell them that, if anything comes up, they can reach us at your number?"

Bridget nodded. "Of course, but what's the problem?"

Tamara answered for Jennifer in an oblique manner. "Does David really pester you that much? New texts every ten minutes?"

Jennifer exhaled. "It's not usually this bad, but it has been today. His wife and kids are out of town for the weekend and, clearly, he has nothing better to do with his time than harass me. Some of the messages are kind of funny, but—" Her phone vibrated again. Message: *And she rly had a thing 4 hairy guys. . . .*

She turned off her phone and pocketed it. "I'm just going to pretend the battery needs charging." She nibbled on her cookie in agitation but, even though she knew it was perfectly and lovingly baked by her friend, it tasted like sawdust in her mouth.

"Okay," Bridget said. "I'll let the kids know. Don't worry."

"Thanks," Jennifer said between mechanical bites. She stared at the beer keg. "What color is it this year?"

"Jet black," Tamara replied, pointing to a handful of people with cups of beer so inky it looked like they were drinking the stuff inside fountain-pen refills.

"Great," Jennifer murmured, filling a plastic cup with the horrid-looking substance anyway and grabbing a glass of some greenish Kool-Aid-like thing that reeked with the distinctive odor of tequila. "All right. I've gotta get back to Michael, but I'll see you both in a bit."

"Hang in there," Tamara said.

"I will." The lead character from the lesser-known Brothers Grimm tale *Hans My Hedgehog* walked by, narrowly missing getting his spines tangled up in some low-hanging cobwebs. "You, too," Jennifer added. "And thanks for the cookie, Bridget. Best thing here."

She scurried away moments before the hosts themselves swept into the room, dressed as Prince Charming and Cinderella gone horribly wrong. The outfits were correct—a flowing pink ball gown for her, a crisp white tux for him—but the details set the fairy tale on its head. The Wieners had managed to turn the romantic pairing into a Goth couple, complete with black fingernail polish, black lipstick, a number of temporary tattoos and a few fake piercings (for realism).

"Oh, my God," Tamara breathed.

Bridget, who'd seen the hosts briefly when she and Graham had arrived, was not nearly so surprised, but she still wasn't thrilled about having to get a close-up view of their outfits a second time. Nevertheless, as Leah and Kip approached them, bearing trays of some beverage, Bridget snatched up a Headless Gingerbread Man Cookie from the refreshments table so she could appear more sociable and accepting of the festivities than she felt. Next to her, Tamara stifled a snicker.

"Hellooo, you two!" Leah enthused. "I hope you're having a marvelous time."

"Oh, indescribably so," Tamara commented.

"Yeah," Bridget said, almost believably. And then, because she hated to lie, she took an inadvertently large bite out of the head-deprived Gingerbread Man. A mistake. She started coughing—an immediate and uncontrollable reaction to a strong, unrecognizable spice. What the heck had Leah baked into this thing?

Kip thrust a small martini-shaped glass at her, a wedge of some fruit—an apple slice?—garnishing the rim. "Here, honey. Have one of these."

Desperate, Bridget took it and gulped. The flame of vodka engulfed her throat and eviscerated her taste buds. For a moment, she coughed even harder but, suddenly, it all stopped. Her esophagus had been sufficiently shocked by the mysterious contents of the cocktail. "Uh, thanks," she murmured.

Kip grinned and put one in Tamara's hand as well.

"What . . . is it?" Tamara asked for them both.

"A Poisoned Appletini, of course," Leah said far too cheerfully.

"It's not really toxic," Kip confided. He winked at them. "Unless you drink too many of 'em."

Then the Goth couple laughed at their own joke and moved on to terrorize the next group of partygoers.

Tamara took a cautious sip of her pinkish drink, and she was pleasantly surprised. There was vodka, yes, but she also detected apple schnapps, Cointreau and a dash of apple cider. Very, very tasty.

And when Kip deposited the remainder of the glasses on the food table and urged her to "Have another one, sweetie," she took him up on it.

Bridget, by contrast, barely drank half of her first Appletini and absolutely begged off a second. Nevertheless, she stayed by Tamara's side for another twenty minutes, talking to her about a couple of great new carryout places in the area, until the Twelve Dancing Princesses descended upon them.

Actually, Tamara noted there were only half a dozen of them— the local instructors at Madame Chelsea's School of Dance—but they pirouetted so much that, to Tamara, it felt as if there were at least twice as many.

The Dancing Princesses knew Bridget's daughter from her years of ballet study, and they flung a seemingly endless stream of questions at Bridget:

"We've missed Cassandra this semester. Is she practicing her *pliés?* Her *chassés?* Her *relevés?*"

"Will you be enrolling her in ballet camp next summer?"

"Might she consider auditioning for *The Nutcracker* in December?"

The flurry of queries naturally left Bridget feeling guilty because she knew she hadn't focused much attention on her daughter during the past two months, but Cassandra had *asked* to take a break from dance this fall. It wasn't as though Bridget was purposely depriving her!

As for Tamara, she only felt old. Although she was personally familiar with all of the dance terms the instructors used, she felt edged out of the discussion. She was long past the age of being a dance student herself and Madame Chelsea's—unlike some of the other dance studios in the area—did not offer classes for middle-aged adults who wanted to relieve their *Swan Lake* days.

So, she left Bridget to the Dancing Princesses in the middle of the room and drifted back toward the food table where she grabbed another Poisoned Appletini. Through what was quickly becoming a shimmery vodka haze, she regarded her increasingly chaotic surroundings with newfound interest.

Really, it was a full-fledged Comedy of the Absurd.

There was a fascinating dynamic playing out in the back corner of the room, a sitcom between two Peters and their diminutive dates. That is, Peter Pan, who'd come to the party with Tinker Bell, seemed to be showing an inappropriate level of interest in Thumbelina, the flirtatious date of Peter Piper. Not good.

Thumbelina, with a high-pitched giggle, a batting of eyelashes and a swinging of her petite hips, declared, "Oh, you're so *funny*, Peter Pan. Tell us *more* about Neverland."

Peter Pan laughed and pretended to sprinkle some pixie dust on her chest, which was surprisingly robust and well-displayed, given her childlike character. Then again, her outfit was kinda skimpy.

Neither Tinker Bell nor Peter Piper looked remotely amused.

Tamara turned her attention to the Arabian Nights contingent at the opposite end of the room, a spectacle involving a threesome this time. She was unsure if Aladdin and Ali Baba were going to draw long swords to fight for the right to take the lovely Scheherazade home, or if they were just going to make it a ménage à trois.

Clearly, she wasn't the only one under the influence of the unusual alcoholic mixtures. She sighed and wondered vaguely what Jon was up to—hunting down the district attorney and a local judge or two, no doubt—but, mostly, she scanned the crowd, nibbled on the apple wedge accompanying her latest drink and chitchatted briefly with a Dwarf, a Sorcerer and a couple of Evil Henchmen.

She'd gotten to the point where her buzz had morphed into a delightfully relaxed awareness, fringed by the smooth and rare edge of self-acceptance. As an added bonus, she found herself able to focus on limited stimuli with the intensity of a toddler. She was completely living in the moment and unusually at peace with the sensation.

Which was why, of course, the very next marvel introduced into her consciousness was the inevitable sight of Aaron slipping into the room.

Dressed as yet another prince (there were too damn many of them already) and carrying a couple of pumpkins suitable for carving, he grinned when he spotted her. Setting down his offerings on the unoccupied ledge of a bookshelf, he strode over to her and said, "Hey, Tamara. Good to see you here."

"You, too. Nice outfit."

"Thanks." He spread his robe like a caped crusader. "I'm a superhero."

"You're a prince."

"Same difference." He shrugged. "Point is, I'm a cool and invincible dude, prepared to battle every obstacle in my path." He motioned to her long, fake Rapunzel braids. "If there's a pair of garden shears around here somewhere, I can fix those for you."

She laughed and reached for her fifth (sixth?) Poisoned Appletini. "Take a swipe at my braids, neighbor, and you're gonna need to be immortal, not just invincible."

Back in the center of the room, Bridget finally wrapped up her conversation with the Dancing Princesses, sending them flitting off to interrogate some other equally negligent ballet mom. She glanced around for Tamara and saw her laughing with a Very Handsome Prince near one end of the table. Graham was a few clusters of people away, talking with a couple of guys from the fire department—a Lion, a Tiger and, yes, a Bear—so she finally had a few moments to herself.

She walked to a semiquiet spot near the candy-covered walls of the room (the Wieners had decorated several areas of their house like the witch's cottage in *Hansel and Gretel*, complete with wrapped chocolates shaped like various creatures of the night, gumdrops and lollipops taped to the walls), pulled out her cell phone and gave the kids a quick call. After she'd let Shelby know about Jennifer's cell phone problem, and just as she was listening to Keaton's long recounting of the "way cool DVDs in Veronica's living room," Graham walked up to her and motioned for her to hang up.

Bridget said goodbye to her son and turned to her husband. "How's it going, my good Woodsman?"

He rolled his eyes. "Checking up on the kids again? Jeez, Bridget. Give 'em a little space. They're fine. Have a Spider Sandwich or one of the Bloody Pigs in a Blanket, why don't 'cha?" He popped a biscuit-covered wienie into his mouth. "They're not half bad."

She bit her lip. She'd been trying to watch her weight by eating healthier things in smaller portions. Trying to avoid reflexively reaching for food as a way to soothe herself. Trying, even though Graham didn't know this, to help out Jennifer by phoning the house at her friend's request.

But why even bother attempting to explain? Graham only saw what he wanted to see, and what he wanted to see was his wife acting in the way he always expected her to act. Which was as a snacker, a worrier, a hovering mother. And maybe she was all of these (not that she didn't have a reason—she'd been right about Evan having a problem, after all!), but Graham didn't stop to listen to her explanations. He hadn't for years. At least not once he thought he *knew* her.

"I just wanted to make sure everyone was okay," she said, pulling her red cloak a little tighter around her shoulders.

Graham shrugged. "They're okay. And they'll let us know if they aren't." He took a step back from her and surveyed her costume. "That's pretty cute on you," he said with a small grin. "Maybe we could play dress up later." He waggled his eyebrows at her.

She smiled weakly.

He studied her expression and shrugged again. "But you're not into games like that, are you?" he said, clearly not expecting an answer because he swiveled around, strode to the table and grabbed himself another black beer. He didn't bring one back for her because, as he said when he returned, she'd already had one drink that night. "And you never drink more than one at a party."

Candy giggled. "Well, I don't remember the ingredients as well as Dr. Luke. He took notes. You wouldn't believe how he listens to everything Bridget says. But I'm pretty sure there was amaretto liqueur in it, and some grated chocolate. . . ."

A few rooms away, in the large living room, Jennifer was struggling to keep drowsiness at bay. One would think that with all the spooky noises and the decoration overload it'd be easy to stay awake, but the green Kool-Aid (aka: "Witch's Brew") was at least 50 percent tequila. When mixed with the monotony of Michael's conversation—he *really* hated this party—the effect was like NyQuil.

For what felt like an hour and a half, he lamented the lost evening, during which he would have rather been at home playing gin rummy with the girls, grading Spanish quizzes or, alternately, cleaning the garage. Then he complained of headaches, which Jennifer could empathize with because the music was . . . odd. Loud, pulsating and far from mainstream.

"Where did they get this awful mix CD?" Michael grumbled, the most recent Halloween "song" coming to a crescendo with screeches that sounded like cats undergoing electrocution.

"No idea," Jennifer murmured as the next selection began to a weirdly syncopated beat. She heard someone else in the room joke that it was by Beauty and the Beastie Boys, and she would have laughed at that except Michael's discontent kept her from so much as cracking a smile.

Michael checked his watch for probably the eighty-seventh time in the past half hour. "It's after eleven," he said. "Veronica should've put Evan and Keaton to bed by now." He held out his palm. "Hand me your phone, would'ya? I'm just gonna give them a quick ring. Make sure they got the tent up and everything's okay." The boys were having a campout in the basement of the house until the party was over, and Cassandra was crashing in a sleeping bag on Shelby's bedroom floor.

Jennifer fought to keep her expression neutral. "Oh, sorry. I forgot to charge it, so the battery died. Don't you have yours with you?"

He shook his head. "I forgot it at home, but I figured it was all right because you *always* have yours with you." Then, because his irritation had eclipsed his good nature and logic had long since fled, he added, in an especially pissy voice, "How the hell are the kids supposed to get a hold of us if we don't have a working phone?"

She took a deep breath. "Don't worry. I told Bridget about it as soon as I realized there was a problem. If anything comes up, the kids will just call her number, but I'm really not wor—"

"Well, *I'm* worried. Look around this house. It's huge. It's filled with people. Bridget and her working cell phone could be anywhere in it." He swiveled from side to side, glancing wildly around them for emphasis. "Right *now* they could be having an emergency and we wouldn't even know it!"

Jennifer tried to speak calmly. "I saw Bridget by the refreshments table not that long ago. I'll go check with her, okay? I'm sure she's talked with the kids and—"

"No, I'll go," Michael said with a huff. "And, swear to God, I'm not staying one minute past midnight. I don't care what the Wieners say about us."

She downed the last of her Witch's Brew as he strode out of the room and, figuring the coast would be clear for at least five minutes, moved to a semiprivate corner to turn on her phone and check for text messages.

There were seven more. All from David.

She blinked at the tiny screen and tried to shield it from the sight of the other guests wandering past her. She knew she should just delete them, unread. But, like a four-car pileup at the end of the interstate, she couldn't help but look. Couldn't stop herself from clicking on each one.

The first message was a clear continuation of the Goldilocks story—David style—that he'd begun earlier in the night: *She was tired of being a good grl. Just Say No to more rules.*

Then: *She snuck in2 the house like a school grl in knee highs & a shrt skirt. Little did she know she'd emerge a woman.*

Jennifer swallowed and scanned the edges of the room for signs of Michael. Still clear. Next message: *She searched til she found something v. tasty.*

Then: *She bit and sucked and licked. . . . Goldilocks was rly good w. her mouth.*

Oh, God. David was such a piece of work. How was it that he always knew how to punch her buttons? He could drive her crazy and turn her on in the same breath. Such a disconcerting quality.

Message number five: *In her excitmnt she broke a few things in the house. Bad grls shd be punished—shdn't they?*

Jennifer blushed. Then: *She turned on the bedrm radio &* "Sister Golden Hair" *was playing. The music made her sleepy so she crawld in2 bed.*

And, finally: *Like the song, she knew someone whod been a poor correspondent & whod been 2 . . . 2 . . . hard 2 find. She dreamd abt him.*

And that made seven. She wished there'd been another installment of the story for her to read. But the flurry of messages had begun earlier in the night, and the last one was time-stamped over a half hour ago. David must've given up on getting a response back from her and gone to bed.

A bit reluctantly, she deleted the messages. She was about to turn off the phone completely again when she spotted Michael's distinctive Bear costume across the room. Not having time to do more than shove the phone into her purse before he reached her, she did that first. "You found Bridget?" she asked, probably too brightly. She stuck her hand into the purse, sniffed loudly and pretended to root around for a tissue.

He nodded. "The kids are fine." His underlying subtext, however, was *No thanks to you.* "Veronica is behaving herself. She and the boys watched some old Indiana Jones movie before they went to bed. Shelby and Cassandra are bonding over video games."

She ignored his tone. "Good." She sniffed again, snatched a tissue with one hand and, without pulling her phone out of her purse, nestled the phone in the padded pocket without looking, just so it wouldn't bump up against any noisy keys or anything and make buzzing sounds if it vibrated again. She feigned blowing her nose. "Did you want to go outside at all? There's a fire pit in the backyard. Some people are roasting marshmallows."

"No." He took a step backward and managed to bump into a woman dressed as the Little Mermaid. "Oh, sorry. Sorry," he told her. He unzipped the part of his furry costume nearest his neck and inhaled. "This thing is so hot." He fanned himself, and perhaps Jennifer was reading too much into it, but there seemed to be a sense of accusation toward her even in that simple gesture. She had, after all, chosen the costumes along with Tamara and Bridget. The Woodsman outfit was most austere, and the Prince outfit more attractive. However, both were "cooler"—in multiple senses of the word—than the Bear. Clearly, on top of all her other faults, she was culpable for bad costume judgment, too.

"I'm feeling a little warm myself," she whispered, thinking about the suggestive fairy tale David had been texting to her. "Do you want me to get you some more beer?"

Michael made a face. "No."

They fell silent for a few moments, although the room around them was alive with activity. Someone had turned up the volume on the spooky mix CD of questionable origin. A couple of woodland creatures were doing the Monster Mash around a leather sofa. And a clique nearby, consisting of Sleeping Beauty, Snow White and Rose Red, were having an inane discussion on the merits of Maybelline Crimson Crush lipstick for keeping their lips "extra red."

Snow White brushed a strand of black-wig hair away from her very fair complexion and pursed her lips for her friends to examine. "See?" she said. "It's the reddest of all."

The Little Mermaid walked by again, rolled her eyes and mouthed, "Mirror, mirror," at Jennifer, which made her laugh for the first time in over two hours.

Michael, apparently startled by the sound of her merriment, took a quick step to the side and banged his shin against a sharp-edged coffee table. "Dammit!"

"Are you okay?" she asked him.

He rubbed his fingers against his injured leg and shook his head. "I think I feel blood."

She winced. "Maybe you should go to the bathroom and check it out. Take off the costume and, if there's a scratch, clean it up.

Here—" She dug into her purse again and retrieved a couple of Band-Aids. "Take these with you."

"Fine," he said, his irritation and self-involvement reminding her of a five-year-old who'd scraped his knee on the playground. He glanced at his watch again. "Thank God this is almost over."

She exhaled as soon as he disappeared through the door and into some other part of the house. The crowd in the living room had begun to thin the closer it got to midnight. More of the guests congregated out back, and Leah, Kip and Kip's police-chief brother busied themselves setting up a structure of some kind near the fire pit.

She pulled out her phone to check for new messages. One!

Jennifer hadn't felt it vibrate, but it was David again. She grinned.

She glanced around her, taking in the scene and wondering how long she had before Michael returned this time. That she was annoyed with him by now was a given. That she was exasperated with his attitude and his klutziness was, likewise, undeniable. That his company bored her when he was in one of these moods was a reality of her married life. The thing she hadn't anticipated, however, was that the mere reminder of David's existence heightened her dissatisfaction. That her ex's playfulness was too much of an emotional contrast in a situation that—with her husband—was stressful and frustrating just on its own.

Granted, David wasn't actually *at* the party. In person, maybe he wouldn't have been any fun. Maybe he, too, would've protested that the gathering was "so unrealistic," like Michael had done earlier, despite the obviousness that it *wasn't supposed to be* realistic. Maybe he would've been offended by the gruesomeness of the upcoming "beheading" and, like Michael, preferred the syrupy sweetness of the Disney versions of the fairy tales as opposed to the gritty violence of the Grimm Brothers' originals.

But she doubted it.

David didn't claim to have the "heart of a poet," so sarcastic humor, earthiness and overt cynicism were natural fixtures in his social toolbox. And, certainly, David had unleashed his share of foul moods in her presence but, at the Hallowiener Party, she could've used a dash of jesting from her husband. The tiny measure of levity she got, she got only from her old boyfriend.

She clicked to read David's text: *The man in Goldilocks's dream is real & he does unspeakably sexy things 2 her in Big Bear's bed. Wanna know what they R?*

Oh, boy.

She wished she had more of that green Witch's Brew. She licked the rim of her glass for the last few droplets and was about to shut off her phone again when it vibrated in her hand.

Not a text this time. A phone call.

David.

Meanwhile, in the Wieners' library loft, her Rapunzel skirt pushed up to her knees, Tamara sat languorously on the carpeted floor, leaned back against the smooth mahogany bookshelf and worked her way through yet another Poisoned Appletini. And while she had lost track (some two hours ago) of just how many she'd had to drink, she was pretty sure she hadn't eaten anything since Bridget's oatmeal-raisin cookie. Good thing she could hold her liquor so well, huh?

She slapped Aaron on his chest with the back of her outstretched palm. Whoa. Solid muscle. How freaky! She laughed at his surprise. "So, w-why'd you start getting into marathons and s-stuff?" she slurred. "Bored at home?"

"Triathlons," Aaron corrected, sliding a couple of inches closer to her from his spot on the floor. "I can do all *three* events. Swim, bike *and* run. I'm talented that way."

"You are," Tamara agreed. "You surely are. I can just play tennis."

Aaron guzzled his sixth (at least) inky black beer. "But I bet'cha you're *great* at it. 'Cuz you're, you know"—he studied her legs with obvious appreciation—"tall."

"Exactly," she said, impressed by Aaron's perceptiveness. He was *such* a good friend to her. She didn't have a lot of good guy friends. Just Aaron . . . and Al. And Al had been kind of avoiding her lately. Well, her phone calls. Sort of. She understood it, though. He wasn't trying to be mean to her or anything. He even explained it. That his grief overwhelmed him when he dwelled on Aunt Eliza's death, and he dwelled on it when he talked for too long with Tamara. So, for the sake of his old, aching heart and for the sake of his worried children and grandchildren, he was making an effort to lighten up a little. To get out a bit more. To start the process of moving on.

She sighed. This grief stuff was *so* exhausting. That was why it was good to just relax. In a quiet, comfortable place. With a friend and a drink . . . or seven.

Every so often, some couple or small group would climb the stairs to the library loft and talk to them for a few minutes. A few partygoers even nabbed extra drinks for them. People could be so *nice* sometimes. One couple even brought them a few Spider Sandwiches. Aaron had one, but Tamara couldn't bring herself to eat it. Who knew what Leah put in there? Maybe they weren't just *shaped* like spiders. It'd be just like Leah to stuff them with real black widows.

Aaron asked her about her favorite story as a child, which was funny because it involved spiders.

"Charlotte's Web," she told him.

He nodded. "I liked that one, too. It's about the cycle of life, and how precious our friendships are." He took another chug of beer. "How they give us meaning. And hope."

This, she decided, was a *really deep* thing to say. But, before she could come up with an equally philosophical point for Aaron to ponder, too, Jon—to her astonishment—staggered into the room.

Her husband took in the sight of her sitting on the floor next to their neighbor, surrounded by their collection of empty martini glasses and empty beer cups. He looked confused and oddly displaced without his mayoral sidekick, but no less arrogant.

So Tamara said, "Hey, there you are. Where'd you hide Rumpelstiltskin?"

"Probably in a very small, windowless room," Aaron suggested thoughtfully before Jon had a chance to answer. "Spinning straw into gold."

Tamara giggled at Aaron's extremely clever comment, and

added, "That's the only way he'll get enough money to pass his stupid referendum."

Aaron thought this was a hilarious response (because—c'mon—everyone knew Mayor West was a pain in the ass, always wanting to raise taxes for his pet projects), but Jon narrowed his eyes at both of them. "Lower your voice, Tamara."

She shrugged and slurped a little more of her Appletini. "So are you having a good time? Getting in lots of n-networking?"

"I've talked with a few people, yeah," Jon said, his Prince crown resting high on his head and his pose making him appear particularly regal. "Men who make things happen in our community." The expression on his face indicated that Aaron wasn't one of those men, and that Tamara—due to the inescapable fact that she was female—was incapable of "making things happen" in their community or, indeed, anywhere.

Huh. Well, fuck that.

Tamara eyed Aaron, whose Prince crown was tilted at a precarious angle and in danger of sliding right off. She was tempted to reach out and straighten it for him, but there was something odd about doing so while her husband was standing there. She couldn't figure out why at the moment, though. She did glance from one guy to the other . . . the same sex and, yet, so different. "Look! Two Princes." She rested her head against the bookshelf and sighed. "There are lots of you out there tonight," she murmured, wondering vaguely how any woman was supposed to choose the right prince when there were so many masquerading as the real deal.

Aaron, who'd been handed an Appletini a half hour ago that he hadn't yet gotten around to drinking, ignored both Jon's insinuations and Tamara's mutterings and took a taster sip. "Not bad," he pronounced. Then he dumped about a quarter of his black beer into it and swirled the two beverages together with the apple slice. "This is a magical potion. A good-health elixir."

"It looks disgusting," Jon commented. And even Tamara couldn't help but silently agree.

"Looks can be deceiving," Aaron said, swigging half his potion. "I spend my life helping men improve their *look*, but really"—he shrugged—"really, it's futile. Really, the truth is"—he leaned forward toward Jon in a sagacious, rumor-divulging mode—"there's no special formula. There's no big secret. A guy can dress up, slap on some expensive aftershave, work out with a trainer four times a week and gel the hell out of his hair, but it won't matter because, in the end . . . All. Will. Be. Revealed. The kind of people who resent you when you're successful will resent you even more if you look good doing it. The kind of people who are there for you when the stock portfolios are down will still be there for you no matter what you're wearing. You can't fool anyone worth fooling. Not for long."

Jon squinted at him, trying to make sense of their neighbor's alcohol-infused logic. Jon had been drinking, too, but not as much as either Aaron or Tamara, so maybe that was what prevented him from making the associate leap. Or, maybe, he just didn't *get it* because he said with a sneer, "Who are *you* trying to fool?"

"No one!" Aaron laughed uproariously. "No one at all."

Jon stood there and shook his head. "Whatever," he told them just before Judge Rhinelander burst into the room, breathless from the climb up the stairs and flushed from too many surreptitious nips of brandy from his hidden trench coat flask.

"The beheading's gonna start, Jon!" the judge exclaimed. "Wanna help?"

Jon suddenly looked excited, like a schoolboy asked to play at the arcade or something. "Of course." Sparing Aaron and Tamara barely a parting glance, he stumbled out of the room even faster than he'd entered it, and took the palpable tension he'd created with him.

Tamara giggled—because what else could she do? This whole thing was ridiculous. What had she been thinking before? Giving marriage to the *real man* a try, not just the *vision* she'd created? What bullshit. Neither the real man nor her vision of him wanted to spend any time with her.

She looked out of the floor-to-ceiling windows to either side. The library loft was ideally situated to expose extensive second-floor views of both the front and back yards. So, even from the floor, if she glanced left, she could see the walkway leading up to the front door, lit with Halloween horrors. If she glanced right, she could spy the fire pit out back, some weird platform or something next to it (complete with a chopping block and a glistening ax, like from one of those atrocious English period dramas they always showed on PBS) and an ever-growing crowd of people gathering around the hosts.

"D'ya wanna see it?" Aaron asked her, pointing toward the right window. "You don't have to stay in here with me or anything. You can go watch Jon, uh, help murder someone."

She giggled again. "I don't think so. But"—she rested her hands on her queasy abdomen—"I think maybe I should eat something."

Aaron nodded, scanned the room and, with some effort, pushed himself to standing. His gaze fixed on a number of foil-wrapped items taped to the wall. He grabbed a couple of them, peeled away the colorful wrapper on a chocolate ghoul and offered it to her. "Start with this," he said, popping it into her mouth. Then he unwrapped one for himself and sank to the floor again.

"Thanks," she whispered, strangely happy to be right there, on the carpet, eating chocolate with him. She had a bad habit of not taking time to appreciate her blessings—maybe everyone was that way—but it was easier to see this flaw in herself when she was drunk, and she wasn't going to make the same mistake that night. "Thanks," she said again, "for being such good company. You've made the evening a lot more fun for me."

"For me, too," he said, but she wasn't sure if he meant it or if he was just being polite.

"And, um, sorry about Jon," she said, finding it was always easier to smooth over her husband's gaffes when he was no longer in the room. "He probably seemed kind of rude. He's not really acquainted with people in creative professions, so—"

"S'okay." Aaron waved off her attempt at an explanation. "I've heard all the insinuations before, Tamara. From raised eyebrows to more overt criticisms. One of Isabelle's work pals said I had a stay-at-home-mom life and another informed me that he *knew* I was really just eating pizza and watching ESPN all day. So, I've dealt with sneers from men besides your husband. Anyway, I meant what I said. I'm not trying to fool anyone. You can't impress people by being some glossed-over version of yourself. The truth comes out. The inner slob is always exposed."

"Or the vain workaholic," Tamara muttered, thinking of her husband.

Aaron exhaled and gazed steadily at her. He didn't comment.

Finally, he broke eye contact and nodded toward the right window. "Can you see what bizarre thing they're doing outside now?"

From what Tamara could tell, Kip and Leah were the reigning King and Queen (though still in their Cinderella story Goth-wear), and they were presiding over the ritualistic killing of the Big Bad Wolf, an honorary sacrificial reenactment, featuring Kip's brother the Wolf/Chief as the symbolic victim. *Bizarre* didn't begin to describe it.

"It's like the worst of the original fairy tales pimped out with Halloween macabre," she said. "I'm *not* going out there."

Aaron shrugged. "Fine with me. Guess we'd better eat more chocolate then." He nabbed another candy from the wall, ripped off the foil and fed it to her.

Back by the refreshments table, Candy and her husband left the room to find a good spot for the show in the backyard, and Graham, not willing to head out of doors without another black beer for sustenance, slid away from Bridget's side.

"I'm just gonna get a refill," Graham said, holding up his cup, "and say hi to Nick over there."

Bridget said, "All right," and watched as he strode over to another of his construction pals and slapped his back.

She stood by the edge of the table, still within hearing distance of her husband, but choosing to zone out a little now that it was so close to midnight. She'd been appropriately social and pleasant all night, but she realized too late that she hadn't explored any room beyond this one and, in fact, hadn't been out of Graham's eyesight for the whole evening. Not that she would have done anything more devious than poke around the Wieners' house (and, okay, maybe take a quick peek in their pantry—not in their medicine cabinet, though!), but it kind of bothered her that she had been so predictable. That she had let herself get harassed by the ballet instructors, hadn't gossiped about anything worth the effort and basically acted like a surrogate hostess whenever someone had a question about the party food.

Not for the first time (or even the first fifty times) that night, she wished Dr. Luke would have been there. Maybe she would have been able to chat with him in another room, like the kitchen. Maybe they would have inspected the Wieners' cookbook collection or checked out their hanging copper saucepans. Maybe he would have spoken *to* her, not *at* her, and she would have been able to lose her self-consciousness in the joy of that.

She tugged at her red cloak until it rested warmly against her shoulders and adjusted her hood. Then she glanced one last time at the table. She and Graham were going to have to go outside in a minute if they wanted to catch the final, gory act of the evening.

She looked at her husband, who was still talking with his friend, reached for a wall chocolate out of habit, then pulled her arm back. No! She wasn't going to blindly grab more junk food. She just *wasn't*. But a cold voice next to her made her jump.

"What? Did the skeleton on the wall scare you? Tell you not to eat anything unless it was *Italian?*" said that frightful voice, and Bridget realized it belonged to none other than Dr. Nina, who'd dressed herself up as Glenda the Good Witch. Yeah. At least she got the witch part right.

Bridget said, "Um," but mostly stared at her. It was odd to even hear the woman speak. The female dentist had spent the past two weeks ignoring her so completely in the office that Bridget had begun to believe she was invisible to Dr. Nina, like an audience member was to a lead performer when the houselights were out and the show was in progress. Glendale Grove's very own production of *Wicked*.

"I talked to my sister Nancy this week," Dr. Nina said loudly. "She said she'd met you downtown. Ran into you and Dr. Luke having lunch together. Said the two of you looked *awfully cozy* for not being related." Her ice-chip eyes pierced Bridget with their frigidity, her narrow lips thinning to painted horizontal lines two inches above her pointy white chin.

This knowledge of Nina's was a revelation to Bridget. Until that moment, she hadn't gotten any vibes from the Witch that clandestine behavior at the dental group was suspected by anyone. Perhaps Bridget and Dr. Luke had been oblivious to the signals they were sending. Perhaps they had been a subject of office gossip without being aware of it. But, still, they were hardly lewd. So what if they chatted a lot? They were friends. Friends talked to each other.

She opened her mouth to tell Dr. Nina this, but the other woman beat her to the punch.

"Oh, I know you both think you're being subtle, but it's a slippery slope, Little Red Riding Hood. Better watch who's riffling through your basket of goodies." Dr. Nina pivoted away from the table, clearly intending to march away, while Bridget was tempted to fling the contents of a Poisoned Appletini at her in hopes that she'd melt. But, to both their surprise, another voice joined the conversation.

"Hey there," Graham said to Dr. Nina, a black beer and a wienie on a toothpick in his left hand, his right hand extended out to her. "Don't think I know you. I'm Graham, Bridget's husband."

Dr. Nina's eyes grew wide and a cloud of some emotion—possibly regret, but Bridget wouldn't bet on it—passed over the woman's face. She swallowed and shook Graham's callused hand with her bony one. "I'm Dr. Nina Brockman-Lew—" She cut herself off and her stiff posture slackened for a moment. "Nina Brockman," she corrected. "It's very nice to . . ." She stopped and sighed. "Oh, hell. Are those things spiked?" She pointed to the green tequila-infused Kool-Aid cups.

Graham nodded. "Sure are."

"Thanks." Nina grabbed one and beat a hasty retreat. Which left Graham and Bridget facing each other with nothing but a basket, a bloody wienie and a black beer between them.

The expression of hurt on her husband's face left her with no doubt that he'd overheard Dr. Nina's allegations. Graham set down his toxic-looking beverage, tossed out the ketchup-dripping snack and turned slowly back to her. "So, you went downtown . . . with another guy? That gay dentist from your office?"

Before Bridget could consider the implication of her words, she blurted in exasperation, "Dr. Luke is *not* gay."

Graham leveled a serious look at her. "Exactly. Sounds like you got lots of little secrets at that office of yours." He paused. "What the hell else has been going on over there that I don't know about?"

The Emperor, still wearing only a crown and those beige briefs, burst into the room with the pronouncement, "The ceremony's starting, everyone!"

Bridget said, "We should talk, Graham. But please—could we do it at home?"

Her husband nodded, the flash of distress in his eyes causing her to feel a scarlet wave of shame as they rushed out of the room. He said, "Yep. Let's get this dumb show over with so we can go."

With a heart full of dread and a silent prayer to the God she felt she'd been disobeying lately (in hopes He would help her anyway), Bridget agreed and followed Graham to the backyard.

In the living room, Jennifer felt the vibration of the phone in her palm and knew David waited on the other end of the line. With Michael still in the bathroom, she figured she'd have at least a few minutes to talk. And she needed to tell David to stop the constant messaging. That was how she talked herself into answering.

"What do you think you're doing?" she told him, cowering in an empty corner of the room, which suddenly seemed much more open considering the mass exodus outside.

"I've been thinking about you," David said simply. "What'cha doing now, Goldilocks? Have any porridge at the party?"

"No. Just an oatmeal-raisin cookie. And kind of a weird green drink."

"Sounds like frat party wackiness. I'm betting you got in some damn good people-watching tonight."

"Yeah," she said, glad someone could understand the incredible level of information overload that hit an introvert like her at one of these gatherings. And how she felt about the social element of it, too. She couldn't lose herself in an event like this, not the way

Tamara could. Nor could she interact in some sweet and meaning-ful way one-on-one like Bridget. No. She could only watch the spectacle like the outsider she was and try to withstand the three-hour-long pummeling. Had Michael truly been *company* for her that night, and not merely another source of tedium, maybe she could have carved out an itty-bitty niche of enjoyment despite the cacophony. But neither "fitting in" nor "fun" were in the cards for her this time.

"Do you have a minute? Can you tell me about it? I miss seeing the world through your window, Jenn."

In spite of her frustration with the evening and her irritation with him for his text intrusions, she agreed. "Fine. But *only* for a minute." She described the trio of lipstick ladies she had over-heard earlier, complete with conversational snippets. She gave him a ten-second rundown of the Wieners and the other party guests in their fairy-tale costumes. And she explained the setup for the "be-heading ceremony" set to begin any moment.

David laughed on the line, injecting a previously absent bolt of amusement into her night. "Thank you," he said when, really, for this tiny sliver of delight he had passed along, she felt she should be thanking *him*. "That was hilarious. I know you need to go. I just don't wanna stop talking to you."

She sighed. "I don't want to stop talking to you either, but this needs to be the end of our conversations for tonight. No more calls. No more texting. Okay?"

There was a long pause on the line. "Okay, Jenn. But just tell me one last thing. You're coming to the reunion for sure, right? Ab-solutely positively for sure? Your husband knows about it and everything?"

It was her turn to pause. She'd kept that weekend clear, yes, but she still hadn't mentioned the reunion to Michael. A noisy group of revelers skipped by, so she walked deeper into the corner, brought the phone closer to her left ear and plugged her right ear with her fingers. "I haven't talked with him about it yet, but I'm coming. I promise. And I'm going to tell him all about it. Soon."

"I'm counting on that," he told her and, indeed, she could de-tect an edge of desperation in his tone. "Without Marcia and the boys here to distract me, I've been alone with my thoughts. And, I know it's my fault and everything, but there are some seriously unresolved things between us, Jenn."

"Look, David. Now's not the time to—"

"I know. I know. You don't have time right this second to discuss this. I get that. But I just wanna know that we *are* going to discuss it. I can't wait another eighteen years, babe." His voice sounded ragged and more tired than she'd thought when he added, "Listen, you were always *my* golden-haired girl. I keep on thinking about you. . . . And I need to see you again."

"You will. I'll be there in a few weeks."

"Good. G'night, Jenn. Be careful which bed you fall asleep in, okay?"

She laughed. "Okay, David. Bye."

She clicked off the phone and exhaled a long slow breath, but she didn't even have a chance to turn around before hearing the growl of the Bear as he cleared his throat behind her. As she swiveled to face him, it would have been impossible to miss the steady, infuriated look on his face. In the animal kingdom, it would have been the deadly silence of preattack. Michael, no longer hiding in his cave and licking his wounds, was not remotely klutzy for once. He deftly stepped around the coffee table, narrowed his eyes at her and said, "You told me the battery needed to be charged, Jennifer. Quite an interesting conversation to have on a dead cell phone."

Oh, crap.

Alone in the library loft, Tamara and Aaron still sat on the floor, the dim glow of the jack-o'-lanterns painting thin streams of golden light on the walls of the otherwise darkened room. A few other candles had burned down to stubs, too, creating the warm cocoon of a fireplace, and she and Aaron remained in the middle, like those final smoldering embers.

Aaron, concentrating intently on the delicate process of building a series of card houses and one multistoried tower in the space between them from one of Kip's card decks, murmured, "Could'ya help me add a wall to my fire department?"

Tamara picked up a card and let it hover dangerously above one of the card fixtures. "Where do you want it?"

"No, not there. That's the library. Here." He pointed to an empty spot on the carpet. "I'm just starting to build it."

She snorted. "What're you doing? Making an entire village? Should we grab some of Leah's Precious Moments kiddies to populate it? Maybe a couple who could stand in for the Wieners and give fund-raising orders?"

"You're laughin' now," he said seriously, "but you're gonna be blown away by my kingdom."

"I think you mean your kingdom is gonna be blown away. Just one big gust of wind and—"

"You wouldn't dare," he said, shooting her a threatening look.

"Oh, yeah? I'm gonna huff . . ." She took a deep breath and leaned forward mockingly, but the unnaturally high level of oxygen threw off what little sense of balance she had left, and she had to pull away from her jest and sink back against the bookshelf. "Why is the room spinning?"

"Because we're on a planet that rotates," he said reasonably. "The earth spins on its axis, making day into night and night into day. And sometimes"—he squinted through one of the windows—"they all kinda blend together."

She tried to follow his gaze out the window. He seemed to be staring at the moon, but when she strained to look through the one to their left, she saw Jennifer scurrying after Michael down the front walkway. Why would they be leaving before the big horrific event? Not that she blamed them, but still. That was odd.

She glanced out the other window where everyone else had congregated, and she spotted Bridget and Graham in the back, although they were standing about a yard apart from each other. Then she saw Jon playacting some role in the ceremony. A palace guard or something, given his princely status. She rolled her eyes and, finally, just squeezed them shut. She couldn't stand to witness any more of that chilling outdoor affair but, inside, she wasn't sure if she could trust what she was seeing either.

She'd passed from *pretty buzzed* into *unequivocally drunk* an hour ago at least, so everything was very, very fuzzy. With her eyes closed, though, she could let the sensations swirl around within her, not making her nearly as dizzy as when she tried to focus on any one thing. Or any one person.

"I knew you wouldn't wreck my village," Aaron confided, knocking all of his card houses over with a sweep of his arm and gathering the cards back into a deck. "You're not a d-destroyer. You're really nice." He laughed briefly. "I hadn't expected that, actually, since I met Jon first."

Most people, unless they were very drunk, weren't honest with her about their first impressions of her husband, which were almost always negative. When Aaron moved into the neighborhood last year, she could see the wariness in Aaron's eyes when Jon introduced them. Maybe she'd tried to be extra nice to Aaron at first because he was so transparent in his caution. Or maybe it was because there was something very much anti-Jon about him. Two very different Princes . . .

"Appearances can be deceiving, remember?" she told him. "S-So can relationships."

She sensed Aaron was struggling to extract her meaning as he balanced the card deck on top of an empty Appletini glass and inched his body over by hers. Soon, he was sitting so close to her that his princely robes touched her peasant blouse. This made her breath inexplicably quicken and, as she shook her head to try to break the enchantment, one of her long Rapunzel braids flopped forward and grazed his elbow.

He lifted it up, the fake strands gingerly pinched between two of his fingers. "This isn't you. I wanna see your real hair." He dropped the braid. "I *like* your real hair."

"Yeah?" She blinked at him, the irritation and general discomfort of the wig suddenly poking through her consciousness. She couldn't wait to be rid of it and began to peel it off just as the library's grandfather clock struck midnight, the chimes reverberating through the entire wing of the house, empty except for the two of them.

Aaron glanced at his watch. "That's weird. I've got five-past-twelve. The Wieners' clock is off."

"Or yours is," Tamara shot back, finally freeing her auburn

waves from the confinement of their bobby pins and the itchy heat of the Rapunzel wig. There were so many mixed up fairy-tale symbols in the house, she'd long since lost track of which should go with which story. In her head and outside it, it was all chaos and disorder—nothing was certain or logical except for her determination not to pretend anymore.

He tugged off his watch and handed it to her. "It's totally right. You check it out later." Then he heaved off his Prince crown and ran his fingers through his blond hair. "'Uneasy lies the head that wears a crown,'" he quoted, grinning at her. "I'm sick of that thing."

She giggled. "A man who can recite from *Henry IV* even when he's drunk? Who are you, Aaron?"

"I'm your neighbor," he said. "'Do onto your neighbor as you would have them do onto you.' Or something like that."

"Isn't it supposed to be "unto" you?"

"Not in my book, and certainly not tonight."

Tamara wasn't quite sure how to take that, so she just said, "First Shakespeare and now warped biblical references? Way to go, show-off."

"But I'm not a show-off. I'm not trying to impress anyone," he insisted, looking closely at her, his fingertips skimming through the twisted ends of her real hair, his tongue darting out to wet his lips, his body flush against hers.

In a moment she couldn't have anticipated until a couple of seconds before it happened, he closed the gap between them and touched his wet lips to her dry ones. The swirl of sensation she'd experienced before intensified and deepened with his kiss. It was like the sounds and the colors and the scents became pulses of feeling. All of her sensory input was channeled into the minute indentations of their lips pressed together in the semidarkness. She wanted to live forever in that tiny but infinitely wonderful space.

Some jolt of sound, however—a cry from outside as the ax swung down upon the hapless Wolf?—distracted them both. For Tamara it was merely a momentary intrusion. She turned her face up toward Aaron's again. But he stopped and pulled away from her.

"Oh, my God," he murmured. "I'm sorry. I can't fucking believe I did that."

He groaned and wrenched himself off the carpeted floor, strode toward the door and stumbled down the stairs. She had no idea where he went or if he'd be back, but she felt the bitterness of his absence immediately. The last of the light and the warmth was sucked from the room.

She still clutched Aaron's watch in her hand a half hour (maybe more?) later when Jon prodded her to standing. "Time to go home, wench," her husband said with the voice of vague boredom, although she supposed he was trying to be amusing. She was aware of trailing after him to their car and dozing off on the short drive home. She did not see Aaron's car in his driveway or any lights on in his house when they passed by, and she was too tired to fight her way through the mental confusion of the evening before bed.

But as she slipped Aaron's watch into her skirt pocket, a motion unseen by Jon, she knew she wouldn't have to check the time for accuracy. Numbers were meaningless. Half the watch's face might as well read "Before" and the other half "After."

She was now living in the After.

❧ 17 ❧

After Midnight

Sunday, October 31

Bridget and Graham drove in silence to Jennifer and Michael's house to pick up their kids, the goriness of the show still making Bridget shudder involuntarily, even though she knew it was all fake blood and feigned screams.

Graham, who had been studying her from a safe distance ever since he overheard Dr. Nina's comments, didn't press her for an explanation yet, which she appreciated. She'd tell him the truth about her luncheon with Dr. Luke, of course—nothing had happened!—but there were other issues they ought to discuss. And, really, Bridget had no idea how to form those clusters of dissatisfaction into coherent and, above all, fair talking points.

The drive was short and, when they got there, their visit even shorter. Jennifer sat on the front steps, as if waiting for them. She was still in her Goldilocks costume, and she looked paler than normal. Bridget was about to ask if she was feeling all right and if Michael was there, but Jennifer wasn't wasting time with chitchat.

"The kids are all asleep," Jennifer whispered. "Even Cassandra and Shelby dozed off. So why don't you let them all stay overnight? No need to wake everybody up. We'll send them home first thing in the morning, okay?"

"Are you sure?" Bridget said. "Having three extra children in your house is a lot of wor—"

"I'm sure," Jennifer interrupted. And there was such an acutely distraught look in her eyes that Bridget didn't dare disagree. "You two have a nice night. A romantic one," Jennifer continued with a very forced-looking smile. "I'll talk to you later."

Then, with a quick squeeze of Bridget's arm that seemed to implore her to *"Go,"* Jennifer waved them off and hurried into her house.

Bridget glanced at Graham.

He swallowed and said, "Well, okay then. Let's go home." He gazed at her sadly. "I'll put on some coffee and we can talk."

She nodded, and when they got home, she had steeled her resolve to be as open and as honest as she possibly could. Graham was her *husband*, after all. Sure, he could be frustrating, and so often she felt as though he didn't see her, but he didn't deserve to be lied to. Or even to have information withheld from him.

She tugged off her red cloak, sat down at the kitchen table and faced him. "I'm sorry," she began. "I should've told you about Dr. Luke asking me to lunch. It was just as a thank-you for the meals I brought into the office, and nothing at all happened between us," she hastened to assure him. "But I still could've mentioned it, and I didn't."

"Why?" Graham asked her. "Why didn't you mention it? D'ya think I wouldn't care? Or that I'd care too much?"

"I'm not sure," she confessed. "Both of those possibilities scared me." She studied the tight line of his jaw, the worried creases on his forehead. "What *would* you have thought?"

"I would've wanted to know why he asked you out. His intentions, you know? And what yours were when you said yes to it. If it'd just been some meal with a friend, you wouldn't have hidden it." He shrugged. "So, what I would've thought—and what I *do* think—is that there's more to the story, Bridget. And that, even if nothing happened, you've got some kind of *thing* for this guy." He glanced away from her. "Coffee's ready."

She bit her lip. "Graham, I—" She watched him pour a cup for each of them, but she couldn't bring herself to drink any of hers yet. "There isn't a *thing*. We're really just frien—"

"Yeah, yeah. 'Just friends.' I heard you before. But, hold that thought for a sec and tell me something. Where'd the idea to add extra work hours come from? You suddenly were thinking we needed more money? You were already planning on changing up your work schedule just a couple of months after you started? Why didn't you tell me about *those* plans?"

She knew she had to tread carefully over this issue or he'd be insulted. Graham had always been a good and solid provider, but they weren't swimming in extra cash. And they had needs as a family now that they hadn't in years past. "No, honey, I'm not changing anything yet. I was asked about it, but I hadn't really explored the idea a whole lot. At first I thought Dr. Jim and Dr. Luke approached me about going full time just to be nice or, maybe, because they liked my cooking. But they've brought it up a few different times now, and they seem serious about wanting someone in the office who's almost always there. Plus, one of the other receptionists is pregnant and likely to reduce her hours in a few months."

Her husband raised his eyebrows at this. "Oh?"

Bridget felt a fresh jab of guilt. She had known about Pamela's pregnancy for a few weeks but hadn't mentioned this detail to Graham. She had been given the information in private and tried to convince herself that she hadn't wanted to break Pamela's confidence by blabbing about it. Of course, that was a total excuse. Pamela would have understood her need to discuss the idea with her husband. Really, Bridget had just wanted to wait because, well, up until now, Graham hadn't really been listening to her.

"Anyway," she continued, "I wouldn't have agreed to anything without talking with you first. I was just trying to figure out how many expenses we might have coming up balanced against my duties with the kids at home. I don't want to shortchange them on either time or experiences."

Graham crossed his arms. "What do you mean?"

"I mean, if Cassandra wants to sign up for dance classes again this winter, I want her to be able to do it. Her ballet teachers think she shows a lot of promise." Bridget shrugged. Their daughter was leaner and more willowy than she'd ever been. The idea of wearing those tight and pointy toe shoes for any length of time sounded like a form of ancient foot-binding torture to Bridget, but Cassandra seemed to like it. "And Evan is having fewer and fewer stomach cramps on this new diet, so he may need special foods and some extra doctor appointments, even if we've found the solution to his problem. Then there's Keaton . . ." She just let this thought trail off because even Graham knew how Keaton always needed them to buy him new things. A new soccer uniform because he'd accidentally ripped holes in the first one. A new retainer because he'd managed to toss his old one out with his lunch one day. A new set of fine-point markers because he'd loaned out his school set and never gotten it back.

Of course, there were also her own fantasies of adding cooking school tuition to the family expense list, but she didn't mention that either. She wasn't prepared to push it too far that night.

"I want the kids to have everything they need," she told him, "but I also don't want to be so scattered between work and home responsibilities that I'm not there for them. It's been a little trickier to juggle the two this fall than I thought."

"Oh, I don't know." Graham took a big gulp of his coffee and winced. "I think you made a bunch of choices already."

Now it was Bridget's turn to ask what he meant.

"You like being at work. You're happy there. At home, you kinda zone out. I don't think I've ever seen you spend half as much time trying to impress *us* as you do the people in your office. Although all your efforts don't seem to be winning over that witchy woman we saw tonight."

She sighed. "Dr. Nina. No."

"And what she said about you and this Luke guy"—he raised his eyebrows at her—"makes it sound like you two are kinda a couple or something. Or at least real obvious about wanting to be."

She swallowed. "That's not how it is at all. I wish you'd go in there and meet him. Then you'd see." Graham was a man of habit and still went to the same dentist he'd had as a teenager, even though that meant a forty-five-minute drive. He'd never so much as visited Smiley Dental. "I think Dr. Luke is a really nice guy.

He's funny and thoughtful and smart but not in a show-offy way. He's good at his job. And friendly. Everyone else likes him a lot, too."

Her husband's eyes narrowed. "So, he takes *everyone else* out for private lunches?"

"No," she said quickly. Then amended, "Well, I don't know, actually. I don't think so." She was finally ready for a shot of caffeine. She let the heat from the mug burn her fingertips for a moment before releasing her grip. Still too hot. "I—I appreciate him. Qualities about him, like the way he listens to me," she admitted.

"And I don't listen to you?"

Ah. There was the big question. The even bigger question was whether she was going to tell him the truth.

She forced herself to take a sip of her scalding coffee, just to stall. She wanted to shrug off Graham's query, but nothing would change if she did. And, actually, thanks to Nina's big mouth, she was beginning to see that her office behavior was, perhaps, not what she'd imagined it'd been. That through no fault of Dr. Luke's, she'd been under his spell a little bit, and maybe the only way to break the enchantment would be to speak fully and honestly to her husband about that relationship, and what it meant to her.

"You . . . you're less interested in some of the things I like to talk about," she managed to say. "I feel like I'm boring you sometimes."

"Like when?" His posture stiffened. "Like when you're describing all those weird foreign foods? Is that what you talk about so much with your dentist friend?"

She squeezed her eyes shut for a moment. "See? That's exactly what I mean. I love describing those 'weird foreign foods.' I love making them, too. But you don't want to hear about it. You don't want to eat it. You give the kids permission, by having that attitude, to treat me the same way and to be judgmental about something I'm really excited about. And, Graham, I'm sick of it." She pushed away her coffee cup and looked him in the eye. "I'm really lonely at home. I try to support all four of you, but none of you can do the same for me. I'm just wallpaper in the house most of the time. Wallpaper that does a lot of cleaning and chauffeuring. So, yeah. I don't just like going to work, I *love* it. I'm a *person* there. I'm someone that nice and smart people listen to and respect. And, no. No, you don't listen to me. And you haven't in *years*."

He stared at her silently for more seconds than she felt comfortable with, his ceramic mug weighting down his hands until he finally set it on the table. He inhaled deeply, opened his mouth to speak and then shut it. Several other seconds went by before he tried it again. "I didn't know you felt that way," he said, bowing his head. "I guess what I want out of life, my idea of a good day, is kinda simple. I do my job, come home, have a nice normal meal with my family, watch some TV and go to bed with my wife. Nothing complicated and nothing different from what I've always wanted. Maybe you need more than that. Maybe I'm holding you back from getting it."

He looked so sad sitting there, she wanted to tell him that everything was okay. That she wanted him to be just the way he was. That it'd all be all right. But that was only partially true and she'd vowed to be fully honest this time.

"Graham, you're not holding me back." She would have liked to stretch her hands across the table and grasp his, but he'd leaned away. "I made choices about what to do with my life that were based on a lot of things. Most of them I don't regret at all. I love you and the kids. I'm glad to be able to be here for you all. But they're growing up and my role in their life is changing. I need—" She hesitated, trying to think of how to explain it. "I need something more than just blindly going through my day and getting work done. I need to have beautiful-smelling flowers in my house. I need to make really interesting meals sometimes. I need to be able to be passionate about something and not have the people I love most ridicule me."

She saw him swallow and nod very slightly. "I'm sorry," he whispered. "I wasn't trying to put you down. I just wasn't—"

"I know." She sighed. "And I wasn't trying to deceive you or keep secrets from you. I was only trying to find a way to be happier. And Dr. Luke is *nice* to me. He wants to hear about appetizers like Smoked Veal and Cucumber Tartlets or Asian Asparagus Rolls."

Graham winced and then tried to mask it. She noticed anyway. "I, uh, I'm not such a big veggie fan," he said, "but w-we can try them if you want. I'll tell the kids they have to eat a couple of bites, and maybe . . . who knows? I'm sure they'll be great." He shot her a forced grin.

She laughed for the first time in hours. He was trying hard, but he looked kind of green at the idea of eating asparagus. Graham hated asparagus even more than Keaton hated shrimp. "That's okay," she told him. "I don't have to make something like that. Something I *know* you'll despise. And maybe it's too much to ask the kids to eat lots of unusual things anyway, beyond one or two new side dishes a week." She paused and finally reached across their kitchen table for his warm, rough hands. He reached back and grabbed her fingers tight. "But maybe you and I could try to have dinner out every once in a while. Maybe we could go someplace sort of romantic, where we could talk and taste-test a few new things."

"Things made with beef?" Graham asked, his tone hopeful.

"Sure," she said.

Though there were many other questions left unasked, and a great many marital issues that hadn't yet been brought to the table to discuss, this was a start. One quiet, honest moment in their own house. A moment that—at least temporarily—tore down one of the unhealthy walls of silence between them and made an attempt at repairing some of the neglect and inattention that had been dogging them for a decade or more.

And, as a pleasant side effect of their candor, it turned out they had a rather romantic night after all.

In Jennifer's neck of the Deep Dark Woods, Michael had completely shut her out. There was no chitchat over coffee at *their* kitchen table and, while she was frustrated by this, the observer in her couldn't help but analyze it. Pick it apart. Examine the implications. Why wasn't her husband doing his usual *emoting* routine? Where was the drama? The bad poetic lines?

The obvious reason was, in fact, the one he'd given her—in two short, snappish sentences—when she dared to ask him if they could talk.

"Not tonight, Jennifer. We have five children in the house," Michael said before switching on the silent treatment and closing the bedroom door in her face. She almost laughed, it was so uncharacteristic of him. Worse still, she couldn't believe she actually kind of missed his usual verbosity, even when it came in the form of his complaints.

The result of being left alone in a house full of sleeping (or silently brooding) people was that she could contemplate her mistakes at length but, for good or bad, could take no action. So she hid in the darkened living room, pushed herself into one corner of their sofa and covered her and her Goldilocks outfit with a comforter. She replayed her damning phone call with David over and over in her mind, trying to garner what Michael might have interpreted from overhearing just her side of the conversation.

Clearly, she couldn't smooth over the fact that she had lied about the phone battery needing to be charged. But to explain *why* she had lied would, likewise, mean explaining about the text messages David had sent her, even if she omitted the inappropriate innuendos of said texts. And *that* would lead to explaining about their prior months of contact . . . because an ex-boyfriend you haven't seen in almost two decades didn't suddenly have access to your cell phone number, did he?

She sighed and buried her head in the comforter. Even if Michael's ability to reason his way through these steps by the use of pure logic didn't happen immediately, eventually he'd get there. And the thought of how that would hurt him made her stomach twist and roil with anxiety.

But, were she to be completely honest with herself, there was also a live wire of excitement sparking beneath her apprehension. As with so many aspects of her life, there weren't many possible areas of change or even frequent opportunities to take simple actions that might shift the course of anything important. But this incident required it of her. She needed things to change, and the certainty that *something* would be altered, some small step taken as a result of this unfortunate incident, gave her hope enough to close her eyes and drift into an uneasy sleep.

The next morning, however, the glare of daily life, especially harsh after the relative peace of the post-midnight hours, sent the nausea and worry flooding back into her system. She had just enough time to sneak into the bedroom—where was Michael?—so she could change out of her costume and comb her hair before the kids raided the kitchen.

"Good morning," she told the children, just as the front door swung open and an exhausted-looking Michael stepped inside.

"I brought home donuts, eggs and sausage patties," he announced, speaking to the kids with jollity so fake Jennifer couldn't believe his daughters didn't comment on it. Refusing to meet her gaze, he set down his carryout bag on the kitchen counter and looked extra-intensely at the collection of children milling around the table. "Got some great stuff for you guys. Veronica, could you grab a few plates?"

"Sure, Dad," their eldest said, padding her way barefoot across the kitchen floor and retrieving enough dishware for all of them. To help, Jennifer dug through the silverware drawer and pulled out forks. She tried to hand them to Michael, but he persistently ignored her. Veronica saw her holding out the utensils, though. She eyed Jennifer strangely, but then grabbed them. "I got it, Mom."

"Thanks, honey," she murmured.

Veronica and Keaton wanted only donuts. Shelby and Evan were served the eggs and sausage (Michael made sure there were no glutens anywhere on Evan's plate). And Cassandra, preferring a donut but wanting to be like Shelby, her new role model, asked for a little of each. Jennifer poured everyone either milk or orange juice and stood to the side, watching.

Michael nabbed a vanilla-glazed long john and disappeared into the basement.

So, this was the way it was going to be.

After the kids gobbled their breakfast and Shelby and Cassandra played one last video game, Michael emerged from downstairs and swept Bridget's three children into his car. On their way out the door, he informed no one in particular that, after he dropped the kids off at their home, he was "going to run errands." A vague statement made in an odd tone of voice, one that militantly refused to ask anyone's permission. Not that she would have tried to stop him.

Jennifer exhaled when they left, not even realizing until the car had zoomed out of the driveway that she had been holding her breath.

Shelby, standing a few feet away from her, yawned loudly. "I am *so* tired."

"Only because you were up playing World of Warcraft until *forever*," her big sister said, snickering.

Shelby shrugged and sauntered into her bedroom, presumably too tired to even answer her sister.

Left by themselves in the kitchen, Veronica helped Jennifer load the dishes into the dishwasher and, while they were clearing the table, Jennifer asked about how the evening went and if the youngsters were well behaved. Typical Mom questions.

Veronica had a wholly different agenda.

"So, what's going on with you and Dad?" her newly fifteen-year-old daughter asked.

"What do you mean?" Jennifer said, feigning surprise.

"Did you two have a fight or something? It's really frosty between you."

Jennifer brushed some stray donut sprinkles into the sink. "It was just a long night. Your dad doesn't enjoy going to the Wieners' house, and I'm not that into it either. That's probably why we both seem a little out of sorts." Her pulse kicked up a couple of notches. She wasn't used to being grilled by her daughter and, even worse, blatantly lying to her.

Veronica wasn't buying it. "Yeah, but you slept on the sofa last night, Mom." Her long, streaked-blond hair brushed her shoulders as she shook her head in disbelief. "Something's wrong."

It was ironic, really, that Veronica was so intensely interested in Jennifer's relationship with Michael, and so persistent in the pursuit of discussing it, especially given her reticence in disclosing so much as one sentence of worthwhile information about her own romantic affairs. Veronica had kept her own confidence over the last several weeks, particularly in regard to the goings-on at the Homecoming Dance. And, while she'd confessed embarrassment for her antics in Mr. Ryerson's history class—only when confronted by it, however—she'd been subdued and secretive about what'd transpired between her and the two boys.

According to Shelby, Tim no longer proclaimed his love of Veronica to his pal on the bus. And Erick, who'd made a nuisance of himself with phone calls to Veronica's cell when she was at home those few days just prior to the dance, hadn't called at all since then, at least not as far as Jennifer knew. So, Jennifer was almost tempted to make a deal with her daughter: *I'll tell you, if you tell me.*

Almost.

"There's nothing wrong, Veronica," she said, injecting a half dose of incredulousness into her voice, laced with a few droplets of amusement. Hopefully she didn't overdo it.

Her daughter blinked at her. "Whatever you say," she muttered. "I'm gonna watch some TV, okay?"

"Okay."

And as Veronica sprinted toward the stairs, her slender legs striding away from Jennifer as purposefully as her father's had a half hour before, Jennifer couldn't help but fear she'd lost a precious opportunity for connecting with her daughter. But what would she have said? *I know what it's like to be attracted to two very different men, honey. What happened between you, Tim and Erick?* Or, even worse: *There's something both worrisome and powerful about being caught in a love triangle, isn't there, sweetie? Your father and I are experiencing something similar. Wanna trade stories?*

For fear she'd blurt out a ridiculously inappropriate line like one of those in a moment of pure desperation, Jennifer took care to avoid conversation with her own children for much of the day. Thankfully, it was a lazy Sunday and both girls preferred to fend for themselves. Too old, they felt, for trick-or-treating, but still young enough to enjoy seeing the kiddie costumes, they dumped bags of candy into Jennifer's giant Halloween bowl and prepared for the onslaught of neighborhood children that evening.

Several hours later, when Jennifer had thrown together a quick dinner for the girls (Michael, of course, was still resolutely absent), she grabbed a sandwich for herself and hid out in her office, claiming to be working on some Web designs for a client. Meanwhile, her daughters—who'd spent the day reading, napping, watching stupid shows on cable and chatting with the occasional friend on the phone—nibbled on whatever food interested them, answered the door to appease the latest candy-toting ghost or skeleton and, again, kept only each other company at the table.

Jennifer tried to put aside all self-accusations of being a neglectful mother. Not that she didn't believe it. She just had to make it through this pretense of parental competence (however sub-par) somehow until Michael returned home. Which, it turned out, wasn't until well after seven.

Upon his quiet reappearance, he bustled into the kitchen and cobbled together some sort of snack. Then, during the remainder of the evening, he once again spoke only to their daughters, although Jennifer made this easy for him by removing herself from the family's public spaces. Also, taking a page from his book, she made her few announcements very general, as if they were intended for the house at large.

During one of these—"Recycling day is tomorrow. So, if you have anything to toss in the bin, please do it tonight."—Veronica strolled by and shot her a disbelieving frown face. Soon after, the girls slipped into bed without either Jennifer or Michael being called in for anything, not even their daughters' usual last-minute queries. The already quiet house suddenly turned morgue-like in its silence.

Jennifer knew the tension between her and Michael couldn't go on indefinitely and, being that she felt herself to be primarily to blame for its emergence, she worked up the courage to seek him out. Downstairs. Where he was gazing at the TV with complete absorption, despite the fact that it was turned off.

"Michael?"

He sighed and turned toward her. He didn't say anything, though.

"Michael, is it possible for us to talk now?"

He shrugged, his jaw tense.

She took a few steps closer to him but stopped when his eyes narrowed. "Look, um, I'm very sorry about misleading you yesterday. About the phone. I'd been getting a lot of . . . messages, and I really just wanted to turn it off."

He raised his eyebrows slowly. "Misleading? Odd choice of word. Don't you mean *lying*, Jennifer?" He crossed his arms and answered his own question. "Yeah. Definitely lying."

She bowed her head. "I'm sorry, Michael."

He didn't acknowledge her response. "And then there's the whole issue of the *nature* of your conversation. That was really . . . something." He smirked, a very odd facial expression for her husband, and stared hard at the side wall, as if recounting the lines of dialogue he'd overheard.

Her entire body cringed at the memory of that. She took a deep breath and forced her mouth open. She wasn't certain yet what she'd say, but she owed him an explanation of some kind. "I—"

"Oh, no, Jennifer," he interrupted. "Don't even think this is something you can take care of by spitting out a few vague sentences and being done with it." His eyes bore right into her face. "You weren't just talking with another man. You were making plans and sharing secrets with that other man. A man whose name I happen to recognize." He paused. "Unless there's more than one David in your life." He paused again. "Was it your old computer geek boyfriend? Answer yes or no."

"Yes," she whispered.

He nodded. "Interesting. Really. It's funny, I've been thinking all day today about what you'd told me about that relationship. About the things he said to you. The things he did. How he'd hurt you. And, yet, out of fucking nowhere, he's calling you. But that's not the interesting part. The interesting part is that, from the sound of it, it wasn't the first time. Or even the fifth time. Was it?"

She shook her head slightly.

He laughed, but it was a raw, hurting sound. *"I don't want to stop talking to you either, David,"* he mocked. *"No, I haven't told my husband about our super special plans, but I will. And I promise I'll be there."* He took a ragged breath. "You wanna explain that?"

She swallowed. "Michael, please don't be so upset—"

"Oh, I passed *upset* hours ago." He pushed himself to standing and began pacing around the room. "What's the big event that's happening in a few weeks?"

"It's just a reunion," she said. "My old computer club from college is having a reunion, okay? That's why David first contacted me."

Something flickered behind his eyes. "How long ago?"

"A few weeks. Not that long, really."

"Well, it's October thirty-first today. And I know you're really good with numbers and dates." He said this like it was a kind of fungal infection. "How about you tell me *exactly* when and how he contacted you."

"August thirteenth," she confessed, not bothering to camouflage the truth. She knew Michael was intent on nailing her no matter what she said. "Via e-mail."

"A little more than a *few* weeks, perhaps?" Again, he didn't wait for an answer before pressing on. "I knew there was something going on with you. I *knew* it." He rubbed his temples briefly. "And this reunion is going to be when and where?"

"November thirteenth. At C-IL-U."

"Ah. Less than two weeks from now. Also interesting, Jennifer. And a fair driving distance away. When, precisely, were you going to mention it to me? Or weren't you? Perhaps you were just going to say you were going out with your friends and would be back really, really late." He studied her expression for a moment, but she had no idea what he saw there. "I wouldn't put it past you. You're one of those sneak-around and do-whatever-the-hell-you-want types. So quiet. And so careful. And so full of your little secrets."

At this, Jennifer could no longer quash her sigh. Granted, Michael wasn't entirely wrong. She *had* snuck away to meet David on campus already. It *had* crossed her mind to make up an excuse for her absence and just go to the reunion without telling him. So, she knew she deserved some of his disdain. But, other than entertaining the notion of what it would have been like to still be with David, she hadn't acted on a single one of her sexual fantasies. Michael was behaving as if he had caught her cheating on him, and she hadn't come close to doing that.

Well, not *very* close.

"I'd rather you didn't go," he pronounced.

She squinted at him. She could have shrugged and consented to stay home, but some angry twenty-two-year-old demon inside her just didn't want to play along. Not with Michael's dictates. Or with David's games. How long would they both just push her around if she didn't set limits somewhere, sometime? And wouldn't *she* be to blame if she let them get away with it?

"I can understand that," she said, working hard to keep her voice even. "But I need to attend."

His eyebrows shot up to midforehead. "You *need* to? Why's that?"

"I need to see everyone for myself. I need closure."

"What the hell kind of closure could you possibly need after eighteen years, Jennifer? Be honest with me for a change. You just want to be with your ex again. Make out with him. Maybe screw him. Your mind has been on him for *months*. And, God, I knew it."

He knew it? How would he have known that? Was he reading her e-mail or something?

She shot him a questioning look, and he laughed—again, that sound like an injured animal.

"I could feel it in the way you'd moved away from me, Jennifer. In the way your attention became so divided. I didn't want to admit it to myself, but I could sense the hugeness of the problem, and it made me . . . very nervous." He looked at her, imploring her to obey his command. "He is a massively bad guy. And I'm telling you, for the sake of our marriage, I don't want you to go to this stupid reunion. I don't want you to see that bastard again."

She could never wrap her mind around this idea of people "just sensing" things. Hard for her to believe that was real and not some projection he had made up. She met his gaze and whispered, "I realize that. But I *have* to go."

"No, you don't *have* to. You *want* to. And you don't care what you destroy." He puffed out some air, pushed past her and vanished upstairs.

Tamara awoke, sometime after ten on Sunday morning, certain the world was going to spin right off its little axis and hurl itself, in pinball fashion, from the moon to Venus to Mars and, probably, to Saturn and Mercury, too, before it was cast out of the solar system altogether and sent crashing into the nearest spiral galaxy.

God almighty. It'd been a hell of a long time since she'd been *this* hung over.

She struggled to remember what it was about the night before that had made it so very deadly. There was that bizarre food at the Wieners' party. And those drinks—what were they? Oh, yeah. Poisoned Appletinis. How very cutesy.

She tried to lift her head off the pillow, but it reverberated in the center, like five-foot-high speakers at a heavy metal concert. And Jon wasn't helping matters. What a bloody racket he was making in his office. He was always pounding away at something, even on the weekends. Compiling litigation materials for upcoming cases. Organizing bank bonds, CDs and insurance papers. Printing out Excel spreadsheets with stock projections and the occasional Super Bowl prediction. Always living for the future instead of experiencing life in the now.

Not that the now was so great.

She sank back into her pillow. The now was, in fact, pretty damn shitty.

Squeezing her eyes closed, she ran her fingers through the snarls of matted hair at the back of her head. That idiotic Rapunzel wig had been a pain. But she remembered taking it off at some point in the night. Sometime during the hours she was up in the library loft with Aar—

Oh, fuck!

Aaron had been there with her. He'd asked her to take the wig off, right? The details were kinda fuzzy, but there were parts she remembered. At least she *thought* she remembered. They were talking and laughing. They were drinking weird things. They were playing with some cards on the floor and looking out the window at all the nut jobs in the yard. She vaguely recalled something about foil-wrapped chocolate ghouls. But, it couldn't have been all true to life because, in her memory, Aaron kissed her, and he didn't actually do that, did he?

Nope.

She rubbed her head again. She was a mess and, clearly, she'd been hallucinating. She wouldn't put it past the Wieners to have slipped something illicit into the drinks of their guests. Something that made people mix up their fantasies with their realities.

Damn, drugs were *dangerous*. She felt like a live-action Just Say No warning commercial.

She slid back into a less-than-restful doze, weaving in and out of sleep like Benji when he was a feverish preschooler. She twisted her body to try to get more comfortable, but she was lying on something metallic—a big button on the side of her costume— that kept jabbing her thigh. It took a few minutes of trying to un-button it before she remembered that the Rapunzel skirt had a zipper in the back and nothing at all on the side. And it wasn't until she reached into her pocket, her fingers hot against the cool sleekness of Aaron's watch, that the reality and the fantasy finally separated . . . like oil and water . . . and she remembered.

Everything.

Holy crap, Batman.

Despite her throbbing head, she pushed herself up to sitting and glanced around the bedroom she and Jon shared as if she were seeing it for the first time. The walls were painted a dark, restful blue, the room meticulously uncluttered, the mattress firm but well cushioned with a thick foam pad, high-thread-count linen sheets and a fluffy teal coverlet. It was a place that should be in-disputably sleep-inducing and, yet, she strongly suspected she wouldn't rest easy in this bedroom anytime soon.

She opened the bottom drawer of her dresser and gently placed the watch underneath some of her carefully folded tennis socks. Like Scarlett O'Hara, she decided she'd deal with that unpleas-antness tomorrow.

Tamara wandered down the hall to where Jon's noisy printer was spewing out pages of some document—legal or financial in origin. She peered at him through the slit in the door, his dark eyes so intent on his project she couldn't help but be reminded of when she'd met him. The intense, incredibly serious law student he'd been, one who lacked the ability to relax even in his early twenties, possessed an earnestness in his expression those years ago that she only caught glimpses of now. But she had once loved the combination of qualities she saw on his face. Solemnity plus industriousness. She had no idea then that they would later manifest as detachment and cool ambition.

Two sides of the same coin, really. Though that was the gift and curse of marriage, too, wasn't it? Novelty and fascination eventually flips to familiarity and indifference.

"Finally up?" Jon said to her, his voice scratchy from lack of use this morning.

She pushed his office door open a few inches more. "Yeah. I'm not feeling great, though. Too many Appletinis."

His lips twisted into a small smirk. "I remember you were really swigging them last night. That runner guy down the street looked wasted, too." Jon shook his head. "People who can't hold their liquor shouldn't drink."

She didn't comment. Not because she didn't want to. Jon had had nearly as much to drink as she, and he hadn't exactly been the poster child for sobriety at other parties they had attended. But the mere mention of Aaron sent her pulse racing and made her throat too dry for speech.

She grunted something about getting a glass of water and drifted away from him. Jon's facial expression stayed with her, however. A captivating photograph on her mind's movie screen for one surprising reason: there was no emotional reaction evident in his eyes at all. His serious intensity was not directed toward her. And she, in the kitchen, combating dehydration with a glassful of spring water, found this far more interesting intellectually than she should have.

Jon wasn't angry with her about lounging in the Wieners' library loft and pouring Appletinis down her throat for hours while he gallivanted around the party and made contacts. Oh, no. He didn't care. As long as her behavior didn't reflect poorly on him. As long as his networking goals weren't hindered by her in any way. As long as she didn't publicly embarrass him, he didn't pay attention to her.

Despite the fuzziness, she thought back and remembered that the only time he had admonished her at all was when she had tangentially criticized the mayor. Jon seemed completely unfazed by the fact that she had been drinking heavily, skirting participation in the outdoor party games and hanging out with another man (aka: "runner guy") for most of the night.

And, come to think of it, she hadn't really spared Jon more than a thought or two throughout the entirety of the evening either.

Thoughts of Aaron, by contrast, were registering seventeen out of ten on her emotional Richter scale. She poured herself a second full glass of water and fought her pounding headache long enough to rationalize this away. An absorbing over-interest in another person was the hallmark of infatuation. It made people's body organs work overtime, their lust hormones kick up a fuss and their imaginations shoot into overdrive. But it *always* disappeared eventually. Even with Jon, at the beginning, they'd had some happyish moments, although those feelings ended sooner rather than later because Benji came into their lives so early.

She meandered into their sunroom and curled into a ball on Benji's old brown beanbag chair. They had a nice house. One that had a spacious den, a brick patio, a raised deck. She had a lovely garden and the luxury of time to tend it. She had an expansive kitchen with gorgeous granite countertops. If she had chosen to have her son on her own . . . if she had insisted on raising him by herself and not testing Jon's dutifulness . . . would she live in a house like this? Would she have been able to afford to send her son to a good college out of state?

Possibly but doubtful. And there was really no fooling herself about the reality of single parenthood. It would have been *very* hard, at least in the beginning. It maybe would have always been hard. So, in a number of ways, she owed Jon for his support of them, even if his reasons for doing it were equally selfish. Even if the *appearance* of the good life was, for him, synonymous with actually *experiencing* the good life. The only thing he had to give up was the notion of ever finding true love himself. And, of course, he made her give that up, too.

A pair of squirrels darted across the lawn. How diligent they were. So productive on this humdrum Sunday morning, gathering and storing nuts for the long winter ahead. She finished her glass of water and could have used another but was still too nauseated to want to move, so she kept her eye on the supposedly simpler creatures in nature.

Only, to her, they seemed kind of wise out there. The squirrels—maybe they were a couple?—worked so well together. Human couples were lucky when they could achieve that kind of marital synchronicity. Relationships were so complicated, and the path strewn with thorns, that everybody struggled somewhere down the line. Early in the dating process. Those rough first years of marriage. Later, when midlife crises and doubts rushed in.

Passion waxed and waned across the board, didn't it? And so many times, people who had dealt with hardships in their relationship at first, grew into mature adults who retained a warm appreciation for each other and for the memories—even the challenges—they had shared. Perhaps their initial fiery ardor evaporated over the years, but a tender respect was forged in its place. Though both parties would have to want that. To be willing to work to reinvent their couplehood.

The threads of these thoughts trailed after her throughout the rest of the day, like loose ends on a fabric, needing to either be tied into a knot or snipped away.

She awoke the next morning with less severe physical symptoms, enabling her to both think and talk more clearly, but Jon had already left for work and the nature of her unanswered questions involved more than just him anyway.

She waited at home for several hours, wondering if Aaron might venture over to retrieve his wristwatch. He did not. Nevertheless, she busied herself by watching a morning talk show, flipping through some dusty old Austen novel, fine-tuning her résumé and e-mailing out a few tester job applications. The employment climate was harsh out there, but she had to start somewhere. And getting feedback of any kind would be useful, whether she ended up working from home or at a company in the city.

Much as she tried to stay active, however, the sensations from Aaron's kiss still lingered like phantom lips on hers. She couldn't stop replaying what she *thought* she remembered. And Tamara, believing introspection could only take a woman so far, decided one real-life encounter was worth five hundred mental simulations.

She snatched the watch from her sock drawer, slipped on her sneakers and strode over to Aaron's house, the frigid gusts of wind reminding her they were headed into the cold season.

At her knock, he yanked the door open. She almost took a step back when she saw him. Dark smudges under his eyes. Puffy face. Wrinkled sweats. Hair that hadn't seen shampoo in a few days.

He looked like hell with a hangover.

Then, again, she wasn't exactly a ray of perkiness and sunshine, was she? But she knew she looked better today than she had yesterday. If this was his *better*, she had a hard time imagining the rotten shape he must have been in the morning after the party.

"Hi," she said. "May I come in for a moment?"

He nodded and held open the screen door for her. Once she was inside, though, he closed it, locked it and leaned against it as if he wouldn't be able to stay upright without support.

"Are you okay?" she asked.

He broke into a cautious grin. "Not so much. Are you?"

"Hmm. I've been better. Um, Aaron—I have something of yours." As she dug into her pocket for the watch, an apology for her part in the party debacle was fashioning itself on her tongue, but she wasn't quite sure yet how to phrase it. First step was getting the watch out of her pocket, which was harder because her hands were inexplicably trembling. Finally, she was able to hold it out to him. "You . . . you'd, uh, given this to me on Saturday night. You were right about the Wieners' clocks being off, by the way. Yours was the accurate one."

His gaze flickered between her eyes and his watch. He reached for it and his fingers grazed hers. *Oh, God.*

He inhaled, then exhaled in a rush. "Tamara, I'm so sorry. You were a good sport to put up with me Saturday night. I was really drunk, as I'm sure you gathered, and not behaving at all as I should have—" His speech faltered and she thought, *Wait. I was a good sport? What the fuck kind of comment is that?*

"You kissed me," she blurted instead.

"Yeah," he said with a heavy nod. "I did. And I'm very, very sorry." He shoved his watch into his sweatpants' pocket, as if needing to keep the offending timepiece out of sight. "I can't even express to you my degree of bad judgment. The only responsible thing I did that night was to walk, not drive, home. It was a helluva long way, but I was actually kinda sober by the time I got here. Sharky took care of me."

She glanced around the room and listened for the distinctive sound of the dog's yaps. "Where *is* Sharky?"

"He earned himself a couple of big bones, so he's out in the backyard gnawing on one now." Aaron studied her for a moment. "So, am I forgiven? Can we," he paused, "put this behind us?"

Tamara smothered a laugh, but she couldn't help wanting to throw her hands up in the air and to start giggling like a brainless teenager. What did a woman say to something like that? *No, you're not forgiven because you made me want you. No, we can't put this behind us because I need you to kiss me again, just so I'll know my feelings weren't a complete fluke of the night.* These were not ideal answers.

So, instead she shrugged and said, "Sure."

"Great." He shot a rueful look at her face and a pensive one at the door. "I don't want this to come out the wrong way, but I think it probably will, so I might have to ask you to forgive me for something else in a minute." He swallowed and wet his lips before speaking again. "Have you shared these talks we've had with your husband? I mean, does he know you and I get together sometimes? That we . . . chat? Would he, for instance, be surprised if he found out you were here, at my house, visiting me right now?"

"Oh, um, well—" She thought about it. Had she ever told Jon she'd visited Aaron at his home? Or that Aaron had dropped by their house a few times when Jon wasn't there? Nope. She'd kept those moments to herself. Precious, jeweled memories that were for her alone. Not that she was going to tell Aaron that. Besides, she had a reasonable excuse, and she figured now was the time to use it. "Jon's not home that much. Lots of out of town business trips and long hours at the firm downtown. Several days might go by between one of our long chats about gardening or something and the next time I have a chance to catch up with Jon about our week. So, the conversations we have"—she motioned between her and Aaron—"don't usually come up with him."

"Don't *usually*, Tamara, or don't *ever?*"

She didn't like the sharpness of his mind at the moment or the gentle firmness with which he was talking to her. She tried to wave it off, but he waited for an answer and, eventually, she was forced to concede that Jon probably had never heard about one of their long conversations, aside from seeing them talking in the loft on Saturday night. "But I'll tell him what a dork you are about growing broccoli, if it makes you feel better," she said.

He granted her a strained smile. "You do that. And, until then, maybe you shouldn't be here without . . . your husband knowing. That's kind of a dangerous game."

"I'm not playing a game, Aaron."

He chuckled to himself and shook his head ever so slightly. "C'mon." He led her to the door, his manner not insulting, exactly, just highly principled and annoyingly responsible. Just before she stepped outside, he squeezed her arm lightly and said, "Marriage is hard enough when there are just two people involved. Trust me on this one."

She shot a look at him over her shoulder as she left, wondering what he meant. Had his ex-wife cheated on him? Had he cheated on her? They did get divorced, after all, for some purportedly good reason. Maybe there was more to their problems than the working-at-home thing. Or, maybe, he was talking about another marriage just now—a couple close to him, like his parents.

She didn't have a chance to ask, not that it was any of her business anyway, because he'd already shut the door behind her. Couldn't get rid of her fast enough, could he? Well, he'd certainly left her with a few things to think about, starting with the fact that she hadn't managed to keep her heart rate under 150 for the past half hour and, except for taking back his watch and squeezing her arm just before she had left, he hadn't touched her at all.

It was hard to stop thinking about his kiss.

An act, she reminded herself (repeatedly) on her chilly walk home, he had apologized for and was clearly embarrassed about. And—just to keep a sense of goddamn perspective—she also reminded herself (repeatedly) that Aaron was *not* Cupid's gift to women. He wasn't involved in a current relationship—must be a reason for that, eh? He had somehow screwed up his marriage—although, to be fair, she was sure Isabelle hadn't been a little doll the whole time either. And he had all but rebuffed Tamara and their friendship until she came clean about their talks to Jon. What kind of a freakin' fantasy man was he?

The cold November wind wafted through her like a ghost through a brick wall. The silliness of Halloween was over, the abundance of autumn gone for another year. Her garden lay fallow now, just a collection of brown twigs and stems in need of clearing. She didn't look forward to the coming months. Nothing grew in winter in this part of the country. Nothing at all.

❧ 18 ❧

The Trio

The trio that gathered at the Indigo Moon Café on Wednesday possessed an unseen sizzle of energy, which surrounded them much like an electric fence and was just as likely to cause a shock if a breach were attempted. But whether this protective measure had been established to keep their secrets contained or to keep others from entering into their sacred circle was, as yet, unclear.

The XM radio songs of the day featured seventies selections from the group Chicago, England Dan & John Ford Coley, a couple of distressingly tender tunes by Michael Johnson ("Bluer Than Blue" and "This Night Won't Last Forever"—Jennifer rolled her eyes when those came on) and then, when they least expected it, a terribly upbeat number from singer Shaun Cassidy. But even Tamara was too frazzled to make any disparaging comments about "Da Doo Ron Ron" that morning.

"That was some event on Saturday," Tamara began, taking a couple of hearty gulps from the triple-shot mocha espresso she ordered. After what she'd been dealing with lately, lattes were for children.

Bridget laughed. "Yeah, it was pretty wild." She, however, was the only one of the three who could laugh with any measure of sincerity about the Hallowiener Party. Not that it hadn't been a source of trauma for her on that night. Simply that it had not branded her marriage with the lingering negative effects her friends were experiencing. Indeed, in Bridget's case, the opposite appeared to be true, although she wasn't yet sure if she should trust Graham's transformation, or if she should even discuss it with anyone.

Jennifer merely nodded. She'd consented to getting together earlier in the week, on Wednesday morning rather than Friday, because Tamara—who'd claimed to have questions about Jennifer's work-from-home experiences—had requested it. But there was really no reason Jennifer could imagine that would entice her to jabber about the text messages from David or the marital freeze-out from Michael.

"Did either of you feel a little, I don't know . . . ill after drinking those Appletinis?" Tamara asked. "I don't think they agreed with me."

Jennifer shrugged. "I didn't try one."

Bridget squinted into the distance. "Those pinkish drinks? I only had half of mine. But, really, *none* of the food at their home agreed with me." And, while she didn't state this aloud, she'd been proud of herself for tasting only tiny portions of the items available on the table at the Wieners' house. It'd been quite a spread, but she'd shown surprising willpower. Even later, when she and Graham were discussing Dr. Luke and Witch Nina's nasty comments, she hadn't lapsed into her usual bad habit of emotional eating. She was really making progress! Maybe this time she'd trim those extra pounds off for good.

She consciously divided her low-fat blueberry muffin into four sections, determined to only eat two parts of it that morning.

Tamara blew out a slow stream of air, ostensibly so as to cool her already lukewarm coffee, but she somehow had to give vent to the frustration brewing within her. She remained unsure how to ask what she wanted to know, which basically came down to questions pertaining to her growing attraction toward Aaron. Was the man himself responsible for her increasing interest? Or were the drinks the culprit, and the fact that she had been grateful to him for easing the tedium of an otherwise lonely evening?

Bridget, whom she had thought too busy with the dissection of her muffin to be particularly perceptive, was the first to actually hint at the direction of Tamara's thoughts.

"When I was getting grilled by the dance instructors, I saw you talking with some guy," Bridget said. "It wasn't long after Leah and Kip brought out those Appletini things. I remember he was dressed as a prince. Tall. Blondish. Pretty good-looking." She looked up from her plate, butter knife gripped like a scalpel in her hand. "Who was he? A friend of Jon's?"

For a split second, Tamara considered trying to feign lack of certainty as to whom Bridget might be referring. She hesitated a beat too long, though, because Bridget smiled and set down her knife, and Jennifer's thin eyebrows rose to midforehead.

"That was Aaron," she stated. "My neighbor."

"*The* neighbor?" Bridget asked gleefully.

Tamara nodded.

"Why didn't I get to meet him?" Jennifer asked, her tone amused.

"Right place, wrong time?" Tamara suggested, going for flippancy but not at all sure she achieved it, especially given her friends' watchfulness of her. "I didn't know he was going to be there."

"Did you two spend a lot of time together?" Bridget asked. "I didn't see you after that for the rest of the night."

Tamara nodded again. "The Wieners have a library, nestled in a loft on the second floor. Aaron discovered it, and it had a nice view of the yard, so we stayed up there and chatted."

"What an opportune location," Jennifer commented.

Tamara shot her a sharp look. Had she guessed? "What do you mean?" she managed to ask.

"Just that it must've been convenient to see all the nonsense going on outside from a nice, safe distance. Why?" Jennifer said slyly. "Was there another reason?"

"Uh, no. Not really." Tamara could finally feel the espresso zipping through her veins. About goddamn time. Of course, caffeine made her more fidgety than usual. "He kissed me up there," she blurted before she could stop herself, and she had the satisfaction of seeing the jaws of both her friends drop and their eyes widen to tennis-ball-sized orbs. Well, she had to tell *somebody*. Might as well be them. "Although I was kind of drunk then."

"Was *he* drunk?" Jennifer asked at the same time that Bridget said, "Was he any good?"

"Yes," Tamara replied. "Very."

"To which question?" Bridget asked, holding her breath.

"To both."

Her friends exchanged a look.

Jennifer set down her calming chai on a brown paper napkin. "Did Jon find out about this? Did he see you, or did you tell him?"

Tamara shook her head. "This really doesn't concern him."

Jennifer, unable to stop ruminating about her own marital crisis or keep herself from playing a compare-and-contrast game between her situation and Tamara's, still could not bring herself to agree with her friend on this one. "I think it does. But I'm not saying you have to take Jon's opinion into consideration, or even that you have to confess what happened to him. Just that, from a logical standpoint, he's involved. Whether or not he knows it."

"Yeah, yeah. I suppose . . ." Tamara ran her long fingers through her hair, skimming over the tangles, but they were there nonetheless. "I don't think telling him about it is a good idea, though. Do you?" She glanced between the two of them. "I mean, what good would it do anyway? It'd only make it harder for us to live with each other."

"You still want to be with him?" Bridget asked, the emotionally stressful nature of this conversation—even though it didn't involve her directly—making her nibble mindlessly on her muffin. She had already finished the second section she had cut up and moved on to the third without realizing it.

"Well, yeah," Tamara said, downing the last of her espresso despite its tepidness. "We have to stay together. For Benji." She stated this as a given, as if the other two women would accept it without question. And, to a degree, they did. What loving mother didn't want to do everything she could for the sake of her child?

The problem, from Bridget's perspective at least, was Jon himself. She'd never liked the guy. The few times she had been in a social situation with him, he acted so smug, so above his company, she always dreaded having to be in the same room with him. Her mom used to say that people who went out of their way to make others feel uncomfortable were just really insecure, so maybe that was it. But he irritated her, and she had never been able to figure out what Tamara saw in the man.

Jennifer was not nearly as mystified. She *got* Tamara and Jon as a couple, or at least she could see how they must have been drawn to each other once. They were both intelligent and outspoken, with a tendency toward sharp edges. If what Tamara had told her about their families was true, neither of them had had particularly strong marital role models growing up, and both desperately wanted to break that pattern. They shared the appreciation for a well-appointed house, a long-held allegiance to moderate liberal politics and an unyielding devotion to their son. These days, though, Jennifer couldn't help but observe their mutual indifference toward each other.

"It's important to consider the children," Jennifer said, thinking of her own daughters and the potential trauma that would be inflicted upon them if she and Michael were ever to separate. The thought of Veronica's face hardening in anger and Shelby's falling in dejection made Jennifer shudder.

"Exactly," Tamara said, although she was starting to believe she had already protested the matter too much. That she was just saying lines from a very old script. However, she couldn't quite break free of her private fantasies of a capricious escape from the constrictions of her wedding vows. The problem, of course, was she no longer knew how to state her true beliefs about marriage because she had no idea anymore what, precisely, they were.

"You still didn't tell us about the kiss," Bridget said. "Other than that it was really good. How did it *happen?*"

Ah. Well, this was concrete. A step-by-step stage direction performed on the library loft's theater in the round. *This* Tamara knew she could do.

She set the scene for them with eloquent detachment: He was drinking, she was drinking, Jon was elsewhere. It was a dark, secluded, intimate cove, away from the eccentricities of the maddening crowd. And, then, like the climactic moment of a soap opera, she described (to the best of her memory) the instant their lips met, attaching no real emotion to the act and none of the mental confusion. Purposely making light and superficial something her friends knew was, unequivocally, a rather big deal.

"And then what?" Bridget asked. "Did he say anything?"

Tamara snickered. "He ran away, and when I saw him on Monday, he apologized. That was it."

Jennifer exhaled. This was making her think too much about David. She didn't have to imagine what it was like to kiss him. She knew. She remembered. "No harm, no foul," she murmured to Tamara, though she didn't believe her own words. "If you're not going to go forward with Aaron, then it's probably better not to mention it to Jon."

Although Bridget nodded in agreement, she couldn't keep from wondering how Jon would be able to miss the signals of restless discontent his wife was sending. Even Graham, who wasn't known for his intuitiveness, had sensed Bridget's unhappiness at home and her greater enjoyment at work. Even Graham, once he realized how important Dr. Luke and Smiley Dental were to her, took steps to try to please her. Little steps, sure, but wholly unexpected ones. Like his surprise visit to the office yesterday. To meet Dr. Luke in person.

"Hey, there," Graham had said, smiling first at both Bridget and her favorite dentist, and then reaching out to shake Dr. Luke's hand while Bridget held her breath.

"Hello," Dr. Luke had replied, returning the smile, grasping her husband's hand and shaking firmly. One man on one side of the dental desk, the other man on the opposite side—with Bridget sitting uncomfortably between them.

Then Dr. Nina had walked by, paused in front of the desk and eyed them all curiously. Bridget resorted to fiddling with her paperwork, Dr. Luke immediately excused himself to go check on a patient, and Graham . . . well, he just stared the Witch down until she rounded the corner. Then he kissed Bridget goodbye and took off himself.

Even the next day, Bridget couldn't quite get over the oddness of it. Of Graham's silent assertion to her coworkers that she had a very present husband and, perhaps, that he supported her and watched over their interactions with her. It pleased her slightly more than it discomfited her but, more than any other reaction, she was surprised.

Might not Tamara's husband, Jon, if he recognized things in his marriage were amiss, do something unpredictable, too?

Tamara concurred with her friends' professed opinions and, not being privy to their unspoken ones—nor really wanting to know them—she pushed aside the baffling nature of Aaron's kiss and moved on to her simmering questions about working from home.

"How do you juggle your day?" Tamara asked Jennifer. "Do you set aside the same hours every week for working on your projects or does it vary wildly depending on what else you have going on?"

Others had asked Jennifer about this a number of times, but she found it interesting that Tamara had never broached the subject before now. Tamara was a different creature from her. Unlike Jennifer, Tamara didn't spend countless hours loitering in the past or projecting herself into the future. She had an altogether idiosyncratic and immediate relationship with time. If she asked about working from home, it wasn't a hypothetical matter. The idea must have taken root in Tamara's present and been of some urgency.

"People have multiple approaches," Jennifer said carefully. "I'm able to be flexible within any given day, but I try to spend at least four or five hours on designs and updates every weekday. A few hours on the weekends, too, if I need to finish something." Or, she added to herself, if Michael wasn't talking to her and she needed a place to escape. "Tomorrow morning I'm meeting with a new client for an hour—Thrifty Gifty, you know?"

The other two nodded. The bargain gift boutique had opened in town just a month ago. To Bridget and Tamara it seemed a cute place, but they'd been too preoccupied with other affairs to shop there yet.

"They have a very basic Web site up already but, now that they've settled in and feel established in the community, they're looking to do more with it. They need a redesign to accommodate additional Web pages, to feature better ads, to optimize the Internet search engines." Jennifer smiled slightly as she spoke about this, enjoying the undivided attention of her friends. It was simple stuff to her, but very strange to recognize how they considered her an expert in something. Stranger still was the fact that she was finally taking her skills more seriously. She needed to do that. If nothing else, being back in contact with David succeeded in reminding her that she'd fantasized about being an innovator once, and she wanted, even in her more limited suburban-mom way, to do more complicated work than she'd done in years.

"Anyway, I'll spend more time today gathering ideas for them and sketching a few design layouts," she continued. "Tomorrow the owner will meet with me and tell me what she's hoping to do with her site. We'll brainstorm and then set a tentative date for completion. Then, I'll just work on it until it's done. Until the client is satisfied." This was underplaying it a bit. Jennifer didn't stop polishing a site until the client reached the point of all-out raving.

Tamara asked a series of follow-up questions that left Jennifer with no doubt her friend was rather determined to reenter the workforce. But, when confronted directly, Tamara hedged.

"I'm just gathering information," Tamara claimed, a statement Jennifer didn't believe in the least and one even Bridget found unlikely. "With Benji away at school now, I think I need some new challenges."

However, from Tamara's point of view, she was being partially honest, which was pretty close to fully truthful, right? To admit openly to her interest in being self-supporting would mean to acknowledge her plan to cut one of the ties binding her to Jon. It was safer to put the blame on her son's absence, and hardly an implausible reason, after all.

The ripple effect these partial truths had on her friends would have surprised the Glendale Grove locals had they learned of it. Tamara's determination to paint as insignificant her kiss with Aaron worked like a floodgate in reverse. All the details and confusion Bridget and Jennifer longed to pour out of their souls were whooshed back in, allowing only trickles of truth to dribble out.

Jennifer refused to discuss David's text messaging or the silent stalemate with Michael, even when Bridget hinted that she'd sensed something amiss on Saturday evening. "It was just a really late night," Jennifer deflected. "We were both really tired after the party."

Bridget, however, had no intention of harshly judging Jennifer's finely honed sense of discretion. Despite a few nebulous allusions, she couldn't bring herself to divulge the brief but momentous occasion of Dr. Luke and Graham's first meeting the day before. Nor did she tell her friends about Dr. Nina's comments at the Wieners' house or how that'd led to Bridget and Graham reaching a new level of understanding with each other. For one thing, it would seem like bragging. And for another, she would then be required to fess up about her luncheon date with Dr. Luke . . . and why would she want to unearth all of that?

She was just about to pop the last bite of muffin in her mouth when she realized she had devoured three-and-three-quarters sections. She dropped the last quarter of the last section on her plate like it was crawling with fire ants, and she bit her lip. Guess she didn't have as much willpower as she'd thought.

Tamara, meanwhile, was pleased to have had, in her opinion, a very open conversation with her friends. Incapable of being truly elusive, she remained relentlessly herself, experiencing a rush of self-congratulation on her (nearly) unguarded disclosure. Her life was, really, quite a mess, though, and she knew it. But in attempting to wade through the ruins and create a small measure of order, she found little nuggets of joy. A joy so dizzying and brief it felt like the thrill of a roller coaster ride once the terror of the big plunge had passed.

The three parted ways after ninety minutes, having had three very different morning encounters:

Bridget—budding with new hope for her marriage but distrustful of most everything outside of it.

Tamara—dealing with those same qualities but neatly swapped. Long-term marital distrust, yes, but a fresh sense of hopefulness on the fringes of her environment.

And Jennifer—who would not have recognized any aspect of

her life were it *not* cloaked in distrust, and who refused to give cre-
dence to the notion that hope could appear out of nowhere and
sweep her away on its air current (that simply wasn't rational),
stayed in the safe cradle of her holding pattern.

Their choice in determining the next correct step varied accordingly. Jennifer returned home and began obsessing about the font
style and page width for her new client. Bridget went grocery
shopping—kiwifruit was in season! And Tamara drove to Aaron's
house and parked in his driveway. She was going to have it out
with him.

❧ 19 ❧

Tamara

Wednesday, November 3 through Friday, November 12

Tamara rang Aaron's doorbell. No answer. She traipsed around to the backyard. No Aaron. She listened for the distinctive bark of a specific dog. No Sharky.

Bloody hell. Her confrontation would have to wait.

But when she was snug in her own house, her irritation gave way to second-guessing. Like an ace whizzing across the net, served by an opponent on the court, it surprised her and forced her to take a step back. It had been so long since she had been mired in any decision worthy of self-doubt, and the simple relief in having shared the kissing incident with her friends dissipated somewhat in the sanctuary of her living room. It left, in its wake, the unease of holding real human emotion in her hands. Emotion, in her case, that was astonishingly contradictory. She hardly knew herself.

Last night, she had spoken with Benji. He had sounded so happy. So full of possibility. And she was reminded of Aunt Eliza and her quest for joy no matter what a person's age. That life was too short not to seek out its lighter side.

Aunt Eliza lived by her own wisdom, and Benji, her darling boy, was well on his way to embracing a similar philosophy. Tamara wished for him every nuance of happiness this life could offer. But—and here was where the oddly disgruntled voice in her head confounded her—she also wished some of that delight for herself. Fully and clearheadedly.

Despite her practical nature, she wanted to feel the elation of life seeping into her body, all the way from her highlighted locks to her professional pedicure.

Despite her acceptance of duty, she wanted there to be the potential for joy even in the midst of mundane tasks.

Above all, and despite her reputation as a woman who could down a few drinks, she wanted to achieve momentary states of happiness without needing to drug herself with 80-proof vodka to do it.

She checked the time. Almost eleven A.M. Might be possible to catch him before he went out to lunch. She snatched her cell phone and punched in Jon's number.

"Everything okay with Benji?" he asked, even before saying hello. Unlike other husbands, he didn't spot his wife's number on the Caller ID and open with, "Hey, honey. How's your morning going?" Nope. Not Jon.

"I think he's fine. That's not why I'm calling."

"Oh." There was a pause and the sound of typing. Jon, ever the multitasker, wasn't going to stop working for so much as forty-five seconds if he didn't have to. "What do you need?"

"We haven't updated the calendar for November," she told him, referring to his work and event calendar they always kept on the fridge at home with the dates of his trips blocked off. "I don't know when you're traveling this month."

He grunted. "Hang on." More super-speedy typing. "I just pulled it up on my computer. Only two trips in November. The eleventh through the sixteenth and a short one just before Thanksgiving—the twenty-first through the twenty-fourth."

"Thanks." Tamara grabbed a pen and inked the dates on her hand.

"Okay. I'll see you later tonigh—"

"One more thing, real quick," she said, her words purposely rushed. "You know our neighbor Aaron?" There was a longish pause on the line, so she added, "Runner guy?"

"Yeah?" Jon must have resumed his typing because she could hear the clickety-clack of his keyboard in the background.

"He's given us a lot of vegetables from his garden this fall, so I thought I'd invite him here for dinner sometime soon. To say thanks. Is that all right with you?"

There was a sigh. "You know, Tamara, I don't care. Invite him if you want. I don't have much to say to the guy, though." More hurried typing.

Almost holding her breath, she said, as if it were the first time it'd occurred to her, "Well, I could have him over for lunch instead. Or for dinner when you're on one of your trips. Would that be better?"

"Yeah. Yeah, it would. Do that." Another sigh and another burst of rapid-fire typing. "Look, I've gotta get some work done here. Do whatever you want with that Aaron guy, but I'd just as soon skip it."

"Okay. No problem." Tamara hung up, unable to neatly braid the mixed strands of emotions: disappointment in her husband's indifference, glee at the cleverness of her machinations and uncertainty over what to tell Aaron. Her neighbor could no longer claim she had kept her objective of getting together with him from Jon. Jon, having stated it quite clearly, "didn't care" what she did with Aaron . . . or when. Although, let's be honest, Jon probably *would* care if he knew they had once done something more physical than steaming broccoli. Or toasting over a few drinks.

The following Thursday, late afternoon, her index finger millimeters from the doorbell, Tamara stood facing Aaron's front door again, this time without any intention of confronting her neighbor and every intention of proceeding with their friendship as if it were a perfectly normal thing and not remotely an act of pushing marital boundaries.

She had *permission*, after all. And she'd had eight days with which to think about the implications of Jon's apathy. If he'd have cared more or acted even minutely interested or concerned, would that have had an impact on her behavior?

Hell, yeah.

Then her feelings of guilt might have been a reasonable thing, not some leftover hang-up from her childhood. She dropped her hand to her side and took a deep breath. She didn't need to be all introspective and philosophical to recognize that she had grown accustomed to her parents' frigid but long-lasting marriage. That she had managed to emulate it in her own. And that the relationship model Aunt Eliza had set forth contrasted greatly from her mom's and Tamara's, but her aunt's way didn't have the ring of familiarity she had come to associate with the state of marriage.

So, hey—finally—she was taking steps to be more like her beloved aunt and less like her neurotic mother. Nothin' wrong with that.

She returned her index finger to its hovering point above the doorbell. She was an open, extroverted, candid woman of action, for chrissake! She could talk to Aaron without Jon present and without any allegations of wrongdoing—at least from her husband's limited vantage point. She sighed and dropped her hand again. So, what the hell was stopping her?

This mental tennis match was driving her crazy. Back and forth. Back and forth. What should she do next? Whose court was the ball in now? She stepped away from the door and reconsidered: She didn't *have* to ask Aaron over for dinner that day. It was only the eleventh and Jon would be gone until the sixteenth. She could come back tomorrow instead. Or even the day after. But where was this uncharacteristic cowardliness coming from? And why—

"You tryin' to drive Sharky mad?" came Aaron's voice from the window above her. She glanced up. Oops. Busted. "He's going nuts in here, barking and jumping. Can't you hear him?"

She forced a grin at him, finally tuning in to the sound of Sharky's deep throaty barks. "Oh, sorry. I was just . . . lost in thought." Even to her own ears this excuse sounded seriously lame.

"Well, stop thinking outside the house, would'ya? The door's unlocked. Come in and pet the poor bastard before he hurts himself."

"Sure." She pushed the front door open and was immediately assaulted by a very excited pooch. She scratched between his ears as he licked her, and she rubbed down the fur covering his back, enjoying the special animal love that was so wholehearted, so physical and so blissfully uncomplicated. This moment required no second-guessing, thank God. Then, she caught her breath as she realized Aaron was eyeing her from midway down the staircase. "Hey," she said. "How are you?"

"Hey," he said back. "I'm not bad. You?"

Her heart rate escalated to speeds medical professionals would find alarming. "Fine," she lied. Then she turned her attention back to Sharky for a few moments because, well, the dog wasn't expecting coherent conversation. "Good, Sharky," she murmured. A happy rumble in his throat and a wag of his tail let her know he, at least, was pleased with her arrival. She wasn't yet sure about Aaron.

"So, what's up?" he asked her, throwing a rawhide ring at Sharky to occupy him and running his fingers through his damp, dark blond hair to push it away from his face. Looked like he'd stepped out of the shower maybe ten minutes ago.

"I come bearing an invitation." She smiled. She had rehearsed these lines in her head, oh, four thousand times in the past week. "I was talking to Jon about you." She paused and let that information sink in to his handsome head. He studied her wordlessly, his brow creased in silent disbelief. "And I told him I wanted to ask you over for dinner. He said that would be no problem, and I was welcome to extend the invitation." She paused again and had the satisfaction of seeing the astonishment in his expression. "Unfortunately, Jon left town on business today and won't be back until Tuesday. However, he encouraged me to invite you over even in his absence, so I wanted to see what your schedule looked like. When you're free. If you'd prefer lunch or dinner. This week with me alone or later next week when Jon can be there. It's all open."

He laughed in a burst of nervous surprise, the corners of his eyes crinkling like an old man's, but the amusement in his voice when he spoke sounded very boyish to her ear. "Thank you, Tamara."

"Well, I'd save the thanks until you've actually eaten something I've made, but you're wel—"

"No." He shook his head for emphasis. "That's not what I'm

thanking you for. Thanks for having that conversation with your husband. And thanks for telling me about it. Since I can't actually imagine Jon wants to bond with me over burgers, I might just take you up on a quick lunch sometime. We can compare strategies for next year's garden or something." He ran his fingers through his hair again, the hand nearest to her catching her eye because she saw a tremor run through it just as it skimmed above the dampness. "Nice of you to ask me," he added.

"Well, pull out your calendar and let's take a look then."

He shook his head. "Don't need to. I'll make myself free. You choose the date and time and let me know. I'll be there."

She took a step closer to him and saw the tremor in his hand again. "You sure you're feeling okay?"

He must have caught her staring at his hands because he shoved them in his jeans' pockets and took a step back. "Yep."

"Well, I—I don't wanna keep you if you've got work to do. Lots of magazine stuff to organize today?"

"Not any more than usual. And, Tamara, you're not keeping me. I *like* talking with you. Sharky loves having you visit. It's . . . always a pleasure to see you."

She took another step toward him and, again, he backed away. *What the hell?* "Uh, thanks. Likewise."

Then, for what felt like two hours (even though it couldn't have been more than ten seconds), the two of them just stood there and looked at each other. He seemed to be scanning her hair and her mouth and she wasn't entirely sure what else because she stared first at his eyes, then his jaw, then her gaze traveled down his chest and—this was crazy. She was a woman of *action*, not endless, pointless rumination. If she wanted to take a step forward—literally, figuratively—she could, dammit.

She inhaled, moved toward him one more time and reached out to snag his arm with her fingers before he could try to slide away again. Oddly, this time, he didn't try. He was so completely motionless she wouldn't have known he was breathing had she not noticed the slightest rise and fall of his chest.

Her gaze returned to his face, his jaw, his lips. The flesh of his arm warmed under her fingertips. His neck muscles tensed as he swallowed and she moved fully into his embrace. Only when there was absolutely no uncertainty left about the direction she was headed did he break the statuesque pose, pull his hands out of his pockets and wrap his arms around her. Not tightly, but it was at least a show of open acceptance in her being there.

By contrast, Tamara exhibited no such restraint. She pressed her body against his, dug the pads of her fingers into his back and touched her lips to the corners of his mouth repeatedly until his lips parted and he finally kissed her in return. At last, his grip on her tightened, and she felt his hands roaming across her lower spine . . . and without the least hint of a tremor.

If Tamara had any lingering convictions that what she had experienced the night of the Hallowiener Party was the direct result of too scant a sense of judgment and too high a dosage of Appletini mix, this was soundly axed when their tongues met and her groan of desire matched one of Aaron's. For a split second, she visualized herself back in her bedroom, alone—her vibrating bunny turned on, her eyes shut, her mind projecting Aaron onto her imaginary screen of passion. How many times had she played out that fantasy? She tried to open her eyes and face the reality of that lonely bedroom, but she couldn't. Her eyes were already open. The moment was real, and she was here. With him.

He broke away from her and sighed. "Look, I'm not apologizing to you right now because *you* started it this time, but we can't . . . do this."

"Maybe not," she said, understanding finally what her fantasies had been telling her for months. Aaron's body may have been mixed in with those fantasies (*heavily* mixed in, if she were being completely truthful), but the jolt of physical attraction she had felt toward him wasn't the only part of those visions. She needed to end the loneliness she felt in that bedroom. In that *life*. Daydreaming about Aaron touching her was really nice, but being trapped in a bleak and lonely world—one decades in the making—was no longer tolerable. Aaron or no Aaron, she had to distance herself from *that*.

"You're married, Tamara. There's no maybe about it." He withdrew his arms and crossed them, putting half a foot of empty space between them again.

She nodded. "Yeah. But I won't be staying that way."

His arms dropped to his side. He cocked his head and squinted. "What?"

"I'll be filing for divorce before the end of the month," she said, marveling at how it was possible to speak these long-dreaded words so evenly. But they were the right words leaving her mouth. They were not partial truths. They were whole, painful, raw truths. Despite all of her mental and verbal protests. Despite all of her wishes otherwise over the years. Despite all of her attempts— and, perhaps, even Jon's—at steering their marriage away from the perils they'd been warned about by their parents.

Bottom line: It hadn't been Aaron's body or his kisses that'd drawn her to him (much). It had been his company. His conversation. The contrast he had provided to the emotional isolation at home.

"W-When did you decide this? And, um, are you—okay?"

She grasped him lightly with both hands straining to span his biceps and kissed him very lightly on the tip of his nose. "I'm okay. Kinda." She shrugged. "I think I actually knew before the Hallowiener Party, but I was trying to avoid admitting it. For years I thought, 'I don't want this to happen to me,' but the focus was wrong, you know? All that energy being used to try to *prevent* something. . . ."

"As opposed to working to *keep* something."

"Exactly," she said.

He reached out to her and ran the side of his thumb from her temple to her chin. "Are you sure there isn't anything left that's worth working to keep? Maybe Jon would really want to try—"

"No, Aaron. Not for any truly good reason anyway. Not wanting to let go of a draining situation because of pride and stubbornness is different from wanting to nurture a relationship."

He nodded. "Okay. I get that. But—" He groaned, and not in that "I'm filled with desire for you" way this time. "What's this thing happening between us? Did that make you, uh . . ."

"No. You weren't what set off the change. I mean, you sort of were but not really."

"What? What do you mean I 'sort of' was?"

She couldn't help but laugh at his expression, which seemed to be almost indignant, but she wasn't precisely sure why. Because he was only *slightly* the cause of her impending marital breakup or because he was implicated in it at all?

"Aaron, look, you're a very attractive guy and talking to you is always fun. But, you're—" She contemplated how best to put this. "Young. It's not like you're a kid or anything, but you're *way* younger than I am. You're barely thirty and—"

"I'm thirty-one, Tamara. Thirty-two in a couple of months. I'm not *that* young. You're not *that* old. Don't use superficial crap like that as shorthand for the real explanation."

Her jaw dropped. "Superficial crap?" she repeated slowly. "Wow. Tell me how you really feel."

"Oh, I plan to tell you more than that." He shot her a small grin. "You know we should probably sit down or something if we're going to have a long discussion. I can put on some tea or coffee if you want."

She poked him with her index finger in the middle of his chest. "And that's what I meant when I said you were sort of the reason. You're annoying and a big braggart, but you want to talk things out. You want to share what you think and feel. I discovered I really appreciate that in a man." She squinted at him and qualified the statement, "In a man-friend. A young man-friend."

He poked her back. "First, I'm not as annoying as you are. And, second, I changed my mind. You don't get coffee or tea. This conversation calls for a much stronger drink." He pointed toward a long cabinet that had a few bottles of alcohol on the top and a row of crystal tumblers and wineglasses beside them. "Pick your poison and pour yourself some."

"I'm not sure after the whole Halloween thing that we should be allowed to drink in each other's company," she said.

"Suit yourself. I'm having wine. At least half a bottle of it."

And he wasn't kidding.

"Huh," she said, after he'd made a serious dent in the chilled,

French-imported Sauvignon Blanc. "Well, I guess I can't let you drink alone."

"Guess not."

So, he poured her a glass, they sat back down and they talked. Just talked. Most of their conversation wasn't earth-shatteringly profound, but it also wasn't antagonistic or abrasive, something that always surprised her when she was in Aaron's company. They merely lobbed their questions and answers back and forth. It was a simple continuation of the way they'd always spoken to each other—affectionately sarcastic, topically divergent, remarkably honest—with one, critical difference: Aaron openly admitted he'd played out this exact scenario in his mind a few times.

"You're saying, you imagined me leaving Jon and . . . and having a fling, or whatever this is, with you?" she asked.

He gulped a healthy amount of white wine. "Yep. I visualized it. Things I visualize tend to happen."

"You don't get to take credit for this."

He laughed. "Credit? Tamara, you're getting a fucking divorce. If anything, I should take some of the blame."

She shook her head. "I don't think so. I keep telling you, this mostly doesn't have anything to do with you. You couldn't have *visualized* my marriage into shambles. It was like that for years before I met you. Besides, I had . . . fantasies of us, too."

"That's great." He grinned. "I wanna hear about those later. But visualizing and fantasizing are two different things. Their intentions are different."

"What? I don't get how—"

"People don't seriously believe their fantasies will come true, Tamara. But when a person visualizes, they're practicing their hoped-for reality. They not only want what they're thinking about to come true but, on some level, they expect it."

"You've been reading too much of your own magazine."

He shrugged. "Probably. Want some more of this?" He held out the nearly empty bottle of Sauvignon Blanc. It was more potent than she'd expected. She could feel her appendages beginning to tingle, but she was a long way from drunk yet.

Better to stop while she was ahead.

She shook her head. "No, thanks. You can have the rest."

But he put the bottle down and turned to her. "I don't know if this thing we have is going to go anywhere. Or even if it should. You've got a lot to deal with in the next several months. Even in the next year or two. But I just want to hang out with you today." He pointed to his fireplace. "It's getting darker and colder out, and I haven't made a fire yet. Let me throw on some logs and make the first one of the season."

She remembered his colossal stack of wood by the side of his house and said, "Sounds great." But she didn't tell him that the simplicity of that gesture—and his statement of wanting to just hang out with her—was the best foreplay she could imagine. It worked better than the wine or any aphrodisiac she could name. So, when the logs were on and the fire built to a medium, easy-burning level, she slid over to him on the sofa and said, "I want to kiss you again."

And she kissed him again.

"You realize the wine I drank, while not enough to make me completely incoherent, keeps me from being able to resist your advances," he told her, when he pulled away to catch his breath.

"Good," she said, her tone deliberately flippant.

"No. Not good," he shot back. "I'm still trying to decide if I'm willing to let myself get used by you. I like you, but I know what you're doing."

"*What?!*" She started to laugh but, then, realized—no, he was serious. "I am not trying—"

"We'll see," he said, cutting her off. "Thing is, I've been wanting to do you in front of the fireplace for, like, a year now. So, this is my chance. I'm weighing my options, but the wine is tipping things in your favor."

Oh, God. Even before he was on *her* radar, she had been on *his?* She had certainly noticed he was attractive, but the fantasizing and the lingering thoughts were, she had to admit, something that had rushed in after they had begun chatting more regularly.

As if reading the question on her lips, he nodded. "Yeah. It was more an immediate attraction thing for me. Guys are visual, you know." He tugged at her light pullover. "Guys wanna see what's under the shirt. It took a while before you started to look at me like that. It didn't happen until—" He paused. Thought. "Late spring of this year. Nine or ten months after we met at that stupid block party last summer."

It was true. She remembered. It wasn't until she and Aaron were out on their respective lawns doing yard work that they had a conversation independent of Jon and Benji. Aaron had been sending her very subtle signals. Signals that he had noticed her. And somewhere along the line, she'd begun responding to them. She was, perhaps, more susceptible to them the closer Benji got to leaving home . . . and as Jon's inattention became more obvious . . . but Aaron's signals to her predated hers to him.

"So, wait a freakin' minute," she told him. "Shouldn't I be the one worried about *you* taking advantage of *me?* You flirted with me first. And I'm the emotionally vulnerable one here. I'm the one about to get divorced."

He pulled her into his arms, a gentle but firm embrace. "Tamara, I've already been where you are. Grief and manipulation are not mutually exclusive. I may have slipped and kissed you the night of that party but, throughout most of this fall, you've been as much of an aggressor as I have, if not more. You stop by here. You flirt with me. You wear provocative outfits—"

She pulled away from him and crossed her arms. "Oh, give me a break. Like you don't stop by my house? Like you don't take your shirt off or wear those really great-fitting jeans on purpose?" She scowled at him, even though a part of her thought the whole argument was kind of funny. "Don't try to claim I'm the only one being manipulative."

"I'm not saying that." He smiled carefully at her. "Just that you're in the position of being even more manipulative than I am. Because there are a bunch of things you need to work out in your head. Your being here with me is not just about liking or not liking *me*. It's also a reaction to your husband. It's also a testing of a new role." He pulled her back toward him and kissed her very lightly on her cheek. "I'm telling you, I've already been where you are. I'm not criticizing as much as explaining."

"So, what kinds of things did *you* do after you and Isabelle separated?"

"Oh, no." He shook his head for emphasis. "We're not going there tonight. 'Cuz, a part of me—maybe more than one—is still trying to get you into bed with me sometime very soon. It's too early in our physical relationship for me to tell you my sordid tales." He winked at her. "But, even though I've been giving you shit, you gotta know, I do get it. I do empathize with you being at this stage. This beginning of the end of the marriage. So, just because in a lot of ways it's a Very Bad Idea for you to sleep with me tonight, and vice versa, I'm not going to discourage it. I'm just trying to be open with you about the dangers. For both of us, really."

Again, it was the ease with which he said stuff like this. The way he perceived it and processed it. She was stepping into brand new territory when they communicated. He was so direct. His understanding of human frailty so strong. He didn't let her get away with anything, yet he was still so compassionate. She'd never met anyone like him. Not ever.

She had walked through his front door having fantasized a thousand times about the two of them having hot sex. Knowing it could be a reality for her, though—and being able to visualize it for real—gave her the courage to pull back. To say to him, "I want to be with you, but you're right. This isn't ideal timing. Maybe tonight we can just talk, snuggle, kiss."

"Sure, Tamara. And while we're doing that, you need to tell me if or when you want it to stop. You especially need to tell me if you think there's even a one-billionth chance that you've changed your mind and you want to stay with Jon. Just don't try to hide from me what you really want and really need. I know it'll be confusing and inconsistent. I know it'll change from one moment to the next. That's okay. Just keep telling me the truth."

She leaned over, and just before she kissed him again, she whispered, "Okay."

And for the longest time, those were the last words spoken aloud. They shifted positions on the sofa until their bodies were stretched out—his partly curling over hers—and they made out like the teenagers they hadn't been for decades. It was passionate, involving, and the tenderness of his touch almost made Tamara cry.

At one point, it must have been an hour or more later, they suddenly realized they were both cold and ravenous. Aaron got up to revive the dwindling fire and to bring them hastily made ham and cheese sandwiches. It was after seven, completely dark outside and a forbiddingly nippy night. Tamara was glad she didn't have to go out there alone and walk back into her equally chilly house.

Aaron caught her staring out the window. "Do you need anything from home? Contact solution? Toothbrush?"

"I don't wear contacts," she said. "And I'll finger brush and borrow your mouthwash. Deal?"

"Oooh. Nothin' says hot to me like a freshly finger-brushed mouth."

She laughed and they ate their sandwiches in companionable silence. Then, revived by the exercise, or maybe the nourishment, they slid back to their languorous spots on the sofa, and Aaron started kissing her again. This time harder, heavier, with more feeling and force.

He was doing it, she realized. He was doing just what he had said he would do: trying to get her to sleep with him. He had candidly admitted to it being a bad idea, but also confessed his intentions for giving it a shot. Aaron was honest that way. And this time, he did more than curl onto half of her. Fully clothed, he put more of his weight on her legs, her hips, her chest. He pressed deeper against her everywhere their bodies touched. With his hands, he explored any region of her not covered by any other part of him. Through his jeans and hers, she could feel his erection. She didn't have to fantasize—or visualize, for that matter—anything at all. It was all right there. It was all too tangible to be trapped in her imagination.

Nevertheless, she broke their kiss long enough to ask a question she'd wondered on a number of occasions. "Do you have a tool belt?"

He groaned. "Oh, God. You're one of those."

"C'mon, Aaron. It's sexy. Tell me you've—"

She didn't have a chance to finish because he rolled fully atop her, crushed his mouth to hers and rammed his pelvis hard against her. She gasped. Guess he wore his tools all day, every day.

He yanked at her waistband. "These need to come off." He sprung off her, pulled her upright and moved about the room, snapping the blinds closed completely and adding another log to the fire. Then he wandered into the bathroom, dug around in there for a minute and returned, only to begin tossing the cushions off the sofa.

"What are you doing?"

He lobbed a handful of Trojans onto the coffee table and pulled out the bed inside the couch. "Sleeper sofa." He pointed to the thin mattress. "My bed's softer, but there's no fireplace upstairs."

"And these?" she asked, waving her open palm at the condoms.

"Better to ask forgiveness than to ask permission. Isn't that what you told me once?"

"Yeah. So?"

"So, I'm breaking that rule. Tell me yes or no. I can escort you home right now because, as I've already been compelled to warn you, this is a supremely bad idea. But I'm not going to fight against well-informed bad judgments. You have all the background. You know we shouldn't be doing this. It's not wise, even if you'll be legally separated soon. But it's also been a long time for me and, like I said, I wanna nail you in front of a roaring fire, so . . ."

Oh, this was interesting. She hadn't asked him much about his love life post-divorce. "How long has it been?"

"Five months, almost six—so, expect enthusiasm."

They met each other's gaze and laughed. And this—this, too—was something she had never had with Jon. Or even with the handful of men she had slept with before getting married.

Suddenly, a conversation with her aunt from years ago finally made sense. Aunt Eliza had said her husband was *funny* in bed. That they could joke about everything, even their sex life. Tamara hadn't experienced that. Jon took every aspect of their life and their relationship seriously. He took himself even more so. In their bedroom, he was either solemn or intense. A workaholic in there as he was everywhere. And, after a while, she'd lost what little bit of humor she'd had about intimacy. When Aunt Eliza told her this about her uncle, Tamara had already been married for a dozen years. She could understand intellectually what her beloved aunt was saying, but it had never seemed real to her. Not until this night.

She unbuttoned her jeans. "I'm staying."

He made a weird sound that seemed to come from the very back of his throat. "Good." He unbuttoned his jeans, too, and pulled them off. He nodded in the direction of her pullover. "I wouldn't cry if you took that off also."

She disrobed to her underwear and planted herself on the now-open sofa bed. She struck a languid pose, waiting for him to slide onto the mattress next to her. Which he did in a matter of seconds.

She ran the tips of her fingers over his bare arm, enjoying the texture of the muscle just below his skin. In a dreamy voice, she said, "So, you're saying, if I stay here tonight, we can just cuddle?"

Through heavy-lidded eyes, she watched his jaw tighten. Watched him swallow and nod. Very slowly. "We can just cuddle," he said through a sigh. "Are you telling me that's what you want?"

She opened her eyes wide and grinned at him. "Nope. I want you to nail me in front of the fire. Try to make me regret this—how did you put it? 'Well-informed bad judgment.' I dare you."

"Did I not say *you* were the manipulative one? Hmm?" Then he embraced her, engulfed her, rocked into her. And, even though she knew this was a fling and it could never last beyond a few plea-surable, transitional months, she had to acknowledge Aaron was *much* better than her vibrating bunny.

Still, in the quiet hours of the night, she couldn't help but suffer the stabs of guilt she would have to be a hard-hearted bitch not to feel. How arrogant she was, really, to act as though she and Aaron had both made these terrible marital choices. Didn't everyone know a spousal crisis took two people to form? Based on both her behavior and Aaron's—it was likely they were each the *causes* of their respective marital rifts, not just the injured victims. In which case, perhaps they deserved each other.

"Hey," he said, his voice sleepy since it was probably two A.M. She was facing away from him, but he caressed her shoulder and pulled higher the blanket he had thrown onto them earlier. "Are you regretting?"

She twisted toward him so she could look him in the eye. "No, Aaron. Not a bit."

They chatted a little longer, finally finished the last of the Sauvignon Blanc, channel surfed until they had watched snippets of about ten different stupid cable sitcoms and made love again. This time so long and leisurely, she was left drained of the energy to even dwell on the mess she would have to deal with at home.

Exhausted, she and Aaron fell deeply asleep and woke up embarrassingly late the next morning.

As it turned out, no one would have been any the wiser if Tamara had not left her cell phone at home.

Jennifer and Bridget stared at each other as the clock inched ten minutes past nine, then twenty minutes past nine, then thirty . . . and, still, Tamara hadn't shown up for their standing coffee date.

"It's not like her to blow us off," Bridget said. "She's never done that before."

Jennifer agreed. "She's always at least called or e-mailed one of us." She pulled out her cell phone, dialed Tamara's home number and got the answering machine.

"She's not there?" Bridget asked.

Jennifer shook her head and tried Tamara's cell number but got the same result.

Bridget bit her lip. "Should we be worried? Maybe go over there?"

"Let's give her a few hours. If we don't hear from her by noon, I can drive over and check up on her. Hard for me to believe she just *forgot*. Something must've happened."

Of course, Tamara did—eventually—wake up. She remembered the Indigo Moon Café and her friends, and she said, "Oh, shit."

Using Aaron's cell, she left an apology message on Bridget's machine. With Jennifer, she got a hold of her in person.

"Sorry. I just overslept," Tamara lied (in principle if not in fact).

Jennifer thought herself quite charitable to go along with this charade. But there was the odd phone number that showed up on her Caller ID and the even odder tone in Tamara's voice, which her friend might have camouflaged on voice mail, but not in a real-time interaction.

Jennifer wasn't fooled. She knew all about covering up.

❧ 20 ❧

Jennifer

In the past couple of weeks since the big Halloween party, the stalemate between Jennifer and Michael only solidified. She wasn't sure how they had managed it, but somehow they both acquired the useful skill of never occupying the same room at the same time. Veronica and Shelby, understandably, found this disconcerting.

Jennifer didn't know how Michael chose to answer their daughters' questions about why one of them always slept on the couch these days (something she and Michael typically did only on rare occasion, when one person was up all night with a bad cold or flu). Her pat response to the girls' expressions of concern was to tell them, "Don't worry. Your father and I are just going through a difficult patch in our relationship. We need time to think." Then, to Shelby's inevitable, "How long is this gonna last?" and Veronica's infuriated, "I *knew* something was going on! What happened?" Jennifer, again, never veered from her answer of "We just had a disagreement about something. It doesn't involve either of you girls. We'll work it out."

Veronica huffed and stalked away, not even bothering to correct her on the use of "girls" versus "women." Shelby just hid in her room.

Michael, whose conversation to her in the past week had been limited to scintillating phrases such as, "I sent in the mortgage payment yesterday," "I'll pick up Shelby from her friend's house" or "I've got a department meeting that goes until four-thirty," addressed her briefly that morning (as he slipped by her, hastily retreating from the kitchen as she entered it). "Are you going to be gone tonight?" he asked.

Over a number of days, she had thought a great deal about her answer to that question and her reason for it, but to Michael she only said, "Yes." She said it, however, very clearly.

He emitted a noise, something she took to be disgust, and sometime around noon he left the house with both of their daughters for a movie day. Shelby shot Jennifer an anxious glance on her way out the door. Veronica narrowed her eyes at her mom and dramatically threw her palms up in a show of chronic irritation.

By two-thirty, however, Jennifer had packed an overnight bag—just in case she needed it (a snowstorm in mid-November wasn't unheard of in the Midwest), finished a number of chores around the house, double-checked her e-mail and voice mail (each contained messages from David, which she returned quickly—"Yes, I'm coming!") and chose an outfit to wear that was both comfortable for driving three hours round-trip and, also, flattering on her. She wasn't a fashion hound like Tamara, but she hadn't seen anyone, except for that one time with David, since graduation. It wouldn't kill her to look nice.

The reunion started at five o'clock (well, 5:07, to be exact), but with weekend traffic to consider, lane closures on the toll roads or any other surprises, she'd give herself an hour's leeway.

There was a familiarity to her drive down to C-IL-U, which made her thankful for her prior excursion last month. She knew precisely which landmarks she could expect to see on the interstate and which radio stations came in clearest in her car. That, at least, was comforting. Just as before, though, she was assaulted by gloomy melodies on the station she'd tuned in to, which convinced her that the seventies were a dreadfully depressing era. ("Fire and Rain" by James Taylor, anyone?) But flipping stations didn't help. Neither the eighties power ballads nor the angsty nineties grunge eased her anxiety. Country hits, rap and alternative were not consistently cheering. And nothing about the new, post-millennium music her daughters loaded onto their iPods could soothe her either.

So, it was back to the decade of disco, bell-bottoms and the original *Star Wars* action figures. But, between Yvonne Elliman belting out "If I Can't Have You" and that disturbing song called—can you believe it?—"Torn Between Two Lovers," Jennifer found herself wishing for one of Luke Skywalker's light sabers so she could slit her wrists.

By the time she reached campus, her road trip (morose melodic accompaniment aside) had successfully helped her transition from her Michael world to her David one. Although, in remembering Tamara's question—"Which world are you in when you're alone?"—Jennifer still had no answer. Was there an independent Jennifer World out there, or was her "world" simply comprised of fractured pieces . . . collected castoffs of her parents' lives, her time with David, her marriage with Michael, her small circle of friends and her daughters? And how did some people instinctively *know* who they were and where they belonged? She felt herself to be little more than camouflage-colored wallpaper on the screen of her own life. A lost chameleon.

Even after a leisurely drive through town and the careful selection of a parking space, she was still too early to venture over to the Vat Building. So, she sat in her car and applied a light layer of powder and a little lipstick. Then she stared out the window, watching as the sun descended on the campus of her youth.

Her cell phone rang. David.

"You here yet?" he asked.

"Yeah."

"Well, come to the lounge. Help me set up."

"Isn't Mitch there helping?" she asked him. "I don't want to get in the way."

"Please, Jenn."

And that was how she found herself facing an assembly of acquaintances—a few who had actually been close friends back then—a full half hour prior to the start of the event. In fact, of the fifteen confirmed attendees, eleven were there early, so eager were they to reestablish that fleeting sense of unity and techie supremacy they'd felt within these walls. It had once flowed like electricity through their fingertips. That night, it was clear this was no longer the case but for a select few.

The first person to see her walk through the door was Pete, one of the CPU regulars from their college years. "Whoa, Jennifer?" he said, grinning. "Time's been good to you. You look great."

She couldn't honestly exclaim the same—he'd grown both bald and pudgy—but what a warm, welcoming smile he still had. She grinned back and said, "Thanks, Pete. It's wonderful to see you, too. How have you been?"

He told her a bit about his wife, their three little ones and the newest baby boy that'd arrived in April. The love he had for his family, however, could not mask the wistfulness he felt in being back in this room. Jennifer understood that. The world had once been limitless inside the Vat Building. They had once been untouchable. Neither was true anymore.

She saw David watching her from across the room. He lifted his hand in a wave and indicated he'd be there in a minute. She turned her attention back to Pete, who was still chattering sweetly about his family.

"Oh, but this story is *really* cute," he said, and launched into a tale about his four-year-old daughter. But before he got out more than one sentence about her attachment to "Dolly" her stuffed llama, he was interrupted by Bill—one of the always obnoxious Ehle brothers—carrying a cheese, sausage and cracker tray into the Techie Lounge.

"Yo, Jennifer. Long time, sunshine," Bill the more annoying twin said. "Hey, Pete, can you set this down on that table over there for me? Thanks, man." He deposited the tray into Pete's hands and, with a turn of his head, dismissed him. Pete blinked and slunk away as if slapped.

Jennifer swallowed and opened her mouth to tell him that wasn't very polite, but he wouldn't have heard her anyway.

"So, what's been up with you? You in IT?"

She began to shake her head, but Bill didn't wait for her to explain.

"You know, me and Bryce, we've been having a *very* good year." He leaned in and she could smell brandy on his breath already, even though the cocktails weren't set to begin for another twenty-some minutes. "We got a bead on a project that—" He leaned in even closer. "I probably shouldn't be tellin' you this, but we think Microsoft is gonna be hot for it." He eyed her up and down as if his clearly embellished "project" gave him the right to inspect everything and everyone that crossed his path.

"Really?" she managed. "How interesting." She took a step toward David, but Bill followed her.

"Yeah, I can't reveal any of the details yet, but, me and Bryce, we're pretty sure we're gonna get a big offer by—"

David strode over and clapped Bill on that back. "You'd better not spill more than that," he told him. "I could hear you over there by the tables." David pointed for good measure. "Just think what would happen if those top-secret details of yours got into the wrong hands?"

Bill's jaw dropped. "Uh . . ."

David threw his arms around Jennifer and gave her a side hug. "Nice to see you," he said to her. Then, to Bill, "You know, if we could find a quiet corner, I'd *really* like to hear more about what you and Bryce are doing after dinner. I mean, if we could be sure it'd be *private*. But, for now, I need Jenn's help, okay?" And with that he steered her away toward the drinks table.

She chuckled low enough so only he could hear. "Thank you," she whispered.

"Don't mention it," he said, his arm still around her. Then, louder, "Could you help me put some ice and a few of these beer bottles in the cooler?"

"No problem," she said, game for anything, even inane tasks, especially when he smiled at her that way, so much like the boy she'd known. Or, rather, thought she'd known.

She dipped her head, remembering, and started pouring ice into the jumbo C-IL-U cooler. It was clear Mitch and David spearheaded the event with a College Life theme in mind. Though everyone in attendance chipped in to cover the cost of the room, the booze and the food, the slogan of the night may well have been

"The Way We Were." She brushed a rogue ice chip off her casual but tastefully tailored outfit. Looking around her at some of the guys in the room, she thought she was the only one who missed the announcement of the jeans and sweatshirts dress code.

Until she spotted Allie.

Allie was wearing jeans—of a type. They were black and form-fitting, tapered to the ankles with black low-cut boots on her feet and some very sheer ivory material for a top. She wouldn't have looked *grossly* out of place, however, if it weren't for her expression of rapt fascination when she was chatting it up with a number of the guys—first Keith, then Charlie, then Bill's twin, Bryce. All of them edging up to talk with her. All of them equally riveting conversationalists, at least from the spellbound look on Allie's face.

"I think it's time for the drinks," David announced, seeing the direction of Jennifer's gaze. "What can I get you?"

"A wine. Something red," she said absently, observing the interplay between Allie and the men. People's personalities remained pretty constant, didn't they?

David handed her a plastic cup of Pinot Noir. "She got divorced five years ago."

"She tell you that?"

"Yeah," David said quickly. "Mitch and I needed to contact everyone, so . . ." He grabbed a bottle of Amstel Light for himself, popped it open and raised it in a private toast with her. "Here's to happy old days."

She clinked with him but couldn't bring herself to drink more than a sip. She was deluged by memories, more with every second that ticked passed. Not all of them were happy. Not even all the ones before David left. She tried another taste of wine. Its acidity seared the back of her throat as she tried to swallow it away.

David, by this time, had finished half of his beer. A *light* beer? Huh. He'd vowed never to drink that "watered-down piss," as she recalled. Maybe times had changed more than she'd thought.

She indicated the snack tray the abominable Bill made Pete bring to the table. "Want a cracker or something?"

David shook his head. "Nope. Cheese and salami—" He shuddered. "Not good for the abs."

She blinked at him. The *abs?* This was a far cry from the guy who'd loaded up on junk food at Kirby's for an all-night snack-a-thon when they were nineteen.

He shrugged at her expression of disbelief. "I know, I know. But it's easy to get a gut after a while. I wanna stay fit."

And, indeed, she hadn't really thought about it because, for her, keeping weight off was easier than for most (she didn't eat when she was stressed out), but he didn't look much heavier around the waist than he had during college. His face was fuller and older, yes, but not his stomach. Even Michael had put on some weight there, and most of the guys in the room were on the heftier side now. David must have worked hard to maintain his shape. Interesting.

"Hey, David," Allie said, sauntering up to them and winking at David. "Good to see you . . . again." She turned to Jennifer. "Wow. If it isn't the happy couple reunited at last, huh? You look"—Allie inspected her—"unchanged. Mostly."

Jennifer cleared her throat. "I was just thinking the same thing about you." She feigned a sweetish smile. "So, what have you been doing lately?" *Besides being an outrageous flirt,* she added silently.

"Oh, you know." She made a rolling motion with her hands. "One day's a lot like the other. Work and get-togethers with friends and weekend softball tournaments and stuff." She winked again at David. "We won our league's championship this year. Got to go on a fun overnighter in Springfield."

"Oh," Jennifer said. What the hell was it with all the winking? "Are you working in programming?"

Allie's eyes narrowed dangerously. "Of course. But I get manicures every week so my fingers don't look like it." Never one to be underestimated, she sloughed off the fluffy-headed act for a second so Jennifer could receive the full impact of her familiar intelligence behind those nasty blue eyes. Then she held up ten perfectly polished fingernails. French-tipped. "David tells me you do . . . Web pages." She laughed brightly, as if something so mundane couldn't *really* be possible. "He said you—"

"Oh, Allie, look." David nodded at the entrance. "Didn't you say you were wondering when Nico was gonna show? The dude's finally here."

"Excellent," Allie murmured, her attention momentarily diverted.

Jennifer wondered why the sudden interest in Nico, especially from somebody like Allie, who'd pointedly ignored the thin, quiet guy during all four years of college, preferring to focus on boys who could score her some good weed or, barring that, a high-tech microprocessor. "What's he been doing lately?" she asked them.

Allie looked at her like she was an uninformed and rather unsightly beetle. "You didn't hear? He owns N-tech Toys. They just went public last spring. Good ole Nico could buy and sell *all* of us three times over." She shook her head and smirked. "Sometimes you just can't call 'em."

Jennifer could see it was true. Even Bill and Bryce were kowtowing to him like he was Steve Jobs, Bill Gates and the CEO of a Japanese electronics firm all rolled into one. Poor guy. And then there was David—for a second his expression registered something like resentment. Huh.

Mitch, who'd been busy setting up an ancient Macintosh Classic II for part of their evening's entertainment, saluted David, then Allie and then her as he plugged in the beast they had all considered state-of-the-art once, despite their preference for PCs. (Well, except for Mitch.) He quickly welcomed Nico to the party and announced, "Who's ready for an original game of Monkey Pong?"

A cheer went up.

Monkey Pong, a game conceived and programmed by Mitch long before he became a designer at Apple, had monkeys swinging from trees and lobbing bananas—boomerang-style—at a range of unsuspecting jungle creatures. Players got points if their monkeys hit an ocelot or an anaconda, even more if they nailed a flying toucan or a scurrying iguana. Some of those suckers could be hard to see. In college, they had set up two consoles side by side and had tournaments in the lounge. That night, there was just one old computer, but the gang surrounded it like it was the newest MacBook Air.

The guys started taking turns playing. Mitch, in his element, grinned and guzzled some kind of vodka slushie thing while annihilating a jaguar and a couple of macaws. Charlie was the closest to giving Mitch a run for his money, but Jennifer also saw Dale, Jake and Ruben jumping in to play a round or two.

Ruben, one of the most tenderhearted guys Jennifer ever knew (David told her he now worked as a branch manager for Sprint), waved them over. Allie ignored him and sidled up to Nico, but David and Jennifer walked over. "Wanna play a round?" Ruben asked them. "For old times' sake?"

David said, "Sure," and when Jake finished his turn, David slid in. Despite the game's sentimental charm, though, Jennifer begged off.

Ruben grinned shyly at her. "Too much excitement for one night already?"

She nodded. "It's a little overwhelming." She watched over David's shoulder as he whacked his first ocelot. The guys whooped for him, but he barely seemed to notice. Ah, the beauty of computer games. Players could focus so hard on the screen and, like hypnosis, lose themselves. All the awkwardness, self-consciousness and the social unease would just disappear. It was one of the things she had loved so much about playing. Something she knew Shelby, if not Veronica, understood.

Jennifer sucked in some air. What was going on in Glendale Grove with her daughters? With Michael? She stole a peek at her cell phone. No messages from home. She didn't know if this was a good thing or a bad one.

The guys played for about an hour more as Jennifer observed the group and answered, with quiet one- or two-line comments, the questions asked by the guys from the old gang. Allie kept Nico hostage by the snack table but, otherwise, it was a gathering much like one of her family's holiday dinners. People who hadn't been together in months or years picked up threads of conversation as if no time had elapsed. It was surprisingly simple to slip into the old patterns of talking and being, and she couldn't help but notice how David reveled in his return to CPU sovereignty.

After that, they milled around, eating appetizers, drinking alcohol and chatting in revolving clusters. Jennifer was glad to see that Nico finally escaped Allie's clutches thanks to some deft maneuverings by Mitch and Pete. David stayed by Jennifer's side or very near it for the next hour, but she watched him shape and lead a number of discussions, crafting them with the skill of his old presidential experience. She, likewise, watched the other guys respond, happy to be in his orbit again.

Just before the pizzas and buffalo wings arrived at ten past seven (Fiorello's Pizzeria didn't follow David's orders for a precise 7:02 delivery—so much for an adherence to multiples of thirteen), Lexi appeared. She stood in the shadow of the doorway for a long moment, seemingly unsure whether she should walk through it. When Jennifer caught her eye, she made her decision.

"Hey, Jennifer," Lexi said. "Am I ever glad to see *you*." She hugged her, said a quick "Hi, there" to the guys, then glanced anxiously around the room.

Jennifer knew the person Lexi was looking for, so she said, "She's supposed to come, but she's late."

"I know," Lexi whispered. "I almost didn't show when Mitch told me Tash was gonna be here, but"—she shrugged— "can't let fear and bad memories ruin our lives, now can we?"

Jennifer shot a look at David and then back at Lexi. "Guess not." The two women shared a smile. Each having a huge club relationship crash-n-burn in public, they had more in common than most.

When Natasha—"Tash"—finally arrived, she gave Jennifer and Lexi a long-distance nod, but hung out in a different corner of the room with Dale, Kyle and a plateful of pizza. David, who was occupied with impressing Allie, Ruben and Bryce in a captivating discussion about his employer's GPS receivers, left Lexi and Jennifer to their "girl talk," as he called it.

Lexi raised her eyebrows at that, but said nothing back to him. To Jennifer, though, she said, "It's so weird seeing Tash again. Or even thinking about her. All those hurt feelings, all that betrayal . . . it's all still there, you know?"

Jennifer laughed faintly. Yeah, she knew. "But you're with someone good now, right? Someone caring?"

Lexi nodded. "Becca's great. We've been together for about twelve years. How about you?"

Jennifer told her about Michael and the girls, judiciously omitting all the marital tension of the past few months.

"Nice," Lexi said. "I'm glad to hear it, 'cuz, man, David was a real jerk to you at the end of college."

"Any idea why he did it? Or why Tash had been such a bitch to you when you two broke up? Was it a deep and permanent character flaw?" Jennifer asked her, not realizing until that moment how helpful it was to finally talk about David with someone who actually knew him. "Or was it just youthful thoughtlessness?"

Lexi pondered this as Jennifer snagged them each a slice of pepperoni. "This is what I think," she said, around a bit of pizza. "I had a few relationships blow up between when Tash and I split and before I met Becca. The thing I learned was that I needed a measuring stick to see whether a relationship was even worth fighting for. That knowledge still might not be enough to save it, but I had to know if there was a threshold below which there was *no way* it could possibly work. You follow?"

She gave a short nod.

"Okay," Lexi said. "I thought of this for the first time right before I left Tash. I kept asking myself if I believed she had my best interests in mind. Not because I was looking for some kind of martyr, but because I needed a girlfriend who, at least most of the time, seemed aware of me and my needs. Who didn't always put her own wants and wishes above mine. Tash might be really great for someone else, but for *me,* she wasn't so good. She didn't have my back, wasn't all that considerate and every time there was a choice to be made about what I wanted versus what she wanted, she assumed we'd go with her choice because she had the more forceful personality." She shrugged. "In the end, my leaving blindsided her and it pissed her off big time, but that was only because she hadn't been paying attention to what I'd been asking for all along."

Jennifer considered this. "So, you'd told her? You'd expressed what you needed and *still* she didn't listen?"

"Yep."

She thought about David at the end of their relationship. She knew she had told him she loved him and she needed him. She knew she had expressed those things as part of the rhythm of their daily interactions. She thought he had expressed them in return. Did she not remember correctly? Could *she* have been the one who didn't recognize the signs of his unhappiness? Might he have tried to tell her what he needed and she just didn't realize it?

A few minutes later David wandered over to them and asked to steal her away for a walk. So, after she and Lexi exchanged e-mail addresses and phone numbers, Jennifer and David slipped on their jackets and headed out into the crisp mid-November night.

They roamed through the campus, soundlessly at first. Past the Weaver Center. ("Want a strawberry milkshake?" he asked, breaking the silence. "Not this time," she replied, knowing his cryptic reference was: "Remember our first date?") They meandered near the Catacombs, where student voices could be heard clearly even out on the walkways, and then alongside TJH. In the dark, if they didn't look at each other directly, Jennifer suspected they could almost delude themselves into believing they were those kids again. David, unspoken and glancing at her askance, reached for the sleeve of her coat, near her wrist, squeezing it as if he were holding her hand.

Because it *wasn't* her hand, she let him keep his grasp on it, but she had waited long enough to question him.

"So, what's going on with you and Marcia?" she began.

He shrugged and, even peripherally, looked uncomfortable. "I told you almost everything already. You know it's not . . . great between us. We're still together because of the boys, but that's all." He shrugged again and Jennifer remembered he'd used those exact sentences when he'd told her of his marital woes via e-mail and text. "What can I say? I made a mistake, Jenn."

She took a big breath. "What happened in those last couple of months of college, David—with us? Was it pressure from Sandra that broke us up? Marcia? Your parents or your friends? Or was it me? Did I not listen to you?"

He paused in the middle of the sidewalk and closed his eyes tight. Then he let his hand slide from her cuff to her chilled palm. The heat of his fingers burned hers, but she held on.

When they began walking again, he said, "It wasn't you, Jenn.

There was pressure . . . from outside of us. Mostly from my sister but, also, I kinda panicked. I caved in to what other people thought was best for me, but I didn't know then what I know now. I realize it's a cliché to say that, but it's true. Time helps a man see things better, and I didn't know what a good thing we had until it was gone."

Jennifer wasn't completely untouched by his speech, but it just seemed so *well practiced*. Her suspicions flared, possibly without reason. Or, maybe, there was a shred of logic that accompanied the unanticipated niggle of "feeling" that shot through her. In fact, had she not been at the reunion to witness the social dynamics with her own eyes, she wouldn't have remembered something. That, in their last few weeks of college, Allie had made herself pretty scarce, too. That David wasn't the only one who was MIA. And on this very night, all those years later, there was so much winking between them.

"David," she said sharply, "did something happen between you and Allie? Did you two have some sort of fling?" She thought of the very first comment Allie had made to David back in the lounge: *"Good to see you"*—and then there was a pause—*"again."* Again?

"When?" he shot back.

And that was when Jennifer snapped the puzzle pieces together. *Oh, my God. When?* as in *Which time?*

"At the end of our senior year, David. And, again, I suspect. Sometime more recently." She wrenched her hand away from his. "Right?"

He halted in the middle of the sidewalk, not more than a few yards away from a constellation of trees in one of the small quads. He tugged her into the shadow of a massive oak and leaned close to her. "Jenn," he whispered, his voice urgent. "Don't waste time thinking about Allie. She's irrelevant. I've missed *you*. How do I get you to understand that? To understand that nothing else matters?"

He positioned her so her back rested against the tree trunk, jagged bits of bark pressing unevenly into her thin jacket. He leaned closer still until his lips connected with hers. Until he had slyly managed to reenact a scene from their senior year in college, one she remembered distinctly.

They had kissed here before. Right at that very spot. On a night like this one, not long before their Thanksgiving break when they knew they would be apart for a whole week. As David's lips moved against hers, that past night and this present one merged. She didn't resist him at first because, well, it was so strangely familiar. Almost not like a new scene at all. They were merely picking up—across the dimension of time—where they had left off.

And then, that very familiarity became creepy. The moment turned a shade peculiar, and the oddness of this recognized duality twisted in her gut, like a coin flipping sides.

She pressed her palms against his chest and pushed him gently away. "Did you have a fling with Allie?" she asked him again. "Ever? At any time?"

He took a step backward and exhaled heavily. "Look, a few years ago, we had a brief . . . tryst, I guess you could call it. We'd gotten in contact again—I can't even remember how that happened now. But she'd just gotten divorced and my marriage really sucked and, so . . ." He tried to shrug it off. "It made me realize how much I missed you, actually. I think I was trying to substitute Allie for you."

His dark eyes bored into her, his ultra-earnestness a poisoned-tipped bayonet. She closed her own eyes for a moment so she wouldn't have to cope with the duplicity. Then she opened them and met his gaze. "And were you trying to substitute Allie for me right before graduation, too?"

He shook his head too vigorously. "No, Jenn, look—"

"Tell me the truth, David. Or I'll ask her myself." She pointed in the direction of the Vat Building. "I know Allie will tell me if you two slept together back then. Gleefully, I'm willing to bet. And in front of the whole CPU gang."

He grunted and swiveled away from her. "Fine. Yes—okay? But just one time. It was a dumb thing. A reaction. I don't know what it was. Anyway, it was a *really* long time ago. It doesn't matter."

She laughed because, truly, this was ludicrous. Did he really not recognize how he had handed her the perfect counterargument?

Did he not see, as she did so clearly now, what a little fool she had been . . . and, in some ways, still was? Maybe he was counting on her to continue her streak of idiocy because he just kept staring at her, his expression one of pathetic pleading.

"David, *we* were a really long time ago, too," she said, surprising even herself with the levelness of her voice given the news she had just been dealt. "But you're right. It doesn't matter. It's over. We're over. In fact, we've been over for more than eighteen years. We need to say good night and go home."

She stayed facing him, awaiting his inevitable argument, but in her mind, she sprinted through all the reasons (even putting aside his involvement with Allie) that had clarified their incompatibility to her already that fall:

The way he had tried to subtly undermine her relationship with Michael and to downplay the significance of his own numerous deceptions to his wife.

The way she had seen him relishing every moment of his club-president omnipotence and trying to recreate the world where she and all their friends revolved around him. A means of bolstering his ego and tapping into the vitality of a now-diminished youth.

The way he had chosen to assert what little potency he had retained with an air of entitlement that wasn't the least bit kind or attractive, in her opinion.

And, in answer to Lexi's excellent question, the way he had repeatedly proven he didn't have her best interests in mind. Not then. Not now.

"Please, Jenn. We're not through with each other yet. There's unfinished business between us. You felt that kiss, didn't you? It felt so right. We're so right together. We *get* each other. You can't deny that."

David was smart, yes. He understood her on many levels—certainly enough to manipulate her well—but he only ever did what he thought was good for himself. Not for her. Not for his wife. Not even for stray lovers. Michael at least demonstrated putting her and the girls ahead of his own needs sometimes. Many times, she realized. She couldn't help but be grateful to him for that. To wish she'd shown him much more appreciation for this trait.

"I'm not denying that, David. I'm not denying anything. I just think we want very different things out of life, and one of the things I want is my family."

He slanted her a speculative look, and said, "The two don't have to be incongruous. I mean, I love my kids, too. We can be together, you and I, and still be good parents and pretty good spouses—if we're careful. It's not like your husband and my wife are such great prizes, right? It's not like they understand us like we deserve to be understood."

She stared at him, amazed the man could look so normal on the outside (with trim abs even) and, yet, be such a pathological liar and all-around bastard. Jennifer was pleased with herself for attaining an undeniable sense of certainty about that. And a sense of peacefulness. She would no longer be haunted by the end of that relationship.

"It's incongruous for *me*, David. So, I don't think we have any unfinished business left now. Really. Good night . . . and good-bye."

She spun around and half walked, half jogged back to her car, breathing deep yoga breaths and saying farewell to each building on campus as she passed it. So long, Vat Building. Bye-bye, Weaver Center. Adios, Thomas Jefferson Hall. David, she was relieved to discover, was intelligent enough not to follow her. And as she slipped into her car and turned the ignition, she knew this part of her life was officially, finally, thankfully *over*.

She drove home without even the comfort of the radio. She found herself tuning in to something different—something internal—but the signal was coming in kind of fuzzily still. She didn't want too many distractions from it, even though it kind of felt more like indigestion than intuition.

But, also, it was late, she was tired and she wanted to be near those she loved. Her daughters, of course, but Michael, too. Despite his negative feelings toward the "massively bad guy" from her past, she was thankful he didn't try to physically prevent her from going to see David. Whether Michael realized it or not, it *was* a necessity for her. And, God, what she'd learned. It sure took her long enough. . . .

Of course, the problem remained that she still really didn't know what Jennifer World was like when she was alone. She had never taken the time to experience it, which was her fault, perhaps, but if she didn't do it soon, she would *still* be to blame. She also wouldn't be doing Michael or even her daughters any favors. She had been a poor guide for Veronica and Shelby lately. She wasn't helping them navigate adolescence well at all. This, she realized, couldn't happen if she didn't know herself. If she just kept blending into whatever environment appeared before her.

Jennifer left her overnight bag in the car and walked into the house, surprised to find Michael still awake at eleven-thirty. He was an early-to-bed, early-to-rise type and, considering how drained he looked, he should've gone to bed at ten.

"Hi," she said.

He raised his hand in a faint wave but didn't speak. With their relationship issues unresolved but at least out in the open, he hadn't been as susceptible to breaking things lately, nor was he as inclined to walk on eggshells around her anymore. She understood this. She gathered he had spent the day trying to shield and reassure their daughters but, by this late in the evening, he was weary. And still very angry with her.

"You're still up?"

"Couldn't sleep." He paused. "You're back, I see."

"Yes, I'm back. And, Michael, you were right about something. David is not a great guy. I knew that before, actually. I remembered it, but tonight . . . I remembered a lot of other things, too. I wanted to see what it was like to be back in the same place with everyone again."

"And?"

"And mostly it was sad. Mostly it was a lot of people wishing they were twenty years younger and they had their choices to make all over again."

He bobbed his head once or twice. "Human nature." But something in his eyes brightened a bit. They didn't have quite the sheen of exhaustion and despondency as when she had first walked in. "So, where are you now? Did you get all that out of your system?"

Something about the way he said this rubbed her the wrong way. They were just words, but it was the implication that she'd been completely mistaken that bothered her. She'd made plenty of mistakes, yes, but not *everything* she'd reacted to in the past few months was erroneous. And not *everything* that was a problem in their marriage was because of her ex-boyfriend.

"I won't be seeing David again. Not anytime soon. Probably not ever," she told him. "If that's what you're wondering. I spoke with another old friend of mine tonight, though. Lexi. And she and I might get together for lunch sometime."

He shrugged as if to say "Whatever."

"And as for 'getting all that out of my system,' I'll have to get back to you on that. I still don't know what's in my . . . system. Or how it works." Then, for the first time in months, since David's original message on August thirteenth, to be precise, she was being honest enough to look her husband in the eye. And she felt—yes, actually *intuited*—that he knew she was no longer their family chameleon.

❧ 21 ❧

The Trio

Friday, November 19

They arrived at the Indigo Moon Café within five minutes of each other. This time, Tamara got there first, a penitent look on her face and a preorder of three lattes and three big hunks of pecan-caramel coffee cake (the November special) on their table.

"What's this for?" Jennifer asked, when she walked in next.

And Bridget, who whisked herself to the table a moment later, exclaimed, "Oh, my goodness. Those look like they have a million calories! Who ordered already?"

"I did," Tamara said. "It's my apology for accidentally skipping out on you two last week."

Was an act of contrition necessary? Bridget thought.

And Jennifer was on the verge of saying, "So, why—really—did you skip out on us?" But Tamara shot her a please-don't-ask look and pointed to the table. "Try the coffee cake, you guys. It's good."

So, they all sat down, started nibbling and began their customary chitchat routine . . . their focus on the usual, predictable subjects, which created a visible degree of ease and emotional weightlessness:

Benji was going to be coming home on Monday, just as Jon was leaving for a few days, but both would be there for Thanksgiving.

Bridget took Evan to the doctor for more follow-up tests, all of them seeming to confirm a diagnosis of celiac disease, which, while good to know, would mean a lifetime of restrictive diets for her son.

Jennifer's daughters were withholding information, especially Veronica, and this was causing parental concern.

And so on and so forth for the first twenty minutes.

They were interrupted only once, by the owner, who'd stopped by their table to ask how they liked the new coffee cake.

"It's delicious," Bridget enthused.

Tamara and Jennifer agreed, but Tamara couldn't help but roll her eyes when Gordon Lightfoot began his 1970s lamentation of "If You Could Read My Mind."

"The cake's excellent," she told the man, "but is there any chance we could bribe you into changing the radio station? I'd take eighties, nineties, alternative, Elvis's greatest hits, *anything* else."

The owner shook his balding head. "No can do, ma'am. The wife loves this station. Only one she'll listen to."

"But *why?*" Tamara had lived through the seventies. Year by agonizing year. She'd had more than enough of its music before the decade ended.

"She says they knew how to write about real heartache back then. She says it's way better than that whiny stuff on the radio today." He leaned closer to Tamara and pointed in the direction of the kitchen. "I'd rather listen to Smashing Pumpkins myself, but I'm gonna give her what she wants, you know? I need her here. She's the one who bakes."

Tamara couldn't think of a counterargument to that, so she shrugged and the owner smiled at her. Then he walked off to the next table.

Bridget, who shared neither Tamara's resentment for the music nor Jennifer's affinity for it, felt she had a lot to be thankful for and expressed her excitement over the upcoming holiday. "It's more of a challenge now to cook recipes Evan can eat," she said. "There are a bunch of traditional dishes he just won't be able to have anymore, like the bread pudding, but I'm having fun coming up with things he can enjoy. It's going to be a pretty big crowd this year."

Jennifer, who thought Bridget's overly packed house for every national and religious holiday was just a few millimeters short of a screaming nightmare, couldn't help but ask, "How many people are coming?"

Bridget stared into space and started counting, her left thumb touching each finger as she named a family cluster. "Well, there's my brother's family, my two sisters and their husbands and kids, my parents, my Auntie Barb and the five of us . . . so, about twenty-two, if everyone shows up."

Tamara groaned. "You're cooking a full Thanksgiving dinner for all of them? Good God, you're insane."

But Bridget shook her head. "No, it's the *best*. Everyone's together. We've all changed a little since the last time we saw everybody, but not so much that we don't recognize each other. We can catch up on news. Spend a few hours with my parents and my aunt, who are getting older. Well, I guess we all are." She smiled faintly. "And I have a captive group of taste-testers at my disposal for my latest recipe acquisitions—like Turkey Tetrazzini al Formaggio and Sweet Potato Dumpling Bake. It's gonna be awesome."

"Knock yourself out, sister," Tamara said.

Bridget knew this wasn't a passion her friends would understand, but, oh, Dr. Luke did! Just yesterday at the dental office, she was flipping through one of her newest cookbooks, *A Tasteful Thanksgiving*, when he stood behind her at the desk and looked over her shoulder as she perused some possible side dish selections.

"How about those?" he said as she turned to the page with recipes for Spinach-Stuffed Zucchini and a very healthy looking Autumn Squash Casserole.

She used a purple Post-It Note to tag the page, but then she saw a picture for the delectable Wild Rice Stuffing on the other side. Oh, and Savory Corn Pudding. Hmm. She skipped to the next page—Brandied Pumpkin Pie!—but before she could even point to it, Dr. Luke said, "Oooh, that one."

"Or maybe the Sherry-Soaked Cranberry Cake?" she suggested, tapping the picture on the facing page. She shot a look back at him and they shared a moment of enchanted expectation. So many possibilities.

"Or both," they said together, laughing. It was like being at the Italian restaurant with him all over again. Like kids playing with an Easy-Bake Oven. Like a free pass back to the imaginary creations and simple pleasures of childhood. No wonder she didn't want to let go of him.

Then, with one eye on her and another on the door, he added, "And you can invite me over for it, too."

It occurred to her then that, perhaps, this was something Dr. Luke missed as well. The whimsy of childhood, the sense of inclusion . . . both of which often seemed to dissipate into the overpowering mist of the adult world. That their ability to have reclaimed a bit of that joy together—in the course of their short *friendship*—was rare.

"We'd love to have you join us, you know," she said, hoping she projected the earnestness she felt. "Do you have plans for Thanksgiving Day?"

Again, his eyes strayed to the door. Graham had popped into the office as a "surprise" more than once this month, and Dr. Nina would just as soon grimace as grin at someone if she walked in. "I'm afraid I do," he said with a gentle smile. "My sister and her family have slotted me into a place at the kids' table already, but thank you."

He was absentmindedly fingering his gold cross, and Bridget remembered something he'd told her one day in passing. That there were times that shook a person's faith. He said he knew all about that. But he also said people needed to do whatever they could to get it back, and being with those they loved and those who loved them in return always helped. "It's fun just imagining what you'll come up with next week," he added. "Your creativity with food astounds me."

"Another time, then," she said. "Promise?"

"Yes," he said. "I promise."

Bridget embraced his words—"your creativity with food astounds me"—and, through them, finally found the courage to give voice to the dream she had held silently but hopefully within her for so many years.

To Jennifer and Tamara that day, she explained, "This is really what I want to do with my life. I want to go to culinary school. I want to cook complicated things for people."

"In other words, you finally figured out who you wanna be when you grow up, and it's a chef," Tamara said, grinning.

"Yes." Bridget nodded emphatically. "Yes, it is." With all her heart and soul, yes! Was she too old? Was it too late for her? God, please make it still be possible.

Jennifer gazed with affection at their sweet friend. "Then don't let anything stop you," she said quietly.

Even Tamara said, seriously this time, "If anyone could do it, it'd be you."

"Thanks, you guys." Bridget wiped away a small drop of wetness that had somehow collected in the corner of her eye. Why was she always so emotional? Of course, admitting her big dream aloud was only the first step. "I just have to break it to Graham now."

"You don't think he'll be supportive?" Jennifer asked.

Bridget shrugged. "There have been a lot of changes for us this year already. Me going back to work. Evan's food issues. The stress of us not being on the same page in our relationship." She thought of the post-Hallowiener Party, their blowup and their reconciliation. The fact that they had both been open and willing to work on their issues had set their marriage on the road to recovery, but Bridget didn't want to push it with Graham. She didn't want to heap on more changes when he was already making a bunch of compromises on her behalf. "I'm sure he'll think that I've got enough on my plate just trying to make gluten-free dishes for Evan. And, in a way, he'd be right. They *are* a challenge."

"Just not the *only* cooking challenge you want," Jennifer discerned.

Bridget nodded. And though she didn't tell her friends this, she couldn't help but worry that Graham's recent attentiveness was just a temporary thing. A knee-jerk reaction to the perceived threat of another man. That Graham might only be willing to take these few cursory steps as a way to thwart Dr. Luke, but he wouldn't necessarily stand for any *real* test. Any major change in their family's lifestyle.

"You might be surprised, Bridget," Tamara suggested, oddly mysterious. "You've really been there for your family all these years. I think they know that. I think each of them might be more willing to support you than you realize."

Jennifer shot Tamara a curious look when she said that, which Bridget didn't notice because she was too preoccupied wrestling the residual jabs of guilt she felt. Though Tamara's statement was awfully kind, it wasn't strictly true. Bridget couldn't forget she'd had months of wayward fantasies and, even though she had never once strayed in her marriage, she knew her "moments" with Dr. Luke had been genuine. That, no matter what she tried to tell herself, her attraction and attachment to the dentist wasn't purely based in "friendship."

"I hope so," Bridget murmured.

Tamara then turned her attention to Jennifer, who seemed to be weaving in and out of a long and dark procession of thoughts. "You've held out on us long enough, Jennifer," she said, showing uncharacteristically high restraint despite her small, sly grin. "I was half hoping you'd call for an emergency coffee meeting this past Monday to tell us what the hell happened at your reunion last weekend. I didn't want to pester you, but I've been dying of curiosity here."

Jennifer bobbed her head. She knew by coming today that she was opening herself up to questions. She'd answer the ones she could. Or at least most of them. Probably.

So, she told them about going to the CPU party. About seeing David again and about crossing paths with the others in her college group of friends.

"I was looking for closure," she told them quietly. "And I got it."

Tamara raised a thin brow. "And?"

"And a part of me is embarrassed. That I'd thought about David for so long and wasted so much time pining over the end of our relationship. Wondering for years 'what if' scenarios—what if he'd never left me or what if I'd somehow gotten him back?" She paused. "The truth is, he *did* leave me, and that said something about him, and about his character, that I didn't want to acknowledge. I also finally understood what a player he is. I guess, on a number of levels, I always knew that, but we were both so young back then. Some players mature over time. Grow out of the worst of it. David only became more skilled. And more desperate. Seeing is believing, I know. But I didn't want to acknowledge what I saw for a long time either."

"Because it made you feel foolish," Tamara said, understanding. It had been a double ego blow for their friend, she realized. Not only had Jennifer been abandoned by a guy she had been imagining a future with, but she had been blindsided—something that made any smart girl feel stupid. Women like Jennifer and Tamara would craft almost any excuse not to feel this way about themselves, even to the point of complete self-delusion. Tamara surmised that Bridget was less calculating by nature and, thus, fortunate in not suffering quite so much from this destructive trait.

"What about Michael?" Bridget asked. "With David out of the picture, how are you feeling about your marriage now? Was it the right decision after all?"

Jennifer swallowed. This was a valid question. The question that had continued to haunt her for months, in fact. Or years. "Bridget, I don't know." She kind of laughed. "And even *I* am starting to get sick of hearing myself say that. The reunion proved a number of things to me. David's a jerk and always has been. People who were truly my friends still are. People who weren't, well, they won't be inviting me to friend them on Facebook anytime soon. The kinds of bad decisions I was vulnerable to making back then, I'm still vulnerable to now. And, above all, I'll only hurt people I care about if I keep floating along with what others tell me I should want, and playing these passive-aggressive games with them." She sighed. "See, it turns out that in my relationship with Michael, *I'm* the player. But I don't want to be anymore."

Again, Tamara was the one who understood immediately and instinctively what Jennifer was saying. Wasn't this a bit like Aaron's accusation of her? That, in his opinion, *she* was the manipulative one? Only her marital scenario with Jon had mostly played itself out already, while Jennifer's domestic drama with Michael was still in the rehearsal stages. Though eighteen years was a long fucking practice run.

Bridget, by contrast, could not fully grasp this whole *player* conundrum and its implications. She did, however, sense how emotionally distraught their friend was, and she had recently witnessed the discord between Jennifer and Michael firsthand. She knew what it felt like to be at odds with one's spouse. It made living together a distancing experience. More like bunking with an indifferent roommate than sharing a home with a loving husband. And that was really, really hard to deal with. Even for people like Jennifer, who weren't overly emotional. Maybe especially then . . . because their intimate inner circle was that much smaller.

"What are you going to do?" Bridget asked.

Jennifer shrugged. "I don't know that either. But I do know I owe it to Michael and the girls to do something." Then, having had the conversational focus on her and her foibles for far longer than was comfortable, Jennifer wanted to turn the tide of attention elsewhere. She suspected she knew just how to do it.

"How are things going for *you?*" she asked Tamara, very tempted to press their friend on the oversleeping issue, but suddenly not sure if she should push it. Perhaps Tamara would be more inclined to share deeply since she'd had an hour's proof that both her friends weren't living in idyllic marriages. But what if she wasn't? She shot Tamara a distressed look.

Bridget stabbed at her coffee cake and glanced between the other two women—unable to hide her concern for Jennifer over her marital uncertainties or her confusion about Tamara over her unusual degree of serenity. What was going on here?

Tamara gulped a few sips of her latte and almost laughed. How often had she been accused of being overly dramatic? Of trying to upstage everyone in a discussion? Yeah. A helluva lot. So, here she was, resisting all urges to blurt out any histrionics, downplaying something *huge*, and what happened? She was getting pleading looks from Jennifer and what-the-fuck looks from Bridget. Both of them saying in nonverbal SOS, "Say something!"

Okay, fine. She'd say it. She could phrase almost anything for shock value, if she tried. But with this news, she didn't have to try.

"So, Jon and I had a long talk a couple of nights ago. We're getting divorced."

"What?" Jennifer exclaimed, in about the loudest tone Tamara had ever heard her use, momentarily drowning out even the Bee Gees crooning "How Deep Is Your Love."

At the same time, Bridget dropped her forkful of coffee cake and the fork along with it. "Oh, my God, Tamara! What happened?"

Ah, well that was kind of a long story, wasn't it?

It happened this way, Tamara explained:

After several days in a row with Aaron (about which she admitted to her friends that, yes, they'd slept together but, no, she wasn't yet prepared to divulge those intimate details), Tamara knew she would have to officially end things with Jon. And soon.

Some people, she reasoned, might be able to go on living with their spouse after a deliberate act of infidelity, but Tamara wasn't one of them. She, in fact, could only justify her unfaithfulness because she had determined that her marriage was over. She remained unwavering on this point.

Jon returned on Tuesday. He had been gone only six days, five nights but, as she had discovered, a lot could happen in that time. Tamara gave him until Wednesday to get settled back into his usual routine, then she suggested carryout for dinner from his favorite restaurant.

"The crispy duck is especially moist tonight," he'd informed her, dipping a forkful into the plum sauce. He had a way of spreading out his stuff all over their dining room table, edging farther and farther into her space until she had to physically move to Benji's old spot in order to have any elbow room. Normally, she found this annoying. That night, she was filled with a tremendous ache for him. For the pain she knew she would be inflicting. No matter how stale their relationship had become, they had weathered years of storms together and, in many ways, she was really grateful to Jon and proud of them both. This point of pure appreciation was, she felt, where she needed to begin.

"Seeing Benji start college, it reminded me of how young we

were when we met," she said to Jon, her voice wavering a bit. "How we'd barely turned into adults before he entered our lives. For you and me, it was an almost instant family, especially since we'd been such loners before."

Jon speared a cucumber wedge and a couple of shredded carrots from his Asian salad. "Yep."

"It was hard for both of us, but we did it. We stuck together. We raised him, and he's turned into a beautiful boy . . . a young man." The tears rushed to her eyes, but she blinked them away and beamed her brightest smile at her husband.

Jon, who was now munching on the end of an eggroll and staring at her a bit strangely, murmured, "Yeah, he's great."

"So, I'm really proud of us. And I'm so thankful for all you did, too."

Goddammit. It was so hard to lead into the end like this. So hard to see the dream of their life together fade. But, if she were being entirely truthful with herself, she'd had too many doubts, down too deep, to have ever believed their marriage was *right*. Maybe that was why she had fought so valiantly for so long to deny the possibility of divorce. She, like Jennifer, hadn't wanted to believe she could make a stupid mistake like that. And, while it was debatable whether she had stayed with Jon too long while Benji was still at home, now—without their son there—she *knew* it was too long. The child who had bound them together had left home, taking their family bond with him.

She snatched a breath and tried to get to the heart of it. "Jon, I think we've reached . . . an ending point." She couldn't help it. She started crying and, though she brushed the wetness away, the tears kept coming. "I'm so sorry. I know you don't like emotional displays."

He put down his eggroll and silently handed her a Beijing Bistro napkin. The look on his face was initially one of surprise, but he quickly veiled it with the lawyerlike poker face of neutrality. He cleared his throat. "What are you saying, Tamara?"

She wiped her eyes again. "I'm saying, the time has come for us to finally separate. Benji held us together for nineteen years. Without him, we never would've lasted that long. You know that."

He nodded, his expression more deflated by the news than she had expected, but it wasn't as though he moved to contradict her. She saw him swallow a few times and glance around them—at the dining room, the kitchen, the visible wall of the living room—as if he were saying goodbye to the house already. "So, are you asking me to move out? Planning to go somewhere else yourself?" He sighed. "What are the details you've worked through from your side so far?"

Tears were now streaming down her face. There weren't enough Beijing Bistro napkins for them all. But Jon had switched to logical, problem-solving mode, and she was required to switch with him. "I haven't made any formal plans yet, Jon. I wanted to discuss everything with you."

His jaw tensed at this, his natural instinct to negotiate obviously rising to the surface, but a rare look of approval flashed behind his eyes in paradoxical negation of any hard-line tactics. She knew then he wasn't going to pull out all the legalistic guns. That they would be able to do this without excessive antagonism or the need for high court fees. That somewhere, despite the initial shock, he had seen this coming for as many years as she had. And, just as she, felt both the sting and the balm of relief.

"Well, the first thing we'll need to do is sell the house." He scanned the rooms around them once again, in appraisal more than wistfulness this time. "The market's poor, but I'll look into it."

"The first thing we'll need to do," she corrected, "is tell Benji."

He nodded. "Of course. He'll be home next week."

"Jon—" She'd been thinking about this, unsure how to ask it. "He's arriving a couple of days before you return from your next trip. W-What would you like me to do? Shall I tell him when he gets here? He might ask something... about us. Or, would you rather I waited until you got back?" How cold these words were. How dispassionate. As if they were telling their son they were merely redecorating his bedroom rather than disbanding the family unit.

Jon almost smiled. Sadly. "If you can avoid painting me as a villain, tell him when he gets home. I doubt it matters, really." He shrugged and pushed away the plate of duck. "You're sure this is what you want?" he asked her, and finally she detected a hint of the pain that lay beneath his protective mask. Finally, he allowed some of it to show through. The real man, not the shadow. But it was just a sliver and it came far too late.

She inhaled. Exhaled. "No, Jon. Not at all. But it's what I need."

And, really, that was it, she explained to her friends. She and Jon put away the leftover Chinese. They made a pot of coffee. And they each worked independently for the next several hours on organizing some of their personal things—Tamara in the bedroom and Jon in his office.

"What do you mean, *that was it?*" Bridget asked, incredulous. "You didn't talk more? Yell at each other? Cry together or anything?"

"Nope. But sometime around eleven, we watched a late-night *Seinfeld* rerun together. He'd turned on the TV in the living room and, so, I wandered in there and stayed with him. Just for the length of the episode. It was the Soup Nazi one," Tamara said, as if that explained her reason for not leaving the room.

Jennifer studied their friend. "No mention of Aaron?"

Tamara shook her head. "Nah. I like Aaron and everything. He's a good guy, all things considered. But this wasn't about him." She lifted her shoulders and palms, then dropped them. "Besides, what he and I have going isn't gonna last. It's just about the sex."

"What?" Bridget exclaimed. "Really and truly? How could that be?" She knew Tamara couldn't possibly believe that! "Aren't you even kind of in love with him?"

Tamara unleashed her most dazzling, win-over-strangers grin. "You're kidding, right? I'm finally on the verge of being *free* after almost twenty years of marriage. The 'other man' is a dozen years younger than I am and a freakin' train wreck in his past relationships. Who needs *that?*"

"Who, indeed," Jennifer murmured.

But Tamara refused to take the bait in any form—subtle or overt. Aaron wasn't someone a woman could easily describe, and revealing her feelings for him—let alone the details of her nights/days with him and the odd, unsettling vibrations he created within her when they talked—this was *not* gonna happen. First, she wasn't a complete bloody idiot. She knew she was in a vulnerable state. She knew she had been skirting the periphery of self-delusion for months or years. And she damn well knew she needed to separate her attraction to Aaron from her desire to be liberated from her marriage to Jon.

Two different Princes. Two different problems.

Second, she couldn't quite bring herself to turn her time with Aaron—chimerical or not—into some cheap, gossipy exercise of Kiss 'n' Tell.

No. Just . . . no.

Thankfully, her friends let her have her way but, when they finished their lattes and their coffee cake, Bridget squeezed Tamara extra hard.

"Please call me if you need to talk," Bridget said. "Even with the crazy holiday stuff coming up. You know I'm here for you, right?"

"Right."

"Me, too," Jennifer added, giving them both one of her unusual side-to-side hugs. "Even if we're not meeting for a few weeks, we can always get together for an emergency coffee date."

Tamara smiled at her friends, genuinely this time. At last not trying to convince anyone (not even herself) of anything.

They'd all agreed, with the several weeks of holidays coming up, to give the Indigo Moon Café gatherings a rest between Thanksgiving and New Year's Day. They did that every year, usually out of necessity. But Tamara appreciated their caring gesture and their willingness to make an exception for her this year, if she called for it. Time with true friends was an unparalleled gift. In the holiday season. In *any* season.

"Thanks, you two," Tamara said. "I'll keep you posted."

And, so, with a sense of unity they hadn't fully felt in a while, the trio went their separate ways for a few weeks—to pick up the threads of their individual tales:

To strengthen them.

To unravel them.

Or, to weave them into new stories fit for telling. . . .

❧ 22 ❧

"Bridget & the Magic Spatula"

Thanksgiving through early December

Once upon a time, a dental office receptionist named Bridget found herself growing weary of the lack of creativity in her life, the seeming inability of her husband and children to understand the depth of her passion for cooking and her own disenchantment with her aging, premenopausal body. She could feel the passage of years in every one of her fat cells, even when she tried to block it out.

She desperately did not want to become one of those unfulfilled suburban housewives who woke up one winter's morning only to find herself retired, without hobbies and certain the best part of the day was over once *Wheel of Fortune* ended after dinner.

No. If she was going to be a frumpy forty-something no matter what she did, something else was gonna have to change. Big time.

As she flipped the omelet in her favorite copper skillet on the Saturday morning after Thanksgiving, and admired the speckled starburst of red and green bell peppers she had carefully chopped and dropped into the egg mixture, she felt a bit of residual magic flowing through her fingertips. She had loved preparing the big turkey feast for her immediate and extended family members a couple of days before, but she couldn't save up her joy to share just on holidays. Daily life *had* to have more to offer than this . . . this

waiting . . . this holding her breath . . . this reining in of her desires. Didn't it?

"Breakfast, everyone," she called. She slid the finished omelet
onto a platter—half would be for her younger son Evan, who had
"a dietary restriction," the other half for whoever else wanted a
taste—and she placed it on the table in between the stack of
freshly made cinnamon-nut pancakes and the big bowl of fruit
salad.

Four pairs of feet raced toward the table.

"Smells great, Mom," her daughter Cassandra said, helping herself to a couple of pancakes and a spoonful of fruit.

Her sons, Keaton and Evan, scooted into their chairs and simply
began eating, while her husband, Graham, came into the kitchen
and put his arms around her. Lightly kissed her cheek. And then
her lips. "Hi, hon. You doing okay?" he asked.

She started to nod (last night, she and her husband locked their
bedroom door after the kids had gone to bed, and they entertained
themselves with Bridget's favorite adult board game: Strip Chocolate). She blushed, remembering, and glanced away momentarily.
But, in that instant, her eyes caught sight of the spatula she'd been
using, resting in the sink now, immersed in the soapy skillet. The
fingers on her right hand began to tingle.

So, instead, she shook her head. "Graham, there's something
I've been wanting to—to talk about with you. Do you have a few
minutes?"

His eyes widened in surprise, a hint of worry racing across his
irises but, nonetheless, he whispered, "Sure."

So, immediately after breakfast, the children having squirreled
themselves away in the living room watching cartoons on Nick-
elodeon, Bridget and Graham stole a half hour alone to talk, side
by side on their staircase.

He opened his palm for her, and she placed her hand on top of
his. He wrapped his warm, strong fingers around hers, and asked,
"What's going on?"

She squeezed his fingers. "It's been a tough fall, and we had a
lot of little challenges to get through. I think, in the end, we han-

dled them okay." She looked at Graham for confirmation and waited, hoping for a nod.

"Yeah. Me, too," he agreed.

"I'm working at the office now and really enjoying it, and I'm so glad you've come in a few times to . . . to meet the staff and see what's going on there."

Her husband's eyes narrowed, ever so slightly. "They're all pretty nice. Mostly."

She smiled, knowing he was thinking of Dr. Nina. "Exactly. But, the thing is, as much as I like being there, and as much as they want me to add even more hours, there's something else I've been dreaming of doing for a long, long time." And she told him about the cooking school programs she'd been researching. How one of them wasn't too far away—just a thirty-minute drive—but that the intro class met twice per week, at night. "I know tuition is expensive," she said, "but if I picked up one more shift at work, that would offset the cost a little. And I know it would be kinda busy, but—"

"Of course," he interrupted. "You don't have to talk me into this, honey. If it's something you really want to do, we'll figure out a way to manage it. I *want* you to follow your dreams. And—" He paused, the emotion and, possibly, the relief that this was all there was to the problem, seemed to require him to take a few additional breaths before continuing. "I know I don't always tell you how much you mean to me, but you're the center of our world, Bridget. We all revolve around *you*. And we're in this marriage and this family together. You've supported me. You've supported all of us. We're here to support you back."

She hugged him. This was quite a speech for her silent, straightforward man. He wasn't just showing his affection to get her attention away from another guy. He was showing it because he knew she needed to see his heart. And he had a big, wonderful one, full of love for her.

Graham said, "I'd planned to take you to one of those fancy-schmancy French restaurants you'd always wanted to try for our anniversary in a few weeks. But maybe you'd rather get something else with the money. Books for this first class? Some new cooking gadget? Just tell me what you need, okay?"

And this, Bridget realized, was precisely what she had been failing to do. She had poured out her excitement to a person besides her husband to the point of being, if not physically unfaithful, then emotionally so. And that had been wrong. That was where she had crossed the line.

The love and gratitude she felt for Graham at that moment couldn't be measured. And, as they talked about a few long-range plans, Bridget felt a surge of compassion for both Tamara and Jennifer, especially the former, for all they were going through in their own marriages. In Tamara's case, she couldn't begin to imagine how difficult it must've been to conceal so much hurt and dissatisfaction. No wonder her friend had been so critical. So edgy.

But, as much sympathy as she felt for her friends and their challenges, she refused to feel guilty for once about her own contentment. Even though she had merely been frustrated with her family life, not wretched, it still had not been an easy road for her and Graham. But they had both stuck with it. They had both worked at it. And maybe that was just good luck or divine intervention—she didn't know. But she felt as though a prayer had been answered.

She beamed a smile at her husband. "I'm so happy!"

He pulled her close to him. "If you are, then I am, too."

At Smiley Dental the following Tuesday, Bridget shared the good news with three of her coworkers.

"You're starting culinary school in January?" Candy said. "That's awesome!"

Pamela agreed and added, "Hey, we'll be happy to taste-test your homework assignments. Will the final exams be something like a *Hell's Kitchen* finale?

They all laughed.

"I have no idea," Bridget admitted. "But you guys will be the first to know."

Dr. Luke glanced between them all, a pensive look on his face. "I'm happy for you, Bridget. You're gonna be top of your class."

His words were sincere, utterly warm, just as always. And she realized how grateful she was to him, too, for being there for her. For being a good friend when she had needed one. For helping her to ferret out her deepest, truest dream. And, in part, for giving her the courage to fight for it.

"Thank you," she said to all of them, but especially to Dr. Luke.

A moment later, when Dr. Nina strode by, shooting glares at all four of them, Dr. Luke winked at her and said in a loud voice, "I hope this doesn't mean you'll need to cut your hours here just because you're gonna be a famous chef soon. Remember us poor dentists, hygienists and receptionists. Protect us from our malnutrition."

Candy and Pamela giggled at this and Bridget, who knew Pamela's pregnancy was public knowledge now, said, "Well, actually, if the offer's still open, I can add one extra shift when Pamela reduces hers."

Cheers went up all around. Dr. Jim peeked around the corner and clapped. A couple of patients in the waiting area (who had, at one time, sampled Bridget's Sugar-Free Mango-Orange Finger Cookies) whistled. And all the others said some variation of "Yay!" Except for Dr. Nina, who stood by the filing cabinets, reactionless.

"This calls for a celebration," Dr. Luke declared. "How about we order a pizza or something?"

Bridget grinned at him. "Sounds great, but save a little room for dessert. I made you all something special."

"Oooh, let's have that first," Dr. Luke suggested, and the others agreed.

So, Bridget unveiled her latest creation: Dark Chocolate and Raspberry Lava Cake. "This, I'm afraid, is *not* sugar free."

"Who cares?" Candy said, already reaching for the knife to start slicing pieces.

Dr. Luke's eyes actually watered after he took the first bite. "This is heavenly. You've outdone yourself again, Bridget." Then, in a lower voice, he murmured, "You bring such good things to our lives. We're so glad to have you here."

She recognized the genuineness of his words and, again, realized how grateful she was to him, too. Without his kindness and attentiveness as a stimulus, she might not have gotten back on track with Graham. Silently but fervently, she thanked God for her friend Luke. He'd helped her regain her passion for life. And passion could change a woman. Make the mundane a delight. She was proof of that.

Dr. Luke turned his gaze away from Bridget and toward Dr. Nina. She was filing paperwork and had refused Candy's offer of a slice of cake. After a few further minutes of office revelry, he picked up the untouched piece and strode over to the female dentist.

"Try it, Nina," he told her. "Just one bite, okay?"

Dr. Nina pursed her lips, sighed but, nevertheless, speared a forkful of gooey cake. "If it means that much to you," she mumbled to Dr. Luke, cautiously putting the fork in her mouth.

As Bridget watched from a distance, she could see Dr. Luke had been trying to be a friend to Dr. Nina, too. He was good at that. As for Dr. Nina, well . . . she had a ways to go before her passions would make her overflowing with happiness, but Bridget wished her well.

Dr. Nina's reaction to the cake wasn't rapturous, but the woman didn't spit it out either. She shrugged, put the fork down and announced, "It's actually not bad."

Dr. Luke laughed and went to talk to Dr. Jim about something before both of them left the room to check on patients. Bridget glanced one last time at Dr. Nina, only to see her eyeing the cake curiously and, then, reaching out to nab one more bite before leaving the room herself. Bridget considered this a moment of culinary triumph.

With her heart filled with joy, she laughed with colleagues and patients alike, saving up bits of conversation to share with Graham and the kids later, over dinner. Knowing she had their affection waiting for her at home.

Sometimes love could be as simple as just that. A twist of the wrist. A flip of the spatula. A chance to start over and do it better the next time around—as long as both parties were ever-vigilant.

Unfortunately, sometimes it was not nearly that simple. . . .

❧ 23 ❧

"Jennifer & the Infinite Journey"

Thanksgiving through mid-December

Once upon a time, in a land of conflicting mental constructs, there lived a woman named Jennifer, who'd experienced a recent incident of marital disruption, thanks to a conniving ex-lover. She and her husband, Michael, had been in a holding pattern of doubt and distrust for over a month, although, in truth, Jennifer's skepticism and matrimonial misgivings had been witnessed by the acutest of observers many years before . . . and ever since.

These gentle observers were their daughters, Veronica and Shelby.

And so it came to pass, one brisk late-November day, Jennifer's daughters returned home from school: One in a foul mood. The other in a fouler one.

Shelby, the younger of the two, tossed her backpack on the floor, slammed her bedroom door shut and lost herself in the fantasy world of online video-gaming. Her mother, understanding the desire for the strategic numbing of brain cells, nevertheless knew this behavior could not last indefinitely. Someday soon, she and Shelby would have to have a chat about the discord in their family and how it led to the pursuit of mindlessness as an escape mechanism.

However, given that Veronica came home crying, the you-need-to-do-something-with-your-time-besides-playing-World-of-Warcraft talk would have to wait.

"Veronica, what's wrong?" Jennifer asked her eldest.

"I am *so* sick of school. That's all," Veronica hissed, swiping angrily at the tears streaming down her smooth skin. "I just need a break from it."

Jennifer mentioned that she, in fact, had just had four days off because of the Thanksgiving holiday.

"Well, that wasn't long enough."

"Clearly." Jennifer took a step toward her daughter. "What happened, sweetheart?" she whispered.

Maybe it was because her child recognized the empathy her mother felt for her, or maybe it was because she just really needed to confide in someone, but Veronica fell into Jennifer's arms and sobbed out a story. From what Jennifer could understand, it seemed that Tim was pissed off about Veronica's flirting with Erick and had proceeded to spread a series of rumors about her at school, including, but not limited to, the assertion that Veronica "went down on Erick at the dance," but she really didn't. And, being that Tim was Mr. Popularity and Student Council Guy, people believed him. While Erick, who was seen as this dangerous bad-boy type just because he was older and already had his driver's license and a couple of tattoos ("Just small ones, Mom!") wasn't believed at all.

"Okay, Veronica. Okay," Jennifer said, trying to soothe her. "What really happened at the dance? Why don't we start there."

Her daughter sniffled. "Almost nothing. Really. Erick met me there. We danced a few times, but the music was lame. And because Tim and his friends were staring at us, we went outside for a walk. Just for, like, fifteen minutes or something. He told me about having to take this history class as a make-up thing because his old high school didn't do U.S. history freshmen year. That it was odd to be the oldest one in the class, but he usually was a loner anyway, so he was kinda used to it. And he asked me what I thought about being in high school and if it was hard." She shrugged. "Nothing weird at all. And then he kissed me once. It was really quick because some other people came outside, too, so we went back into the gym and danced to another couple of songs before the whole thing ended."

"That was it?"

"Yeah. But the next week at school, the rumors started. Tim said I'd changed and that I was a slut." She bit her lip and the tears started leaking out again. "Everyone was whispering about me. Even my friends. And Erick was totally avoiding me. When I asked him about it, he said it was because he didn't want people talking about me even more. He said he could see how upset I was and he didn't know what I wanted him to do. That maybe he should back off. So I said, 'Yeah, okay.' But it didn't make it all stop. I mean, the rumors about Erick stopped, but people liking me and trusting me like they used to—that was gone. Even with the teachers. It was like they believed whatever the other kids believed. That if an 'upstanding class leader' like Tim thought I was bad, then they didn't question it. And I'm in a different building now, so none of my old teachers could defend me. See what I mean?"

Jennifer saw. "So, have any of the teachers accused you of anything? Lying, cheating, stealing . . . anything like that?"

Veronica shook her head. "Not yet. But I can tell they look at me differently than they do the kids in Tim's clique, or even most of my friends. And the expression someone like Mr. Ryerson gets on his face when he looks at Erick—Mom, it's mean. Erick isn't perfect or anything but, deep down, he's a *lot* nicer of a guy than Tim, who just pretends to be nice."

Jennifer sighed. "Guys like Tim will do stuff like that. They'll be sneaky, and they'll lash out in whatever way they can when they're hurt. In some ways, you played into this by flirting with both of those guys in class. You see that, right?"

Her daughter pulled a tissue out of her jeans' pocket, blew her nose and nodded.

"And, if I'm understanding correctly, you really did like them both. These two guys were like two different sides of you. Who you were and, maybe, a little bit of who you wanted to be. Yes?"

"Yes," Veronica said.

"And I'll bet at first there was a really exciting sense of power that came with flirting with them. That you could get both of these very different boys, who were each cool in their own way, to be attracted to you. To want to ask you out. Am I close?"

Veronica squinted at her. "So, this happened to you, too?"

Jennifer nodded and projected all the love in her heart at her daughter. "Unfortunately, yes. But here's something I had to learn and I wish someone would've told me this years and years ago. Those opposing sides of yourself? They're strong and crazy powerful, and they don't *ever* go away. You'll get rewarded by one group of people for displaying one side, and you'll be despised by another for doing the same thing. Teachers will trust you if you act 'good,' whether or not you really *are* good. Outcasts will respect you if they think you're bucking authority, even if your deepest values keep you from being as rebellious as you appear. Either way, you'll be judged, which isn't fair, but it's how the world works. I just think the most interesting people are multifaceted, and that their personalities can't be confined to any one category. So, from my point of view, it's *important* to try out different sides of yourself. Just recognize that consequences always come with that kind of experimentation." She let out a long, long breath. "Actually, consequences come no matter what you do, which is something I'm still learning myself."

"Like with you and Dad?"

"Exactly like with me and Dad," Jennifer admitted, rubbing her forehead. "It's better not to commit to one lifestyle before you know for sure what you want. But, eventually, we all *do* need to choose. Waffling back and forth between different sides of yourself is exhausting, and it's not good for anybody involved. If you're confused, it's okay to step back and reevaluate. The journey never ends, so don't let anybody tell you that you need to choose right away. Take all the time you need."

Veronica leaned against her, much like she used to do when she was an elementary schooler and had had a hard day. "So, you don't think it's too late with Erick? For me to go out with him, even with Tim and his friends talking trash about me?"

Jennifer embraced her daughter. "If you think about it seriously and decide that's really what you want, and if you tell him the truth about what happened and why you changed your mind, then no. I don't think it's ever too late. Not for any of us."

Over the next couple of weeks, Jennifer ruminated on Veronica's situation and her own. Michael's behavior had settled into a routine of coolness rather than frigidity, but the essential issues between them remained unchanged.

At least Jennifer had the pleasure of seeing her eldest daughter take steps to renew her friendship with this Erick kid. And, despite his "small" tattoos, she'd listened to what Veronica had said about the guy, and she approved. Jennifer and her daughter had reached a new phase in their relationship, and it was one of slightly better understanding. So, when Erick called Veronica at home for the first time in weeks, Jennifer gave her daughter a thumbs-up and, in return, earned a rare, jubilant grin from her not-so-little girl.

Shelby still sequestered herself in her room more often than not, but Jennifer was well versed in this form of escapism and, on a few occasions, had managed to slip into her youngest daughter's fantasy world by joining her in a video game. Baby steps but, over time, they could get a person pretty far.

Jennifer was still struggling to unite emotion and logic in her attempt at figuring out the next leg of her marital journey. Like the song "Both Sides Now," she'd looked at love from every possible angle, yet she couldn't help but feel she didn't understand the concept much at all. That she required a more definitive period of reflection, if only to make the distinction of *taking a break* more visible to herself. That, in fact, she needed to physically remove herself from the household for a little while.

So, when the chill of mid-December had fully seeped into her bones and her husband and children were about to begin their two-week winter break, she could no longer ignore the obvious. She sat down with Michael. She told him she had to take the advice she had given their daughter and take a few steps back.

"Your situations aren't similar at all," Michael informed her after Jennifer explained about the long talks she'd been having with

Veronica lately. "The girls will feel abandoned if you leave the house. It's selfish of you even to consider it."

Jennifer inhaled deeply and, for a second, closed her eyes, so as to better listen for that quiet voice she had been training herself to hear.

"Michael, this isn't easy for me to say, but I've been trying to sort this out at home and not create a disruption in all of our lives for a long time now. If I thought I could do it while I was here at home, I would. But it's not working for me anymore to just fake it and hope I can feel the way you want me to. You deserve better than that. And I believe it's more selfish to stay with someone and unfairly hobble their growth than it is to pull away for a few weeks or a month. It's time for me to finally be honest with you about my doubts."

"What the hell, Jennifer? You couldn't have dealt with your *doubts* before we got married?" he spit out.

She bobbed her head. "It would've been much better if I had." She took a step toward him and gently touched his arm. He didn't look as though he liked the gesture, but he didn't move away either. "Listen, please. I know I haven't been fair to you or to the girls, but I'm really trying to right this wrong . . . finally. I'm trying to make a true commitment to *you*, Michael. It's just that loyalty to oneself has to come before loyalty to others. And I want a chance to start over more slowly, more mindfully."

She swallowed away the bitterness she could still taste over her own indecision. Maybe marriage had never been the right path for her. Maybe she was someone who should just live alone. Or, maybe, she and Michael simply needed to get to know one another as new people, as they were *right now*, not as twenty-somethings. But, no matter what, she felt an acute responsibility to her daughters to get this right. This problem between them was no longer just about her own growth. For once, she needed to guide her children by good example.

"Does this sudden decision have anything to do with that David bastard?" he asked coldly.

She shook her head. "No. That chapter is over. He isn't any part of my life, Michael. And this decision, it isn't sudden."

She was being fully truthful on both points. Even when David sent her a text message or an e-mail, as he was sometimes inclined to do, she usually deleted those missives, unread. And she never answered them. Until recently, the burden of having carried around her past had been like lugging twice her body weight in rocks. The relief she had felt in being able to let all that go was intoxicating. Next, though, she had to face her marriage and hope she would be able to achieve some sense of certainty again, especially now that the cobwebs of the past had been cleared away.

So, Jennifer took her laptop (so she could continue her Web design work) and checked into a cheap motel for the duration of the winter break. "Think of it like an artist's retreat," she told her daughters, promising they would still see her or talk to her every day for a little while. She reiterated how much she loved them and that she just needed to sort out a few thoughts.

"You'll try to be back soon?" Michael murmured to her before she drove away.

"I'll really try," she said, but she refused to set a definitive time line for herself. She would take whatever weeks, or months, she needed, and the experience would likely be far harder than she wanted it to be, but she had tamped down her true emotions for too many years, and she wanted to get them back. The journey to recognizing her natural instincts was like Peter Frampton's road— long and winding—but Jennifer suspected it would be worth the trip.

And last but not least . . .

❧ 24 ❧

"Tamara & the Perplexing Prince"

Thanksgiving through Late December

Once upon a time, in a neighborhood of some riches—in property, if not in affection—resided Tamara. She was known as a woman who would willingly plunge her hands into the subterranean depths of her garden's soil bed to make its bountifulness bloom, but who was, conversely, afraid of digging too deeply into the well of her own psyche.

A resident of a nearby kingdom (some five houses down the street and on the left, to be exact), presented a most baffling problem for her: He was markedly different from any man she had ever met. She did not *like* this. Aaron was his name, and he had an unsettling way of challenging her. She *really* did not like *that*.

She did, however, like the way he looked in tight pants, a fact she had been ruminating about for some time at the airport while waiting for her son's flight to arrive. A piece of her heart was coming home for Thanksgiving break, and she could not be happier.

"Benji!" she cried when her lanky nineteen-year-old hugged her at O'Hare's arrival terminal. "I'm so glad you're here."

He pecked the top of her head with a kiss. "It's not like I'm back from a war zone, Mom. Just Texas."

"Well, you can never be sure. 'Remember the Alamo' and all . . . y'all."

He laughed.

They returned to the house, empty of any other residents. Benji's father, Jon, was still away on his latest business trip, and Tamara had yet to explain to their son that, while Jon would return for the holiday, he would not be staying. The fear of inflicting pain on her only child weighed heavily upon her heart, but she could no longer delay telling Benji about his parents' impending divorce.

So, after bringing her son his choice of a refreshing carbonated beverage, the two of them chatted in his childhood bedroom while Benji unpacked his belongings for his week-long visit.

"What's your roommate doing this week?" Tamara asked, finding herself mesmerized as she watched him pull out a couple of sweaters from his suitcase, refold them and place them—almost neatly—in his oak dresser drawer. She remembered getting him that sturdy piece of furniture when he was about nine. The way he used to always shove his T-shirts and sweatpants in there—cripes, what a mess! He'd stuff the drawers to full capacity and slam them shut, always trapping a sleeve or a pant leg between the planks of wood, so the drawers had colorful bits of fabric peeking out everywhere. She smiled to herself. He was so grown up now.

"Lance is staying in Austin for the break. He's gonna go home to Atlanta for Christmas, but it was a little too expensive for him to fly back right now, only to do it again in a few weeks. Plus, he's got his job and already signed up to work a bunch of extra hours. He's a great guy."

Tamara nodded. "Sounds like it." She paused when she saw him set his shaving kit down right between his prized Cubs baseball (autographed by ten team members when he was thirteen) and his old rubber alligator (that he'd tried to scare her with a million times when he was in junior high). She swallowed. "So, any girlfriends or anything?"

Her mostly adult son blushed and shook his head. "Just girls who are friends, Mom."

"For now," she said, suspecting the truth behind his embarrassment. "But you're hoping that'll change with one of them, right?"

"Right." He grinned at her. "Okay, fine. Her name's Abby. She's a sociology major. And she's from Ohio. Can we stop talking about this now?"

Tamara laughed. She'd let him talk about whatever the hell he wanted for a while, which turned out to be a lengthy monologue on the bizarreness of his physics prof, Dr. Shane.

"He smokes a pipe in his office," Benji said, rolling his eyes. "It's like a tobacco shop in there. We all had to go in to talk about our semester projects, and I thought I was gonna suffocate. And, oh! There was this one time when he lugged this freakin' huge engine into class to demonstrate the properties of thermodynamics. . . ."

But when he began to run out of steam on college tales, Tamara knew she had to direct the conversation elsewhere.

"Benji," she began. "There's something I need to tell you." And, with that, she explained how she and his father had both been rather frustrated with each other. That they tended to be happier people when doing things independently. And that, really, they'd been having some problems for a few years, but they were—

Benji stopped her, midspeech. "Not for a *few* years, Mom. You and Dad have been at each others' throats for as long as I can remember." He sighed. "So, what are you telling me? You two are finally calling it quits?"

"Afraid so, sweetheart."

He grunted and bobbed his head at her. "You okay?"

She wasn't sure how to answer that. She'd seen the flash of hope in his eyes dissipate the moment she confirmed his theory, but there were other emotions visible on his face, too, and she'd been trying hard to read them. In some ways, he was as transparent as always. She definitely spotted sadness in his eyes. A little anger, too. A hint of deflation at being forced to give up the fantasy of a warm and fuzzy family life. But there was something else in his expression, as well. Was she wrong or had she, maybe, called this right? In addition to all of the above, did he also seem . . . relieved?

"I'm okay," she said. "Are *you* okay?"

He chuckled, kind of, and covered her hand with his. "Well, it's not like it's great news or anything. But, yeah. I'm okay." Then he glanced around the room and squinted at a few of his high-school posters. One famous athlete. One rock star. One scantily clothed

Miss September. "So, uh, are you selling the house?" A touch of worry graced his brow, but he quickly camouflaged it by running his palm across his forehead.

In this at least, Tamara suspected she could ease her son's anxiety a tiny bit. "Your dad and I discussed it, but once we took a serious look at the housing market, we realized now wouldn't be a good time to sell. Perhaps things will pick up in a few years, but we knew we wouldn't get the price we were looking for in the next year, so I offered to buy out your dad. That way the house will stay in my possession, and your room will look just as it does now. Only, perhaps, a little tidier." She grinned at him, and he grinned back.

He had a few questions, of course: "How can you afford to do that?" To which she explained about her inheritance from Aunt Eliza and how this would use up over half of it, but that she considered it a good long-term real-estate investment. Plus, she really loved the house because it held so many of her happiest memories. "Are you giving Dad a fair deal?" Absolutely. She was paying Jon half of what they'd decided the house was worth, not what it would currently sell for. (She did not add that, from her point of view, it was well worth the financial risk, even if she didn't recoup her profits later. This was the home where her son had grown up. She wanted it to still be here for him.) "Do you really want to stay in the neighborhood?" Unequivocally, yes.

She also explained the Christmas plans. That Jon would tell him more about his road-trip idea when they were all together for Thanksgiving, but that Jon was taking a couple of weeks off at the end of the year and wanted to spend some father-son time with him. That he'd hoped Benji would be up for a pilgrimage to the Baseball Hall of Fame and, maybe, some cool science museums and exhibits.

Benji looked pleased with the plan and even more pleased with his parents' seeming amicability. When Jon returned from his business trip a few days later, the three of them spent a calm, cordial and, alternately, heartbreaking Thanksgiving together. Tamara couldn't help but feel pangs of wistfulness, wishing her marriage would have lasted forever, but she realized the freedom of their imminent separation was what it took for them to achieve this peaceful, easy companionship now.

In the weeks that followed—with Benji back at school, Jon based in an apartment downtown and both of them planning to be away on their road trip until the end of the year—Tamara had the house completely to herself. She started putting out feelers for marketing consulting positions and was pleased to receive a bit of interest from a couple of small companies for one-time jobs that might lead to further appointments. It wouldn't be enough to live on, but it was enough to help her get her feet wet after so many years away.

Of course, in addition to rebuilding her professional life from the ground up, she also had to deal with her relationship with Aaron.

On the first day of December, the ink on her divorce papers (on which she'd marked the Irreconcilable Differences box) having barely dried, she walked over to Aaron's house, her stomach fluttering, and rang the bell.

He opened the door, unsmiling. "Long time, no see."

She pushed her way in, closed the door behind her and pulled his very unyielding body into her arms. "Hi to you, too," she said. "I've missed you."

He cleared his throat, stepped back and regarded her with a look she could only describe as suspicious.

"What?" she said when he refused to hug her. "I've been busy. Benji was home for a week. Jon was in and out, on business trips and moving into his own apartment. There was the whole Thanksgiving thing, *and* we had to meet with the attorneys yesterday and sign the freakin' divorce papers. So, don't look at me like I've been ignoring you or something."

"Tamara." He took a deep breath. "You do not sleep with a guy for six straight days and then not talk to him *at all* for two weeks." He crossed his arms. "You understand that, right?"

She rolled her eyes. "Well, yes. I wouldn't *normally* do that, but I was kind of preoccupied with the ending of my marriage." She looked around the room. "Where's Sharky?"

"At the groomer. My sisters were giving me shit over Thanksgiving about his doggy hygiene, and one of them insisted on taking him to her dog's groomer guy. She picked him up an hour ago and"—he glanced at his watch—"said she'd have him back in less than two. So . . ."

"So, I can't talk you into a quickie on the couch, huh?"

He blinked at her and, in spite of a very obvious attempt to keep a stern expression, smirked ever so slightly. "Nope. Not this time."

"But you're *tempted*, right? Even though I'm an awful neighbor and a wildly inconsiderate lover, who probably should've stopped by to give you flowers or something after our first week of sex, you still kinda want me, don't you?"

His smile grew more conspicuous. "Well, you did bring me those roses once, I suppose."

"And about the wanting me part?"

He shook his head in apparent negation—Tamara's heart almost stopped beating—but then he whispered, "Yes."

"Good," she said. And this time he brought her to him and kissed her.

After making out for a few minutes, though, he pulled back and said, "Just so you know, I don't appreciate this laissez-faire attitude of yours. I understand how you must've been very busy, but don't act as though how you treat me doesn't matter one way or another. It matters."

She stared at him. "Are you for real? I wasn't blowing you off. I was caught up with telling my son that his parents were getting divorced and helping my soon-to-be ex-husband move out."

"So, call me up and tell me that. You're saying you didn't have time for a five-minute phone call anywhere in the past fifteen days? That's bullshit, Tamara."

Despite the December chill seeping between the edges of the front door, she felt herself perspiring underneath her cable-knit sweater. "The phone lines work both ways, you know."

"Not at this stage, they don't."

"What do you mean?"

"I *mean*," he said, "I didn't want to put you in a compromising position in the eyes of your family. I didn't know who was still living in your house this past month and who wasn't. I wouldn't want Benji or Jon to see my number on the Caller ID and wonder why I was calling you. I didn't want them to read a text message, even an innocently worded one, and have that create some kind of unforeseen problem. I sure as hell didn't want to just stop by and interfere with what you were doing there. So I've been waiting for you to contact me." He exhaled. "And, until today, you didn't."

She squinted at him. What was his problem? Why was he getting so intense about this? "I thought you understood that I'm not ready for any big commitments, Aaron. I'm just getting out of a nearly twenty-year marriage. I really like you and everything, but I'm not looking for a serious relationship."

He threw his hands up in the air and shot her a look of pure exasperation. "I'm not asking for a big commitment or a serious relationship. But it shouldn't be too much to ask for you to treat our friendship with respect and a little depth. I'm not just some sex toy you can stuff back in your drawer when you're too busy and pull out again when the coast is clear. Trust me, you're capable of keeping the relationship light while still being considerate, Tamara."

"Yeah, okay," she told him, more to pacify him than because she agreed. And she left shortly after that, promising to call or stop by before the end of the week. But she didn't think she had been inconsiderate or disrespectful of him, just not as available as he might have wanted. His attitude really confused her. He was acting as if this little fling of theirs might actually mean something to him. Which was kind of bizarre since—c'mon—how many affairs like theirs lasted longer than a few weeks, maybe a couple of months?

Spending time with him was certainly an improvement over playing with her vibrating bunny, and he was a nice, intelligent guy, despite his disconcerting need to debate everything so openly. But, dammit, she had a *lot* on her mind these days. Didn't he see that? Didn't he understand that, although she knew he considered her an interesting challenge now, she also knew his curiosity would wear off soon enough? This was what *always* happened.

And then, if she let herself get too attached, she would have to deal with that mess, too. . . . How naive did he think she was?

Despite her desire not to dig too deeply into Aaron's motives for wanting this heightened level of attentiveness from her, Tamara played the part of a dutiful girlfriend for several weeks, nonetheless. She called him every day, even if it was just for a few minutes. She visited him at his invitation a number of times, and invited him over to her house, too. She seduced him several of those times (she quite enjoyed *that*), and she pretended not to be so surprised whenever he showered her with continued interest.

But she *was* surprised.

Was it supposed to be like this? How come the mystery hadn't started to dissipate yet? Had she been living with Jon's pointed indifference for so long that she was constitutionally incapable of recognizing the natural rhythms of a normal, functional relationship?

Hmm. Maybe.

She had, however, promised Aaron she would be honest with him if she ever had any real concerns. Well, after spending half a day sobbing over old photo albums (why the hell did she have to go look at those, anyway?), she was in an uncomfortably vulnerable state when he knocked at the door. And guess what? She had enough concerns to fill a fucking Mack truck.

"Hey," he said, stepping inside. "You look awful."

"Bastard."

He laughed. "What happened? Did Jon do something evil? Benji giving you a guilt trip? See a particularly poignant greeting card commercial?"

She shook her head. "Vacation pictures from about ten years ago. St. Thomas."

His eyebrows shot up. "Ah. Stupid memories . . . and way too much blue water. All that tropical sun and surf is just depressing."

She managed a small smile. "Exactly."

"Anything else?"

"Yeah." She hugged him, struggled for a good breath and

blurted, "Why am I not indifferent to you? Why hasn't my attraction to you faded yet? I don't want to like you this much."

He kissed her cheek, then held her at arm's length so as to see more of her. "Tell me something, Tamara. Is this what's really bothering you, or is it, maybe, a projection? Because I'm a *great* guy. I'm witty. I have a paying job. I work out regularly—you've seen my awesome muscles." He nodded at her in mock seriousness, tensed his left bicep and pointed at it. "I stopped making my mother do my laundry *years* ago. Hell, I'm even pretty much over the drama with my bitchy ex-wife, give or take a few nightmares. So, really, who wouldn't find me a fantastic catch?"

Tamara opened her mouth to contradict him, but he winked and held up his hand. "No, no. None of those snotty comebacks of yours." He kissed her other cheek and whispered, "I like you, too."

"But this cannot possibly last?"

"You said that as a question, not a statement. It could," he said. "It might not but, yes, it *could*. Why do you find that so hard to believe?"

What could she say? That she had dreamed of having deeper intimacy with the man in her life—both physically and emotionally—but she had been convinced that avenue was cut off for her? That she had been coming to the unsettling realization that in order for her most secret fantasy to be possible, she would have to expose all her fears and insecurities? That she knew life was too short to be so afraid, but she didn't know how to break out of old patterns?

"I don't know," she murmured.

"I think you do," he said, his voice infinitely gentle.

But he didn't push her. Instead, he requested they go on a date together. Their first out in public. An evening with all the Christmastime trimmings: a dinner of roast goose and stuffing, a snowy sleigh ride offered by kids at the nearest community college, an hour of caroling followed by peppermint-schnapps-infused hot cocoa in front of his fireplace.

It was a fun and active night, but it ended with them just talking. About their childhoods. About their most memorable marital blowups. About how they had both resisted their initial attraction to each other. She found herself telling him things about her parents and her early boyfriends that she hadn't thought about in years, let alone verbalized.

And he shared his personal philosophy, too. At one point (after, admittedly, a number of heavily spiked cocoas) he explained, "You have to work through pain to create a life worth having. Joy is out there, but you don't just *find* it, you *earn* it. In order for happiness to bloom inside you, you have to be what you seem."

She considered this. "So, how do I do that, Aaron? Where do I start?"

"You just start with yourself. With what you know is true about you. All you have to do is just be honest about what you really want . . . and what you really fear. Know thyself."

"Thanks a lot, Socrates," she teased him, but in many ways, she realized Jon had tried to tell her this, too. Jon's claim when they were in Texas that she didn't know what she really wanted had haunted her for two months. But Jon had hinted at some version of this same accusation for years, and she hadn't wanted to listen. So, perhaps, by persistently ignoring his words, she contributed as much to their marriage's failure as had his unrelenting indifference.

Armed with this bud of self-knowledge, she studied Aaron's expression as he looked at her: calm, kind, confident. He wasn't indifferent. And, while he wasn't perfect either, he had faced a similar fire before and come out stronger. He had gained courage from his marital struggles and, best of all, being with him made her hopeful that she could, too. Cautiously but genuinely optimistic.

And wasn't optimism what a true fairy tale was all about? Optimistic stories were intended to inspire readers, right alongside the characters. And, if one hopeful narrator should be so fortunate as to achieve this feat, the readers wouldn't want the tale to come immediately to a close, would they?

Yet, if those same readers were familiar with fairy-tale convention, either modern or traditional, they would know the end would most likely be the best, most satisfying part of all. That the end of the original story would be the very place theirs would begin . . . should they be so inclined to tell it.

❧ 25 ❧

And They All Lived . . .

New Year's Eve, Friday, December 31

The trio did not, of course, meet at the Indigo Moon Café on New Year's Eve. It closed for the celebratory weekend at five-thirty. But, sometime around ten P.M., Tamara, Bridget and Jennifer got together at Robin's Nest Bar & Grille, just down the road and overlooking a small private lake. Not a glitzy hot spot and hardly Glendale Grove's answer to Navy Pier, but nice. Very nice.

Robin, the owner, brought out their pitcher of frozen strawberry margaritas, three large glasses and a platter of the house nachos, fully loaded. "Here you go, ladies," she said. "Have fun."

"Oh, we will," Tamara replied, tipping the pitcher to expertly fill the three margarita glasses with the red concoction. No coffee on this night. They'd get it tomorrow, when they would undoubtedly need it. But tonight, it was all about celebration.

"So, here's to us," Tamara said, raising her glass. "May the coming year bring only good things to us all. A new year, a new beginning."

They clinked glasses and took healthy sips, each of them reflecting on the changes in their lives over the past few months and projecting into their near futures the dream of even greater love and happiness.

Bridget, pleased by the current trajectory of her marriage, beamed pure joy at her friends and delighted in the rich vermilion of the frozen margarita. Such a pretty color and so tasty, too! "Oh, these are scrumptious," she declared, surreptitiously checking out the multihued loaded-nacho platter and weighing just how many calories she wanted to ingest in one night.

It was New Year's Eve, after all. A once a year celebration, yes, but also an homage to the cyclical nature of relationships. *To everything there is a season*, she reminded herself. *And a time to every purpose under heaven*. For Bridget, this was going to be the season for a healthy pursuit of passions, a healthy kind of friendship, a healthy marriage and a healthy body she could feel comfortable moving around in every day.

So, two margaritas and one reasonable serving of nachos were her limit, she cheerfully decided. She could live with that. And, in the spirit of moderation and honesty, she said to her friends, "For me, the best part of tonight is spending it with you both."

"Thanks," Jennifer said, her smile reaching her eyes, albeit temporarily, and giving them a much-needed sparkle.

Tamara set down her glass. "So, Graham was okay with watching the kids tonight so you could come out with us?"

Bridget laughed. "He's off for ten days, remember? We've spent *all week* together already, and tomorrow I'll be cooking a seven-course meal for the entire family. Graham knows I needed to get out of the house for a few hours." She turned to Jennifer. "How are your girls? Are they enjoying their winter break?"

Jennifer appreciated Bridget's gentleness in broaching the subject. "They're doing all right. We all are," she murmured.

In truth, of course, it had been a challenging couple of weeks for her, living on her own in the sanctuary of the motel and meeting her daughters at the mall, a nearby bookstore or some local diner every day. Michael would drop them off, pick them up and kindly entrust her not to decimate their family bond in the hours in between, but he couldn't camouflage his frustration at her extended break from them and his residual anger over her lingering indecision.

Really, she couldn't blame him.

However, she persisted in standing up for herself and to the world at large, despite their judgments of her. She would, for once, not be swayed by anyone's demands nor allow a single solitary person to dictate the way she should manage her fears. Time had proved none of their suggestions were effective anyway. It left her with some gaps as far as appearing to be a model parent, but it also forced her to be much more real, raw and present with Veronica and Shelby, and their conversations over the past two weeks had been among the more memorable and truthful of their lives.

"I love that, away from the house, we've managed to break some of the patterns of inattention that were so easy to slip into before," Jennifer added. Her two friends nodded. They both knew the danger of inattention in one's closest relationships. "There's really no escape from each other now," she said, "so that part is mostly good. But the girls are embarrassed by the current living arrangements, I think, and even confessed to being relieved that they're on vacation and don't have to face their friends right now. I know they're hoping it'll all go away before school starts again so they can pretend it never happened. Michael would like that, too."

"So, he's not quite accepting, but just dealing with it, right?" Tamara asked.

Jennifer bobbed her head. "It's hard for him, but I really appreciate that he's been open, however grudgingly, to giving me this time. And maybe even realizing, without actually admitting it, that I'd needed it. We've had lunch together, too. Just us. Twice so far." She sighed. "It's awkward, but we keep trying to talk. And all four of us will be meeting up for dinner tomorrow. At least for a few hours."

"Do you ever hear from David?" Bridget blurted.

"No," Jennifer said just as quickly. Then, "Well, yes. He e-mailed me a couple more times, but I deleted his messages. I can't help but think of him, but I'm not tempted by him anymore," she told them, realizing this was completely true. David was like an addictive drug for which she had finally been given the full side effect report. She had known he was bad for her, but since when did an addict voluntarily cease abusing her vice of choice? Not until she was confident that the other choices presented to her were equally powerful and far less damaging. Not until she was *sure* she wanted to live life in full consciousness, despite the risk and the potential pain of reality. And much to her surprise, over these past few weeks, Jennifer realized she *did* want that. Badly.

Tamara said, "Kind of like 'Auld Lang Syne,' right? We never forget old acquaintances. Old exes. Or old boinking buddies." She grinned. "Do we?"

The trio laughed, Jennifer most of all. "Okay, now that's one song I still don't understand the lyrics to," she said. "Google was no help at all. The words just don't make much sense."

Tamara waved her palms in the air in a show of mock exasperation. "You don't get the meaning of a traditional English holiday song but *Stevie Nicks* is so fucking comprehensible? What the hell, Jennifer?"

They giggled like teenagers and toasted to the longevity of Fleetwood Mac.

Around a sensibly sized bite of cheesy nachos, Bridget asked Tamara, "Any news from Benji?"

"Yep. He and Jon are hitting the big museums in the state of New York right now and, apparently, the Baseball Hall of Fame is 'the bomb.'" With a thin swizzle stick she nabbed from the middle of the table, she swirled the remaining half of her margarita thoughtfully. "They're having a good time together, and I'm glad they're doing this road trip. I think Jon really needed to reconnect with Benji, and, to an extent, I got in the way of that for him. He loves to travel—for work or for pleasure—and he gets to share a little of that with our son now."

She, by contrast, enjoyed staying right where she was. She appreciated her independence, loved having the house to herself and, even though she didn't say this aloud, believed ardently that both she and Jon were better parents and better people when they were apart.

"And Aaron?" Jennifer asked, a small smile lifting both corners of her lips.

Tamara could in no way disguise her own smile. "He's good," she said, purposely enigmatic.

Bridget rolled her eyes. "Aw, come on! We want *details*."

Tamara shook her head, reconsidered, then said, "Well . . . okay.

Maybe a few." So, she told them about her Christmas date with Aaron, about a handful of topics they had discussed and about a New Year's Day brunch they had planned for tomorrow. She also told them about some of her worries, but that she was determined to let this relationship play out in spite of them. "Oh, yeah. And we exchanged Christmas gifts. I got him a new watch."

"Really? What did he get you?" Bridget asked.

"A tool belt," Tamara said, laughing until tears streamed down her face.

Jennifer glanced at Bridget in amusement and feigned a sigh. "I think she left out a few details."

"Tamara," Bridget said, grinning. "Spill . . ."

The music had been in a range of genres and decades at this place. Jennifer in particular noted a decided absence of the 1970s songs they had grown accustomed to hearing during their gatherings. But, just before the last stroke of midnight and during the obligatory "Auld Lang Syne," the friends hugged each other, tossed the confetti that Robin the owner had so helpfully provided for everyone high into the air and joined hands, wordlessly.

Then, when the final strains of the annual melody with the bewildering lyrics had faded into the mist of the past year, Eric Clapton's "After Midnight" came on. Tamara, Bridget and Jennifer—hands still clasped—stood up, shook the confetti out of their hair and rang in the New Year, dancing.

FRIDAY MORNINGS AT NINE

Marilyn Brant

ABOUT THIS GUIDE

The suggested questions are included to enhance your group's reading of Marilyn Brant's *Friday Mornings at Nine*.

DISCUSSION QUESTIONS

1. Discuss the personalities of the three main characters in the novel—Bridget, Tamara and Jennifer. How are they different? Are there any similarities between them?

2. This novel is told from multiple points of view. Which character was the most compelling to you? Who did you most relate to? Did you find that you had a different favorite character at the end of novel than you did at the beginning?

3. Consider the role of friendship in the book. Were these women good friends? Did they become closer or more distant as the novel progressed? Did one woman have a better understanding of the behavior and/or motivation of one friend versus another at different points in the story? How are your friendships similar or different from those of these women?

4. A fairy-tale theme is present throughout the book. Which woman was tied to which famous fairy tale? Was it a good fit? Do you think women in modern society have been conditioned to look at relationships, particularly marriage, as a kind of fairy tale come true? If so, is this a healthy expectation to bring to a committed relationship?

5. Has there ever been a person from your past whom you considered "the one who got away"?—a romantic relationship you've never had closure on, and which has haunted you for years? Perhaps a powerful physical chemistry with somebody, but you didn't follow through on it, and you secretly still wish you would—or could—have acted upon that impulse? How far do you take those fantasies? Do you Google these people? Ask mutual acquaintances about them? And to what degree do you regret not having the chance to find out what might have happened?

6. Should people in a marriage be required to be faithful? Why or why not? Is your belief based upon religious principles? Family values? Personal experiences? And should fidelity be judged only by the crossing of a physical line? If so, where is that line (i.e., When a married individual hugs someone other than his/her spouse? Kisses another? Has sex with another?)? Or is the line an emotional one? Is an act of infidelity committed when emotions and confidences are shared with someone outside the marriage?

7. How does the author use the season of fall as a metaphor in the story? Do you see anything symbolic in having one of the major turning points of the novel happening at Halloween, specifically, at a party devoted to games of pretense and disguise?

8. Music from the 1970s provides the soundtrack for this novel, even though the story takes place in the present day. Were you familiar with the songs referenced in the book? If so, did you feel they were good choices for the musical subtext?

9. Discuss the roles of women as wives, mothers and working professionals. What challenges do women face when they return to the workforce after devoting time to raising their children? What fears do they have about themselves and their relationships when those children leave the nest and the couple goes back to being alone at home again?

10. What do you think the future holds for each of the women in the story? Will they all find happiness in love? What does it take to have a good relationship? A successful marriage? Can a marriage survive an affair? If not, why not? If so, what would need to happen next to strengthen the married couple's bond?

Please turn the page
for a special conversation with
Marilyn Brant.

A Real Coffee Date with Marilyn Brant and Her Friends

Marilyn (pulling out a notebook while having coffee with her friends one morning): So, I had this idea. Because *Friday Mornings at Nine* involves a group of friends who meet regularly for coffee, I thought it'd be fun to have a transcript from one of our morning coffee dates at the end of the book. You know, I could write down what we chat about when we *really* get together, so readers could get to know the three of you, too.

Karen (smiling): To know us is to love us.

Marilyn: Exactly!

Sarah (with a snarky mumble): Or at least "to know us . . ."

Joyce: But we wouldn't have to use our real names, would we? Because I can't discuss the kinds of things we talk about if my real name will be out there.

Karen (furrowing her brow): Oooh. Hadn't thought of that.

Marilyn: Well, it isn't like we're going to be talking about anything too wild or gossipy or inappropriate, so—

Sarah: Why not? I *want* to talk about wild, gossipy and inappropriate stuff.

Joyce: But not with our real names, Sarah.

Karen: It could be fun with fake names. (contemplating) I want to be Gretchen.

Sarah: Why Gretchen?

Joyce (squinting at Karen): Hmm. Don't you think she kind of looks like a Gretchen? I do. The hair and the scarf and the—

Karen: Because I like the name Gretchen, okay? It's very Germanic.

Sarah: And that's important to you . . . why?

Marilyn: No, wait, you guys. I already *have* a pseudonym. You're saying I have to choose another one now?

Sarah: Well, according to Joyce, everybody would know it was *you* if you don't.

Marilyn: See, while that might be true, the thing is that it *is* me. It's supposed to be "a coffee date with the author."

Joyce: *And* her friends.

Marilyn: Right. And I don't have any friends named Gretchen. I don't even *know* anybody named Gretchen.

Karen/Gretchen: Well, you should. Starting now.

Joyce (nodding): I think I want to be Annette.

Sarah: Really? Why? Oh, you know what—never mind. I'll be Alexandra then.

Marilyn: You guys, seriously. I don't think we need to have made-up names, but if we're going to do that, two of us shouldn't use a name that starts with the same first letter. That gets confusing for readers. They'll start mixing up Annette and Alexandra in the text. Think of this like a few main characters in a book, chatting around a table—

Sarah/Alexandra (in a totally mocking aside to the other two): You'd think she was a writer or something.

Marilyn (shooting Sarah a well-deserved look of disapproval before clearing her throat and continuing): You'd want each person's dialogue to come across as distinctly as possible, right? So, we want our names to be as different as possible, too.

Joyce/Annette: Sarah, how about a shortened version of Alexandra? Like Lexie?

Karen/Gretchen: I like that. It's cute.

Sarah/Lexie: Fine, that works. What about you, Author Girl?

Marilyn: I don't *know*. The first name I thought of was Adriana, but that starts with an A, so—

Joyce/Annette: That's okay. I'll change mine. I'll be Millie instead.

Karen/Gretchen: Good. Now we've got Gretchen, Lexie, Adriana and Millie.

Marilyn/Adriana (agitated and scribbling some notes): But I wasn't prepared for this. I wasn't even thinking about a pseudonym. And I'm not sure I'd really make a good "Adriana". . . (losing her pen cap under the table) Can't we just talk normally?

Sarah/Lexie: Joyce, why do you want to be Millie?

Joyce/Millie (shrugging): Because I like it, and I had a Grandma Millie, who was really sweet. Well, no—not really. *She* was German.

Karen/Gretchen: Oh! Oh, I want to change mine. I'm going to be Betty. Definitely Betty.

Sarah/Lexie, Joyce/Millie and Marilyn/Adriana: *Betty?!*

Karen/Betty: It was my grandmother's name.

Sarah/Lexie (groaning): Well, now I can't be Lexie, not if you two are choosing names that are meaningful to you. I'll be Erma.

Marilyn/Adriana (retrieving the pen cap): Like the restaurant? Max & Erma's?

Sarah/Erma: No, like Bombeck. Because she was funny and I always liked her. Now, if you're not going to be Adriana, who *are* you going to be?

Marilyn/Adriana (with an exasperated sigh): I'm the author. The one who's trying to write this conversation down or, you know, I *would* write it down if we all had names chosen.

Sarah/Erma: Seems to me, you're the only one who doesn't have a name picked out yet.

Karen/Betty (wagging her finger): Sarah, that's not helpful. What about one of your relatives, Marilyn?

Marilyn/Adriana: Um, my grandmother's name is Lily, and my aunts are—

Joyce/Millie: Lily's nice! How about that?

Marilyn/Adriana (finally realizing the name thing isn't a battle that can be won): Thanks, ladies. That's a good idea. I'll be Lily. So— at last—we have our assumed identities. That only took a half hour. Perhaps *now* we can actually talk about some stuff over coffee, like we're supposed to.

Joyce/Millie: Oh, the coffee! (taking a cautious sip from her mug) I'd almost forgotten about it. I think we should stop and drink some of this before it gets cold.

Karen/Betty (sipping hers): Mmm, this is good.

Joyce/Millie: We need some biscotti. Oh, wait! (clapping) I've got something we can talk about. A few weeks ago I went to this birthday party—

Sarah/Erma (sipping her drink also): Great coffee. I have a shot of espresso in mine.

Karen/Betty: You ordered it that way?

Sarah/Erma: Yeah. I just told the lady to—

Marilyn/Lily: Hey, you two! The coffee *itself* might be an excellent topic for later, but Joyce—I mean, Millie—wanted to say something.

Karen/Betty (blatantly ignoring this attempt at redirection): Well, it would make me really wired if I did that. Too much caffeine.

Sarah/Erma: No, no. The extra caffeine is a good thing. Trust me.

Joyce/Millie (waving her hands in front of the group): Okay, am I going to be able to speak?

Marilyn/Lily: *Yes*. Please talk. I'm ready. I'm taking notes.

Sarah/Erma (sifting through her bag and pulling out her phone): You don't have to take notes. I have a recording feature on my cell. See?

Joyce/Millie: Oh, fun. (grabbing it) Let me look at that.

Marilyn/Lily: Excellent. That'll really help.

Karen/Betty (looking suspiciously at Sarah's phone): Those electronic devices don't really work, do they?

Sarah/Erma (raising a single mischievous eyebrow): Depends on the device—and what you're using it for. . . .

(Everyone laughs as Joyce hands the phone back to Sarah.)

Marilyn/Lily: *Now* we're edging toward inappropriate.

Joyce/Millie: Good thing we have those fake names, eh?

Marilyn/Lily (grinning): Start recording, Sarah. Our conversation is going off on all of these tangents. Maybe if I listen to it later it'll help me organize my notes.

Joyce/Millie: Hey, when am I going to get to tell my story?

Karen/Betty: I know the one she's talking about! It's funny. She told it to me already.

Marilyn/Lily: I want to hear it, too. I know it'll be really great—

Karen/Betty: Oh, but Joyce. You can't say anything about . . . *you know what* . . . not if Sarah's recording.

Marilyn/Lily (shaking her head and muttering to herself): You see how I can't write this down? This conversation is All Over The Place.

(Joyce and Karen whisper indistinctly to each other.)

Sarah/Erma: Marilyn, that's because the closer a group of women are, the more likely they are to have multilinear conversations.

Marilyn/Lily (in a sarcastic tone): Sure. Pull out the whole psychologist thing on me now, Sarah. Complicate my task even more. But here's the problem—I need to somehow give readers a sense of our conversations. And I'm making a mess of this. All we've managed to do is choose names that aren't ours and interrupt one another. Well, and drink a little coffee. (pauses) I do love this hazelnut mocha, though.

Sarah/Erma: But it would sound more realistic if you wrote it that way. A lot of times when you read a scripted conversation, the characters sound stilted. It's hard to show the overlapping dialogue—the cross-talking—of a real conversation.

Marilyn/Lily: No kidding.

Joyce/Millie (interjecting): Eventually we get around to a point. It just takes a while.

Sarah/Erma: Yeah. Conversations with true friends circle around. We hit lots of different notes, not just one. There's a theme, but not everybody plays the melody.

Karen/Betty: And there are variations on that theme, too.

Marilyn/Lily: Oh, that's cool. It's the symphony of us.

Sarah/Erma: Yes! Totally right. Go with that. Say something lyrical about us.

Marilyn/Lily: Okay, how about this. We're like a string quartet, each playing a different instrument. The violin might have the solo, then the cello, and so on, but we all support each others' songs. When we're together, we try to play harmoniously, but the tunes change, depending on the topic.

Sarah/Erma: Yeah, it's like classical to talk about the fam.

Karen/Betty: The *fam?*

Sarah/Erma: You know, family, husband, children—

Joyce/Millie: Blah, blah, nice things.

(Laughter at the table and more coffee drinking)

Marilyn/Lily: Yeah, that makes sense. The family stuff is like classical music. What else?

Karen/Betty: There are movie sound tracks, too.

Joyce/Millie: And Broadway show tunes.

Sarah/Erma: Right, that's like the funny things we have conversations about. It shows our range. Our intelligence, humor—

Karen/Betty: And passion!

Sarah/Erma: Yes, and passion. The hot stuff.

Karen/Betty (bobbing her head): That sounds exactly like us.

Joyce/Millie: We're obviously very smart.

Sarah/Erma: And we say brilliant, insightful things all the time, but no one ever knows about it.

Marilyn/Lily: This time they will.

(All nod sagely.)

Joyce/Millie: Now, can we talk about the party . . . ?

Addendum (a week or two later):

Marilyn: Hey, you guys, I wrote down our conversation from last time. Well, I kind of did. The parts I could transcribe, anyway. Wanna see?

Joyce: Sure.

Marilyn (passing out copies): Okay, if you want to change anything—if I didn't quote you accurately, spell your pseudonym correctly, anything like that—just mark it on the page and I'll fix it. I'm used to revising.

Karen: *I'm* not changing anything.

Joyce: That's because you have a problem with change.

Marilyn and Sarah: Oooooooh.

Karen (rolling her eyes at Joyce): Nice. Let's make sure we put *that* in there.

Sarah (chuckling as she reads the first page): This is hilarious. It sounds just like us.

Marilyn: It *does*, but readers don't know us. Are we the only ones who are going to think this is funny?

Joyce: Probably.

Marilyn (to Joyce): Do you want to make any changes to the text?

Joyce: Look, if I've got a pen in my hand and am making changes, I want some royalties.

Marilyn (laughing): Well, *Millie*, you'll get acknowledgments and a free copy.

Joyce: You know, maybe we should keep our real names. . . .

Marilyn: What?! After all the time we spent—

Karen (yawning): I'm tired. You guys wear me out.

Joyce: And I never did get to tell my story.

Sarah: Yeah, I wanted to hear that.

Marilyn: Sure you did.

Sarah (narrowing her eyes at Marilyn): I *did*.

Karen (glancing around the table): Does anyone even remember it now?

Joyce (considering): Actually, I don't. But I know I want some more coffee.

Marilyn (making a final note on the page): To be continued . . .